A Treasury of Doctor Stories by The World's Great Authors

A TREASURY OF

Doctor Stories

BY THE WORLD'S GREAT AUTHORS

COMPILED BY

NOAH D. FABRICANT AND HEINZ WERNER

FREDERICK FELL · NEW YORK · 1946

FOR

PHOEBE FABRICANT

AND

BETH WERNER

Acknowledgments

For arrangements made with authors, publishers, and authors' agents, the following acknowledgments are gratefully made:

"Lord Mountdrago" by W. Somerset Maugham. From THE MIXTURE AS BEFORE by W. Somerset Maugham. Copyright 1939 by Doubleday, Doran and Company, Inc.

"The Witch Doctor of Rosy Ridge" by MacKinlay Kantor. Copyright 1939 by Curtis Publishing Company; reprinted by permission of Coward-McCann, from AUTHOR'S CHOICE by MacKinlay Kantor. Copyright 1944 by MacKinlay Kantor.

"Indian Camp" by Ernest Hemingway. From IN OUR TIME by Ernest Hemingway. Copyright 1925, 1930, by Charles Scribner's Sons.

"A Day's Wait" by Ernest Hemingway. From THE FIFTH COLUMN AND THE FIRST FORTY-NINE by Ernest Hemingway. Copyright 1938 by Ernest Hemingway, published by Charles Scribner's Sons.

"Zone of Quiet" by Ring W. Lardner. From THE LOVE NEST AND OTHER STORIES by Ring W. Lardner. Copyright 1926 by Charles Scribner's Sons.

"Who Lived and Died Believing" by Nancy Hale. Copyright 1943 by Nancy Hale, published by Charles Scribner's Sons.

"A Movie Scenario" by Ben Hecht. From A GUIDE FOR THE BEDEVILLED by Ben Hecht. Copyright 1944 by Charles Scribner's Sons.

"The Operation" by Roger Martin Du Gard. From THE THIBAULTS by Roger Martin Du Gard. Copyright 1939 by The Viking Press, Inc. By permission of The Viking Press, Inc., New York.

"Birth" by A. J. Cronin. From THE CITADEL by A. J Cronin. Reprinted by permission of Little, Brown & Company.

"The Medicine Man" by Erskine Caldwell. Reprinted by permission of the publishers, Duell, Sloan & Pearce, Inc.

Contents

xiii

Introduction

It has been said that an anthology is largely a scissors and paste job. The editors of a treasury of doctor stories have not found the anthological life so simple. Compiling a treasury of doctor stories has been an arduous but not unpleasant task. First of all, it involved a major sleuthing project to locate sources of literary materia medica. Then, it meant plodding through masses of extraneous material in order to unearth stories pertinent to the medical scene. Finally came the difficulties of proper selection.

After much reading, rereading and elimination, a treasury of doctor stories took form. Here are stories and experiences which reflect the moods, sentiments and behavior of men, women and children under the duress of varying stages of illness. Here, too, are stories of doctors and nurses living their personal as well as their professional lives. Here are stories whimsical and robust, serious and gay.

One element these stories have in common is the uniform excellence of their literary craftsmanship. The authors have not been interested primarily in the medical scene but in a tale well told. It is interesting to note that without relaxing their literary standards these stories maintain a real medical interest. As a matter of fact, only a few of the authors have had formal medical education. A number of the stories have been accorded literary recognition for their outstanding merit.

The medical scene is so far-flung in all of its ramifications that it is very difficult, if not impossible, to define what material an anthology covering it should include. An encyclopedic anthology, one dealing with all human ailments and depicting physicians in all their aspects, would be theoretically ideal—but, in fact, profoundly boring.

A treasury of doctor stories is by no means all-inclusive and, we hope, by no means boring.

Noah D. Fabricant • *Heinz Werner*

A Treasury of Doctor Stories by The World's Great Authors

Doc Mellhorn and the Pearly Gates

STEPHEN VINCENT BENÉT

Doc Mellhorn had never expected to go anywhere at all when he died. So, when he found himself on the road again, it surprised him. But perhaps I'd better explain a little about Doc Mellhorn first. He was seventy-odd when he left our town; but when he came, he was as young as Bates or Filsinger or any of the boys at the hospital. Only there wasn't any hospital when he came. He came with a young man's beard and a brand-new bag and a lot of newfangled ideas about medicine that we didn't take to much. And he left, forty-odd years later, with a first-class county health record and a lot of people alive that wouldn't have been alive if he hadn't been there. Yes, a country doctor. And nobody ever called him a man in white or a death grappler that I know of, though they did think of giving him a degree at Pewauket College once. But then the board met again and decided they needed a new gymnasium, so they gave the degree to J. Prentiss Parmalee instead.

They say he was a thin young man when he first came, a thin young man with an Eastern accent who'd wanted to study in Vienna. But most of us remember him chunky and solid, with white hair and a little bald spot that always got burned bright red in the first hot weather. He had about four card tricks that he'd do for you, if you were a youngster—they were always the same ones—and now and then, if he felt like it, he'd take a silver half dollar out of the back of your neck. And that worked as well with the youngsters who were going to build rocket ships as it had with the youngsters who were going to be railway engineers. It always worked. I guess it was Doc Mellhorn more than the trick.

But there wasn't anything unusual about him, except maybe the card

3

tricks. Or, anyway, he didn't think so. He was just a good doctor and he knew us inside out. I've heard people call him a pig-head, obstinate old mule—that was in the fight about the water supply. And I've heard a weepy old lady call him a saint. I took the tale to him once, and he looked at me over his glasses and said, "Well, I've always respected a mule. Got ten times the sense of a—horse." Then he took a silver half dollar out of my ear.

Well, how do you describe a man like that? You don't—you call him up at three in the morning. And when he sends in his bill, you think it's a little steep.

All the same, when it came to it, there were people who drove a hundred and fifty miles to the funeral. And the Masons came down from Bluff City, and the Poles came from across the tracks, with a wreath the size of a house, and you saw cars in town that you didn't often see there. But it was after the funeral that the queer things began for Doc Mellhorn.

The last thing he remembered, he'd been lying in bed, feeling pretty sick, on the whole, but glad for the rest. And now he was driving his Model T down a long straight road between rolling, misty prairies that seemed to go from nowhere to nowhere.

It didn't seem funny to him to be driving the Model T again. That was the car he'd learned on, and he kept to it till his family made him change. And it didn't seem funny to him not to be sick any more. He hadn't had much time to be sick in his life—the patients usually attended to that. He looked around for his bag, first thing, but it was there on the seat beside him. It was the old bag, not the presentation one they'd given him at the hospital, but that was all right too. It meant he was out on a call and, if he couldn't quite recollect at the moment just where the call was, it was certain to come to him. He'd wakened up often enough in his buggy, in the old days, and found the horse was taking him home, without his doing much about it. A doctor gets used to things like that.

All the same, when he'd driven and driven for some time without raising so much as a traffic light, just the same rolling prairies on either hand, he began to get a little suspicious. He thought, for a while, of stopping the car and getting out, just to take a look around, but he'd always hated to lose time on a call. Then he noticed something else. He was driving without his glasses. And yet he hadn't driven without his glasses in fifteen years.

"H'm," said Doc Mellhorn. "I'm crazy as a June bug. Or else—Well, it might be so, I suppose."

But this time he did stop the car. He opened his bag and looked inside it, but everything seemed to be in order. He opened his wallet and looked at that, but there were his own initials, half rubbed away, and he recognized them. He took his pulse, but it felt perfectly steady.

"H'm," said Doc Mellhorn. "Well."

Then, just to prove that everything was perfectly normal, he took a silver half dollar out of the steering wheel of the car.

"Never did it smoother," said Doc Mellhorn. "Well, all the same, if this is the new highway, it's longer than I remember it."

But just then a motorcycle came roaring down the road and stopped with a flourish, the way motor cops do.

"Any trouble?" said the motor cop. Doc Mellhorn couldn't see his face for his goggles, but the goggles looked normal.

"I am a physician," said Doc Mellhorn, as he'd said a thousand times before to all sorts of people, "on my way to an urgent case." He passed his hand across his forehead. "Is this the right road?" he said.

"Straight ahead to the traffic light," said the cop. "They're expecting you, Doctor Mellhorn. Shall I give you an escort?"

"No; thanks all the same," said Doc Mellhohn, and the motor cop roared away. The Model T ground as Doc Mellhorn gassed her. "Well, they've got a new breed of traffic cop," said Doc Mellhorn, "or else—"

But when he got to the light, it was just like any light at a crossroads. He waited till it changed and the officer waved him on. There seemed to be a good deal of traffic going the other way, but he didn't get a chance to notice it much, because Lizzie bucked a little, as she usually did when you kept her waiting. Still, the sight of traffic relieved him, though he hadn't passed anybody on his own road yet.

Pretty soon he noticed the look of the country had changed. It was parkway now and very nicely landscaped. There was dogwood in bloom on the little hills, white and pink against the green; though, as Doc Mell-horn remembered it, it had been August when he left his house. And every now and then there'd be a nice little white-painted sign that said TO THE GATES.

"H'm," said Doc Mellhorn. "New State Parkway, I guess. Well, they've fixed it up pretty. But I wonder where they got the dogwood. Haven't seen it bloom like that since I was East."

. Then he drove along in a sort of dream for a while, for the dogwood reminded him of the days when he was a young man in an Eastern col-lege. He remembered the look of that college and the girls who'd come to dances, the girls who wore white gloves and had rolls of hair. They were pretty girls, too, and he wondered what had become of them. "Had babies, I guess," thought Doc Mellhorn. "Or some of them, anyway." But he liked to think of them as the way they had been when they were just pretty, and excited at being at a dance.

He remembered other things too—the hacked desks in the lecture rooms, and the trees on the campus, and the first pipe he'd ever broken in, and a fellow called Paisley Grew that he hadn't thought of in years—a raw-boned fellow with a gift for tall stories and playing the jew's-harp.

"Ought to have looked up Paisley," he said. "Yes, I ought. Didn't amount to a hill of beans, I guess, but I always liked him. I wonder if he still plays the jew's-harp. Pshaw, I know he's been dead twenty years."

He was passing other cars now and other cars were passing him, but he didn't pay much attention, except when he happened to notice a license you didn't often see in the state, like Rhode Island or Mississippi. He was too full of his own thoughts. There were foot passengers, too, plenty of them—and once he passed a man driving a load of hay. He wondered what the man would do with the hay when he got to the Gates. But prob-ably there were arrangements for that.

"Not that I believe a word of it," he said, "but it'll surprise Father Kelly. Or maybe it won't. I used to have some handsome arguments with that man, but I always knew I could count on him, in spite of me being a heretic."

Then he saw the Wall and the Gates, right across the valley. He saw them, and they reached to the top of the sky. He rubbed his eyes for a while, but they kept on being there.

"Quite a sight," said Doc Mellhorn.

No one told him just where to go or how to act, but it seemed to him that he knew. If he'd thought about it, he'd have said that you waited in line, but there wasn't any waiting in line. He just went where he was expected to go and the reception clerk knew his name right away.

"Yes, Doctor Mellhorn," he said. "And now, what would you like to do first?"

"I think I'd like to sit down," said Doc Mellhorn. So he sat, and it was a comfortable chair. He even bounced the springs of it once or twice, till he caught the reception clerk's eye on him.

"Is there anything I can get you you?" said the reception clerk. He was young and brisk and neat as a pin, and you could see he aimed to give service and studied about it. Doc Mellhorn thought, "He's the kind that wipse off your windshield no matter how clean it is."

"No," said Doc Mellhorn. "You see, I don't believe this. I don't believe any of it. I'm sorry if that sounds cranky, but I don't."

"That's quite all right, sir," said the reception clerk. "It often takes a while." And he smiled as if Doc Mellhorn had done him a favor.

"Young man, I'm a physician," said Doc Mellhorn, "and do you mean to tell me—"

Then he stopped, for he suddenly saw there was no use arguing. He was either there or he wasn't. And it felt as if he were there.

"Well," said Doc Mellhorn, with a sigh, "how do I begin?"

"That's entirely at your own volition, sir," said the reception clerk briskly. "Any meetings with relatives, of course. Or if you would prefer to get yourself settled first. Or take a tour, alone or conducted. Perhaps these will offer suggestions," and he started to hand over a handful of leaflets. But Doc Mellhorn put them aside.

"Wait a minute," he said. "I want to think. Well, naturally, there's Mother and Dad. But I couldn't see them just yet. I wouldn't believe it. And Grandma—well, now, if I saw Grandma—and me older than she is —was—used to be—well, I don't know what it would do to me. You've got to let me get my breath. Well, of course, there's Uncle Frank—he'd be easier." He paused. "Is he here?" he said.

The reception clerk looked in a file. "I'm happy to say that Mr. Francis V. Mellhorn arrived July 12, 1907," he said. He smiled winningly.

"Well!" said Doc Mellhorn. "Uncle Frank! Well, I'll be—well! But it must have been a great consolation to Mother. We heard—well, never mind what we heard—I guess it wasn't so. . . . No, don't reach for that phone just yet, or whatever it is. I'm still thinking."

"We sometimes find," said the reception clerk eagerly, "that a person not a relative may be the best introduction. Even a stranger sometimes—a distinguished stranger connected with one's own profession—"

"Well, now that's an idea," said Doc Mellhorn heartily to keep his mind off how much he disliked the reception clerk. He couldn't just say why he disliked him, but he knew he did.

It reminded him of the time he'd had to have his gall bladder out in the city hospital and the young, brisk interns had come to see him and called him "Doctor" every other word.

"Yes, that's an idea," he said He reflected. "Well, of course, I'd like to see Koch," he said. "And Semmelweiss. Not to speak of Walter Reed. But, shucks, they'd be busy men. But there is one fellow—only he lived pretty far back—"

"Hippocrates, please," said the reception clerk into the telephone or whatever it was. "*H* for horse—"

"No!" said Doc Mellhorn quite violently. "Excuse me, but you just wait a minute. I mean if you can wait. I mean, if Hippocrates wants to come, I've no objection. But I never took much of a fancy to him, in spite of his oath. It's Aesculapius I'm thinking about. George W. Oh, glory!" he said. "But he won't talk English. I forgot."

"I shall be happy to act as interpreter," said the reception clerk, smiling brilliantly.

"I haven't a doubt," said Doc Mellhorn. "But just wait a shake." In a minute, by the way the clerk was acting, he was going to be talking to Aesculapius. "And what in time am I going to say to the man?" he thought. "It's too much." He gazed wildly around the neat reception room—distempered, as he noticed, in a warm shade of golden tan. Then his eyes fell on the worn black bag at his feet and a sudden warm wave of relief flooded over him.

"Wait a minute," he said, and his voice gathered force and authority. "Where's my patient?"

"Patient?" said the reception clerk, looking puzzled for the first time.

"Patient," said Doc Mellhorn. *"P* for phlebitis." He tapped his bag.

"I'm afraid you don't quite understand, sir," said the reception clerk.

"I understand this," said Doc Mellhorn. "I was called here. And if I wasn't called professionally, why have I got my bag?"

"But, my dear Doctor Mellhorn—" said the reception clerk.

"I'm not your dear doctor," said Doc Mellhorn. "I was called here, I tell you. I'm sorry not to give you the patient's name, but the call must have come in my absence and the girl doesn't spell very well. But in any well-regulated hospital—"

"But I tell you," said the reception clerk, and his hair wasn't slick any more, "nobody's ill here. Nobody can be ill. If they could, it wouldn't be He—"

"Humph," said Doc Mellhorn. He thought it over, and felt worse. "Then what does a fellow like Koch do?" he said. "Or Pasteur?" He raised a hand. "Oh, don't tell me," he said. "I can see they'd be busy. Yes, I guess it'd be all right for a research man. But I never was ... Oh, well, shucks, I've published a few papers. And there's that clamp of mine—always meant to do something about it. But they've got better ones now. Mean to say there isn't so much as a case of mumps in the whole place?"

"I assure you," said the reception clerk, in a weary voice. "And now, once you see Doctor Aesculapius—"

"Funny," said Doc Mellhorn. "Lord knows there's plenty of times you'd be glad to be quit of the whole thing. And don't talk to me about the healer's art or grateful patients. Well, I've known a few ... a few. But I've known others. All the same, it's different, being told there isn't any need for what you can do."

"A for Ararat," said the reception clerk into his instrument. *"E* for Eden."

"Should think you'd have a dial," said Doc Mellhorn desperately. "We've got 'em down below." He thought hard and frantically. "Wait a shake. It's coming back to me," he said. "Got anybody named Grew here? Paisley Grew?"

"*S* for serpent . . ." said the reception clerk. "What was that?"

"Fellow that called me," said Doc Mellhorn. "G-r-e-w. First name, Paisley."

"I will consult the index," said the reception clerk.

He did so, and Doc Mellhorn waited, hoping against hope.

"We have 94,183 Grews, including 83 Prescotts and one Penobscot," the reception clerk said at last. "But I fail to find Paisley Grew. Are you quite sure of the name?"

"Of course," said Doc Mellhorn briskly. "Paisley Grew. Chronic indigestion. Might be appendix—can't say—have to see. But anyhow, he's called." He picked up his bag. "Well, thanks for the information," he said, liking the reception clerk better than he had yet. "Not your fault, anyway."

"But—but where are you going?" said the reception clerk.

"Well, there's another establishment, isn't there?" said Doc Mellhorn. "Always heard there was. Call probably came from there. Crossed wires, I expect."

"But you can't go there!" said the reception clerk. "I mean—"

"Can't go?" said Doc Mellhorn. "I'm a physician. A patient's called me."

"But if you'll only wait and see Aesculapius!" said the reception clerk, running his hands wildly through his hair. "He'll be here almost any moment."

"Please give him my apologies," said Doc Mellhorn. "He's a doctor. He'll understand. And if any messages come for me, just stick them on the spike. Do I need a road map? Noticed the road I came was all one way."

"There is, I believe, a back road in rather bad repair," said the reception clerk icily. "I can call Information if you wish."

"Oh, don't bother," said Doc Mellhorn. "I'll find it. And I never saw a road beat Lizzie yet." He took a silver half dollar from the doorknob of the door. "See that?" he said. "Slick as a whistle. Well, good-by, young man."

But it wasn't till he'd cranked up Lizzie and was on his way that Doc Mellhorn felt safe. He found the back road and it was all the reception clerk had said it was and more. But he didn't mind—in fact, after one particularly bad rut, he grinned.

"I suppose I ought to have seen the folks," he said. "Yes, I know I ought. But—not so much as a case of mumps in the whole abiding dominion! Well, it's lucky I took a chance on Paisley Grew."

After another mile or so, he grinned again.

"And I'd like to see old Aesculapius' face. Probably rang him in the middle of dinner—they always do. But shucks, it's happened to all of us."

Well, the road got worse and worse and the sky above it darker and darker, and what with one thing and another, Doc Mellhorn was glad enough when he got to the other gates. They were pretty impressive gates, too, though of course in a different way, and reminded Doc Mellhorn a little of the furnaces outside Steeltown, where he'd practised for a year when he was young.

This time Doc Mellhorn wasn't going to take any advice from reception clerks and he had his story all ready. All the same, he wasn't either registered or expected, so there was a little fuss. Finally they tried to scare him by saying he came at his own risk and that there were some pretty tough characters about. But Doc Mellhorn remarked that he'd practiced in Steeltown. So after he'd told them what seemed to him a million times that he was a physician on a case, they finally let him in and directed him to Paisley Grew. Paisley was on Level 346 in Pit 68,953, and Doc Mellhorn recognized him the minute he saw him. He even had the jew's-harp, stuck in the back of his overalls.

"Well, Doc," said Paisley finally, when the first greetings were over, "you certainly are a sight for sore eyes! Though, of course, I'm sorry to see you here," and he grinned.

"Well, I can't see that it's so different from a lot of places," said Doc Mellhorn, wiping his forehead. "Warmish, though."

"It's the humidity, really," said Paisley Grew. "That's what it really is."

"Yes, I know," said Doc Mellhorn. "And now tell me, Paisley; how's that indigestion of yours?"

"Well, I'll tell you, Doc," said Paisley. "When I first came here, I thought the climate was doing it good. I did for a fact. But now I'm not so sure. I've tried all sorts of things for it—I've even tried being transferred to the boiling asphalt lakes. But it just seems to hang on, and every now and then, when I least expect it, it catches me. Take last night. I didn't have a thing to eat that I don't generally eat—well, maybe I did have one little snort of hot sulphur, but it wasn't the sulphur that did it. All the same, I woke up at four, and it was just like a knife. Now . . ."

He went on from there and it took him some time. And Doc Mellhorn listened, happy as a clam. He never thought he'd be glad to listen to a hypochondriac, but he was. And when Paisley was all through, he examined him and prescribed for him. It was just a little soda bicarb and pepsin, but Paisley said it took hold something wonderful. And they had a fine time that evening, talking over the old days.

Finally, of course, the talk got around to how Paisley liked it where he was. And Paisley was honest enough about that.

"Well, Doc," he said, "of course this isn't the place for you, and I can see you're just visiting. But I haven't many real complaints. It's hot, to be sure, and they work you, and some of the boys here are rough. But they've had some pretty interesting experiences, too, when you get them talking—yes, sir. And anyhow, it isn't Peabodyville, New Jersey," he said with vehemence. "I spent five years in Peabodyville, trying to work up in the leather business. After that I bust out, and I guess that's what landed me here. But it's an improvement on Peabodyville." He looked at Doc Mellhorn sidewise. "Say, Doc," he said, "I know this is a vacation for you, but all the same there's a couple of the boys—nothing really wrong with them of course—but—well, if you could just look them over—"

"I was thinking the office hours would be nine to one," said Doc Mellhorn.

So Paisley took him around and they found a nice little place for an office in one of the abandoned mine galleries, and Doc Mellhorn hung out his shingle. And right away patients started coming around. They didn't get many doctors there, in the first place, and the ones they did get weren't exactly the cream of the profession, so Doc Mellhorn had it all to himself. It was mostly sprains, fractures, bruises and dislocations, of course, with occasional burns and scalds—and, on the whole, it reminded Doc Mellhorn a good deal of his practice in Steeltown, especially when it came to foreign bodies in the eye. Now and then Doc Mellhorn ran into a more unusual case—for instance, there was one of the guards that got part of himself pretty badly damaged in a rock slide. Well, Doc Mellhorn had never set a tail before, but he managed it all right, and got a beautiful primary union, too, in spite of the fact that he had no X-ray facilities. He thought of writing up the case for the State Medical Journal, but then he couldn't figure out any way to send it to them, so he had to let it slide. And then there was an advanced carcinoma of the liver—a Greek named Papadoupolous or Prometheus or something. Doc Mellhorn couldn't do much for him, considering the circumstances, but he did what he could, and he and the Greek used to have long conversations. The rest was just everyday practice—run of the mine—but he enjoyed it.

Now and then it would cross his mind that he ought to get out Lizzie and run back to the other place for a visit with the folks. But that was just like going back East had been on earth—he'd think he had everything pretty well cleared up, and then a new flock of patients would come in. And it wasn't that he didn't miss his wife and children and grandchildren—he did. But there wasn't any way to get back to them, and he knew it. And there was the work in front of him and the office crowded every day. So he just went along, hardly noticing the time.

Now and then, to be sure, he'd get a suspicion that he wasn't too popular with the authorities of the place. But he was used to not being popular with authorities and he didn't pay much attention. But finally they sent an inspector around. The minute Doc Mellhorn saw him, he knew there was going to be trouble.

Not that the inspector was uncivil. In fact, he was a pretty high-up official—you could tell by his antlers. And Doc Mellhorn was just as polite, showing him around. He showed him the free dispensary and the clinic and the nurse—Scotch girl named Smith, she was—and the dental chair he'd rigged up with the help of a fellow named Ferguson, who used to be an engineer before he was sentenced. And the inspector looked them all over, and finally he came back to Doc Mellhorn's office. The girl named Smith had put up curtains in the office, and with that and a couple of potted gas plants it looked more homelike than it had. The inspector looked around it and sighed.

"I'm sorry, Doctor Mellhorn," he said at last, "but you can see for yourself, it won't do."

"What won't do?" said Doc Mellhorn, stoutly. But, all the same, he felt afraid.

"Any of it," said the inspector. "We could overlook the alleviation of minor suffering—I'd be inclined to do so myself—though these people are here to suffer, and there's no changing that. But you're playing merry Hades with the whole system."

"I'm a physician in practice," said Doc Mellhorn.

"Yes," said the inspector. "That's just the trouble. Now, take these reports you've been sending," and he took out a sheaf of papers. "What have you to say about that?"

"Well, seeing as there's no county health officer, or at least I couldn't find one—" said Doc Mellhorn.

"Precisely," said the inspector. "And what have you done? You've condemned fourteen levels of this pit as unsanitary nuisances. You've recommended 2136 lost souls for special diet, remedial exercise, hospitalization—Well—I won't go through the list."

"I'll stand back of every one of those recommendations," said Doc Mellhorn. "And now we've got the chair working, we can handle most of the dental work on the spot. Only Ferguson needs more amalgam."

"I know," said the inspector patiently, "but the money has to come from somewhere—you must realize that. We're not a rich community, in spite of what people think. And these unauthorized requests—oh, we fill them, of course, but—"

"Ferguson needs more amalgam," said Doc Mellhorn. "And that last batch wasn't standard. I wouldn't use it on a dog."

"He's always needing more amalgam!" said the inspector bitterly, making a note. "Is he going to fill every tooth in Hades? By the way, my wife tells me I need a little work done myself—but we won't go into that. We'll take just one thing—your entirely unauthorized employment of Miss Smith. Miss Smith has no business working for you. She's supposed to be gnawed by a never-dying worm every Monday, Wednesday and Friday."

"Sounds silly to me," said Doc Mellhorn.

"I don't care how silly it sounds," said the inspector. "It's regulations. And, besides, she isn't even a registered nurse."

"She's a practical one," said Doc Mellhorn. "Of course back on earth a lot of her patients died. But that was because when she didn't like a patient, she poisoned him. Well, she can't poison anybody here and I've kind of got her out of the notion of it anyway. She's been doing A-1 work for me and I'd like to recommend her for—"

"Please!" said the inspector. "Please! And as if that wasn't enough, you've even been meddling with the staff. I've a note here on young Asmodeus—Asmodeus XIV—"

"Oh, you mean Mickey!" said Doc Mellhorn, with a chuckle. "Short for Mickey Mouse. We call him that in the clinic. And he's a young imp if I ever saw one."

"The original Asmodeus is one of our most prominent citizens," said the inspector severely. "How do you suppose he felt when we got your report that his fourteenth great-grandson had rickets?"

"Well," said Doc Mellhorn, "I know rickets. And he had 'em. And you're going to have rickets in these youngsters as long as you keep feeding 'em low-grade coke. I put Mickey on the best Pennsylvania anthracite and look at him now!"

"I admit the success of your treatment," said the inspector, "but, naturally—well, since then we've been deluged with demands for anthracite from as far south as Sheol. We'll have a float a new bond issue. And what will the taxpayers say?"

"He was just cutting his first horns when he came to us," said Doc

Mellhorn reminiscently, "and they were coming in crooked. Now, I ask you, did you ever see a straighter pair? Of course, if I'd had cod liver oil—My gracious, you ought to have somebody here that can fill a prescription; I can't do it all."

The inspector shut his papers together with a snap. "I'm sorry, Doctor Mellhorn," he said, "but this is final. You have no right here, in the first place; no local license to practice in the second—"

"Yes, that's a little irregular," said Doc Mellhorn "but I'm a registered member of four different medical associations—you might take that into account. And I'll take any examination that's required."

"No," said the inspector violently. "No, no, no! You can't stay here! You've got to go away! It isn't possible!"

Doc Mellhorn drew a long breath. "Well," he said, "there wasn't any work for me at the other place. And here you won't let me practice. So what's a man to do?"

The inspector was silent.

"Tell me," said Doc Mellhorn presently. "Suppose you do throw me out? What happens to Miss Smith and Paisley and the rest of them?"

"Oh, what's done is done," said the inspector impatiently, "here as well as anywhere else. We'll have to keep on with the anthracite and the rest of it. And Hades only knows what'll happen in the future. If it's any satisfaction to you, you've started something."

"Well, I guess Smith and Ferguson between them can handle the practice," said Doc Mellhorn. "But that's got to be a promise."

"It's a promise," said the inspector.

"Then there's Mickey—I mean Asmodeus," said Doc Mellhorn. "He's a smart youngster—smart as a whip—if he is a hellion. Well, you know how a youngster gets. Well, it seems he wants to be a doctor. But I don't know what sort of training he'd get—"

"He'll get it," said the inspector feverishly. "We'll found the finest medical college you ever saw, right here in West Ball. We'll build a hospital that'll knock your eye out. You'll be satisfied. But now, if you don't mind—"

"All right," said Doc Mellhorn, and rose.

The inspector looked surprised. "But don't you want to—" he said. "I mean my instructions are we're to give you a banquet, if necessary—after all, the community appreciates—"

"Thanks," said Doc Mellhorn, with a shudder, "but if I've got to go, I'd rather get out of town. You hang around and announce your retirement, and pretty soon folks start thinking they ought to give you a testimonial. And I never did like testimonials."

All the same, before he left he took a silver half dollar out of Mickey Asmodeus' chin.

When he was back on the road again and the lights of the gates had faded into a low ruddy glow behind him, Doc Mellhorn felt alone for the first time. He'd been lonely at times during his life, but he'd never felt alone like this before. Because, as far as he could see, there was only him and Lizzie now.

"Now, maybe if I'd talked to Aesculapius—" he said. "But pshaw, I always was pigheaded."

He didn't pay much attention to the way he was driving and it seemed to him that the road wasn't quite the same. But he felt tired for a wonder —bone-tired and beaten—and he didn't much care about the road. He hadn't felt tired since he left earth, but now the loneliness tired him.

"Active—always been active," he said to himself. "I can't just lay down on the job. But what's a man to do?"

"What's a man to do?" he said. "I'm a doctor. I can't work miracles."

Then the black fit came over him and he remembered all the times he'd been wrong and all the people he couldn't do anything for. "Never was much of a doctor, I guess," he said. "Maybe, if I'd gone to Vienna. Well, the right kind of man would have gone. And about that Bigelow kid," he said. "How was I to know he'd hemorrhage? But I should have known.

"I've diagnosed walking typhoid as appendicitis. Just the once, but that's enough. And I still don't know what held me back when I was all ready to operate. I used to wake up in a sweat, six months afterward, thinking I had.

"I could have saved those premature twins. if I'd known as much then as I do now. I guess that guy Dafoe would have done it anyway—look at what he had to work with. But I didn't. And that finished the Gorhams' having children. That's a dandy doctor, isn't it? Makes you feel fine.

"I could have pulled Old Man Halsey through. And Edna Biggs. And the little Lauriat girl. No. I couldn't have done it with her. That was before insulin. I couldn't have cured Ted Allen. No, I'm clear on that. But I've never been satisfied about the Collins woman. Bates is all right— good as they come. But I knew her, inside and out—ought to, too—she was the biggest nuisance that ever came into the office. And if I hadn't been down with the flu . . .

"Then there's the flu epidemic. I didn't take my clothes off, four days and nights. But what's the good of that, when you lose them? Oh, sure, the statistics looked good. You can have the statistics.

"Should have started raising hell about the water supply two years before I did.

"Oh, yes, it makes you feel fine, pulling babies into the world. Makes you feel you're doing something. And just fine when you see a few of them, twenty-thirty years later, not worth two toots on a cow's horn. Can't say I ever delivered a Dillinger. But there's one or two in state's prison. And more that ought to be. Don't mind even that so much as a few of the fools. Makes you wonder.

"And then, there's incurable cancer. That's a daisy. What can you do about it, Doctor? Well, Doctor, we can alleviate the pain in the last stages. Some. Ever been in a cancer ward, Doctor? Yes, Doctor, I have.

"What do you do for the common cold, Doctor? Two dozen clean linen handkerchiefs. Yes, it's a good joke—I'll laugh. And what do you do for a boy when you know he's dying, Doctor? Take a silver half dollar out of his ear. But it kept the Lane kid quiet and his fever went down that night. I took the credit, but I don't know why it went down.

"I've only got one brain. And one pair of hands.

"I could have saved. I could have done. I could have.

"Guess it's just as well you can't live forever. You make fewer mistakes. And sometimes I'd see Bates looking at me as if he wondered why I ever thought I could practice.

"Pigheaded, opinionated, ineffective old imbecile! And yet, Lord, Lord, I'd do it all over again."

He lifted his eyes from the pattern of the road in front of him. There were white markers on it now and Lizzie seemed to be bouncing down a residential street. There were trees in the street and it reminded him of town. He rubbed his eyes for a second and Lizzie rolled on by herself—she often did. It didn't seem strange to him to stop at the right house.

"Well, Mother," he said rather gruffly to the group on the lawn. "Well, Dad. . . . Well, Uncle Frank." He beheld a small, stern figure advancing, hands outstretched. "Well, Grandma," he said meekly.

Later on he was walking up and down in the grape arbor with Uncle Frank. Now and then he picked a grape and ate it. They'd always been good grapes, those Catawbas, as he remembered them.

"What beats me," he said, not for the first time, "is why I didn't notice the Gates. The second time, I mean."

"Oh, that Gate," said Uncle Frank, with the easy, unctuous roll in his voice that Doc Mellhorn so well remembered. He smoothed his handle-bar mustaches. "That Gate, my dear Edward—well, of course it has to be there in the first place. Literature, you know. And then, it's a choice," he said richly.

"I'll draw cards," said Doc Mellhorn. He ate another grape.

"Fact is," said Uncle Frank, "that Gate's for one kind of person. You pass it and then you can rest for all eternity. Just fold your hands. It suits some."

"I can see that it would," said Doc Mellhorn.

"Yes," said Uncle Frank, "but it wouldn't suit a Mellhorn. I'm happy to say that very few of our family remain permanently on that side. I spent some time there myself." He said, rather self-consciously, "Well, my last years had been somewhat stormy. So few people cared for refined impersonations of our feathered songsters, including lightning sketches. I felt that I'd earned a rest. But after a while—well, I got tired of being at liberty."

"And what happens when you get tired?" said Doc Mellhorn.

"You find out what you want to do," said Uncle Frank.

"My kind of work?" said Doc Mellhorn.

"Your kind of work," said his uncle. "Been busy, haven't you?"

"Well," said Doc Mellhorn. "But here. If there isn't so much as a case of mumps in—"

"Would it have to be mumps?" said his uncle. "Of course, if you're aching for mumps, I guess it could be arranged. But how many new souls do you suppose we get here a day?"

"Sizable lot, I expect."

"And how many of them get here in first-class condition?" said Uncle Frank triumphantly. "Why, I've seen Doctor Rush—Benjamin Rush—come back so tired from a day's round he could hardly flap one pinion against the other. Oh, if it's work you want—And then, of course, there's the earth."

"Hold on," said Doc Mellhorn. "I'm not going to appear to any young intern in wings and a harp. Not at my time of life. And anyway, he'd laugh himself sick."

" 'Tain't that," said Uncle Frank. "Look here. You've left children and grandchildren behind you, haven't you? And they're going on?"

"Yes," said Doc Mellhorn.

"Same with what you did," said Uncle Frank. "I mean the inside part of it—that stays. I don't mean any funny business—voices in your ear and all that. But haven't you ever got clean tuckered out, and been able to draw on something you didn't know was there?"

"Pshaw, any man's done that," said Doc Mellhorn. "But you take the adrenal—"

"Take anything you like," said Uncle Frank placidly. "I'm not going to argue with you. Not my department. But you'll find it isn't all adrenalin. Like it here?" he said abruptly. "Feel satisfied?"

"Why, yes," said Doc Mellhorn surprisedly, "I do." He looked around the grape arbor and suddenly realized that he felt happy.

"No, they wouldn't all arrive in first-class shape," he said to himself. "So there'd be a place." He turned to Uncle Frank. "By the way," he said diffidently, "I mean, I got back so quick—there wouldn't be a chance of my visiting the other establishment now and then? Where I just came from? Smith and Ferguson are all right, but I'd like to keep in touch."

"Well," said Uncle Frank, "you can take that up with the delegation." He arranged the handkerchief in his breast pocket. "They ought to be along any minute now," he said. "Sister's been in a stew about it all day. She says there won't be enough chairs, but she always says that."

"Delegation?" said Doc Mellhorn. "But—"

"You don't realize," said Uncle Frank, with his rich chuckle. "You're a famous man. You've broken pretty near every regulation except the fire laws, and refused the Gate first crack. They've got to do something about it."

"But—" said Doc Mellhorn, looking wildly around for a place of escape.

"Sh-h!" hissed Uncle Frank. "Hold up your head and look as though money were bid for you. It won't take long—just a welcome." He shaded his eyes with his hand. "My," he said with frank admiration, "you've certainly brought them out. There's Rush, by the way."

"Where?" said Doc Mellhorn.

"Second from the left, third row, in a wig," said Uncle Frank. "And there's—"

Then he stopped, and stepped aside. A tall grave figure was advancing down the grape arbor—a bearded man with a wise majestic face who wore robes as if they belonged to him, not as Doc Mellhorn had seen them worn in college commencements. There was a small fillet of gold about his head and in his left hand, Doc Mellhorn noticed without astonishment, was a winged staff entwined with two fangless serpents. Behind him were many others. Doc Mellhorn stood straighter.

The bearded figure stopped in front of Doc Mellhorn. "Welcome, Brother," said Aesculapius.

"It's an honor to meet you, Doctor," said Doc Mellhorn. He shook the outstretched hand. Then he took a silver half dollar from the mouth of the left-hand snake.

The Nurse

BEN AMES WILLIAMS

THERE is a curious institution, widely distributed, called the waiting room. You will find specimens almost everywhere, in railroad stations, in hotels, in department stores, and in business offices of every description. The waiting room is a fearful thing. At best it offers boredom, and at the worst it is a place where one sits through minutes that seem interminable, filled with apprehension or with despair.

Millie had had some experience of waiting rooms, and she dreaded them. She had been sitting in this particular waiting room at the employment agency for three days. She was a little woman, one of those women whose appearance suggests that they have been wrung dry by the torque and torsion of their own emotions; a little woman thin and taut and just now curiously tremulous. She was probably about forty-five years old and she sat among the others without taking any part in the occasional passages of conversation among them. She seemed to be unconscious of their presence, and her eyes, inflamed and weary, looked blankly straight before her. And sometimes, for no apparent reason, they became suffused with tears; not merely misted with moisture, but drowned in a swimming, drenching flood which flowed over her lids and down her dry cheeks until she remembered to wipe away these evidences of the grief which racked her.

On her first day, when she had tried to talk with a prospective employer, she had been unable to control her voice; and her eyes had thus gushed tears till the other woman said impatiently:

"Well, I certainly don't want you if you're the crying kind," and turned away.

Millie had then been rather relieved than disappointed. She always dreaded this necessity of seeking new employment while she was still in the throes of her latest loss. So she sat all that day and the next and into the third. And whenever it appeared that she must talk with one of those who came here seeking servants, she averted her eyes, weakly endeavoring to avoid attracting their notice, willing to put off the inevitable adventure of new employment.

But on the third day she found herself replying in a dull voice to the questions put to her by a woman, perhaps thirty years old, who introduced herself by a name which Millie scarcely heard. She was not interested in the names of her mistresses; she had had so many of them. They were a shadowy procession in the background of her life, those in the past no more definite in her mind than those who waited for her in the future. This woman's name might have been Smith or Brown. It happened to be Mrs. Jones.

Millie answered her questions in a dull and lifeless tone, telling as impersonally as though she spoke of someone else what her life had been. She had been a baby nurse since she was seventeen years old. It would be hard to pack into one sentence a more tragic biography. A woman who has loved one baby and lost it wears forever after in her eyes the mark of her grief like a pale flower. But Millie had been condemned by life to love many babies and to lose them all.

Mrs. Jones asked question upon question, but Millie asked only one. "Is it a boy or a girl?"

"A little girl," Mrs. Jones replied, and Millie's ravaged face seemed to lighten faintly at the word.

"I always like the girls best," she confessed.

They arranged for Millie to come the next morning to take the place, and Millie was for the rest of that day a little more cheerful. Her aching grief found anodyne in the prospect of having another baby to love.

There is hardly another ordeal comparable to that of entering the home of strangers and finding yourself there at once an alien, an outsider, liable to instant dismissal, and at the same time in such an intimate relation to the life of the family as that held by the baby nurse. Millie was still sick with sorrow over the loss of her last baby, a loss as irrevocable and a grief as poignant as though the baby had died. But she had no more tears, and she entered this new household, hiding her misery behind a stony countenance.

Mrs. Jones was a friendly, kindly young woman, competent, sure of what she wanted, and at once firm and conciliatory. She was just out of the hospital, and there was still a trained nurse in the house. The little girl who was to be Millie's baby now was about six weeks old.

"Her name is Joan," Mrs. Jones explained to Millie. "This is her room, and you will use this bathroom, and you can keep her things on these shelves, and you will sleep here across the hall."

Millie, with every desire in the world to conciliate her new mistress, nevertheless found herself saying in an exacting tone:

"I always want to sleep in the room with my babies, so I can hear them in the night."

Mrs. Jones nodded willingly enough.

"If you prefer, that is quite all right," she assented. "I will have a cot put in here for you; but I think by the time Joan is three months old we can give up her night feedings altogether. We did with Johnnie."

Millie had already seen Johnnie, the son of the house, about six years old and a lively youngster. Although she had an infinite and understanding tenderness for little babies, she had long since learned that when they grew old enough to walk and to talk they began to escape from her. She knew that she could not, as the saying is, "get along with older children"; and she asked Mrs. Jones now:

"Do you want I should take care of Johnnie too?"

"He can dress himself," Mrs. Jones said proudly. "And he sleeps all night, and he has breakfast and lunch with us. Charles gives him his supper, and he goes to bed before our dinner. I will want you to keep his room in order; but you won't have much to do with him."

"I like to give all my time to my baby," Millie explained, and Mrs. Jones agreed:

"You'll have very little else to do."

The trained nurse left the next day, and Millie threw herself at once into the interminable routine of petty tasks which the care of a small baby brings in its train. Mrs. Jones had been unable to nurse the child more than two weeks, so that Joan was already on the bottle. Millie roused at about half-past five every morning, heated the first bottle over the small electric plate in the bathroom, and held it while Joan absorbed its contents. Afterward the baby slept for an hour or more, while Millie had time to dress, to have her breakfast in the kitchen with Charles and Laura, and to do some of the enormous amount of washing which had to be done every day. At eight o'clock she took Joan up and bathed her.

Another bottle, another sleep, another waking and another bottle, fresh clothing, and so to sleep again. Thus the recurring days.

In the care of Joan, Millie was perfectly and passionately happy; but not in her other relations. From the beginning she disliked young Johnnie so definitely that at times her feeling amounted to hatred. He was, of course, disorderly, and even though she might be tired and her back might be aching, it was necessary for her to busy herself about his room, forever putting back in their places things which he as continually threw into confusion again. Also, he was noisy, and whenever his shrill voice was upraised she expected him to wake Joan; and if she was near enough, she always tried to command him to silence. But the second or third time this occurred, Mrs. Jones reproved her.

"You must expect Johnnie to be noisy, Millie," she told the nurse.

"He'll wake my baby," Millie jealously retorted.

Mrs. Jones smiled a little, and said, "I'm afraid we're a noisy household. Joan will have to get used to living with us. You mustn't keep hushing Johnnie. After all, he has his rights as well as Joan."

Millie was silenced, because she knew by experience that those considerations which seemed to her so overwhelming would have no weight with her mistress; and her position was weak, since Joan was from the first a sound sleeper, quite undisturbed by anything that went on in the big house. But the fact that Joan never did waken could not prevent Millie's being constantly afraid she would, and a remonstrance at Johnnie's noise was forever on the tip of her tongue.

There were many other disturbing sounds in the house, and they all jarred on her taut nerves; so that after each burst of laughter, or cry, or concussion of a slamming door, she would sit tensely listening for long seconds, expecting a wail of distress from the room where Joan was sleeping.

It did not matter what the source of these noises might be, she resented them all equally. When Johnnie was to blame she was furious; and when older folk were responsible her anger was even more intense. One night two guests came in to dinner and, since the weather was bad, Mr. and Mrs. Jones insisted that they stay over night. When the four of them came upstairs to go to bed, there was a good deal of talking and laughing in the halls; and Millie's anger overcame her prudence so that she put on her dressing gown, and—an absurd little figure with her small braid hanging between her shoulders—she came out into the hall and faced them with burning eyes, and said sharply:

"Joan has just gone to sleep. You'll have to keep quiet. I can't have her waked up now."

Mr. Jones himself replied sternly, "She never wakes, Millie. And even if she did, she cannot expect us to go whispering about the house all the time." He was a large man, his very bulk impressive, and Millie hated him as much as she feared him. But she dared make no reply and retreated to her own room full of bitter rage.

She soon found herself involved in continual discord with Charles, the house man who did the chores and served the meals, and with Laura, his wife, the cook. Millie had her meals with them in the kitchen, and it seemed to her that they were extravagant in their use of electricity and gas, and that they wasted food. The great love which she always gave her babies left in her nothing but angry resentment at the rest of the world; and, although she knew from experience that only trouble could come from any altercation between her and the other servants, she was unable to refrain from criticising their methods to them and to Mrs. Jones.

Mrs. Jones at first received these reports without comment; but the situation became more and more acute until she was compelled at last to silence Millie and to bid her attend to her own work and let the others attend to theirs.

"You are here to take care of Joan, Millie," she said definitely. "I do not ask you to supervise Charles and Laura. That is my business. They do their work and you do yours, and what they do or how they do it does not concern you."

Millie, knowing the danger in such a course, nevertheless could not refrain from a protesting word. "I can't have them wasting electric light the way they do," she said stridently. And Mrs. Jones replied:

"If you can't be happy here, Millie, you are perfectly free to go at any time; but I will not have you interfering with the other servants."

Millie made no reply. At this word, this suggestion of her leaving, she had been struck with such stark terror that she could not speak. At this time she had been only about two months in the Jones household. In the normal course of events she might expect to stay until Joan was two years old, and there was always a chance that another baby might appear in the meantime to prolong her sojourn. To leave now, while Joan was still small, would be to lose her baby; and she could not bear to contemplate that possibility. Already Joan had ascended to that throne in her heart which so many babies had occupied before. They had become shades, shadows of lost loved ones in the background of her thoughts; but Joan was alive, actual, twelve or fourteen pounds of substantial, tangible, sweet flesh; and she began already to know Millie, to look forward to her appearances, and to respond to her caresses and endearments with wide and toothless smiles.

This is the tragedy of the baby nurse, that she loves her baby so completely that she will endure anything human flesh can endure rather than be separated from her charge. Millie would go to any length to avoid this catastrophe; and that afternoon, in a desperate desire to placate Mrs. Jones and to ameliorate the impatience which the other might be feeling, she made a cup of tea and took it up to her mistress with an apologetic word.

"I thought you might like it," she explained.

And Mrs. Jones thanked her, and the world was thereafter for a while serene.

Millie's life during the next few months was a succession of irritating incidents from which she found escape in the hours she spent with the baby. Joan now slept less. Her night feedings had been abandoned. She had bottles four times a day; and from about seven o'clock in the morning till the ten-o'clock bottle, and from the two-o'clock bottle until that which she had at six, she was awake. In the morning Millie brought her downstairs to sit in the dining room while Mr. and Mrs. Jones and Johnnie had their breakfast. In the afternoon she took the baby for a ride in her perambulator and stayed away from the house, when the weather was fair, as late as it was possible, revelling in the long hours alone with Joan. But she could not always be with her baby, and in her relations with Charles and Laura and with Johnnie there were continual irritations.

Between her and Charles there was a continuing feud. Charles was devoted to Johnnie, and he so contrived his time as to be able to help the little boy dress in the morning and undress at night. The two were born companions. But Millie hated Johnnie, and he returned this feeling, not with hatred, because he was too young to feel that passion, but with resentment of her attentions and with an inclination to become fretful and angry at her ministrations. She hated Johnnie; but the fact that he welcomed Charles and liked to be with the man aroused in Millie an infuriating jealousy. Sometimes she and Charles became involved in arguments as to the simple business of keeping Johnnie's room in order; and it seemed to Millie that Charles encouraged Johnnie to rebel at her authority and to be impudent to her.

One morning, when she brought Joan to the dining room, she had had such a passage with the man, and it had so wrought upon her nerves that she was in tears. When she came in, Mr. and Mrs. Jones and Johnnie were already at the table; and she burst out in explosive complaint, hating herself for doing it, knowing the risk she ran, yet unable to control her tongue. With tears streaming down her face she cried:

"Mrs. Jones, I want you to tell Johnnie that he isn't to talk back to me the way he does."

Mrs. Jones said quietly, "We'll discuss that by and by, Millie."

"He won't do anything I tell him to," Millie insisted. "And him and Charles just laugh at me."

Charles, coming in just then with the coffee, was driven to self-defence.

"Johnnie's all right, Mrs. Jones," he said stoutly. "She won't let him alone. She don't understand boys. I can take care of Johnnie all right if she'd just leave him alone."

Mrs. Jones said decisively, "That will do, Charles!"

"Yes, ma'am," Charles agreed, and left the room.

But Millie, unutterably exasperated, cried again, "Johnnie's got to be made to behave, ma'am."

Mrs. Jones repeated, "We'll discuss that later, Millie!"

And Millie, though she was almost beside herself with weeping rage, felt the menace in the other's tone and left the room.

After her husband had gone, Mrs. Jones summoned Millie and said to her steadily:

"You are not to do such a thing as that again, Millie. I don't want Mr. Jones bothered by anything that goes on at home. If you have anything to say to me, wait until he has gone and come to me quietly."

Millie cried, "Well, I can't stand the way Johnnie treats me."

"Hereafter," Mrs. Jones told her, "you need have no contact with Johnnie except to keep his room in order. Charles will take care of him, and I am sure you will get along all right if you avoid trouble with Johnnie or with Charles."

"I can't stand it," Millie cried.

"If you can't be happy here with us," Mrs. Jones told her, "I would rather you did not stay. I don't want anyone in the house who is unhappy."

The words struck Millie with a sobering effect, as though Mrs. Jones had dashed cold water in her face. They silenced her utterly, and drove her from the room to fight down all that day her desperate fear. That afternoon she made Mrs. Jones another cup of tea.

She thought Joan the most beautiful of babies and she thought of Joan always as her baby, and Joan seemed to Millie to feel that Millie was her whole world, too. When Millie came to her in the morning, even before the nurse entered the room, Joan was apt to begin to crow with delight at her coming. And when Millie bathed her, changed her garments, talked to her in that cheering, reassuring tone which, no matter what her own mood, she was always able to summon for Joan, Joan fairly wriggled with delight. When in the morning it came time for Mrs. Jones to go to town and Millie was summoned to take the baby Joan always came to her eagerly. And sometimes when either Mr. or Mrs. Jones offered to take the baby from Millie, Joan would laugh aloud and throw her arms around Millie's neck and snuggle her face into the nurse's shoulder as though it were a game which she played.

Millie used to nurse the memory of these scenes, and to tell herself over and over that Joan loved her more than she loved either her father or her mother; and thus thinking, she would hug Joan with a fierce tenderness full of passion. At such times Joan chuckled and babbled with delight as though these ferocious caresses were delightful to her. Millie revelled in these hours when she had Joan to herself, the rest of the world apart. But at those moments when she perceived that Joan had passed from one of the phases of babyhood to another, abandoning one little trick for the next, Millie felt a poignant alarm at the approach of the time when Joan would no longer be a baby at all and so would escape from her.

She stifled these forebodings, clinging to the present, refusing to consider the future, blinding herself to the inevitable end of all this happiness, insistently declining to look forward to the day when—one way or another—she would lose this baby, whom she loved, as she had lost so many before. Yet these fears, though they were stifled, had their effect upon her; her furtive dread sharpened her tongue, and she found herself saying and doing irritating things. At such moments she was full of regret, regret not so much because of what she had done as because by such actions she laid herself open to dismissal, ran the risk of losing Joan. And afterward she would seek to make amends, throwing herself into her work with new zeal, seeking tasks outside her appointed duties, paying her mistress small attentions, bringing her a potted plant, making a dress for Joan, or serving Mrs. Jones a cup of tea in the afternoon.

Thus her life was a succession of crimes and repentances, a series of passions each followed by fearful remorse. And there were days, occasionally weeks, when she held such a rigid bridle upon her tongue that her silence made her seem sulky; and there were other days when the check which she kept upon herself slipped, and she loosed in bitter words the blind and venomous anger which she felt against the whole world.

Once or twice she caught herself talking to Charles and Laura of Mr. and Mrs. Jones in terms frankly slanderous, and for days thereafter she was full of bitter and terrified self-reproach, moving cautiously, watching the demeanour of her mistress for any sign that her words had been reported, shrinking with fear of the destruction she had invited. She was her own worst enemy and she knew this as well as anyone, but it became more and more difficult for her to keep a curb upon her tongue.

As Joan approached her first birthday, half a dozen influences combined to produce a cumulative nervous strain which Millie found more and more tormenting. For one thing, the baby was maturing. Millie had wished to keep her as long as possible completely helpless and dependent, so she had prisoned her in her crib or in her perambulator, and Joan had not yet learned to creep. But Mrs. Jones at last insisted that Millie put the baby on the floor for an hour or two a day, to exercise those muscles which were ready to assume their functions.

The result was an increasingly rapid development of Joan's powers. She set herself to the task of learning to manipulate her small body with a persistency as deliberate as though she were quite conscious of what she did. And she would sit upon the floor, pull herself forward over her legs until she lay on her face, push herself back up to a sitting posture again, pull herself forward once more and roll on her back, and from this position again push herself up until she was sitting erect, following this routine over and over as though she had been set these tasks to do. She began also to exercise her voice, no longer in the meaningless outcries of infancy, but trying different tones, now shrill, now guttural; and some of these utterances assumed a form suggestive of speech, till it was easy to imagine she was trying to say something.

Millie had cared for so many babies that she knew what these signs portended. She knew that Joan would soon escape from her ministering care, and this knowledge oppressed her dreams.

The nurse was also at this time under an increased physical strain. Mrs. Jones was planning a birthday party for Joan, to which half a dozen other babies, a little younger or a little older, would be invited. Millie decided to make a dress which Joan should wear on that occasion; and into this work she threw all her energies, spending upon it every hour not directly devoted to Joan herself, working at it in the early morning, at moments snatched during the day, and late at night when she might better have been asleep. The result was that she was tired almost all the time, and this weariness served to break down in large and larger measure her self-control, till she was in continual conflict within herself, fighting to stifle the resentment which she felt against those among whom her life was cast.

There had long existed between her and Charles a state of open warfare; and this was brought to something like a crisis one evening when Mr. and Mrs. Jones had gone out to dinner. Charles, as he liked to do on such occasions, had put the young son of the house to bed. Millie was moved by some blind and senseless impulse, after Charles had gone downstairs, to get Johnnie up again and insist upon giving him a bath.

The little boy felt the injustice of this. "I don't want to take a bath," he cried.

"You're dirty," Millie told him. "You ought to be ashamed to go to bed as dirty as you are; and Charles ought to be ashamed to let you. Now, you come right along into the bathroom and Millie will give you a nice bath."

"I had a bath this morning," Johnnie insisted bitterly. "I'm not going to take a bath now."

Millie's tone was soothing, yet there was in it at the same time something acidly venomous.

"Come right along," she retorted. "There's no use fussing. You've got to have a bath the way Millie says."

Johnnie still resisting, she undertook to compel him; but the result was such an outcry that Charles heard and came swiftly upstairs, and there followed a bitter altercation between the two servants, Johnnie clinging to Charles for protection, Millie reduced to a state of blind and incoherent frenzy.

But there was no way she could carry her point, since Charles was quite obviously the physical master of the situation. She surrendered because she had to surrender; but the episode remained in her mind and accentuated the developing enmity between her and Charles to such a point that the least incident was sufficient to set them into open wrangling. Millie, out of necessity, ate in the kitchen with Charles and Laura, and it is not to be wondered at that under the circumstances she had no relish for her meals, and her digestion suffered.

Yet still she tried desperately to control herself, to avoid giving further offence to her mistress in any way. But the very desperation of her efforts in this direction led her into error. Millie's greatest virtue had always been that she gave her babies perfect care; but now, once and then again, she was guilty of negligence even toward Joan. The first occasion followed a night when she had worked late upon the dress for Joan's birthday party, and her resultant weariness made her oversleep the hour for the morning bottle. The baby awoke and cried, and Millie did not even hear till Mrs. Jones came to her door. Millie's bitter self-reproach translated itself into anger against her mistress. She said sharply:

"You don't have to come after me. I heard her. She's all right to cry a little while. I'll get to her in a minute. You can't expect me to keep on the run all the time."

Mrs. Jones hesitated, as though to control her voice, but she only said:

"You had better take her up now, Millie. I don't want her to cry when it isn't necessary," and turned away.

The final incident occurred one afternoon when she was about to take Joan out for a ride in her perambulator. Joan was by this time more and more vigorous and active, and when Millie put her in the baby carriage she did not buckle the safety strap sufficiently tight. She went back into the house to get her own hat and coat and while she was gone Joan, wriggling this way and that, managed to twist herself till she was hanging half out of the carriage and forthwith began to scream with fright and despair.

As luck would have it, Charles heard her and ran out from the kitchen in time to avoid any serious result from the mishap. But Millie also had heard Joan crying and was only a second behind Charles; and the fact that he had interfered seemed to her so bitter a wrong that she upbraided him violently.

"Take your hands off my baby," she cried in a shrill and exasperated voice. "I won't have you touching her. I won't have you bothering her."

Charles said sternly, "It's lucky I did touch her. She'd have bumped her head. You ought to take more care the way you buckle her in."

"I don't need any man to tell me how to take care of babies," Millie screamed at him. "You get back into your kitchen, you scullery maid."

Charles laughed shortly. "Hard names never hurt anybody," he retorted. "If they did, I could think up one or two myself."

But the fact that he stood his ground, as though passing judgment upon the manner in which she now bestowed Joan in the perambulator, whetted Millie's anger to a pitch near delirium; and when Mrs. Jones, attracted by the sound of the nurse's shrill and frenzied voice, came to the door, Millie was in a perfect paroxysm of fury.

The result of this culminating incident was her dismissal.

"If you can't control yourself," Mrs. Jones said in a tone of finality, "I can't let you be about Joan any longer. I'm sorry, Millie, but you will have to go. I'll have a taxi come for you at three this afternoon."

Millie cried all that day, not silently, but with wild and explosive sounds, the tears streaming from her eyes. She at first accepted her dismissal without argument, but when Mrs. Jones insisted upon bathing Joan herself, and told Millie to go to her room and pack her things, the old woman for the first time fully realized that sentence had been passed upon her. Her agony of spirit was like that of a man condemned to death;

and when Joan was asleep—for even now Millie would not do anything calculated to disturb the routine of the baby's life—the nurse went to Mrs. Jones's room and sought to bring about a change in the other's decision. Her abject grief, the craven pleadings to which in the end she was at last driven, worked upon her mistress intolerably; and there was a moment when one of these women was almost as unhappy as the other. But although she perceived how much of a tragedy this was to Millie, Mrs. Jones had made her decision and was strong enough to hold to it.

"I've only kept you so long," she said, "because you've been so good to Joan. You're a good nurse, Millie, but you're a most uncomfortable person to have around. If you would learn to be civil and to attend to your own affairs, you'd avoid so much trouble. I've made up my mind. I'll have to let you go."

Millie left the house in mid-afternoon. As her belongings were being packed into the taxicab which Mrs. Jones had summoned, she wept unbearably, and Mrs. Jones could not refrain from asking:

"Where do you plan to go, Millie?"

Millie said desperately, "I'll go somewhere. I don't know where."

"Shall I send you to a hotel till you can get another place?" Mrs. Jones suggested, and Millie shook her head.

"No," she replied. And she named a woman whom she knew and said, "I'll go to her house for a day or two."

When she said good-bye to Joan she tried to control herself. She had dried her eyes and she fought to achieve the smile and the soothing and agreeable tone which she always used to the baby. Mrs. Jones had Joan in her sitting room on the second floor, and Millie went in there, and Joan saw her enter and lifted both arms in an appeal to be taken up from the floor. Millie picked her up, pouring out upon her that meaningless flood of words which Joan always found so delightful, while Mrs. Jones watched the two unhappily.

After a moment Millie said:

"I'll not be here for her birthday party."

"You might like to come in that afternoon," Mrs. Jones suggested; but

Millie shook her head, and the tears burst from her eyes.

"I left a dress for her on my bed," she explained. "I've been making it the last month."

"She shall wear it," Mrs. Jones assured her, unable to feel anything but pity for the little old woman, and fighting for strength to maintain her decision that Millie must go.

Joan was pounding at Millie's face with her small hands, and Millie for a moment forgot Mrs. Jones, turning her attention to the baby again. "Good-bye," she said. Joan wrinkled her nose and screamed with delight, and as she slapped Millie's cheeks the tears splashed under her hands. "I'm sorry I'm going, Joan," Millie told the baby. And Joan crowed, and Millie turned to Mrs. Jones and said:

"Take her."

Mrs. Jones held out her arms to the baby, but Joan had played that game before, and she knew what was expected of her. She laughed glee-fully, threw her arms around Millie's neck, and snuggled her face into the nurse's shoulder; and Millie gave a little gasping cry and turned abruptly and set Joan down upon the floor and fled from the room. Only in the doorway she paused for a moment to turn and look back and to say over and over:

"I'm so sorry, Joan. I'm so sorry. Millie's so sorry. Good-bye, Joan. Good-bye."

She stood there a moment longer, drenched in tears; and Joan, sobered by this spectacle, stared at her in perplexity and waved a small hand in a doubtful way.

"Yes, yes," Millie gasped. "Yes, Joan! Bye-bye!"

So she waved an answering hand; then turned and fled, blind and stumbling, toward where the taxi waited at the door.

A waiting room is a fearful place. Millie had had some experience of waiting rooms and she dreaded them. She had been sitting in this par-ticular waiting room at the employment agency for three days; a little woman, thin and taut, and just now curiously tremulous. Her eyes, in-flamed and weary, looked blankly straight before her. And sometimes, for no apparent reason, they became suffused with tears; not merely misted with moisture, but drowned in a swimming, drenching flood which flowed over her lids and down her dry cheeks until she remembered to wipe away these evidences of the grief which racked her.

On the third day she found herself replying in a dull voice to the questions put to her by a woman who introduced herself by a name which Millie scarcely heard. She was not interested in the names of her mistresses; she had so many of them. This woman's name might have been Brown or Jones. It happened to be Mrs. Smith.

Mrs. Smith asked question upon question, but Millie asked only one. "Is the baby a boy or a girl?"

"A little girl," Mrs. Smith replied. And Millie's ravaged face seemed to lighten faintly at the word.

"I like little girls best," she confessed.

They arranged for Millie to come next morning; and Millie was for the rest of that day a little more cheerful. Her aching grief found anodyne in the prospect of having another baby to love.

The Enemy

PEARL BUCK

Dr. Sadao Hoki's house was built on a spot of the Japanese coast where as a little boy he had often played. The low square stone house was set upon rocks well above a narrow beach that was outlined with bent pines. As a boy Sadao had climbed the pines, supporting himself on his bare feet, as he had seen men do in the South Seas when they climbed for coconuts. His father had taken him often to the islands of those seas, and never had he failed to say to the little grave boy at his side, "Those islands yonder, they are the steppingstones to the future for Japan."

"Where shall we step from them?" Sadao had asked seriously.

"Who knows?" his father had answered. "Who can limit our future? It depends on what we make it."

Sadao had taken this into his mind as he did everything his father said, his father who never joked or played with him but who spent infinite pains upon him who was his only son. Sadao knew that his education was his father's chief concern. For this reason he had been sent at twenty-two to America to learn all that could be learned of surgery and medicine. He had come back at thirty, and before his father died he had seen Sadao become famous not only as a surgeon but as a scientist. Because he was now perfecting a discovery which would render wounds entirely clean he had not been sent abroad with the troops. Also, he knew, there was some slight danger that the old General might need an operation for a condition for which he was now being treated medically, and for this possibility Sadao was being kept in Japan.

Clouds were rising from the ocean now. The unexpected warmth of

38

the past few days had at night drawn heavy fog from the cold waves. Sadao watched mists hide outlines of a little island near the shore and then come creeping up the beach below the house, wreathing around the pines. In a few minutes fog would be wrapped about the house too. Then he would go into the room where Hana, his wife, would be waiting for him with the two children.

But at this moment the door opened and she looked out, a dark blue woolen haori over her kimono. She came to him affectionately and put her arm through his as he stood, smiled and said nothing. He had met Hana in America, but he had waited to fall in love with her until he was sure she was Japanese. His father would never have received her unless she had been pure in her race. He wondered often whom he would have married if he had not met Hana, and by what luck he had found her in the most casual way, by chance literally, at an American professor's house. The professor and his wife had been kind people anxious to do something for their few foreign students, and the students, though bored, had accepted this kindness. Sadao had often told Hana how nearly he had not gone to Professor Harley's house that night—the rooms were so small, the food so bad, the professor's wife so voluble. But he had gone and there he had found Hana, a new student, and had felt he would love her if it were at all possible.

Now he felt her hand on his arm and was aware of the pleasure it gave him, even though they had been married years enough to have the two children. For they had not married heedlessly in America. They had finished their work at school and had come home to Japan, and when his father had seen her the marriage had been arranged in the old Japanese way, although Sadao and Hana had talked everything over beforehand. They were perfectly happy. She laid her cheek against his arm.

It was at this moment that both of them saw something black come out of the mists. It was a man. He was flung up out of the ocean—flung, it seems, to his feet by a breaker. He staggered a few steps, his body outlined against the mist, his arms above his head. Then the curled mists hid him again.

"Who is that?" Hana cried. She dropped Sadao's arm and they both leaned over the railing of the veranda. Now they saw him again. The man was on his hands and knees crawling. Then they saw him fall on his face and lie there.

"A fisherman perhaps," Sadao said, "washed from his boat." He ran quickly down the steps, and behind him Hana came, her wide sleeves flying. A mile or two away on either side there was fishing villages, but here was only the bare and lonely coast, dangerous with rocks. The surf beyond the beach was spiked with rocks. Somehow the man had managed to come through them—he must be badly torn.

They saw when they came toward him that indeed it was so. The sand on one side of him had already a stain of red soaking through.

"He is wounded," Sadao exclaimed. He made haste to the man, who lay motionless, his face in the sand. An old cap stuck to his head soaked with sea water. He was in wet rags of garments. Sadao stooped, Hana at his side, and turned the man's head. They saw the face.

"A white man!" Hana whispered.

"Yes, it was a white man. The wet cap fell away and there was his wet yellow hair, long, as though for many weeks it had not been cut, and upon his young and tortured face was a rough yellow beard. He was unconscious and knew nothing that they did to him.

Now Sadao remembered the wound, and with his expert fingers he began to search for it. Blood flowed freshly at his touch. On the right side of his lower back Sadao saw that a gun wound had been reopened. The flesh was blackened with powder. Sometime, not many days ago, the man had been shot and had not been tended. It was bad chance that the rock had struck the wound.

"Oh, how he is bleeding!" Hana whispered again in a solemn voice. The mists screened them now completely, and at this time of day no one came by. The fishermen had gone home and even the chance beachcombers would have considered the day at an end.

"What shall we do with this man?" Sadao muttered. But his trained hands seemed of their own will to be doing what they could to stanch the fearful bleeding. He packed the wound with the sea moss that strewed the beach. The man moaned with pain in his stupor but he did not awaken.

"The best thing that we could do would be to put him back in the sea," Sadao said, answering himself.

Now that the bleeding was stopped for the moment he stood up and dusted the sand from his hands.

"Yes, undoubtedly that would be best," Sana said steadily. But she continued to stare down at the motionless man.

"If we sheltered a white man in our house we should be arrested and if we turned him over as a prisoner, he would certainly die," Sadao said.

"The kindest thing would be to put him back into the sea," Hana said. But neither of them moved. They were staring with a curious repulsion upon the inert figure.

"What is he?" Hana whispered.

"There is something about him that looks American," Sadao said. He took up the battered cap. Yes, there, almost gone, was the faint lettering. "A sailor," he said, "from an American warship." He spelled it out: "U. S. Navy." The man was a prisoner of war!

"He has escaped," Hana cried softly, "and that is why he is wounded."

"In the back," Sadao agreed.

They hesitated, looking at each other. Then Hana said with resolution:

"Come, are we able to put him back into the sea?"

"If I am able, are you?" Sadao asked.

"No," Hana said. "But if you can do it alone . . ."

Sadao hesitated again. "The strange thing is," he said, "that if the man were whole I could turn him over to the police without difficulty. I care nothing for him. He is my enemy. All Americans are my enemy. And he is only a common fellow. You see how foolish his face is. But since he is wounded . . ."

"You also cannot throw him back to the sea," Hana said. "Then there is only one thing to do. We must carry him into the house."

"But the servants?" Sadao inquired.

"We must simply tell them that we intend to give him to the police—as indeed we must, Sadao. We must think of the children and your position. It would endanger all of us if we did not give this man over as a prisoner of war."

"Certainly," Sadao agreed. "I would not think of doing anything else."

Thus agreed, together they lifted the man. He was very light, like a fowl that has been half starved for a long time until it is only feathers and skeleton. So, his arms hanging, they carried him up the steps and into the side door of the house. This door opened into a passage and down the passage they carried the man toward an empty bedroom. It had been the bedroom of Sadao's father and since his death it had not been used. They laid the man on the deeply matted floor. Everything here had been Japanese to please the old man, who would never in his own home sit on a chair or sleep in a foreign bed. Hana went to the wall cupboards and slid back a door and took out a soft quilt. She hesitated. The quilt was covered with flowered silk and the lining was pure white silk.

"He is so dirty," she murmured in distress.

"Yes, he had better be washed," Sadao agreed. "If you fetch hot water I will wash him."

"I cannot bear for you to touch him," she said. "We shall have to tell the servants he is here. I will tell Yumi now. She can leave the children for a few minutes and she can wash him."

Sadao considered a moment. "Let it be so," he agreed. "You tell Yumi and I will tell the others."

But the utter pallor of the man's unconscious face moved him first to stoop and feel his pulse. It was faint but it was there. He put his hand against the man's cold breast. The heart too was yet alive.

"He will die unless he is operated on," Sadao said, considering. "The question is whether he will not die anyway."

Hana cried out in fear. "Don't try to save him! What if he should live?"

"What if he should die?" Sadao replied. He stood gazing down on the motionless man. This man must have extraordinary vitality or he would have been dead by now. But then he was very young—perhaps not yet twenty-five.

"You mean die from the operation?" Hana asked.

"Yes," Sadao said.

Hana considered this doubtfully, and when she did not answer Sarao turned away. "At any rate something must be done with him," he said, "and first he must be washed." He went quickly out of the room and Hana came behind him. She did not wish to be left alone with the white man. He was the first she had seen since she left America and now he seemed to have nothing to do with those whom she had known there. Here he was her enemy, a menace, living or dead.

She turned to the nursery and called, "Yumi!"

But the children heard her voice and she had to go in for a moment and smile at them and play with the baby boy, now nearly three months old.

Over the baby's soft black hair she motioned with her mouth, "Yumi—come with me!"

"I will put the baby to bed," Yumi replied. "He is ready."

She went with Yumi into the bedroom next to the nursery and stood with the boy in her arms while Yumi spread the sleeping quilts on the floor and laid the baby between them.

Then Hana led the way quickly and softly to the kitchen. The two servants were frightened at what their master had just told them. The old gardener who was also a house servant pulled the few hairs on his upper lip.

"The master ought not to heal the wound of this white man," he said bluntly to Hana. "The white man ought to die. First he was shot. Then the sea caught him and wounded him with her rocks. If the master heals what the gun did and what the sea did they will take revenge on us."

"I will tell him what you say," Hana replied courteously. But she herself was also frightened, although she was not superstitious as the old man was. Could it ever be well to help an enemy? Nevertheless she told Yumi to fetch the hot water and bring it to the room where the white man was.

She went ahead and slid back the partitions. Sadao was not yet there. Yumi, following, put down her wooden bucket. Then she went over to the white man. When she saw him her thick lips folded themselves into stubbornness. "I have never washed a white man," she said, "and I will not wash so dirty a one now."

Hana cried at her severely, "You will do what your master commands you!"

"My master ought not to command me to wash the enemy," Yumi said stubbornly.

There was so fierce a look of resistance upon Yumi's round dull face that Hana felt unreasonably afraid. After all, if the servants should report something that was not as it happened?

"Very well," she said with dignity. "You understand we only want to bring him to his senses so that we can turn him over as a prisoner?"

"I will have nothing to do with it," Yumi said. "I am a poor person and it is not my business."

"Then please," Hana said gently, "return to your own work."

At once Yumi left the room. But this left Hana with the white man alone. She might have been too afraid to stay had not her anger at Yumi's stubbornness now sustained her.

"Stupid Yumi," she muttered fiercely. "Is this anything but a man? And a wounded, helpless man!"

In the conviction of her own superiority she bent impulsively and untied the knotted rags that kept the white man covered. When she had his breast bare she dipped the small clean towel that Yumi had brought into the steaming hot water and washed his face carefully. The man's skin, though rough with exposure, was of a fine texture and must have been very blond when he was a child.

While she was thinking these thoughts, though not really liking the man better now that he was no longer a child, she kept on washing him until his upper body was quite clean. But she dared not turn him over. Where was Sadao? Now her anger was ebbing and she was anxious again and she rose, wiping her hands on the wrung towel. Then lest the man be chilled she put the quilt over him.

"Sadao!" she called softly.

He had been about to come in when she called. His hand had been on the door and now he opened it. She saw that he had brought his surgeon's emergency bag and that he wore his surgeon's coat.

"You have decided to operate!" she cried.

"Yes," he said shortly. He turned his back to her and unfolded a sterilized towel upon the floor of the *takonoma* alcove, and put his instruments out upon it.

"Fetch towels," he said.

She went obediently, but how anxious now, to the linen shelves and took out the towels. There ought also to be old pieces of matting so that the blood would not ruin the fine floor covering. She went out to the back veranda where the gardener kept strips of matting with which to protect delicate shrubs on cold nights and took an armful of them.

But when she went back into the room she saw this was useless. The blood had already soaked through the packing in the man's wound and had ruined the mat under him.

"Oh, the mat!" she cried.

"Yes, it is ruined," Sadao replied, as though he did not care. "Help me to turn him," he commanded her.

She obeyed him without a word, and he began to wash the man's back carefully.

"Yumi would not wash him," she said.

"Did you wash him, then?" Sadao asked, not stopping for a moment his swift concise movements.

"Yes," she said.

He did not seem to hear her. But she was used to his absorption when he was at work. She wondered for a moment if it mattered to him what was the body upon which he worked so long as it was for the work he did so excellently.

"You will have to give the anesthetic if he needs it," he said.

"I?" she repeated blankly. "But never have I!"

"It is easy enough," he said impatiently.

He was taking out the packing now and the blood began to flow more quickly. He peered into the wound with the bright surgeon's light fastened on his forehead. "The bullet is still there," he said with cool interest. "Now I wonder how deep this rock wound is. If it is not too deep it may be that I can get the bullet. But the bleeding is not superficial. He has lost much blood."

At this moment Hana choked. He looked up and saw her face the color of sulphur.

"Don't faint," he said sharply. He did not put down his exploring instrument. "If I stop now the man will surely die." She clapped her hands to her mouth and leaped up and ran out of the room. Outside in the garden he heard her retching. But he went on with his work.

"It will be better for her to empty her stomach," he thought. He had forgotten that of course she had never seen an operation. But her distress and his inability to go to her at once made him impatient and irritable with this man who lay like dead under his knife.

"This man," he thought, "there is no reason under heaven why he should live."

Unconsciously this thought made him ruthless and he proceeded swiftly. In his dream the man moaned, but Sadao paid no heed except to mutter at him.

"Groan," he muttered, "groan if you like. I am not doing this for my own pleasure. In fact, I do not know why I am doing it."

The door opened and there was Hana again. She had not stopped even to smooth back her hair.

"Where is the anesthetic?" she asked in a clear voice.

Sadao motioned with his chin. "It is as well that you came back," he said. "This fellow is beginning to stir."

She had the bottle and some cotton in her hand.

"But how shall I do it?" she asked.

"Simply saturate the cotton and hold it near his nostrils," Sadao replied without delaying for one moment the intricate detail of his work. "When he breathes badly move it away a little."

She crouched close to the sleeping face of the young American. It was a piteously thin face, she thought, and the lips were twisted. The man was suffering whether he knew it or not. Watching him, she wondered if the stories they heard sometimes of the sufferings of prisoners were true. They came like flickers of rumor, told by word of mouth and always that wherever the Japanese armies went the people received them gladly, with cries of joy at their liberation. But sometimes she remembered such men as General Takima, who at home beat his wife cruelly, though no one mentioned it now that he had fought so victorious a battle in Manchuria. If a man like that could be so cruel to a woman in his power, would he not be cruel to one like this for instance?

She hoped anxiously that this young man had not been tortured. It was at this moment that she observed deep red scars on his neck, just under the ear. "Those scars," she murmured, lifting her eyes to Sadao.

But he did not answer. At this moment he felt the tip of his instrument strike against something hard, dangerously near the kidney. All thought left him. He felt only the purest pleasure. He probed with his fingers, delicately, familiar with every atom of this human body. His old American professor of anatomy had seen to that knowledge. "Ignorance of the human body is the surgeon's cardinal sin, sirs!" he had thundered at his classes year after year. "To operate without as complete knowledge of the body as if you had made it—anything less than that is murder."

"It is not quite at the kidney, my friend," Sadao murmured. It was his habit to murmur to the patient when he forgot himself in an operation. "My friend," he always called his patients and so now he did, forgetting that this was his enemy.

Then quickly, with the cleanest and most precise of incisions, the bullet was out. The man quivered but he was still unconscious. Nevertheless he muttered a few English words.

"Guts," he muttered, choking. "They got ... my guts ..."

"Sadao!" Hana cried sharply.

"Hush," Sadao said.

The man sank again into silence so profound that Sadao took up his wrist, hating the touch of it. Yes, there was still a pulse so faint, so feeble, but enough, if he wanted the man to live, to give hope.

"But certainly I do not want this man to live," he thought.

"No more anesthetic," he told Hana.

He turned as swiftly as though he had never paused and from his medicines he chose a small vial and from it filled a hypodermic and thrust it into the patient's left arm. Then, putting down the needle, he took the man's wrist again. The pulse under his fingers fluttered once or twice and then grew stronger.

"This man will live in spite of all," he said to Hana and sighed.

The young man woke, so weak, his blue eyes so terrified when he perceived where he was, that Hana felt compelled to apology. She served him herself, for none of the servants would enter the room.

When she came in the first time she saw him summon his small strength to be prepared for some fearful thing.

"Don't be afraid," she begged him softly.

"How come . . . you speak English?" he gasped.

"I was a long time in America," she replied.

She saw that he wanted to reply to that but he could not, and so she knelt and fed him gently from the porcelain spoon. He ate unwillingly, but still he ate.

"Now you will soon be strong," she said, not liking him and yet moved to comfort him.

He did not answer.

When Sadao came in the third day after the operation he found the young man sitting up, his face bloodless with the effort.

"Lie down," Sadao cried. "Do you want to die?"

He forced the man down gently and strongly and examined the wound. "You may kill yourself if you do this sort of thing," he scolded.

"What are you going to do with me?" the boy muttered. He looked just now barely seventeen. "Are you going to hand me over?"

For a moment Sadao did not answer. He finished his examination and then pulled the silk quilt over the man.

"I do not know myself what I shall do with you," he said. "I ought of course to give you to the police. You are a prisoner of war—no, do not tell me anything." He put up his hand as he saw the young man about to speak. "Do not even tell me your name unless I ask it."

They looked at each other for a moment, and then the young man closed his eyes and turned his face to the wall.

"Okay," he whispered, his mouth a bitter line.

Outside the door Hana was waiting for Sadao. He saw at once that she was in trouble.

"Sadao, Yumi tells me the servants feel they cannot stay if we hide this man here any more," she said. "She tells me that they are saying that you and I were so long in America that we have forgotten to think of our own country first. They think we like Americans."

"It is not true," Sadao said harshly, "Americans are our enemies. But I have been trained not to let a man die if I can help it."

"The servants cannot understand that," she said anxiously.

"No," he agreed.

Neither seemed able to say more, and somehow the household dragged on. The servants grew daily more watchful. Their courtesy was as careful as ever, but their eyes were cold upon the pair to whom they were hired.

"It is clear what our master ought to do," the old gardener said one morning. He had worked with flowers all his life, and had been a specialist too in moss. For Sadao's father he had made one of the finest moss gardens in Japan, sweeping the bright green carpet constantly so that not a leaf or a pine needle marred the velvet of its surface. "My master's son knows very well what he ought to do," he now said, pinching a bud from a bush as he spoke. "When the man was so near death why did he not let him bleed?"

"That young master is so proud of his skill to save life that he saves any life," the cook said contemptuously. She split a fowl's neck skillfully and held the fluttering bird and let its blood flow into the roots of a wistaria vine. Blood is the best of fertilizers, and the old gardener would not let her waste a drop of it.

"It is the children of whom we must think," Yumi said sadly. "What will be their fate if their father is condemned as a traitor?"

They did not try to hide what they said from the ears of Hana as she stood arranging the day's flowers in the veranda near by, and she knew they spoke on purpose that she might hear. That they were right she knew too in most of her being. But there was another part of her which she herself could not understand. It was not sentimental liking of the prisoner. She had come to think of him as a prisoner. She had not liked him even yesterday when he had said in his impulsive way, "Anyway, let me tell you that my name is Tom." She had only bowed her little distant bow. She saw hurt in his eyes but she did not wish to assuage it. Indeed, he was a great trouble in this house.

As for Sadao, every day he examined the wound carefully. The last stitches had been pulled out this morning, and the young man would in a fortnight be nearly as well as ever. Sadao went back to his office and carefully typed a letter to the chief of police reporting the whole matter. "On the twenty-first day of February an escaped prisoner was washed up on the shore in front of my house." So far he typed and then he opened a secret drawer of his desk and put the unfinished report into it.

On the seventh day after that two things happened. In the morning the servants left together, their belongings tied in large square cotton kerchiefs. When Hana got up in the morning nothing was done, the house not cleaned and the food not prepared, and she knew what it meant. She was dismayed and even terrified, but her pride as a mistress would not allow her to show it. Instead she inclined her head gracefully when they appeared before her in the kitchen, and she paid them off and thanked them for all that they had done for her. They were crying, but she did not cry. The cook and the gardener had served Sadao since he was a little boy in his father's house, and Yumi cried because of the children. She was so grieving that after she had gone she ran back to Hana.

"If the baby misses me too much tonight send for me. I am going to my own house and you know where it is."

"Thank you," Hana said, smiling. But she told herself she would not send for Yumi however the baby cried.

She made the breakfast and Sadao helped with the children. Neither of them spoke of the servants beyond the fact that they were gone. But after Hana had taken morning food to the prisoner she came back to Sadao.

"Why is it we cannot see clearly what we ought to do?" she asked him.

"Even the servants see more clearly than we do. Why are we different from other Japanese?"

Sadao did not answer. But a little later he went into the room where the prisoner was and said brusquely, "Today you may get up on your feet. I want you to stay up only five minutes at a time. Tomorrow you may may try it twice as long. It would be well that you get back your strength quickly as possible."

He saw the flicker of terror on the young face that was still very pale.

"Okay," the boy murmured. Evidently he was determined to say more. "I feel I ought to thank you, Doctor, for having saved my life."

"Don't thank me too early," Sadao said coldly. He saw the flicker of terror again in the boy's eyes—terror as unmistakable as an animal's. The scars on his neck were crimson for a moment. Those scars! What were they? Sadao did not ask.

In the afternoon the second thing happened. Hana, working hard on unaccustomed labor, saw a messenger come to the door in official uniform. Her hands went weak and she could not draw her breath. The servants must have told already. She ran to Sadao, gasping, unable to utter a word. But by then the messenger had simply followed her through the garden and there he stood. She pointed at him helplessly.

Sadao looked up from his book. He was in his office, the outer partition of which was thrown open to the garden for the southern sunshine.

"What is it?" he asked the messenger, and then he rose, seeing the man's uniform.

"You are to come to the palace," the man said, "the old General is in pain again."

"Oh," Hana breathed, "is that all?"

"All!" the messenger exclaimed. "Is it not enough?"

"Indeed it is," she replied: "I am very sorry."

When Sadao came to say good-by she was in the kitchen, but doing nothing. The children were asleep and she sat merely resting for a moment, more exhausted from her fright than from work.

"I thought they had come to arrest you," she said.

He gazed down into her anxious eyes. "I must get rid of this man for your sake," he said in distress. "Somehow I must get rid of him."

"Of course," the General said weakly, "I understand fully. But that is because I once took a degree in Princeton. So few Japanese have."

"I care nothing for the man, Excellency," Sadao said, "but having operated on him with such success . . ."

"Yes, yes," the General said. "It only makes me feel you more indispensable to me. Evidently you can save anyone—you are so skilled. You say you think I can stand one more attack as I have had today?"

"Not more than one," Sadao said.

"Then certainly I can allow nothing to happen to you," the General said with anxiety. His long, pale, Japanese face became expressionless, which meant that he was in deep thought. "You cannot be arrested," the General said, closing his eyes. "Suppose you were condemned to death and the next day I had to have my operation?"

"There are other surgeons, Excellency," Sadao suggested.

"None I trust," the General replied. "The best ones have been trained by Germans and would consider the operation successful even if I died. I do not care for their point of view." He sighed. "It seems a pity that we cannot better combine the German ruthlessness with the American sentimentality. Then you could turn your prisoner over to execution and yet I could be sure you would not murder me while I was unconscious." The General laughed. He had an unusual sense of humor. "As a Japanese, could you not combine these two foreign elements?" he asked.

Sadao smiled. "I am not quite sure," he said, "but for your sake I would be willing to try, Excellency."

The General shook his head. "I had rather not be the test case," he said. He felt suddenly weak and overwhelmed with the cares of his life as an official in times such as these when repeated victory brought great responsibilities all over the south Pacific. "It is very unfortunate that this man should have washed up on your doorstep," he said irritably.

"I feel it so myself," Sadao said gently.

"It would be best if he could be quietly killed," the General said. "Not by you, but by someone who does not know him. I have my own private assassins. Suppose I send two of them to your house tonight—or better, any night. You need know nothing about it. It is now warm—what would be more natural than that you should leave the outer partition of the white man's room open to the garden while he sleeps?"

"Certainly it would be very natural," Sadao agreed. "In fact, it is so left every night."

"Good," the General said, yawning. "They are very capable assassins—they make no noise and they know the trick of inward bleeding. If you like I can even have them remove the body."

Sadao considered. "That perhaps would be best, Excellency," he agreed, thinking of Hana.

He left the General's presence then and went home, thinking over the plan. In this way the whole thing would be taken out of his hands. He would tell Hana nothing, since she would be timid at the idea of assassins in the house, and yet certainly such persons were essential in an absolute state such as Japan was. How else could rulers deal with those who opposed them?

He refused to allow anything but reason to be the atmosphere of his mind as he went into the room where the American was in bed. But as he opened the door, to his surprise he found the young man out of bed, and preparing to go into the garden.

"What is this!" he exclaimed. "Who gave you permission to leave your room?"

"I'm not used to waiting for permission," Tom said gaily. "Gosh, I feel pretty good again! But will the muscles on this side always feel stiff?"

"Is it so?" Sadao inquired, surprised. He forgot all else. "Now I thought I had provided against that," he murmured. He lifted the edge of the man's shirt and gazed at the healing scar. "Massage may do it," he said, "if exercise does not."

"It won't bother me much," the young man said. His young face was gaunt under the stubby blond beard. "Say, Doctor, I've got something I want to say to you. If I hadn't met a Jap like you—well, I wouldn't be alive today. I know that."

Sadao bowed but he could not speak.

"Sure, I know that," Tom went on warmly. His big thin hands, gripping a chair, were white at the knuckles. "I guess if all the Japs were like you there wouldn't have been a war."

"Perhaps," Sadao said with difficulty. "And now I think you had better go back to bed."

He helped the boy back into bed and then bowed. "Good night," he said.

Sadao slept badly that night. Time and time again he woke, thinking he heard the rustling of footsteps, the sound of a twig broken or a stone displaced in the garden—a noise such as men might make who carried a burden.

The next morning he made the excuse to go first into the guest room. If the American were gone he then could simply tell Hana that so the General had directed. But when he opened the door he saw at once that it was not last night. There on the pillow was the shaggy blond head. He could hear the peaceful breathing of sleep and he closed the door again quietly.

"He is asleep," he told Hana. "He is almost well to sleep like that."

"What shall we do with him?" Hana whispered her old refrain.

Sadao shook his head. "I must decide in a day or two," he promised.

But certainly, he thought, the second night must be the night. There rose a wind that night, and he listened to the sounds of bending boughs and whistling partitions.

Hana woke too. "Ought we not to go and close the sick man's partition?" she asked.

"No," Sadao said. "He is able now to do it for himself."

But the next morning the American was still there.

Then the third night of course must be the night. The wind changed to quiet rain and the garden was full of the sound of dripping eaves and running springs. Sadao slept a little better, but he woke at the sound of a crash and leaped to his feet.

"What was that?" Hana cried. The baby woke at her voice and began to wail. "I must go and see."

But he held her and would not let her move.

"Sadao," she cried, "what is the matter with you?"

"Don't go," he muttered, "don't go!"

His terror infected her and she stood breathless, waiting. There was only silence. Together they crept back into the bed, the baby between them.

Yet when he opened the door of the guest room in the morning there was the young man. He was very gay and had already washed and was now on his feet. He had asked for a razor yesterday and had shaved himself, and today there was a faint color in his cheeks.

"I am well," he said joyously.

Sadao drew his kimono round his weary body. He could not, he decided suddenly, go through another night. It was not that he cared for this young man's life. No, simply it was not worth the strain.

"You are well," Sadao agreed. He lowered his voice. "You are so well that I think if I put my boat on the shore tonight, with food and extra clothing in it, you might be able to row to that little island not far from the coast. It is so near the coast that it has not been worth fortifying. Nobody lives on it because in storm it is submerged. But this is not the season of storm. You could live there until you saw a Korean fishing boat pass by. They pass quite near the island because the water is many fathoms deep there."

The young man stared at him, slowly comprehending. "Do I have to?" he asked.

"I think so," Sadao said gently. "You understand—it is not hidden that you are here."

The young man nodded in perfect comprehension. "Okay," he said simply.

Sadao did not see him again until evening. As soon as it was dark he had dragged the stout boat down to the shore and in it he put food and bottled water that he had bought secretly during the day, as well as two quilts he had bought at a pawnshop. The boat he tied to a post in the water, for the tide was high. There was no moon and he worked without a flashlight.

When he came to the house he entered as though he were just back from his work, and so Hana knew nothing. "Yumi was here today," she said as she served his supper. Though she was so modern, still she did not eat with him. "Yumi cried over the baby," she went on with a sigh. "She misses him so."

"The servants will come back as soon as the foreigner is gone," Sadao said.

He went into the guest room that night before he went to bed and himself checked carefully the American's temperature, the state of the wound, and his heart and pulse. The pulse was irregular, but that was perhaps because of excitement. The young man's pale lips were pressed together and his eyes burned. Only the scars on his neck were red.

"I realize you are saving my life again," he told Sadao.

"Not at all," Sadao said. "It is only inconvenient to have you here any longer."

He had hesitated a good deal about giving the man a flashlight. But he had decided to give it to him after all. It was a small one, his own, which he used at night when he was called.

"If your food runs out before you catch a boat," he said, "signal me two flashes at the same instant the sun drops over the horizon. Do not signal in darkness, for it will be seen. If you are all right but still there, signal me once. You will find fish easy to catch but you must eat them raw. A fire would be seen."

"Okay," the young man breathed.

He was dressed now in the Japanese clothes which Sadao had given him, and at the last moment Sadao wrapped a black cloth about his blond head.

"Now," Sado said.

The young American without a word shook Sadao's hand warmly and then walked quite well across the floor and down the step into the darkness of the garden. Once—twice—Sadao saw his light flash to find his way. But that would not be suspected. He waited until from the shore there was one more flash. Then he closed the partition. That night he slept.

"You say the man escaped?" the General asked faintly. He had been operated upon a week before, an emergency operation to which Sadao had been called in the night. For twelve hours Sadao had not been sure the General would live. The gall bladder was much involved. Then the old man had begun to breathe deeply again and to demand food. Sadao had not been able to ask about the assassins. So far as he knew they had never come. The servants had returned and Yumi had cleaned the guest room thoroughly and had burned sulphur in it to get the white man's smell out of it. Nobody said anything. Only the gardener was cross because he had got behind with his chrysanthemums.

But after a week Sadao felt the General was well enough to be spoken to about the prisoner.

"Yes, Excellency, he escaped," Sadao now said. He coughed, signifying that he had not said all he might have said but was unwilling to disturb the General further. But the old man opened his eyes suddenly.

"That prisoner," he said with some energy, "did I not promise you I would kill him for you?"

"You did, Excellency," Sadao said.

"Well, well!" the old man said in a tone of amazement, "so I did! But you see, I was suffering a good deal. The truth is, I thought of nothing but myself. In short, I forgot my promise to you."

"I wondered, Your Excellency," Sadao murmured.

"It was certainly very careless of me," the General said. "But you understand it was not lack of patriotism or dereliction of duty." He looked anxiously at his doctor. "If the matter should come out you would understand that, wouldn't you?"

"Certainly, Your Excellency," Sadao said. He suddenly comprehended that the General was in the palm of his hand and that as a consequence he himself was perfectly safe. "I can swear to your loyalty, Excellency," he said to the old General, "and to your zeal against the enemy."

"You are a good man," the General murmured, and closed his eyes. "You will be rewarded."

But Sadao, searching the spot of black in the twilighted sea that night, had his reward. There was no speck of light in the dusk. No one was on the island. His prisoner was gone—safe, doubtless, for he had warned him to wait only for a Korean fishing boat.

He stood for a moment on the veranda, gazing out to the sea from whence the young man had come that other night. And into his mind, although without reason, there came other white faces he had known —the professor at whose house he had met Hana, a dull man, and his wife had been a silly, talkative woman, in spite of her wish to be kind. He remembered his old teacher of anatomy, who had been so insistent on mercy with the knife, and then he remembered the face of his fat and slatternly landlady. He had had great difficulty in finding a place to live in America because he was a Japanese. The Americans were full of prejudice and it had been bitter to live in it, knowing himself their superior. How he had despised the ignorant and dirty old woman who had at last consented to house him in her miserable home! He had once tried to be grateful to her because she had in his last year nursed him through influenza, but it was difficult, for she was no less repulsive to him in her kindness. But then, white people were repulsive of course. It was a relief to be openly at war with them at last. Now he remembered the youthful, haggard face of his prisoner—white and repulsive.

"Strange," he thought, "I wonder why I could not kill him?"

Lord Mountdrago

W. SOMERSET MAUGHAM

Dr. Audlin looked at the clock on his desk. It was twenty minutes to
six. He was surprised that his patient was late, for Lord Mountdrago
prided himself on his punctuality; he had a sententious way of expressing himself which gave the air of an epigram to a commonplace remark,
and he was in the habit of saying that punctuality is a compliment you
pay to the intelligent and a rebuke you administer to the stupid. Lord
Mountdrago's appointment was for five-thirty.

There was in Dr. Audlin's appearance nothing to attract attention. He
was tall and spare, with narrow shoulders and something of a stoop; his
hair was grey and thin; his long, sallow face deeply lined. He was not
more than fifty, but he looked older. His eyes, pale blue and rather large,
were weary. When you had been with him for a while you noticed that
they moved very little; they remained fixed on your face, but so empty
of expression were they that it was no discomfort. They seldom lit up.
They gave no clue to his thoughts nor changed with the words he spoke.
If you were of an observant turn it might have struck you that he blinked much less often than most of us. His hands were on the large side,
with long, tapering fingers; they were soft but firm, cool but not clam-
my. You could never have said what Dr. Audlin wore unless you had
made a point of looking. His clothes were dark. His tie was black. His
dress made his sallow lined face paler and his pale eyes more wan. He
gave you the impression of a very sick man.

Dr. Audlin was a psychoanalyst. He had adopted the profession by
accident and practised it with misgiving. When the war broke out he

had not been long qualified and was getting experience at various hospitals; he offered his services to the authorities, and after a time was sent out to France. It was then that he discovered his singular gift. He could allay certain pains by the touch of his cool, firm hands, and by talking to them often induce sleep in men who were suffering from sleeplessness. He spoke slowly. His voice had no particular colour, and its tone did not alter with the words he uttered, but it was musical, soft and lulling. He told the men that they must rest, that they mustn't worry, that they must sleep; and rest stole into their jaded bones, tranquillity pushed their anxieties away, like a man finding a place for himself on a crowded bench, and slumber fell on their tired eyelids like the light rain of spring upon the fresh-turned earth. Dr. Audlin found that by speaking to men with that low, monotonous voice of his, by looking at them with his pale, quiet eyes, by stroking their weary foreheads with his long firm hands, he could soothe their perturbations, resolve the conflicts that distracted them and banish the phobias that made their lives a torment. Sometimes he effected cures that seemed miraculous. He restored speech to a man who, after being buried under the earth by a bursting shell, had been struck dumb, and he gave back the use of his limbs to another who had been paralyzed after a crash in a plane. He could not understand his powers; he was of a sceptical turn, and though they say that in circumstances of this kind the first thing is to believe in yourself, he never quite succeeded in doing that; and it was only the outcome of his activities, patent to the most incredulous observer, that obliged him to admit that he had some faculty, coming from he knew not where, obscure and uncertain, that enabled him to do things for which he could offer no explanation. When the war was over he went to Vienna and studied there, and afterwards to Zurich; and then settled down in London to practise the art he had so strongly acquired. He had been practising now for fifteen years, and had attained, in the specialty he followed, a distinquished reputation. People told one another of the amazing things he had done, and though his fees were high, he had as many patients as he had time to see. Dr. Audlin knew that he had achieved some very extraordinary results; he had saved men from suicide, others from the lunatic asylum, he had assuaged griefs that embittered useful lives, he had turned unhappy marriages into happy ones, he had eradicated abnormal instincts and thus delivered not a few from a hateful bondage, he had given health to the sick in spirit; he had done all this, and yet at the back of his mind remained the suspicion that he was little more than a quack.

It went against his grain to exercise a power that he could not understand, and it offended his honesty to trade on the faith of the people he treated when he had no faith in himself. He was rich enough now to live without working, and the work exhausted him; a dozen times he had been on the point of giving up practice. He knew all that Freud and Jung and the rest of them had written. He was not satisfied; he had an intimate conviction that all their theory was hocus-pocus, and yet there the results were, incomprehensible, but manifest. And what had he not seen of human nature during the fifteen years that patients had been coming to his dingy back room in Wimpole Street? The revelations that had been poured into his ears, sometimes only too willingly, sometimes with shame, with reservations, with anger, had long ceased to surprise him. Nothing could. shock him any longer. He knew by now that men were liars, he knew how extravagant was their vanity; he knew far worse than that about them; but he knew that it was not for him to judge or to condemn. But year by year as these terrible confidences were imparted to him his face grew a little greyer, its lines a little more marked and his pale eyes more weary. He seldom laughed, but now and again when for relaxation he read a novel he smiled. Did their authors really think the men and women they wrote of were like that? If they only knew how much more complicated they were, how much more unexpected, what irreconcilable elements coexisted within their souls and what dark and sinister contentions afflicted them!

It was a quarter to six. Of all the strange cases he had been called upon to deal with, Dr. Audlin could remember none stranger than that of Lord Mountdrago. For one thing the personality of his patient made it singular. Lord Mountdrago was an able and a distinguished man. Appointed Secretary for Foreign Affairs when still under forty, now after three years in office he had seen his policy prevail. It was generally acknowledged that he was the ablest politician in the Conservative Party, and only the fact that his father was a peer, on whose death he would no longer be able to sit in the House of Commons, made it impossible for him to aim at the premiership. But if in these democratic times it is out of the question for a Prime Minister of England to be in the House of Lords, there was nothing to prevent Lord Mountdrago from continuing to be Secretary for Foreign Affairs in successive Conservative administrations and so for long directing the foreign policy of his country.

Lord Mountdrago had many good qualities. He had intelligence and industry. He was widely travelled and spoke several languages fluently. From early youth he had specialized in foreign affairs and had conscientiously made himself acquainted with the political and economic circumstances of other countries. He had courage, insight and determination. He was a good speaker, both on the platform and in the House, clear, precise and often witty. He was a brilliant debater and his gift of repartee was celebrated. He had a fine presence: he was a tall, handsome man, rather bald and somewhat too stout, but this gave him solidity and an air of maturity that were of service to him. As a young man he had been something of an athlete and had rowed in the Oxford boat, and he was known to be one of the best shots in England. At twenty-four he had married a girl of eighteen whose father was a duke and her mother a great American heiress, so that she had both position and wealth, and by her he had had two sons. For several years they had lived privately apart, but in public united, so that appearances were saved, and no other attachment on either side had given the gossips occasion to whisper. Lord Mountdrago indeed was too ambitious, too hard-working, and it must be added too patriotic, to be tempted by any pleasures that might interfere with his career. He had in short a great deal to make him a popular and successful figure. He had unfortunately great defects.

He was a fearful snob. You would not have been surprised at this if

his father had been the first holder of the title. That the son of an en-
nobled lawyer, manufacturer or distiller should attach an inordinate
importance to his rank is understandable. The earldom held by Lord
Mountdrago's father was created by Charles II, and the barony held
by the first earl dated from the Wars of the Roses. For three hundred
years the successive holders of the title had allied themselves with the
noblest families of England. But Lord Mountdrago was as conscious
of his birth as a *nouveau riche* is conscious of his money. He never
missed an opportunity of impressing it upon others. He had beautiful
manners when he chose to display them, but this he did only with
people whom he regarded as his equals. He was coldly insolent to
those whom he looked upon as his social inferiors. He was rude to his
servants and insulting to his secretaries. The subordinate officials in the
government offices to which he had been successively attached feared
and hated him. His arrogance was horrible. He knew that he was a
great deal cleverer than most of the persons he had to do with, and
never hesitated to apprise them of the fact. He had no patience with
the infirmities of human nature. He felt himself born to command and
was irritated with people who expected him to listen to their arguments or wished to hear the reasons for his decisions. He was immeas-
urably selfish. He looked upon any service that was rendered him as
a right due to his rank and intelligence and therefore deserving of no
gratitude. It never entered his head that he was called upon to do anything for others. He had many enemies: he despised them. He knew
no one who merited his assistance, his sympathy or his compassion. He
had no friends. He was distrusted by his chiefs, because they doubted
his loyalty; he was unpopular with his party, because he was overbear-
ing and discourteous; and yet his merit was so great, his patriotism so
evident, his intelligence so solid and his management of affairs so brilliant, that they had to put up with him. And what made it possible to
do this was that on occasion he could be enchanting: when he was with
persons whom he considered his equals, or whom he wished to capti-
vate, in the company of foreign dignitaries or women of distinction, he

could be gay, witty and debonair; his manners then reminded you that in his veins ran the same blood as had run in the veins of Lord Chesterfield; he could tell a story with point, he could be natural, sensible and even profound. You were surprised at the extent of his knowledge and the sensitiveness of his taste. You thought him the best company in the world; you forgot that he had insulted you the day before and was quite capable of cutting you dead the next.

Lord Mountdrago almost failed to become Dr. Audlin's patient. A secretary rang up the doctor and told him that his lordship, wishing to consult him, would be glad if he would come to his house at ten o'clock on the following morning. Dr. Audlin answered that he was unable to go to Lord Mountdrago's house, but would be pleased to give him an appointment at his consulting room at five o'clock on the next day but one. The secretary took the message and presently rang back to say that Lord Mountdrago insisted on seeing Dr. Audlin in his own house and the doctor could fix his own fee. Dr. Audlin replied that he saw patients only in his consulting room and expressed his regret that unless Lord Mountdrago was prepared to come to him he could not give him his attention. In a quarter of an hour a brief message was delivered to him that his lordship would come not next day but one, but next day, at five.

When Lord Mountdrago was then shown in he did not come forward, but stood at the door and insolently looked the doctor up and down. Dr. Audlin perceived that he was in a rage; he gazed at him, silently, with still eyes. He saw a big heavy man, with greying hair, receding on the forehead so that it gave nobility to his brow, a puffy face with bold regular features and an expression of haughtiness. He had somewhat the look of one of the Bourbon soveigns of the eighteenth century.

"It seems that it is as difficult to see you as a Prime Minister, Dr. Audlin. I'm an extremely busy man."

"Won't you sit down?" said the doctor.

His face showed no sign that Lord Mountdrago's speech in any way affected him. Dr. Audlin sat in his chair at the desk. Lord Mountdrago still stood, and his frown darkened.

"I think I should tell you that I am His Majesty's Secretary for Foreign Affairs," he said acidly.

"Won't you sit down?" the doctor repeated.

Lord Mountdrago made a gesture, which might have suggested that he was about to turn on his heel and stalk out of the room; but if that was his intention he apparently thought better of it. He seated himself. Dr. Audlin opened a large book and took up his pen. He wrote without looking at his patient.

"How old are you?"

"Forty-two."

"Are you married?"

"Yes."

"How long have you been married?"

"Eighteen years."

"Have you any children?"

"I have two sons."

Dr. Audlin noted down the facts as Lord Mountdrago abruptly answered his questions. Then he leaned back in his chair and looked at him. He did not speak; he just looked, gravely, with pale eyes that did not move.

"Why have you come to see me?" he asked at length.

"I've heard about you. Lady Canute is a patient of yours, I understand. She tells me you've done her a certain amount of good."

Dr. Audlin did not reply. His eyes remained fixed on the other's face, but they were so empty of expression that you might have thought he did not even see him.

"I can't do miracles," he said at length. Not a smile, but the shadow of a smile flickered in his eyes. "The Royal College of Physicians would not approve of it if I did."

Lord Mountdrago gave a brief chuckle. It seemed to lessen his hostility. He spoke more amiably.

"You have a very remarkable reputation. People seem to believe in you."

"Why have you come to me?" repeated Dr. Audlin.

Now it was Lord Mountdrago's turn to be silent. It looked as though he found it hard to answer. Dr. Audlin waited. At last Lord Mountdrago seemed to make an effort. He spoke.

"I'm in perfect health. Just as a matter of routine I had myself examined by my own doctor the other day, Sir Augustus Fitzherbert, I daresay you've heard of him, and he tells me I have the physique of a man of thirty. I work hard, but I'm never tired, and I enjoy my work. I smoke very little and I'm an extremely moderate drinker. I take a sufficiency of exercise and I lead a regular life. I am a perfectly sound, normal, healthy man. I quite expect you to think it very silly and childish of me to consult you."

Dr. Audlin saw that he must help him.

"I don't know if I can do anything to help you. I'll try. You're distressed?"

Lord Mountdrago frowned.

"The work that I'm engaged in is important. The decisions I am called upon to make can easily affect the welfare of the country and even the peace of the world. It is essential that my judgment should be balanced and my brain clear. I look upon it as my duty to eliminate any cause of worry that may interfere with my usefulness."

Dr. Audlin had never taken his eyes off him. He saw a great deal. He saw behind his patient's pompous manner and arrogant pride an anxiety that he could not dispel.

"I asked you to be good enough to come here because I know by experience that it's easier for someone to speak openly in the dingy surroundings of a doctor's consulting room than in his accustomed environment."

"They're certainly dingy," said Lord Mountdrago acidly. He paused. It was evident that this man who had so much self-assurance, so quick and decided a mind that he was never at a loss, at this moment was embarrassed. He smiled in order to show the doctor that he was at his ease, but his eyes betrayed his disquiet. When he spoke again it was with unnatural heartiness.

"The whole thing's so trivial that I can hardly bring myself to bother you with it. I'm afraid you'll just tell me not to be a fool and waste your valuable time."

"Even things that seem very trivial may have their importance. They can be a symptom of a deep-seated derangement. And my time is entirely at your disposal."

Dr. Audlin's voice was low and grave. The monotone in which he spoke was strangely soothing. Lord Mountdrago at length made up his mind to be frank.

"The fact is I've been having some very tiresome dreams lately. I know it's silly to pay any attention to them, but—well, the honest truth is that I'm afraid they've got on my nerves."

"Can you describe any of them to me?"

Lord Mountdrago smiled, but the smile that tried to be careless was only rueful.

"They're so idiotic, I can hardly bring myself to narrate them."

"Never mind."

"Well, the first I had was about a month ago. I dreamt that I was at a party at Connemara House. It was an official party. The King and Queen were to be there, and of course decorations were worn. I was wearing my ribbon and my star. I went into a sort of cloakroom they have to take off my coat. There was a little man there called Owen Griffiths, who's a Welsh member of Parliament, and to tell you the truth, I was surprised to see him. He's very common, and I said to myself: 'Really, Lydia Connemara is going too far, whom will she ask next?' I thought he looked at me rather curiously, but I didn't take any notice of him; in fact I cut the little bounder and walked upstairs. I suppose you've never been there?"

"Never."

"No, it's not the sort of house you'd ever be likely to go to. It's a rather vulgar house, but it's got a very fine marble staircase, and the Connemaras were at the top receiving their guests. Lady Connemara gave me a look of surprise when I shook hands with her, and began to giggle; I didn't pay much attention—she's a very silly, ill-bred woman, and her manners are no better than those of her ancestress whom King Charles

II made a duchess. I must say the reception rooms at Connemara House are stately. I walked through, nodding to a number of people and shaking hands; then I saw the German Ambassador talking with one of the Austrian archdukes. I particularly wanted to have a word with him, so I went up and held out my hand. The moment the Archduke saw me he burst into a roar of laughter. I was deeply affronted. I looked him up and down sternly, but he only laughed the more. I was about to speak to him rather sharply, when there was a sudden hush, and I realized that the King and Queen had come. Turning my back on the Archduke, I stepped forward, and then, quite suddenly, I noticed that I hadn't got any trousers on. I was in short silk drawers, and I wore scarlet sock suspenders. No wonder Lady Connemara had giggled; no wonder the Archduke had laughed! I can't tell you what that moment was. An agony of shame. I awoke in a cold sweat. Oh, you don't know the relief I felt to find it was only a dream."

"It's the kind of dream that's not so very uncommon," said Dr. Audlin.

"I daresay not. But an odd thing happened next day. I was in the lobby of the House of Commons, when that fellow Griffiths walked slowly past me. He deliberately looked down at my legs, and then he looked me full in the face, and I was almost certain he winked. A ridiculous thought came to me. He'd been there the night before and seen me make that ghastly exhibition of myself and was enjoying the joke. But of course I knew that was impossible because it was only a dream. I gave him an icy glare, and he walked on. But he was grinning his head off."

Lord Mountdrago took his handkerchief out of his pocket and wiped the palms of his hands. He was making no attempt now to conceal his perturbation. Dr. Audlin never took his eyes off him.

"Tell me another dream."

"It was the night after, and it was even more absurd than the first one. I dreamt that I was in the House. There was a debate on foreign affairs which not only the country, but the world, had been looking forward to with the gravest concern. The government had decided on a change in their policy which vitally affected the future of the Empire.

The occasion was historic. Of course the House was crowded. All the ambassadors were there. The galleries were packed. It fell to me to make the important speech of the evening. I had prepared it carefully. A man like me has enemies—there are a lot of people who resent my having achieved the position I have at an age when even the cleverest men are content with situations of relative obscurity—and I was determined that my speech should not only be worthy of the occasion, but should silence my detractors. It excited me to think that the whole world was hanging on my lips. I rose to my feet. If you've ever been in the House you'll know how members chat to one another during a debate, rustle papers and turn over reports. The silence was the silence of the grave when I began to speak. Suddenly I caught sight of that odious little bounder on one of the benches opposite, Griffiths, the Welsh member; he put out his tongue at me. I don't know if you've ever heard a vulgar music-hall song called 'A Bicycle Made for Two.' It was very popular a great many years ago. To show Griffiths how completely I despised him I began to sing it. I sang the first verse right through. There was a moment's surprise, and when I finished they cried 'Hear, hear,' on the opposite benches. I put up my hand to silence them and sang the second verse. The House listened to me in stony silence and I felt the song wasn't going down very well. I was vexed, for I have a good baritone voice, and I was determined that they should do me justice. When I started the third verse the members began to laugh; in an instant the laughter spread; the ambassadors, the strangers in the Distinguished Strangers' Gallery, the ladies in the Ladies' Gallery, the reporters, they shook, they bellowed, they held their sides, they rolled in their seats; everyone was overcome with laughter except the ministers on the Front Bench immediately behind me. In that incredible, in that unprecedented, uproar they sat petrified. I gave them a glance, and suddenly the enormity of what I had done fell upon me. I had made myself the laughing-stock of the whole world. With misery I realized that I should have to resign. I woke and knew it was only a dream."

Lord Mountdrago's grand manner had deserted him as he narrated this, and now having finished he was pale and trembling. But with an effort he pulled himself together. He forced a laugh to his shaking lips.

"The whole thing was so fantastic that I couldn't help being amused. I didn't give it another thought, and when I went into the House on the following afternoon I was feeling in very good form. The debate was dull, but I had to be there, and I read some documents that required my attention. For some reason I chanced to look up, and I saw that Griffiths was speaking. He has an unpleasant Welsh accent and an unprepossessing appearance. I couldn't imagine that he had anything to say that it was worth my while to listen to, and I was about to return to my papers when he quoted two lines from 'A Bicycle Made for Two.' I couldn't help glancing at him, and I saw that his eyes were fixed on me with a grin of bitter mockery. I faintly shrugged my shoulders. It was comic that a scrubby little Welsh member should look at me like that. It was an odd coincidence that he should quote two lines from that disastrous song that I'd sung all through in my dream. I began to read my papers again, but I don't mind telling you that I found it difficult to concentrate on them. I was a little puzzled. Owen Griffiths had been in my first dream, the one at Connemara House, and I'd received a very definite impression afterwards that he knew the sorry figure I'd cut. Was it a mere coincidence that he had just quoted those two lines? I asked myself if it was poscible that he was dreaming the same dreams as I was. But of course the idea was preposterous, and I determined not to give it a second thought."

There was a silence. Dr. Audlin looked at Lord Mountdrago and Lord Mountdrago looked at Dr. Audlin.

"Other people's dreams are very boring. My wife used to dream occasionally and insist on telling me her dreams next day with circumstantial detail. I found it maddening."

Dr. Audlin faintly smiled.

"You're not boring me."

"I'll tell you one more dream I had a few days later. I dreamt that I went into a public house at Limehouse. I've never been to Limehouse in my life and I don't think I've ever been in a public house since I was at Oxford, and yet I saw the street and the place I went into as exactly as if I were at home there. I went into a room—I don't know whether they call it the saloon bar or the private bar; there was a fireplace and a large leather armchair on one side of it, and on the other a small sofa; a bar ran the whole length of the room, and over it you could see into the public bar. Near the door was a round marble-topped table and two armchairs beside it. It was a Saturday night, and the place was packed. It was brightly lit, but the smoke was so thick that it made my eyes smart. I was dressed like a rough, with a cap on my head and a handkerchief round my neck. It seemed to me that most of the people there were drunk. I thought it rather amusing. There was a gramophone going, or the radio, I don't know which, and in front of the fireplace two women were doing a grotesque dance. There was a little crowd round them, laughing, cheering and singing. I went up to have a look, and some man said to me: ' 'Ave a drink, Bill.' There were glasses on the table full of a dark liquid which I understand is called brown ale. He gave me a glass, and not wishing to be conspicuous I drank it. One of the women who were dancing broke away from the other and took hold of the glass. ' 'Ere, what's the idea?' she said. 'That's my beer you're putting away.' 'Oh, I'm so sorry,' I said, 'this gentleman offered it me, and I very naturally thought it was his to offer.' 'All right, mate,' she said, 'I don't mind. You come an' 'ave a dance with me.' Before I could protest she'd caught hold of me and we were dancing together. And then I found myself sitting in the armchair with the woman on my lap and we were sharing a glass of beer. I should tell you that sex has never played any great part in my life. I married young because in my position it was desirable that I should marry, but also in order to settle once for all the question of sex. I had the two sons I had made up my mind to have, and then I put the whole matter on one side. I've always been too busy to give much thought to that kind of thing, and living so much in the public eye as I do, it would have been madness to do anything that might give rise to scandal. The greatest asset a politician can have is a blameless record as far as women are concerned. I have no patience with the men who smash up their careers for women. I only despise them. The woman I had on my knees was drunk; she wasn't pretty and she wasn't young: in fact, she was just a blowsy old prostitute. She filled me with disgust, and yet when she put her mouth to mine and kissed me, though her breath stank of beer and her teeth were decayed, though I loathed myself, I wanted her—I wanted her with all my soul. Suddenly I heard a voice: 'That's right, old boy, have a good time.' I looked up, and there was Owen Griffiths. I tried to spring out of the chair, but that horrible woman wouldn't let me. 'Don't you pay no attention to 'im,' she said, ' 'e's only one of them nosy parkers.' 'You go to it,' he said. 'I know Moll. She'll give you your money's worth all right.' You know, I wasn't so much annoyed at his seeing me in that absurd situation as angry that he should address me as old boy. I pushed the woman aside and stood up and faced him. 'I don't know you, and I don't want to know you,' I said. 'I know you all right,' he said. 'And my advice to you, Molly, is, see that you get your money, he'll bilk you if he can.' There was a bottle of beer standing on the table close by. Without a word I seized it by the neck and hit him over the head with it as hard as I could. I made such a violent gesture that it woke me up."

"A dream of that sort is not incomprehensible," said Dr. Audlin. "It is the revenge nature takes on persons of unimpeachable character."

"The story's idiotic. I haven't told it you for its own sake. I've told it you for what happened next day. I wanted to look up something in a hurry, and I went into the library of the House. I got the book and began reading. I hadn't noticed when I sat down that Griffiths was sitting in a chair close by me. Another of the Labour Members came in and went up to him. 'Hullo, Owen,' he said to him, 'you're looking pretty dicky to-day.' 'I've got an awful headache,' he answered, 'I feel as if I'd been cracked over the head with a bottle.' "

Now Lord Mountdrago's face was grey with anguish.

"I knew then that the idea I'd had and dismissed as preposterous was true. I knew that Griffiths was dreaming my dreams and that he remembered them as well as I did."

"It may also have been a coincidence."

"When he spoke he didn't speak to his friend, he deliberately spoke to me. He looked at me with sullen resentment."

"Can you offer any suggestion why this same man should come into your dreams?"

"None."

Dr. Audlin's eyes had not left his patient's face and he saw that he lied. He had a pencil in his hand, and he drew a straggling line or two on his blotting paper. It often took a long time to get people to tell the truth, and yet they knew that unless they told it he could do nothing for them.

"The dream you've just described to me took place just over three weeks ago. Have you had any since?"

"Every night."

"And does this man Griffiths come into them all?"

"Yes."

The doctor drew more lines on his blotting paper. He wanted the silence, the drabness, the dull light of that little room to have its effect on Lord Mountdrago's sensibility. Lord Mountdrago threw himself back in his chair and turned his head away so that he should not see the other's grave eyes.

"Dr. Audlin, you must do something for me. I'm at the end of my tether. I shall go mad if this goes on. I'm afraid to go to sleep. Two or three nights I haven't. I've sat up reading and when I felt drowsy put on my coat and walked till I was exhausted. But I must have sleep. With all the work I have to do I must be at concert pitch; I must be in complete control of all my faculties. I need rest; sleep brings me none. I no sooner fall asleep than my dreams begin, and he's always there, that vulgar little cad, grinning at me, mocking me, despising me. It's a monstrous persecution. I tell you, Doctor, I'm not the man of my dreams; it's not fair to judge me by them. Ask anyone you like. I'm an honest, upright, decent man. No one can say anything against my moral character either private or public. My whole ambition is to serve my country and maintain its greatness. I have money, I have rank, I'm not exposed to many of the temptations of lesser men, so that it's no credit to me to be incorruptible; but this I can claim, that no honour, no personal advantage, no thought of self would induce me to swerve by a hairsbreadth from my duty. I've sacrificed everything to become the man I am. Greatness is my aim. Greatness is within my reach, and I'm losing my nerve. I'm not that mean, despicable, cowardly, lewd creature that horrible little man sees. I've told you three of my dreams; they're nothing; that man has seen me do things that are so beastly, so horrible, so shameful, that even if my life depended on it I wouldn't tell them. And he remembers them. I can hardly meet the derision and disgust I see in his eyes, and I even hesitate to speak because I know my words can seem to him nothing but utter humbug. He's seen me do things that no man with any self-respect would do, things for which men are driven out of the society of their fellows and sentenced to long terms of imprisonment; he's heard the foulness of my speech; he's seen me not only ridiculous, but revolting. He despises me and he no longer pretends to conceal it. I tell you that if you can't do something to help me I shall either kill myself or kill him."

"I wouldn't kill him if I were you," said Dr. Audlin coolly, in that soothing voice of his. "In this country the consequences of killing a fellow creature are awkward."

"I shouldn't be hanged for it, if that's what you mean. Who would know that I'd killed him? That dream of mine has shown me how. I told you, the day after I'd hit him over the head with a beer bottle he had such a headache that he couldn't see straight. He said so himself. That shows that he can feel with his waking body what happens to his body asleep. It's not with a bottle I shall hit him next time. One night, when I'm dreaming, I shall find myself with a knife in my hand or a revolver in my pocket—I must because I want to so intensely—and then I shall seize my opportunity. I'll stick him like a pig; I'll shoot him like a dog. In the heart. And then I shall be free of this fiendish persecution."

Some people might have thought that Lord Mountdrago was mad; after all the years during which Dr. Audlin had been treating the diseased souls of men he knew how thin a line divides those whom we call sane from those whom we call insane. He knew how often in men who to all appearance were healthy and normal, who were seemingly devoid of imagination, and who fulfilled the duties of common life with credit to themselves and with benefit to their fellows, when you gained their confidence, when you tore away the mask they wore to the world, you found not only hideous abnormality, but kinks so strange, mental extravagances so fantastic, that in that respect you could only call them lunatic. If you put them in an asylum, not all the asylums in the world would be large enough. Anyhow, a man was not certifiable because he had strange dreams and they had shattered his nerve. The case was singular, but it was only an exaggeration of others that had come under Dr. Audlin's observation; he was doubtful, however, whether the methods of treatment that he had so often found efficacious would here avail.

"Have you consulted any other member of my profession?" he asked.

"Only Sir Augustus. I merely told him that I suffered from nightmares. He said I was overworked and recommended me to go for a cruise. That's absurd. I can't leave the Foreign Office just now when the international situation needs constant attention. I'm indispensable, and I know it. On my conduct at the present juncture my whole future depends. He gave me sedatives. They had no effect. He gave me tonics. They were worse than useless. He's an old fool."

"Can you give any reason why it should be this particular man who persists in coming into your dreams?"

"You asked me that question before. I answered it."

That was true. But Dr. Audlin had not been satisfied with the answer.

"Just now you talked of persecution. Why should Owen Griffiths want to persecute you?"

"I don't know."

Lord Mountdrago's eyes shifted a little. Dr. Audlin was sure that he was not speaking the truth.

"Have you ever done him an injury?"

"Never."

Lord Mountdrago made no movement, but Dr. Audlin had a queer feeling that he shrank into his skin. He saw before him a large, proud man who gave the impression that the questions put to him were an insolence, and yet for all that, behind that facade, was something shifting and startled that made you think of a frightened animal in a trap. Dr. Audlin leaned forward and by the power of his eyes forced Lord Mountdrago to meet them.

"Are you quite sure?"

"Quite sure. You don't seem to understand that our ways lead along different paths. I don't wish to harp on it, but I must remind you that I am a minister of the Crown and Griffiths is an obscure member of the Labour Party. Naturally there's no social connection between us; he's a man of very humble origin, he's not the sort of person I should be likely to meet at any of the houses I go to; and politically our respective stations are so far separated that we could not possibly have anything in common."

"I can do nothing for you unless you tell me the complete truth."

Lord Mountdrago raised his eyebrows. His voice was rasping.

"I'm not accustomed to having my word doubted, Dr. Audlin. If you're going to do that, I think to take up any more of your time can only be a waste of mine. If you will kindly let my secretary know what your fee is, he will see that a cheque is sent to you."

For all the expression that was to be seen on Dr. Audlin's face you might have thought that he simply had not heard what Lord Mountdrago said. He continued to look steadily into his eyes, and his voice was grave and low.

"Have you done anything to this man that *he* might look upon as an injury?"

Lord Mountdrago hesitated. He looked away, and then, as though there were in Dr. Audlin's eyes a compelling force that he could not resist, looked back. He answered sulkily:

"Only if he was a dirty, second-rate little cad."

"But that is exactly what you've described him to be."

Lord Mountdrago sighed. He was beaten. Dr. Audlin knew that the sigh mean he was going at last to say what he had till then held back. Now he had no longer to insist. He dropped his eyes and began again drawing vague geometrical figures on his blotting paper. The silence lasted two or three minutes.

"I'm anxious to tell you everything that can be of any use to you. If I didn't mention this before, it's only because it was so unimportant that I didn't see how it could possibly have anything to do with the case. Griffiths won a seat at the last election, and he began to make a nuisance of himself almost at once. His father's a miner, and he worked in a mine himself when he was a boy; he's been a school-master in the board schools and a journalist. He's that half-baked, conceited intellectual, with inadequate knowledge, ill-considered ideas and impractical plans, that compulsory education has brought forth from the working classes. He's a scrawny, grey-faced man who looks half starved, and he's always very slovenly in appearance; heaven knows members nowadays don't bother much about their dress, but his clothes are an outrage to the dignity of the House. They're ostentatiously shabby, his collar's never clean, and his tie's never tied properly; he looks as if he hadn't had a bath for a month, and his hands are filthy. The Labour Party have two or three fellows on the Front Bench who've got a certain ability, but the rest of them don't amount to much. In the kingdom of the blind the one-eyed man is king: because Griffiths is glib and has a lot of superficial information on a number of subjects, the Whips on his side began to put him up to speak whenever there was a chance. It appeared that he fancied himself on foreign affairs, and he was continually asking me silly, tiresome questions. I don't mind telling you that I made a point of snubbing him as soundly as I thought he deserved. From the beginning I hated the way he talked, his whining voice and his vulgar accent; he had nervous mannerisms that intensely irritated me. He talked rather shyly, hesitatingly, as though it were torture to him to speak and yet he was forced to by some inner passion, and often he used to say some very disconcerting things. I'll admit that now and again he had a sort of tub-thumping eloquence. It had a certain influence over the ill-regulated minds of the members of his party. They were impressed

by his earnestness, and they weren't, as I was, nauseated by his sentimentality. A certain sentimentality is the common coin of political
debate. Nations are governed by self-interest, but they prefer to believe
that their aims are altruistic, and the politician is justified if with fair
words and fine phrases he can persuade the electorate that the hard
bargain he is driving for his country's advantage tends to the good of
humanity. The mistake people like Griffiths make is to take these fair
words and fine phrases at their face value. He's a crank, and a noxious
crank. He calls himself an idealist. He has at his tongue's end all the
tedious blather that the intelligentsia have been boring us with for years.
Non-resistance. The brotherhood of man. You know the hopeless rubbish. The worst of it was that it impressed not only his own party, it
even shook some of the sillier, more sloppy-minded members of ours.
I heard rumours that Griffiths was likely to get office when a Labour
Government came in; I even heard it suggested that he might get the
Foreign Office. The notion was grotesque but not impossible. One day
I had occasion to wind up a debate on foreign affairs which Griffiths
had opened. He'd spoken for an hour. I thought it a very good opportunity to cook his goose, and by God, sir, I cooked it. I tore his speech
to pieces. I pointed out the faultiness of his reasoning and emphasized
the deficiency of his knowledge. In the House of Commons the most
devastating weapon is ridicule: I mocked him; I bantered him; I was
in good form that day and the House rocked with laughter. Their
laughter excited me, and I excelled myself. The Opposition sat glum
and silent, but even some of them couldn't help laughing once or twice;
it's not intolerable, you know, to see a colleague, perhaps a rival, made a
fool of. And if ever a man was made a fool of, I made a fool of Griffiths.
He shrank down in his seat; I saw his face go white, and presently he
buried it in his hands. When I sat down I'd killed him. I'd destroyed
his prestige for ever; he had no more chance of getting office when a
Labour Government came in than the policeman at the door. I heard
afterwards that his father, the old miner, and his mother had come up
from Wales, with various supporters of his in the constituency, to watch

the triumph they expected him to have. They had seen only his utter humiliation. He'd won the constituency by the narrowest margin. An incident like that might very easily lose him his seat. But that was no business of mine."

"Should I be putting it too strongly if I said you had ruined his career?" asked Dr. Audlin.

"I don't suppose you would."

"That is a very serious injury you've done him."

"He brought it on himself."

"Have you never felt any qualms about it?"

"I think perhaps if I'd known that his father and mother were there I might have let him down a little more gently."

There was nothing further for Dr. Audlin to say, and he set about treating his patient in such a manner as he thought might avail. He sought by suggestion to make him forget his dreams when he awoke; he sought to make him sleep so deeply that he would not dream. He found Lord Mountdrago's resistance impossible to break down. At the end of an hour he dismissed him.

Since then he had seen Lord Mountdrago half a dozen times. He had done him no good. The frightful dreams continued very night to harass the unfortunate man, and it was clear that his general condition was growing rapidly worse. He was worn out. His irritability was uncontrollable. Lord Mountdrago was angry because he received no benefit from his treatment, and yet continued it, not only because it seemed his only hope, but because it was a relief to him to have someone with whom he could talk openly. Dr. Audlin came to the conclusion at last that there was only one way in which Lord Mountdrago could achieve deliverance, but he knew him well enough to be assured that of his own free will he would never, never take it. If Lord Mountdrago was to be saved from the breakdown that was threatening, he must be induced to take a step that must be abhorrent to his pride of birth and his self-complacency. Dr. Audlin was convinced that to delay was impossible. He was treating his patient by suggestion, and after several visits found him more susceptible to it. At length he managed to get him into a condition of somnolence. With his low, soft, monotonous voice he soothed his tortured nerves. He repeated the same words over and over again. Lord Mountdrago lay quite still, his eyes closed; his breathing was regular, and his limbs were relaxed. Then Dr. Audlin in the same quiet tone spoke the words he had prepared.

"You will go to Owen Griffiths and say that you are sorry that you caused him that great injury. You will say that you will do whatever lies in your power to undo the harm that you have done him."

The words acted on Lord Mountdrago like the blow of a whip across his face. He shook himself out of his hypnotic state and sprang to his feet. His eyes blazed with passion, and he poured forth upon Dr. Audlin a stream of angry vituperation such as even he had never heard. He swort at him. He cursed him. He used language of such obscenity that Dr. Audlin, who had heard every sort of foul word, sometimes from the lips of chaste and distinguished women, was surprised that he knew it.

"Apologize to the filthy little Welshman? I'd rather kill myself."

"I believe it to be the only way in which you can regain your balance."

Dr. Audlin had not often seen a man presumably sane in such a condition of uncontrollable fury. Lord Mountdrago grew red in the face, and his eyes bulged out of his head. He did really foam at the mouth. Dr. Audlin watched him coolly, waiting for the storm to wear itself out, and presently he saw that Lord Mountdrago, weakened by the strain to which he had been subjected for so many weeks, was exhausted.

"Sit down," he said then, sharply.

Lord Mountdrago crumpled up into a chair.

"Christ, I feel all in. I must rest a minute and then I'll go."

For five minutes perhaps they sat in complete silence. Lord Mountdrago was a gross, blustering bully, but he was also a gentleman. When he broke the silence he had recovered his self-control.

"I'm afraid I've been very rude to you. I'm ashamed of the things I've said to you, and I can only say you'd be justified if you refused to have anything more to do with me. I hope you won't do that. I feel that my visits to you do help me. I think you're my only chance."

"You mustn't give another thought to what you said. It was of no consequence."

"But there's on thing you mustn't ask me to do, and that is to make excuses to Griffiths."

"I've thought a great deal about your case. I don't pretend to understand it, but I believe that your only chance of release is to do what I proposed. I have a notion that we're none of us one self, but many, and one of the selves in you has risen up against the injury you did Griffiths and has taken on the form of Griffiths in your mind and is punishing you for what you cruelly did. If I were a priest I should tell you that it is your conscience that has adopted the shape and lineaments of this man to scourge you to repentance and persuade you to reparation."

"My conscience is clear. It's not my fault if I smashed the man's career. I crushed him like a slug in my garden. I regret nothing."

It was on these words that Lord Mountdrago had left him. Reading through his notes, while he waited, Dr. Audlin considered how best he could bring his patient to the state of mind that, now that his usual methods of treatment had failed, he thought alone could help him. He glanced at his clock. It was six. It was strange that Lord Mountdrago did not come. He knew he had intended to because a secretary had rung up that morning to say that he would be with him at the usual hour. He must have been detained by pressing work. This notion gave Dr. Audlin something else to think of: Lord Mountdrago was quite unfit to work and in no condition to deal with important matters of state. Dr. Audlin wondered whether it behooved him to get in touch with someone in authority, the Prime Minister or the Permanent Under Secretary for Foreign Affairs, and impart to him his conviction that Lord Mountdrago's mind was so unbalanced that it was dangerous to leave affairs of moment in his hands. It was a ticklish thing to do. He might cause needless trouble and get roundly snubbed for his plans. He shrugged his shoulders.

"After all," he reflected, "the politicians have made such a mess of the world during the last five-and-twenty years, I don't suppose it makes much odds if they're mad or sane."

He rang the bell.

"If Lord Mountdrago comes now, will you tell him that I have another appointment at six-fifteen and so I'm afraid I can't see him."

"Very good, sir."

"Has the evening paper come yet?"

"I'll go and see."

In a moment the servant brought it in. A huge headline ran across the front page: Tragic Death of Foreign Minister.

"My God!" cried Dr. Audlin.

For once he was wrenched out of his wonted calm. He was shocked, horribly shocked, and yet he was not altogether surprised. The possibility that Lord Mountdrago might commit suicide had occurred to him several times, for that it was suicide he could not doubt. The paper said that Lord Mountdrago had been waiting in a tube station, standing on the edge of the platform, and as the train came in was seen to fall on the rail. It was supposed that he had had a sudden attack of faintness. The paper went on to say that Lord Mountdrago had been suffering for some weeks from the effects of overwork, but had felt it impossible to absent himself while the foreign situation demanded his unremitting attention. Lord Mountdrago was another victim of the strain that modern politics placed upon those who played the more important parts in it. There was a neat little piece about the talents and industry, the patriotism and vision, of the deceased statesman, followed by various surmises upon the Prime Minister's choice of his successor. Dr. Audlin read all this. He had not liked Lord Mountdrago. The chief emotion that his death caused in him was dissatisfaction with himself because he had been able to do nothing for him.

Perhaps he had done wrong in not getting into touch with Lord Mountdrago's doctor. He was discouraged, as always when failure frustrated his conscientious efforts, and repulsion seized him for the theory and practice of this empiric doctrine by which he earned his living. He was dealing with dark and mysterious forces that it was perhaps beyond the powers of the human mind to understand. He was like a man blindfold trying to feel his way to he knew not whither. Listlessly he turned the pages of the paper. Suddenly he gave a great start, and an exclamation once more was forced from his lips. His eyes had fallen on a small paragraph near the bottom of a column. Sudden Death of an M.P., he read. Mr. Owen Griffiths, member for so-and-so, had been taken ill in Fleet Street that afternoon and when he was brought to Charing Cross Hospital life was found to be extinct. It was supposed that death was due to natural causes, but an inquest would be held. Dr. Audlin could hardly believe his eyes. Was it possible that the night before Lord Mountdrago had at last in his dream found himself possessed of the weapon, knife or gun, that he had wanted, and had killed his tormentor, and had that ghostly murder, in the same way as the blow with the bottle had given him a racking headache on the following day, taken effect a certain number of hours later on the waking man? Or was it, more mysterious and more frightful, that when Lord Mountdrago sought relief in death, the enemy he had so cruelly wronged, unappeased, escaping from his own mortality, had pursued him to some other sphere, there to torment him still? It was strange. The sensible thing was to look upon it merely as an odd coincidence. Dr. Audlin rang the bell.

"Tell Mrs. Milton that I'm sorry I can't see her this evening, I'm not well."

It was true; he shivered as though of an ague. With some kind of spiritual sense he seemed to envisage a bleak, a horrible void. The dark night of the soul engulfed him, and he felt a strange, primeval terror of he knew not what.

Zone of Quiet

RING W. LARDNER

"**W**ELL," said the Doctor briskly, "how do you feel?"

"Oh, I guess I'm all right," replied the man in bed. "I'm still kind of drowsy, that's all."

"You were under the anesthetic an hour and a half. It's no wonder you aren't wide awake yet. But you'll be better after a good night's rest, and I've left something with Miss Lyons that'll make you sleep. I'm going along now. Miss Lyons will take good care of you."

"I'm off at seven o'clock," said Miss Lyons. "I'm going to a show with my G. F. But Miss Halsey's all right. She's the night floor nurse. Anything you want, she'll get it for you. What can I give him to eat, Doctor?"

"Nothing at all; not till after I've been here tomorrow. He'll be better off without anything. Just see that he's kept quiet. Don't let him talk, and don't talk to him; that is, if you can help it."

"Help it!" said Miss Lyons. "Say, I can be old lady Sphinx herself when I want to! Sometimes I sit for hours—not alone, neither—and never say a word. Just think and think. And dream.

"I had a G. F. in Baltimore, where I took my training; she used to call me Dummy. Not because I'm dumb like some people—you know—but because I'd sit there and not say nothing. She'd say, 'A penny for your thoughts, Eleanor.' That's my first name—Eleanor."

"Well, I must run along. I'll see you in the morning."

"Good-by, Doctor," said the man in bed, as he went out.

84

"Good-by, Doctor Cox," said Miss Lyons as the door closed.

"He seems like an awful nice fella," said Miss Lyons. "And a good doctor, too. This is the first time I've been on a case with him. He gives a girl credit for having some sense. Most of these doctors treat us like they thought we were Mormons or something. Like Doctor Holland. I was on a case with him last week. He treated me like I was a Mormon or something. Finally, I told him, I said, 'I'm not as dumb as I look.' She died Friday night."

"Who?" asked the man in bed.

"The woman; the case I was on," said Miss Lyons.

"And what did the doctor say when you told him you weren't as dumb as you look?"

"I don't remember," said Miss Lyons. "He said, 'I hope not,' or something. What *could* he say? Gee! It's quarter to seven. I hadn't no idear it was so late. I must get busy and fix you up for the night. And I'll tell Miss Halsey to take good care of you. We're going to see 'What Price Glory?' I'm going with my G. F. Her B. F. gave her the tickets and he's going to meet us after the show and take us to supper.

"Marian—that's my G. F.—she's crazy wild about him. And he's crazy about her, to hear her tell it. But I said to her this noon—she called me up on the phone—I said to her, 'If he's so crazy about you, why don't he propose? He's got plenty of money and no strings tied to him, and as far as I can see there's no reason why he shouldn't marry you if he wants you as bad as you say he does.' So she said maybe he was going to ask her tonight. I told her, 'Don't be silly! Would he drag me along if he was going to ask you?'

"That about him having plenty of money, though, that's a joke. He told her he had and she believes him. I haven't met him yet, but he looks in his picture like he's lucky if he's getting twenty-five dollars a week. She thinks he must be rich because he's in Wall Street. I told her, I said, 'That being in Wall Street don't mean nothing. What does he do there? is the question. You know they have to have janitors in those buildings just the same like anywhere else.' But she thinks he's God or somebody.

"She keeps asking me if I don't think he's the best looking thing I ever saw. I tell her yes, sure, but between you and I, I don't believe anybody'd ever mistake him for Richard Barthelmess.

"Oh, say! I saw him the other day, coming out of the Algonquin! He's the best looking thing! Even better looking than on the screen. Roy Stewart."

"What about Roy Stewart?" asked the man in bed.

"Oh, he's the fella I was telling you about," said Miss Lyons. "He's my G. F.'s B. F."

"Maybe I'm a D. F. not to know, but would you tell me what a B. F. and G. F. are?"

"Well, you *are* dumb, aren't you!" said Miss Lyons. "A G. F., that's a girl friend, and a B. F. is a boy friend. I thought everybody knew that.

"I'm going out now and find Miss Halsey and tell her to be nice to you. But maybe I better not."

"Why not?" asked the man in bed.

"Oh, nothing. I was just thinking of something funny that happened last time I was on a case in this hospital. It was the day the man had been operated on and he was the best looking somebody you ever saw. So when I went off duty I told Miss Halsey to be nice to him, like I was going to tell her about you. And when I came back in the morning he was dead. Isn't that funny?"

"Very!"

"Well," said Miss Lyons, "did you have a good night? You look a lot better, anyway. How'd you like Miss Halsey? Did you notice her ankles? She's got pretty near the smallest ankles I ever saw. Cute. I remember one day Tyler—that's one of the internes—he said if he could just see our ankles, mine and Miss Halsey's, he wouldn't know which was which. Of course we don't look anything alike other ways. She's pretty close to thirty and—well, nobody'd ever take her for Julia Hoyt. Helen."

"Who's Helen?" asked the man in bed.

"Helen Halsey. Helen; that's her first name. She was engaged to a man in Boston. He was going to Tufts College. He was going to be a doctor. But he died. She still carries his picture with her. I tell her she's silly to mope about a man that's been dead four years. And besides a girl's a fool to marry a doctor. They've got too many alibis.

"When I marry somebody, he's got to be a somebody that has regular office hours like he's in Wall Street or somewhere. Then when he don't come home, he'll have to think up something better than being 'on a case.' I used to use that on my sister when we were living together. When I happened to be out late, I'd tell her I was on a case. She never knew the difference. Poor sis! She married a terrible oil can! But she didn't have the looks to get a real somebody. I'm making this for her. It's a bridge table cover for her birthday. She'll be twenty-nine. Don't that seem old?"

"Maybe to you; not to me," said the man in bed.

"You're about forty, aren't you?" said Miss Lyons.

"Just about."

"And how old would you say I am?"

"Twenty-three."

"I'm twenty-five," said Miss Lyons. "Twenty-five and forty. That's fifteen years' difference. But I know a married couple that the husband is forty-five and she's only twenty-four, and they get along fine."

"I'm married myself," said the man in bed.

"You would be!" said Miss Lyons. "The last four cases I've been on was all married men. But at that, I'd rather have any kind of a man than a woman. I hate women! I mean sick ones. They treat a nurse like a dog, especially a pretty nurse. What's that you're reading?"

"'Vanity Fair,'" replied the man in bed.

"'Vanity Fair.' I thought that was a magazine."

"Well, there's a magazine *and* a book. This is the book."

"Is it about a girl?"

"Yes."

"I haven't read it yet. I've been busy making this thing for my sister's birthday. She'll be twenty-nine. It's a bridge table cover. When you get that old, about all there is left is bridge or cross-word puzzles. Are you a puzzle fan? I did them religiously for a while, but I got sick of them. They put in such crazy words. Like one day they had a word with only

three letters and it said 'A e-longated fish' and the first letter had to be
an *e*. And only three letters. That *couldn't* be right. So I said if they put
things wrong like that, what's the use? Life's too short. And we only
live once. When you're dead, you stay a long time dead.

"That's what a B. F. of mine used to say. He was a caution! But he
was crazy about me. I might of married him only for a G. F. telling him
lies about me. And called herself my friend! Charley Pierce."

"Who's Charley Pierce?"

"That was my B. F. that the other girl lied to him about me. I told
him, I said, 'Well, if you believe all them stories about me, maybe we
better part once and for all. I don't want to be tied up to a somebody that
believes all the dirt they hear about me.' So he said he didn't really
believe it and if I would take him back he wouldn't quarrel with me no
more. But I said I thought it was best for us to part. I got their announcement two years ago, while I was still in training in Baltimore."

"Did he marry the girl that lied to him about you?"

"Yes, the poor fish! And I bet he's satisfied! They're a match for each
other! He was all right, though, at that, till he fell for her. He used to be
so thoughtful of me, like I was his sister or something.

"I like a man to respect me. Most fellas wants to kiss you before they
know your name.

"Golly! I'm sleepy this morning! And got a right to be, too. Do you
know what time I got home last night, or this morning, rather? Well,
it was half past three. What would mama say if she could see her little
girl now! But we did have a good time. First we went to the show—
'What Price Glory?'—I and my G. F.—and afterwards her B. F. met us
and took us in a taxi down to Barney Gallant's. Peewee Byers has got
the orchestra there now. Used to be with Whiteman's. Gee! How he can
dance! I mean Roy."

"Your G. F.'s B. F.?"

"Yes, but I don't believe he's as crazy about her as she thinks he is.
Anyway—but this is a secret—he took down the phone number of the
hospital while Marian was out powdering her nose, and he said he'd

give me a ring about noon. Gee! I'm sleepy! Roy Stewart!"

"Well," said Miss Lyons, "how's my patient? I'm twenty minutes late, but honest, it's a wonder I got up at all! Two nights in succession is too much for this child!"

"Barney Gallant's again?" asked the man in bed.

"No, but it was dancing, and pretty near as late. It'll be different to-night. I'm going to bed just the minute I get home. But I did have a dandy time. And I'm crazy about a certain somebody."

"Roy Stewart?"

"How'd you guess it? But honest, he's wonderful! And so different than most of the fellas I've met. He says the craziest things, just keeps you in hysterics. We were talking about books and reading, and he ask-ed me if I liked poetry—only he called it 'poultry'—and I said I was wild about it and Edgar M. Guest was just about my favorite, and then I asked him if he liked Kipling and what do you think he said? He said he didn't know; he'd never kipled.

"He's a scream! We just sat there in the house till half past eleven and didn't do nothing but just talk and the time went like we was at a show. He's better than a show. But finally I noticed how late it was and I asked him didn't he think he better be going and he said he'd go if I'd go with him, so I asked him where could we go at that hour of night, and he said he knew a roadhouse just a little ways away, and I didn't want to go, but he said we wouldn't stay for only just one dance, so I went with him. To the Jericho Inn.

"I don't know what the woman thought of me where I stay, going out that time of night. But he *is* such a wonderful dancer and such a perfect gentleman! Of course we had more than one dance and it was after two o'clock before I knew it. We had some gin, too, but he just kissed me once and that was when we said good night."

"What about your G. F., Marian? Does she know?"

"About Roy and I? No. I always say that what a person don't know don't hurt them. Besides, there's nothing *for* her to know—yet. But listen: If there was a chance in the world for her, if I thought he cared anything about her, I'd be the last one in the world to accept his intentions. I hope I'm not that kind! But as far as anything serious between them is concerned, well, it's cold. I happen to *know* that! She's not the girl for him.

"In the first place, while she's pretty in a way, her complexion's bad and her hair's scraggy and her figure, well, it's like some woman in the funny pictures. And she's not peppy enough for Roy. She'd rather stay home than do anything. Stay home! It'll be time enough for that when you can't get anybody to take you out.

"She'd never make a wife for him. He'll be a rich man in another year; that is, if things go right for him in Wall Street like he expects. And a man as rich as he'll be wants a wife that can live up to it and entertain and step out once in a while. He don't want a wife that's a drag on him. And he's too good-looking for Marian. A fella as good-looking as him needs a pretty wife or the first thing you know some girl that is pretty will steal him off of you. But it's silly to talk about them marrying each other. He'd have to ask her first, and he's not going to. I know! So I don't feel at all like I'm trespassing.

"Anyway, you know the old saying, everything goes in love. And I—— But I'm keeping you from reading your book. Oh, yes; I almost forgot a T. L. that Miss Halsey said about you. Do you know what a T. L. is?"

"Yes."

"Well, then, you give me one and I'll give you this one."

"But I haven't talked to anybody but the Doctor. I can give you one from myself. He asked me how I liked you and I said all right."

"Well, that's better than nothing. Here's what Miss Halsey said: She said if you were shaved and fixed up, you wouldn't be bad. And now I'm going out and see if there's any mail for me. Most of my mail goes to where I live, but some of it comes here sometimes. What I'm looking for is a letter from the state board telling me if I passed my state examination. They ask you the craziest questions. Like 'Is ice a disinfectant?'

Who cares! Nobody's going to waste ice to kill germs when there's so much of it needed in high-balls. Do you like high-balls? Roy says it spoils whisky to mix it with water. He takes it straight. He's a terror! But maybe you want to read."

"Good morning," said Miss Lyons. "Did you sleep good?"

"Not so good," said the man in bed. "I——"

"I bet you got more sleep than I did," said Miss Lyons. "He's the most persistent somebody I ever knew! I asked him last night, I said, 'Don't you never get tired of dancing?' So he said, well, he did get tired of dancing with some people, but there was others who he never got tired of dancing with them. So I said, 'Yes, Mr. Jollier, but I wasn't born yesterday and I know apple sauce when I hear it and I bet you've told that to fifty girls." I guess he really did mean it, though.

"Of course most anybody'd rather dance with slender girls than stout girls. I remember a B. F. I had one time in Washington. He said dancing with me was just like dancing with nothing. That sounds like he was insulting me, but it was really a compliment. He meant it wasn't any effort to dance with me like with some girls. You take Marian, for instance, and while I'm crazy about her, still that don't make her a good dancer and dancing with her must be a good deal like moving the piano or something.

"I'd die if I was fat! People are always making jokes about fat people. And there's the old saying, 'Nobody loves a fat man.' And it's even worse with a girl. Besides people making jokes about them and don't want to dance with them and so forth, besides that they're always trying to reduce and can't eat what they want to. I bet, though, if I was fat, I'd eat everything in sight. Though I guess not, either. Because I hardly eat anything as it is. But they do make jokes about them.

"I'll never forget one day last winter, I was on a case in Great Neck and the man's wife was the fattest thing! So they had a radio in the house and one day she saw in the paper where Bugs Baer was going to talk on the radio and it would probably be awfully funny because he writes so crazy. Do you ever read his articles? But this woman, she was awfully sensitive about being fat and I nearly died sitting there with her listening to Bugs Baer, because his whole talk was all about some fat woman and he said the craziest things, but I couldn't laugh on account of she being there in the room with me. One thing he said was that the woman, this woman he was talking about, he said she was so fat that she wore a wrist watch on her thumb. Henry J. Belden."

"Who is Henry J. Belden? Is that the name of Bugs Baer's fat lady?"

"No, you crazy!" said Miss Lyons. "Mr. Belden was the case I was on in Great Neck. He died."

"It seems to me a good many of your cases die."

"Isn't it a scream!" said Miss Lyons. "But it's true; that is, it's been true lately. The last five cases I've been on has all died. Of course it's just luck, but the girls have been kidding me about it and calling me a jinx, and when Miss Halsey saw me here the evening of the day you was operated, she said, 'God help him!' That's the night floor nurse's name. But you're going to be mean and live through it and spoil my record, aren't you? I'm just kidding. Of course I want you to get all right.

"But it *is* queer, the way things have happened, and it's made me feel kind of creepy. And besides, I'm not like some of the girls and don't care. I get awfully fond of some of my cases and I hate to see them die, especially if they're men and not very sick and treat you half-way decent and don't yell for you the minute you go out of the room. There's only one case I was ever on where I didn't mind her dying and that was a woman. She had nephritis. Mrs. Judson.

"Do you want some gum? I chew it just when I'm nervous. And I always get nervous when I don't have enough sleep. You can bet I'll stay home tonight, B. F. or no B. F. But anyway he's got an engagement tonight, some directors' meeting or something. He's the busiest somebody in the world. And I told him last night, I said, 'I should think you'd need sleep, too, even more than I do because you have to have all your wits about you in your business or those big bankers would take advantage and rob you. You can't afford to be sleepy,' I told him.

"So he said, 'No, but of course it's all right for you, because if you go to sleep on your job, there's no danger of you doing any damage except maybe give one of your patients a bichloride of mercury tablet instead of an alcohol rub.' He's terrible! But you can't help from laughing.

"There was four of us in the party last night. He brought along his B. F. and another girl. She was just blah, but the B. F. wasn't so bad, only he insisted on me helping him drink a half a bottle of Scotch, and on top of gin, too. I guess I was the life of the party; that is, at first. Afterwards I got sick and it wasn't so good.

"But at first I was certainly going strong. And I guess I made quite a hit with Roy's B. F. He knows Marian, too, but he won't say anything, and if he does, I don't care. If she don't want to lose her beaus, she ought to know better than to introduce them to all the pretty girls in the world. I don't mean that I'm any Norma Talmadge, but at least— well—but I sure was sick when I *was* sick!

"I must give Marian a ring this noon. I haven't talked to her since the night she introduced me to him. I've been kind of scared. But I've got to find out what she knows. Or if she's sore at me. Though I don't see how she can be, do you? But maybe you want to read."

"I called Marian up, but I didn't get her. She's out of town but she'll be back tonight. She's been out on a case. Hudson, New York, that's where she went. The message was waiting for her when she got home the other night, the night she introduced me to Roy.

"Good morning," said Miss Lyons.

"Good morning," said the man in bed. "Did you sleep enough?"

"Yes," said Miss Lyons. "I mean no, not enough."

"Your eyes look bad. They almost look as if you'd been crying."

"Who? Me? It'd take more than—I mean, I'm not a baby! But go on and read your book."

"Well, good morning," said Miss Lyons. "And how's my patient?

And this is the last morning I can call you that, isn't it? I think you're mean to get well so quick and leave me out of a job. I'm just kidding. I'm glad you're all right again, and I can use a little rest myself."

"Another big night?" asked the man in bed.

"Pretty big," said Miss Lyons. "And another one coming. But tomorrow I won't ever get up. Honest, I danced so much last night that I thought my feet would drop off. But he certainly is a dancing fool! And the nicest somebody to talk to that I've met since I came to this town. Not a smart Alex and not always trying to be funny like some people, but just nice. He understands. He seems to know just what you're thinking. George Morse."

"George Morse!" exclaimed the man in bed.

"Why yes," said Miss Lyons. "Do you know him?"

"No. But I thought you were talking about this Stewart, this Roy."

"Oh, him!" said Miss Lyons. "I should say not! He's private property; other people's property, not mine. He's engaged to my G. F. Marian. It happened day before yesterday, after she got home from Hudson. She was on a case up there. She told me about it night before last. I told her congratulations. Because I wouldn't hurt her feelings for the world! But heavens! what a mess she's going to be in, married to that dumbbell. But of course some people can't be choosey. And I doubt if they ever get married unless some friend loans him the price of a license.

"He's got her believing he's in Wall Street, but if he ever goes there at all, it's to sweep it. He's one of these kind of fellas that's got a great line for a little while, but you don't want to live with a clown. And I'd hate to marry a man that all he thinks about is to step out every night and dance and drink.

"I had a notion to tell her what I really thought. But that'd only of made her sore, or she'd of thought I was jealous or something. As if I couldn't of had him myself! Though even if he wasn't so awful, if I'd liked him instead of loathed him, I wouldn't of taken him from her on account of she being my G. F. And especially while she was out of town.

"He's the kind of a fella that'd marry a nurse in the hopes that some day he'd be an invalid. You know, that kind.

"But say—did you ever hear of J. P. Morgan and Company? That's where my B. F. works, and he don't claim to own it neither. George Morse.

"Haven't you finished that book yet?"

A Movie Scenario

BEN HECHT

(RESEARCH NOTE): Ignatz Philip Semmelweis was born in Budapest on the Danube in July, 1818. He was the fourth son of a grocer. There were eight children in the house. They were noisy and full of song.

(HISTORICAL NOTE): Napoleon was through with pulling Europe through his ego and there was an end to all foolish warring in the world.

(EDUCATIONAL NOTE): Philip Semmelweis was sent to the Pest Academy where he learned Latin, won no prizes and left behind no memories of Minerva passing. It was his father's dream that he should be a lawyer.

In 1837 Philip went to Vienna to obtain his degree as a barrister.

NO CAMERAS YET

Philip, the young law student, has an aversion for the legerdemain of legalistic philosophy. There is in his mind a pre-echo of a line Sandburg will write: "Why does a hearse horse snicker carrying a lawyer's bones?"

No hearse horse will snicker at Philip. He will hear, instead, the guffaw of a lynching mob. He will hear the world shriek with derision as he rides to rest behind the black plumes. But this he does not know. And, with broken heart (to be explained in a moment), and full of the love of humanity, he goes to become a doctor. He attends courses under Skoda, the greatest surgeon in Vienna.

NOTE TO PRODUCER

I would begin the picture with Semmelweis getting married. His

96

bride is shy and pretty. I would show them during the year that follows. They are happy. Philip is full of love and hope because his wife is to present him with a child.

I would show the scene in which Semmelweis waits for his first-born. He is a poor law student and his wife has gone for delivery to the big hospital in Vienna.

He waits at the end of a dark corridor. He hears a bell tolling. Two figures appear—a priest in vestments and before him an attendant tolling a little bell. They are going with the viaticum to the bedside of a dying woman. This is prescribed by the rules of the hospital.

Semmelweis sees the little procession stop at the door behind which his wife lies.

A doctor emerges and tells young Philip that nothing can be done. His wife? Dying. The child? Dead. The bell tolls.

Semmelweis looks wildly around. Two, five, nine, fifteen priests move down the corridors. Each has an attendant in front of him who rings the soft bell. Each procession moves toward the bed of a woman dying in childbirth.

Semmelweis weeps—and the bell tolling is his heart beating against iron tragedy.

APOLOGY TO CELINE

This is not in your book—the marriage, the tragic death in childbirth. But it is a case history from Hippocrates, medical ancestor of Semmelweis, written down by Hippocrates twenty-three hundred years ago— the case of Philinas, who stood by with the Greek physician and watched helplessly the dying of his beautiful wife, Thasus, in childbirth. She died of childbed fever. I add it to your book because it fits. Trust me.

OPENING SEQUENCES

Philip enrolls in the medical school under the great Skoda. He is moody, haunted by the shy face of his bride, by the tolling of the little bell in the corridor.

He has come to a school where the professors will teach him the answers to death, rather than legal answers to greed and vengeance.

Skoda is a renowned man. He is strong, audacious, experimental. He laughs at controversy—and medicine is a controversy almost as vicious as politics. A corpse runs for election, and always wins. The doctors conduct the campaign.

Philip venerates Skoda. He will learn everything from him but his laughter.

Our Philip works like a steam engine. It is not grief that makes him work. It is the avidity that is always the first disordered sign of genius. He pries everywhere. He travels through miles of viscera. And a bell is always tolling faintly over his books and his cadavers.

A new character appears—Professor Rokitansky. He occupies the first chair of Pathological Anatomy in the school. He is not as famous as Skoda, but he has a deft hand with the scalpel. He is a beer drinker and a man who roars poetry at the night.

Skoda and Rokitansky are the ordained Godfathers of Semmelweis. Says Celine: "They will follow with anxious eyes the labors and efforts of their unforgettable disciple. With anguish they will watch him staggering along the road of his Calvary—and they will be able neither to help nor yet always understand."

CHARACTERIZATION

Philip Semmelweis is not an easy character, even now. There is a hole in his heart. He has looked into a grave and never quite looked out of it. This is the beginning of his new love story—his hunt among the cadavers.

Philip's eyes are not on the world. He is insolent to his superiors. He explodes easily—like all concentrated matter. He is oversensitive to the ancient jokes of medical students. He toils, broods, snarls, and behaves like a man full of slivers. Yet there is only love in his heart.

The trouble with Philip is that he has the genius for smelling out stupidity in others—which is unpardonable in a man who has as yet no other gift to offer to the world. (It will be even more unpardonable when he brings the unwanted gift.)

Harassed by his own nature, by his own ignorance, by the strutting ignorance around him, Philip abandons the clinics and cadavers for happier surroundings. He becomes a beachcomber in the Royal Botanical Gardens. Here he meets Herr Bazatov—a shy man and a great expert on plant life. He talks with Bazatov week after week about the wonders and secrets of blossoms.

Philip is delighted by the flowers. He is never to know any other sweetness for the rest of his life than these garden months. No faces will ever smile on him as do the petunias, the roses, the calla lilies.

It is of flowers he writes (in Latin) when he submits his doctorate thesis to the medical school. Skoda and Rokitansky smile. It is bad Latin and worse botany and has no bearing on the medical arts. But they are in a beer stube. The music is playing. The brew is good. And Semmelweis is a stormy one who touches their hearts. They give their wayward Godson an official diploma. In May, 1844, Semmelweis is pronounced a doctor.

SCENES IN SHADOW FOR THE CAMERA

Philip's personality continues to stand in his way like a hippopotamus. But with the aid of his Godfathers, he manages to vault over it. He becomes an assistant to Rokitansky.

He becomes one of the death dealing surgeons of that era. It is the time before Pasteur and asepsis. Nine major operations out of ten terminate with immediate death, or infection—which is death walking.

Young Semmelweis watches the other death-dealers at work over the tables with their little guillotine knives. They are neither disturbed nor ashamed. They are full of strut and wisdom. Young Semmelweis sees that this is the way of the world—to be smug in error, content with stupidity and hateful of all that challenges it.

He listens to learned discourses in which the death-dealers explain the mystery of the tolling bell. They speak of "thickened pus," of "benign pus" and "laudable pus." Celine calls these phrases "the sonorities of impotence."

Semmelweis has also something to say. Vague words, but not smug ones. Remember that he is a man of his time, that he sits among the satraps of ignorance, that he has not seen tomorrow. Yet he writes (out of tomorrow): "Everything they are doing here seems to me quite futile, deaths follow one another with regularity. They go on operating, however, without seeking to find out why one patient succumbs in exactly the same circumstances in which another survives."

Rokitansky sighs over his beer mug as he reads this heresy. Skoda frowns and is thoughtful. Their godson is a question-asker. Dangerous calling. They have flirted with questions themselves. But they know how to laugh and drink beer.

ENTER, THE VILLAIN

Master Surgeon Philip Semmelweis, with a hundred dead patients already in the bag, moves to a new department. It is new only to his science. His tears were there before. It is the department where women die in childbirth. The professor at its head is the gallant Dr. Klein.

Dr. Klein is now known in medical history as one of its super villains. This is unfair. Medical history, like world history, likes to condemn the great error-makers of the past. This gives the present always the illusion that it has progressed beyond admiring and defending error. Vain boast! With error constantly disproved and exposed, what remains triumphant in the world? Only this—the genius for admiring and defending further error. The trouble lies in our education. It doesn't begin till we are almost ready to die. Except for a few precocious people like Semmelweis.

Dr. Klein was no villain at all, for he was the friend of his time, the associate of current error. This made him an authority. Patients adored him—on the few occasions when they survived his ministrations. The medical press fawned on him. He was not the kind of presumptuous booby who knew more than the Editors. Nobody defends ignorance as savagely as an Editor. His job depends on holding off tomorrow—like the little boy with his finger in the dyke. Editors always stand behind authorities. Authorities are the dykes.

To boot, Professor Klein wore a frock coat and his beard pointed the way to righteousness. He was all-knowing. Nobody could win an argument from him. His was a firm mind. But there was nothing in it. Nothing but yesterday in a coat of armor.

NOTE TO THE CASTING DIRECTOR

To cast this man right in our movie, we must have him played by the most dignified actor in all of Hollywood and the most heroic. Gary Cooper would do if he could sigh like Charles Boyer and beam with indulgent humor like Clark Gable. He must win the hearts of the audience at once. For in our movie, he, and not Semmelweis, is their man. He is the robust, clever, chuckling, fascinating Know-It-All. The fatuous Weisenheimer World masquerading as Hero. He is a man the audience believes automatically—the moment he says anything about Medicine, God, Politics, or the stupidity of all opposition. Just as Semmelweis is a man the audience wants to turn over to the police the moment *he* starts gabbing.

This is the great casting difficulty in our movie—but a most vital issue. Right is not on the side of the audience and the audience is not on the side of right. This oddity must be underscored.

THE BELL GROWS LOUDER

Semmelweis comes to work on his first day as scientist in the Lying-in Pavilion through February snows. There are two separate pavilions in the hospital for lying-in cases. The Second Pavilion is presided over by Dr. Bartsch—a professor who likes his job a little more than anything else. Dr. Klein commands the First Pavilion.

Semmelweis remembers the day he paced the waiting room full of hope and heard the bell tolling. His wife died here and his child. He has come to avenge them.

He sits down at a desk. His duty is to register the admission of pregnant women. They are from the poor districts of Vienna, from the slums, from the cafe street corners. They have no money for private obstetrics.

We see Semmelweis surrounded by women come for delivery. They weep. They cry out as if before a firing squad. It is Tuesday and Bartsch's Pavilion Number 1 is closed. They plead to be entered in Bartsch's. But the Hospital has rules. On alternate days pregnant women seeking free medical service must be entered in Klein's pavilion. This is the Klein day.

Around Semmelweis' feet, the Klein women moan. They tell him there is no hope for them. All who come to have children in the Klein pavilion must die. All Vienna knows this. All the basement and tenement brides and the poor girls of the streets know this.

Semmelweis sends for the records. It is true. The percentage of women dying in childbirth from puerperal fever is three times higher in the Klein pavilion than in the Bartsch pavilion.

What can this mean? Semmelweis frowns at this curious fact. But he can do nothing. Twenty penniless women, wailing their farewells to life, are admitted on this Tuesday into Klein's childbirth inferno. Others scream and run out and refuse to be coaxed back again by the relatives who brought them in. They prefer to give birth in the streets. Their chances of survival are better.

For this group of twenty, the little bell that goes before the priests tolls nineteen times. Semmelweis hears the priests chanting as they walk slowly, and the bell tolling. He knows the hope and love that die at this sound. He sits at his desk and hurls his mind at the dark.

SCENES OF TERROR AND SMUGNESS

Day after day Semmelweis sits at his registrar's desk in the Klein Pavilion—not a doctor, but a Charon embarking terrified women for the shores of death.

Around him are many doctors. They are a little nervous from their toil in the charnel house. But the mighty Klein commands them. There is no nervousness in the face of this hero. It beams. It knows that a best of all possible worlds lies around it. If you are worried, look at Klein—and peace comes back into your heart. Thus do Prime Ministers and Foreign Secretaries and all High Authorities look when the smells of disaster touch their noses. They look proud and All-Knowing, and the world cheers them.

The mortality rate in the Klein Pavilion has risen to 96%. A hundred mothers come in to have babies. Ninety-six go out as corpses. It is a very bad situation.

But Klein has an answer. He points to London, Paris, Berlin, Rome. It is not much better in those great cities. The pregnant women of the poor die off in all the free hospitals of the world. The percentages vary from thirty percent to fifty, to ninety. It is obvious to Professor Klein and to the world that venerates him and all his colleagues in Edinburgh, London, Paris, Rome, and Berlin, that puerperal fever is a curse of nature. It is a sort of pox that belongs among the divine mysteries. God is restive with his sinful children. Did He not once send a flood? Now he sends puerperal fever. Perhaps because it is easier to transport than water.

Nevertheless, there is a scandal in Vienna. The poor have clung only to one basic right—the right of producing more poor. This has been always the single joy that no monarchs or taxes or hellish laws could rob them of. And this right is now in jeopardy.

Investigations are started. The professors meet, listen to each other speak (using many Latin phrases), and finally figure out the professorial cure for puerperal fever. Close all the lying-in hospitals. Then there will be no hospital statistics to frighten and depress anybody.

Semmelweis does not attend these learned conferences. He sits in the gloomy reception room. His heart is burdened and he hurls his mind into the darkness.

A RAY OF LIGHT

A student stops to talk to the brooding, snarling Charon at his desk. The student says humorously, "I bet you the reason there are fewer deaths in Bartsch's pavilion than in Klein's is because the work over there is done by midwives—and not by doctors."

The student has a hangover and a grudge. He walks on chuckling at his mot.

But Semmelweis is on his feet, staring at something he cannot see. But it is there. And it is not a joke. It is a Fact, a ray of light from God, or from His only child—Genius.

Semmelweis rushes to Pavilion No. 2. He drags out all the record books. It is true. It has been true for fifty years. Always a half, a third as many dead mothers at Bartsch's as at Klein's.

Semmelweis makes his first move. It is more the move of a checker player than a scientist. Skoda and Rokitansky support him. He moves all the midwives from Bartsch's to Klein's. He moves all the doctors from Klein's to Bartsch's. Bartsch and Klein are amused at this childish game.

The move is an overwhelming success. Semmelweis has moved Death from one space to another. The doctors are Death. Two weeks after the doctors have taken over Bartsch's Pavilion, its mortality rate has doubled. The mortality rate in the Klein Pavilion, where the midwives now deliver babies, has been cut in half.

LIGHT BEATS ON DISASTER

Why do doctors carry death—and not midwives? Why are men, nobly trained in medicine and surgery, villains of the darkest hue—and ignorant midwives medical heroines?

Semmelweis puts these questions to Klein. The Professor with the beard is outraged. Says Klein, these are not questions. They are insults. They impugn. They defy authority.

Semmelweis, Master Surgeon and question-asker, is fired.

LIGHT DIMS AND THE WORLD TRIUMPHS

Semmelweis has lost his badge. He is no longer the official Charon. He has no other standing in the Klein Pavilion now but busybody.

And he is a daily busybody at the Pavilion of the 96%. He sits at the bedsides of the dying women. This is now his love affair. He loves these agonized ones who try to bring life into the world—and die trying. His heart bursts with a hope for them. He would take their fever away. He would open their eyes and let them see the new face of a child of which they had been dreaming so long. He would place life at their breasts to feed.

Such is his desire. Not his own dead but all the dead torment him. Not his own lost hope, but all lost hope aches in his heart.

All day the priests in their vestments march with the viaticum. The attendant in front of them tolls his bell. Semmelweis, lover of life, hears only the tongue of death. He sits and weeps beside the dying ones, snarls over them when they are dead, not at them, but at Death. He is the poet who has found a Cross from which to look on the world. It is not yet a big Cross, but it will enlarge.

THE CROSS GROWS BIGGER

How does it happen that Semmelweis suddenly looks into tomorrow, suddenly looks on the truth—a flash, a tittle, a finger of it? The Camera will have to explain this. The Camera will come close to his face as he sits at a bedside and holds the hand of a dying mother. It will see his eyes widen, see a stare come into them and register a grimace as of terror that fills his face.

Sitting at the bedside of the poor dead one, Semmelweis knows suddenly why women die of puerperal fever. Women in Rome, London, Berlin, Paris, Edinburgh, Boston, New York. With what he knows in this moment of light, Semmelweis can save a million lives a year in Europe alone.

Skoda and Rokitansky hear the news. It is so simple and Semmelweis speaks so violently that the thing is hard to understand. But they manage to figure out what he is saying. He wants wash bowls placed beside all the lying-in beds. He wants all the doctors to wash their hands— before delivering babies. This is the great Semmelweis discovery—that there is dirt on the hands of authority that needs washing off.

Skoda and Rokitansky abet this mad plot. The washstands are installed, the orders given to the doctors. The results are astonishing. In one week the Klein mortality rate drops to 70%—a twenty per cent fall.

But Professor Klein is outraged once more. The Devil is loose again.

He summons this laundryman of a scientist, this washerwoman savant Semmelweis, into his office. He demands to know—why does he want doctors to wash their hands? What in God's name does Semmelweis think is on their hands? Are doctors evil people? Does he think scientists are witches?

Semmelweis replies a little wildly. He has not the facts of tomorrow's Pasteur. He cannot name the thing. But it is there—on the hands of doctors. He has seen it kill.

"Why do you want theories now?" he cries at Klein. "Look at the facts. Facts are enough for the time being. Fewer women are being killed by doctors with washed hands."

The thing drives Professor Klein out of his head. How does a priest feel if he hears God called dirty? How does a patriot feel if he hears his land slandered? How does a citizen feel if he listens to criticism of his reason? Klein is all these things. He rises up like a trinity. No priest, no patriot, no citizen was ever more righteous. He calls for the dismissal of Semmelweis from the hospital.

Hospital directors, physicians, surgeons, journalists and believers in authority, make an army around Professor Klein. They sustain him. They chant his praises. He is defending his Time. He is saving authority from an enemy.

Semmelweis, who had almost saved a million women a year, is thrown out of the hospital. His Godfathers Skoda and Rokitansky can do nothing. Scandal shakes the pillars of medicine. Not the scandal of a numbskull slayer of poor women, named Professor Klein—and named all the obstetricians of Europe and America, great and small. But the scandal of a man who dares question Professor Klein, dares challenge today—who dares ask a few men to wash their hands and save a million lives.

HIDEAWAY IN LAUGHTER

Disgraced, derided, Semmelweis leaves medicine, leaves Vienna—city of science. He is a little mad. The worried Godfathers send a friend to look after him.

Semmelweis goes gasping to Venice. Here he drinks, paddles around in gondolas, laughs in bagnios and sings at the top of his voice. He plays pagan in Venice. He is never still, rarely sober. He falls in love with Art. Art is noble and serene and has triumphed over the Kleins. He rhapsodizes over paintings and sunsets, over women and barcarolles.

He is trying to put out of his mind the memory of a light that was in it, and out of his ears the tolling of a bell. But this bell rings through all his revelries. It wakens him in the bagnios. Drunk, he hears it. It comes through kisses and sounds out of emptied wine bottles. And it pulls him back to Vienna—and the death beds.

MELODRAMA OF A FACT

Semmelweis arrives in Vienna to find that his best friend, Dr. Kolletschka, is dead. Kolletschka was Professor of Anatomy and dear to him. He had died in the night as a result of infection through a finger wound. He had been dissecting a corpse.

Semmelweis weeps. He weeps—but he investigates. No one else is investigating the death of the estimable Kolletschka. But Semmelweis has genius. Genius is a quality that knows nothing but works as if it knows. This is the way answers are found—by not knowing them. And Semmelweis finds an answer. He investigates not Kolletschka, but the cadaver on which he operated. He finds the same death in the cadaver as in his friend. He finds that pericarditis, peritonitis, and meningitis can come from the exudations of a corpse. It is all theory, for he has no microscope to identify the villains. Nor has he enough chemical learning to make a scientific case of it. But he has light without words, logic and the gift for truth. And he proclaims his discovery.

Up to the moment of Semmelweis' proclamation, corpses were considered to be objects thoroughly done with living. Semmelweis proclaims that corpses are alive—with death.

Thus the plot is solved—for Semmelweis. He has an answer now for the mighty Klein. He gives the answer.

"The fingers of the medical students soiled by recent dissections carry death dealing cadaveric particles into the genital organs of women in childbirth—and cause their deaths."

He speaks again.

"Disinfect the hands of the students. Every mother will then be saved."

The great Professor Klein is outraged for a third time. In fact, he is more outraged this time than ever. He summons his cohorts about him. They are also outraged. Why? A man has not only questioned authority but answered it. Toppled it. Outwitted it. Disproved it. Made it suddenly seem little as a match flicker in an abyss. There are thus two lines of action. Either Authority capitulates. Or it gets rid of this man.

It gets rid of the man. Semmelweis is ordered out of Pavilion Number 1. There is no room for a busybody charlatan in the sacred death chambers of science.

Skoda and the beer drinker, Rokitansky, intercede. They have enough power to effect compromises. Through their efforts Semmelweis is permitted to experiment in Bartsch's Pavilion Number 2.

The "charlatan" orders the doctors brought again from Klein's to Bartsch's. The midwives are moved once more from Bartsch's to Klein's. But Semmelweis is doing something more than playing checkers this time. He is taking his place now beside Pasteur, Lister, Koch, Banning, Ehrlich, and all the great of medical history.

Naturally nobody is aware of this. The little world of Authority around Semmelweis scowls as he toils—and busies itself organizing a lynching mob.

In two weeks, with doctors delivering the babies, the death rate doubles in Bartsch's. Semmelweis bides his time. Up goes the death rate—thirty per cent, fifty per cent, seventy-five per cent. Now is the moment for Truth. Semmelweis gives his epic order. "Every medical student who has touched a corpse must wash his hands thoroughly in an antiseptic chlorine solution before undertaking the examination of obstetrical cases."

Such is the order. It is put into operation. And Semmelweis watches—and gloats. The tolling of the bell subsides. In a month of handwashing in chlorine water, the mortality rate falls from 70% to 12%.

But Semmelweis is not content. The bell must stop—forever. He insists on more thorough and longer washings. And the bell stops! For the first time in history the mortality figures in Semmelweis' wards are lowered to those of the best maternity wards of modern science—two-tenths of one per cent!

VICTORY!

And does the world rejoice? Does medicine raise its head proudly to the light? Do the Professors of Europe and America join hands in hosannahs?

No. Here, where our movie should end, it begins. Here where truth smacks the world, error alone triumphs.

Semmelweis has completed his love affair. He has brought hope and life to the bedsides of birth. Nobody rejoices. Nobody sings. Instead, a roar of laughter rises from all the professors in Berlin, Paris, Rome, Boston, Edinburgh, and New York who hear of the goings-on of this charlatan.

How can they laugh? How can these pontifical fools pontificate? Are there not facts? Is not truth evidence?

But what are facts and truth to the unyielding and ferocious stupidity of the world? Science in all its centers asserts itself as wiser than Semmelweis, more All-Knowing. It kills off one million, five, ten million mothers in order to make its statement of contempt for Semmelweis. But what are ten million mothers beside the triumph of Authority? A hill of beans.

Everybody is for the magnificent Professor Klein. This is no mystery and no Devil's work. The world is Klein—yesterday, today, and tomorrow. The world is never Semmelweis. It will stumble forward, our world, out of exhaustion, out of the proddings of disaster. It will never move forward honorably or gracefully.

Supported by communications from great men all over the world, Professor Klein storms into Board of Directors meetings. Skoda, Rokitansky and a few others oppose the righteous beard and the thundering communications. But they are the immemorial disciples. They have power only to beat their bosoms—and turn their heads from the crucifixion.

Science from all over the world stands firmly behind Professor Klein. Blaming doctors for infection is like blaming politicians for economic distress or blaming rich people for the woes of poverty. It is not to be contemplated. The medical students stand firmly behind Professor Klein. They cry they are bored with those "filthy washings."

And imagine who else stands behind Professor Klein? The Press, of course, but who else? The government, naturally, but who else? The mothers. The howling, frightened pregnant ones. The poor sufferers whom Semmelweis loved, for whom he toiled, snarled, wept and won. His loved ones—the people. His dream girl—humanity. These join Professor Klein in the denunciation of Semmelweis. They call him a fool, a busybody, a crazy man. They defend the doctors with beards. Doctors are clean people. How can anyone dare fly in the face of enlightened Authority like that Semmelweis! Semmelweis, if the truth were only known, is the only dirty one!

Thus the common people—the Audience. The pack at the heels of Authority. The black hearts who go to the movies to hear how white they are. The fierce echo that echoes only ignorance, that repeats like a parrot the screeches of Authority. That dies rather than surrender its hatred of poets, Christs and Semmelweises.

TWO CAMERAS FOR THIS SCENE

There is a meeting of the Academy of Sciences in Vienna, foremost city of medical learning. All the Big Wigs assemble. Skoda, valiant but no longer laughing, reports to the meeting the absolutely conclusive results supporting the theory of Semmelweis. He has verified the theory by the "experimental infection from the exudations of corpses of a certain number of animals." The animals infected died—like Dr. Kolletschka. What does this prove? It proves that Skoda is a fool and had better watch his step.

Another Semmelweis friend, Dr. Hebra, speaks to the august Society.

"Semmelweis' discovery presents so great an interest for the future of Surgery and Obstetrics that I ask for the immediate naming of a Commission to examine with complete impartiality the results he has obtained."

This is an excellent movie scene. It is full of action. The scientists scream. Five Big Wigs knock Skoda to the floor. Eight more of them beat up Dr. Hebra with their fists.

The government is shocked. Vienna has been disgraced—by Semmelweis. It forbids the appointment of any such Commission. It orders Semmelweis—the alien—to quit Vienna.

The Press exults. The Professors breathe with relief. The women return to Klein's Pavilion Number 1 to die. Nobody minds this. Authority has been vindicated. Semmelweis, the charlatan, the anarch, the undesirable question-asker, is back in Budapest, where he came from. He lies weeping in bed, beating the walls with his fists. He has seen God—and is paying for the privilege.

THE FIDDLES TUNE UP

Now our movie must move faster. Its points are in the bag. What we do now is sock away at a finale. And what a finale! You can take any finish you want—even Calvary. I take Semmelweis in Budapest.

Outside his window he hears music and shouting. Hungary has troubles. It is demanding freedom from the Austrian tyrant. Semmelweis gets up. He joins the mobs screaming, "Down with the Austrians." He knows an Austrian named Klein.

The screaming revives him. War comes. Men fight for freedom. They fight against Croats, against Russians and against Austrians. Semmelweis goes almost mad laughing at this. Can Freedom be fought for? And when Freedom is won—what is free? Does the little bell of human wickedness stop tolling?

Hungary fights and loses and Semmelweis falls down a flight of stairs and breaks an arm and a leg. He is laid up in splints. He becomes silent. He speaks to no one. He lies staring at a wall.

Skoda sends the friend who went with Semmelweis to Venice. They speak of Venice. No word of the 96 per cent or of the chlorine water. Or of the two tenths of one per cent. No whisper of the truth that lies like an oak tree seed in Semmelweis' brain.

Skoda gets him a job under famous Professor Birly, head of St. Rochus Hospital in Budapest. Birly loves beer, pastry, and sensible attitudes. He soothes Semmelweis. What does it all matter—life, death, wars for freedom, puerperal fevers, genius, stupidity? It is all alike. Eat, work, amuse yourself—and be a human being. That is the best.

And Semmelweis agrees. He learns to dance like a faun. He is at all the Balls. At thirty he learns to ride a horse like a master. He rides in all the parks. Society people meet and adore him. This dancing, riding, bubbling, handsome young man! What a fellow to have around to make the day cheerful! What jokes, what cynicism, what wit! "Come and meet Dr. Semmelweis tonight at our party. You'll adore him."

But the dancing and adorable Semmelweis, the gay blade doctor, is only playing a joke. He is quite mad but nobody smells this out, not even Professor Birly. For at night he hides in his room, like a criminal engaged on a crime, and he writes his book, "Etiology of Puerperal Fever." It is all going into a book—the oak seed burgeoning in his head. They may deride and hate a man—Semmelweis looks furtively out of his window. But a book can outlive even Professor Klein—and Authority.

While composing he writes also letters to the Medical Academies of the world. He submits his findings and posts the letters secretly at night. No letters come back from the world. The Medical Academies have no time for cranks.

DANSE MACABRE

Birly dies. Semmelweis, the gay horseback rider, is made head of St. Rochus Hospital.

He arrives, bows, is installed. Authority shakes him by the hand. Presto! Semmelweis is Klein. Students salute him. He has only to grow a pointed beard and chuckle All-Knowingly.

And at this very moment Semmelweis explodes. The oak seed is thriving in his head.

He issues on Open Letter to All Professors of Obstetrics. It begins,

"Assassins! So I call all those who have defied the rules prescribed to combat puerperal fever. Against those I stand as one should stand against a band of criminals!"

Now Budapest is shocked, the same as was Vienna. Good God, that old nonsense again—about saving a million mothers! And Semmelweis seemed so sane, so gay and witty. What a sad thing! The society folk, the counts and barons and fine ladies are sincerely hurt.

In Paris at a conclave of the world's greatest scientists in July 1858, held at the Academy of Medicine, the most celebrated obstetrician of his time—the great Professor Dubois—rises and proclaims. Semmelweis is an ass. His theories are nonsense. They have been proved worthless. Some minor statistics juggled by a charlatan. Vienna, itself, has abandoned him and cast him out. Let us be sensible men and ignore Semmelweis and his vaporings and get down to business.

And what is the business of this conclave of the world's greatest scientists? The business is to study the menace of puerperal fever—to find out how God can be induced to withdraw it from the better hospitals.

In the streets of Budapest you can now see Semmelweis. He is putting up posters on the walls. "Fathers, the doctors are killing your wives when they go to the hospitals to have children. Don't let them. Demand that the doctors wash their hands."

The head of a hospital cannot go around pasting up stickers on a wall like a small boy on Hallowe'en. The doctors shake their heads sadly at poor Semmy's monomania. And he is removed.

People step aside as Semmelweis passes in the street. His head is big with an oak seed growing. This makes it difficult for him to walk. He takes to tottering, to standing still, to screaming at the sky. And to laughing suddenly when people look at him. He is a spectacle for Budapest.

Screams come from his room. The authorities call and discover nobody is bothering Semmelweis. He is alone. He is howling at phantoms.

Do you remember Cyrano under the oak tree in the convent garden, mortally wounded and drawing his sword for the last time—to fight the shadows around him?

Here is another Cyrano. He fights Klein and a hundred great men. He fights a hundred thousand. He fights a whole world that has trampled truth. He charges down the stairs of his rooming house, haggard and pursuing phantoms.

The good people of Budapest stare at a madman howling.

History looks back and smiles tenderly at a man of wisdom pleading.

CROWN OF BACTERIA

It is a spring afternoon in Budapest, 1856. A man is running through the street. That crazy Semmelweis again!

He runs to a building, runs inside, runs into a room full of doctors. It is the anatomical amphitheater of the Medical Faculty.

A cadaver ready for demonstration lies on the marble slab under a bright light. Semmelweis knocks over doctors and runs to it. He seizes a scalpel from a student. He cuts his own finger with it. Then he plunges his bleeding finger and the scalpel into the liquescent and oozing interior of a dead man.

This is what Kolletschka did and died—proving that there was death in corpses. Semmelweis wants to prove it all over again—the theory of the cadaveric particles.

He holds up his bescummed and bleeding hand. His head is too mad with truth to talk. But his hand will speak for him. His hand will rot. His body will rot. His eyes will go blind. The world can then look on a great tube of pus called Semmelweis and know the truth.

Skoda comes to Budapest. He takes Semmelweis from his bed, full of fever already, full of pus. He rides the case of lymphangitis and peritonitis back to Vienna. Semmelweis waves his putrescence in the air. He cries only the word, "Look! look!"

He is put in an insane asylum in Vienna. Here he demonstrates the truth for three weeks with his dying.

But the world looks on Semmelweis dying and sees no truth. It is conscious only of a horrid smell.

Semmelweis dies—and they open the windows.

They said—even his friends—that Semmelweis died a madman. He screamed with pain and something worse. Nobody could understand him. Therefore, he was mad. They did not see that the last action of Semmelweis was full of courage and clarity. They did not see that his desperation was a cry of love, that his pain, his reek and his death were a plea for truth. There is sometimes nothing else one can do for the truth—but die for it.

They did not see that the only madness involved was the madness of the world that buried Ignatz Philip Semmelweis, and millions of helpless women—rather than pause to wash its hands.

She Walks in Beauty

MARTHA FOLEY

Emily had the mumps. She had discovered funny lumps in her throat and made the mistake of showing them to her father. He immediately said 'mumps' and sent her to bed. That was the worst of having a doctor for a father. Or should it be a father for a doctor? They made you sick whether you wanted to be or not. Sometimes it was nice. She would never have got these lovely shiny spectacles to wear if her father weren't Dr. Graham. She told him one day about her lesson in school. You know Miss Lunt says you can't see the air and the books say you can't but I can see the air. Well, well. That's a lot for a little girl to see. I've never seen the air. What does it look like? A lot of little black specks going round and round. Do you see the air all the time? All the time, except when I am asleep. Hm-m-m, we shall have to look into this. The next day Emily was taken to Dr. Prentiss whose sign said OCULIST and he tried all kinds of spectacles on her nose while he made her read something she couldn't read and the day after she was given a pair all for herself. Some of the children called her Four-Eyes but that was really because they were jealous and wanted to have glasses, too. Oh, Emily, let me wear them! Let me wear them, they all said the first day she went to school with the glasses. Emily had picked out her best friends. I'll let Ruth wear them until recess, and after recess Alice can wear them. But don't forget to give them back to me at noon, Alice. The last time I lent you my locket you went home with it and the family wouldn't believe I hadn't lost my very best locket which belonged to my grandmother and has the turquoises in it. This afternoon I'll let Helen take my eyeglasses until

116

recess and then Mary can have them until school is over. Tomorrow! Tomorrow! I want them tomorrow! But Emily had decided it would mix her up too much to promise them for the next day so she had said, we'll wait until tomorrow and those girls who are the very nicest to me today can have my eyeglasses tomorrow. She would have lent them to Joan and Hazel and Violet and Dorothy too if Miss Crowell hadn't come into her classroom and said to Miss Lunt have you a little girl here who wears glasses and Miss Lunt said no. But Emily raised her hand and said I do. Miss Lunt had looked surprised and said but are you sure Emily? I've never seen you wearing glasses. Oh, yes, Miss Lunt. Don't you remember I was excused from school last week so I could have my eyes examined? But you've never worn any glasses. That's because I've lent them. Emily! Don't you know you can't lend eyeglasses? That only the person they are made for can wear them? Besides if you're supposed to wear glasses they're not doing you any good on some other little girl's nose. Miss Crowell hadn't been so strict. She had smiled and said I guess Emily was trying to be generous. I have brought her glasses back for her. She took her hand from behind her back and there were the eyeglasses. Emily took them and while the whole class watched Emily wiped each glass carefully with a little pink cloth out of her eyeglass case and then she put the glasses on her nose and looked at Miss Lunt out of them. Miss Lunt smiled and Miss Crowell laughed. Emily was afraid at first she might have been kept after school, Miss Lunt had been so severe, but when she saw her smile she knew it was all right.

And now just when everybody in the school had got used to Emily's glasses and she couldn't be proud of them any more she had got the mumps. All the girls at recess had felt her neck and Emily had kept going up to the school window where it was dark like a mirror to see how much bigger her neck was getting all the time. Her throat hadn't been sore at all at first. Just bigger and bigger. It was funny trying to turn her neck like this and like that. One minute it would turn so far and the next it wouldn't turn nearly so far. She must be getting a fat neck like Mrs. Pierce. Probably that was where women first began putting on weight. She had kept her neck quiet in school so Miss Lunt wouldn't notice and then she had made the mistake of telling her father when she got home.

She was to stay out of school three weeks. The first ten days she was to stay in bed. After that she could sit up and then a few days later she could go out. That is she could go out if she promised not to go near her brothers or any other children. But what was the fun of having the mumps if you couldn't tell people you had them while you were having them? After the mumps were all over nobody would get excited about them. Then there was nasty little Josephine Parkerson. She was bound to say I don't believe you ever had the mumps. You're just making believe again. Of course Emily did make believe a lot but it was interesting and a lot of girls liked to have her make believe. Oh, Emily, let's make believe something! They would all sit down together while Emily made believe they were little girls a giant with big eyes and hairy arms and hands had captured and he was about to eat them all up and then she would jump up and say oh here! he's coming, run! run! And they would all run screaming. She couldn't make believe the giant eating little girls any more though because Ruth's mother had been scared when she heard them all running screaming from the giant. So Emily had to play more quiet make-believe like Queen Titania's court when she sat on a throne and the other little girls all sat around with their hair unbraided and made believe they were good fairies who could do all kinds of things with a touch of the long wands they carried which were sticks from bushes with just a little tuft of leaves left on the ends. They pretended they were turning everything they touched to candy until one of them accidentally touched Dorothy's baby brother. And Dorothy who really was too little to be playing make-believe anyway had cried and cried and said she didn't want her baby brother to be eaten up for candy and everybody had got terribly excited and tried to make Dorothy stop crying and told her not to be such a baby that it was all only make-believe and that nobody was going to eat her brother. Then Emily had remembered something about a man-witch named Merlin and she said, Wait! Wait! We'll get Merlin! Everybody asked who Merlin was and she told them and Dorothy stopped crying about her brother being candy. Emily went away and in a little time she came back and she was wearing a long black cloth over her head so you could hardly see her face and in a low deep voice she said I am Merlin who wants me here and Dorothy started to cry again so Emily said as quickly as she could this baby won't be candy any more I'll make him a real baby again and she said Hoochy-Poochy pronto changeo! He was still asleep so to prove he was changed she pinched him and he cried and the baby was real again. And Dorothy instead of saying thank you had got mad and wheeled her brother off in his baby carriage and said I'm never going to bring my brother here again to be made into candy and get pinched so he cries! Something like that was always happening when Emily played make-believe and she couldn't make the other children understand how something you made believe was so really wasn't so. Anyhow she was getting to be eleven years old and that was pretty big for make-believe except to one's self. In fact making believe to one's self was much more fun. It was like having a secret.

She could do a lot of make-believing while she was staying in bed for ten days having the mumps. Sometimes she would pretend the bed was a boat. It was out in the middle of the ocean and she was floating along in it. She would pass beautiful islands with palm trees and birds in them singing. There would be caves on the islands and beautiful women with long golden hair singing in the cave openings. She would float and float and that was a good make-believe for going to sleep. Then she would make believe that her bed was in a hospital and that she had been a soldier wounded doing his duty on the battlefront. Nurses were hovering around her and people were telling her how brave she was. She could hear cannons bombarding in the distance and the enemy shouting. People would run in and out of the hospital room saying, Oh, what a brave man you are! You have saved your country! Hear the enemy shouting. You fought so bravely you made them run. They don't like it. Hear the way they are shouting. The cannon would roar and the enemy shout. A band leading her conquering army to victory would be playing Hail Columbia the Gem of the Ocean. She sat up in bed and said I have given all for my country. And fell back dead.

Let's see, what else could she be? She could hitch the spread up to the top of the bed and pretend she was in a tent. That she was a pioneer camping out on the cold, cold ground. Listen to the winds howl! And the snow was coming down fast, covering up the earth and the bushes and the trees and the tent. It was a terrible blizzard, the worst in many years. Oh, it was good to lie here in bed—in the tent snug and warm.

Emily put the sheet back. She could also, by holding the sides of the spread tight under her arms, pretend she was a prisoner of the Indians lying on the ground. But she was tired of making believe. And she had read all the big green Dickens volumes lying on the chair beside her bed. The Uncommercial Traveler and Bleak House and even The Mystery of Edwin Drood. She felt a little cross about Edwin Drood. After all Dickens had no right to begin a novel and then leave it right in midair even if it wasn't his fault that he did die. But somehow those tall thin volumes that always seemed so reliable to her had failed her. She would never be able to look into them again sure they would satisfy her interest. Edwin Drood bothered her. She tried to figure it out but none of her endings for the book, Drood murdered, Drood posing as the other man, Drood back from the colonies with lots of money, seemed to be right. So she gave it up and went back to The Uncommercial Traveler, the least liked of the Dickens stories which she read only after she had read everything else.

She would polish her glasses, Emily decided. She carefully took the little pink cloth the optician had given her out of her black leather case and wiped her glasses. The world always seemed brighter when she put them on.

Her glasses sparkling bright she lay back in bed, facing the window which opened on a neighbor's garden. She looked at the green of a budding tree and other trees beyond.

Suddenly Emily looked up—and she knew what beauty was. It was the corner of the house next door against the sky. The sky was blue. The house corner a simple angle painted yellow. But, oh, it was beautiful! The house corner, the sky. A little yellow and a lot of blue. And it was the first really beautiful thing she had ever seen. Or the first thing she knew for herself was beautiful.

Emily lay back in bed, holding her vision. So that was beauty! What she felt. It was what poets and artists had, it was what people were always talking about when they said the word beautiful and she had thought it was something pretty like her turquoise locket or Alice's long curls. But beauty such as this was different from all the turquoise lockets in the world. This beauty made you tremble and made you happy and sad and excited. Beauty! She had beauty!

All the rest of the time Emily had the mumps she lay quietly in bed. Her books she didn't read except one day to turn over the leaves looking for all references to beauty. She stopped playing the games of make-believe and she paid no attention to the cards and the other games her family gave her. Instead she looked constantly out of the window, not always at the corner of the house next door. She tried again and again to come upon it suddenly as she had that first day when the sight had given her such an unknown feeling. But it never gave her quite the same start although she learned it could act as a rousing thing from which to go on to other loveliness.

Emily would look at the corner of the house and then at the leaves on the tree. She saw for the first time how delicate they were and how lightly the sun glistened on them. She watched first the leaves and then the branches take a pattern on the blue of the sky. She watched the clouds in the sky coming up slowly and whitely. At night she looked at the stars and listened to the stirring of the leaves in the winds of the darkness. Beauty! I have beauty!

Are you sure you are feeling better?' Her family bothered her with questions. Oh, thought Emily, if they would only go away and leave me alone. I want to look at the corner of the house. 'Why don't you play with the nice games we brought you?' Or 'Do you miss all your little playmates? Only a few days, now, dear, and you can get up and go out and play.'

She heard her mother and her aunt discussing her in the next room.

'I'm a little worried about Emily. She lies in bed so quietly and doesn't seem to take an interest in anything any more. Andrew says it's just an ordinary case of mumps such as all children have but it doesn't seem natural for her to be so quiet. She's always been so full of spirits.'

And her aunt's voice. 'Probably the mumps make her feel tired and lethargic. I wouldn't worry about it. And doesn't she look a funny little owl lying there so solemnly with her big spectacles and swollen throat?'

Emily began to hate the thought of getting up until one day it occurred to her that perhaps other things might make her feel beautiful the way the corner of the house did. Perhaps that old bridge over the river where her father liked to walk so often. He always said when she asked him why do you come this way all the time, because it is beautiful along here. She would go and see how beautiful it was as soon as she was well. She wanted to go back into the art museum too and see if the statues and pictures everyone said were so beautiful made her feel the way the corner of the house did. The last time she had been taken to the art museum she tried to stay in the mummy room and when her father took her into the classical statue room she had kept trying to look at the undressed men without having anyone notice what part she was looking at. Funny that men should be made that way, all outside. It ought to seem heavy to them or perhaps it was just the same as having an arm or a leg.

The day she got up for the first time she wanted to run everywhere looking for beauty. She was made to stay in the garden or on the porch lying in the hammock. So all she could do in the way of finding beauty was to study flowers. Nasturtiums and hollyhocks, somehow, never seemed very nice to her anyway. Too ordinary. Yet the corner of that house was ordinary and it made her feel beauty. Emily concentrated on a tall, swaying hollyhock hooked with great pink flowers. No, hollyhocks suggested barnyards where most of them were planted and what could be less beautiful than a barnyard? Now the syringa wasn't so bad. The more you looked the lovelier it became, the flowers were small white stars and to close your eyes and breathe their fragrance was sweet.

For a long time after she got better Emily didn't play much with the other children. Near the school was an office building with wide steps where the girls liked to play jackstones. The steps looked down the street toward the west. One late afternoon Emily sat on the steps watching the sky turn rose. She was thinking how beautiful it was and how much more beautiful it would be if only she could hear music as she watched the coloring sky.

'Oh, come on, Emily, why don't you play? If you're no good at jackstones we can play jump rope but if you don't hold the rope first why we can't play jump rope because that wouldn't be fair.'

'I can't. I'm watching the sunset.'

'What are you doing that for?'

'It's beautiful.'

The other children turned and looked surprised at the sunset.

'It's just the same as it always is.'

'Yes, but it's always beautiful. And a thing of beauty is a joy forever. Didn't you ever read poetry? A thing of beauty . . .'

'Beauty! Oh, you're crazy!'

Ruth turned away and picked up the jump rope.

'She's crazy! Emily's crazy! Emily's crazy!' They skipped in time to the refrain. 'Emily's crazy!'

But Emily sat on the steps, her face held tight in her hands, her eyes behind her glasses fixed on the sky. She had a secret. Beauty was her secret. She would never talk about it to Alice or Ruth again.

A Work of Art

ANTON CHEKHOV

Holding under his arm an object wrapped in a newspaper, Sasha Smirnov, the only son of his mother, walked nervously into the office of Doctor Koshelkov.

"Well, my dear boy," exclaimed the doctor warmly, "how do you feel today? What's the good news?"

Sasha began to blink with his eyes, put his hand over his heart, and stammered nervously:

"My mother sends her regards and begs to thank you. . . . I am my mother's only son, and you have saved my life . . . and we both hardly know how to thank you."

"Come, come, my young friend, let us not speak of it," interrupted the doctor, literally melting with pleasure. "I have only done what anybody else in my place would have done."

"I am the only son of my mother. . . . We are poor people and consequently we are not in position to pay you for your trouble . . . and it makes it very embarrassing for us, Doctor, although both of us, mother and I, who am the only son of my mother, beg of you to accept from us, a token of our gratitude, this object which . . . is an object of rare worth, a wonderful masterpiece in antique bronze."

The doctor made a grimace.

"Why, my dear friend," he said, "it is entirely unnecessary. I don't need this in the least."

"Oh, no, no," stammered Sasha. "I beg you please accept it!"

He began to unwrap the bundle, continuing his entreaties in the meantime:

124

"If you do not accept this, you will offend both my mother and myself. . . . This is a very rare work of art . . . an antique bronze. It is a relic left by my dead father. We have been prizing it as a very dear remembrance. . . . My father used to buy up bronze antiques, selling them to lovers of old statuary. . . . And now we continue in the same business, my mother and myself."

Sasha undid the package and enthusiastically placed it on the table.

It was a low candelabrum of antique bronze, a work of real art representing a group: On a pedestal stood two figures of women clad in the costume of Mother Eve and in poses that I have neither the audacity nor the temperament to describe. These figures were smiling coquettishly and in general gave one the impression that, were it not for the fact that they were obliged to support the candle-stick, they would lean down from their pedestal and exhibit a performance which . . . my dear reader, I am even ashamed to think of it!

When the doctor espied the present, he slowly scratched his head, cleared his throat and blew his nose.

"Yes, indeed, a very pretty piece of work," he mumbled. . . . "But,— how shall I say it—not quite . . . I mean . . . rather unconventional . . . not a bit literary, is it? . . . You know . . . the devil knows. . . ."

"Why?"

"Beelzebub himself could not have conceived anything more ugly. Should I place such a phantasmagoria upon my table I would pollute my entire home!"

"Why, Doctor, what a strange conception you have of art!" cried Sasha in offended tones. "This is a real masterpiece. Just look at it! Such is its harmonious beauty that just to contemplate it fills the soul with ecstasy and makes the throat choke down a sob! When you see such loveliness you forget all earthly things. . . . Just look at it! What life, what motion, what expression!"

"I quite understand all this, my dear boy," interrupted the doctor. "But I am a married man. Little children run in and out of this room and ladies come here continually."

"Of course," said Sasha, "if you look at it through the eyes of the rabble, you see this noble masterpiece in an entirely different light. But you certainly are above all that, Doctor, and especially when your refusal to accept this gift will deeply offend both my mother and myself, who am the only son of my mother. . . . You have saved my life . . . and in return we give you our dearest possession and . . . my only regret is that we are unable to give you the mate to this candelabrum."

"Thanks, friend, many thanks. . . . Remember me to your mother and . . . But for God's sake! You can see for yourself, can't you? Little children run in and out of this room, and ladies come here continually. . . . However, leave it here! There's no arguing with you."

"Don't say another word!" exclaimed Sasha joyously. "Put the candelabrum right here, next to the vase. By Jove, but it's a pity that I haven't got the mate to give you. But it can't be helped. Well, good-bye, Doctor!"

After the departure of Sasha the doctor looked for a long time at the candelabrum and scratched his head.

"This is beautiful, all right," he thought. "It would be a pity to throw it away. . . . And yet I dare not keep it. . . . Hm! . . . Now who in the world is there to whom I can present or donate it?"

After long deliberation he hit upon a good friend of his, the lawyer Ukhov, to whom he was indebted for legal services.

"Fine!" chuckled the doctor. "Being a close friend of his, I cannot very well offer him money, and so I will give him this piece of indecency instead. . . . And he's just the man for it . . . single, and somewhat of a gay bird, too."

No sooner thought than done. Dressing himself, the doctor took the candelabrum and went to the home of Ukhov.

"Good morning, old chap!" he said. "I have come here to thank you for your trouble. . . . You will not take money, and I will therefore repay you by presenting you with this exquisite masterpiece. . . . Now say for yourself, isn't it a dream?"

As soon as the lawyer caught sight of it he was exhilarated with its beauty.

"What a wonderful work of art!" he laughed uproariously. "Ye gods, what conceptions artists will get in their heads! What alluring charm! Where did you get this little dandy?"

But now his exhilaration had oozed away and he became frightened. Looking stealthily toward the door, he said:

"But, I can't accept it, old chap. You must take it right back."

"Why?" asked the doctor in alarm.

"Because . . . because . . . my mother often visits me, my clients come here . . . and besides, I would be disgraced even in the eyes of my servants."

"Don't say another word!" cried the doctor gesticulating wildly. "You simply have got to accept it! It would be rank ingratitude for you to refuse it! Such a masterpiece! What motion, what expression. . . . You will greatly offend me if you don't take it!"

"If only this were daubed over or covered with fig leaves. . . ."

But the doctor refused to listen to him. Gesticulating even more wildly, he ran out of Ukhov's house in the thought that he was rid of the present.

When the doctor was gone the lawyer carefully examined the candelabrum, and then, just as the doctor had done, he began to wonder what in the world he could do with it.

"A very beautiful object," he thought. "It is a pity to throw it away, and yet it is disgraceful to keep it. I had best present it to someone . . . I've got it! . . . This very evening I'm going to give it to the comedian Shoshkin. The rascal loves such things, and besides, this is his benefit night. . . ."

No sooner thought than done. That afternoon the well-packed candelabrum was brought to the comedian Shoshkin.

That whole evening the dressing-room of the comedian Shoshkin was besieged by men who hastened to inspect the present. And during all the time the room re-echoed with hilarious laughter which most closely resembled the neighing of horses.

If any of the actresses approached the door and said, "May I enter?" the hoarse voice of Shoshkin was immediately heard to reply:

"Oh, no, no, my darling, you mustn't. I am not dressed!"

After the performance the comedian shrugged his shoulders, gesticulated with his hands and said:

"Now what in the world am I to do with this? I live in a private apartment! I am often visited by actresses! And this isn't a photograph that one could conceal in a drawer!"

"Why don't you sell it?" suggested the wig maker. "There is a certain old woman who buys up antique bronzes.... Her name is Smirnova.... You had better take a run over there; they'll show you the place all right, everybody knows her...."

The comedian followed his advice....

Two days later Koshelkov, his head supported on his hand, was sitting in his office concocting pills. Suddenly the door was opened and into the office rushed Sasha. He was smiling radiantly and his breast heaved with joy.... In his hands he held something wrapped in a newspaper.

"Doctor!" he cried breathlessly. "Imagine my joy! As luck would have it, I've just succeeded in getting the mate to your candelabrum! Mother is so happy! I am the only son of my mother.... You have saved my life."

And Sasha, quivering with thankfulness and rapture, placed a candelabrum before the doctor. The latter opened his mouth as if to say something, but uttered not a word.... His power of speech was gone....

Who Lived and Died Believing

NANCY HALE

IT WAS a strange, hot summer. The days throbbed and the nights were
exhausted and melancholy. In August the temperature rose over ninety
and hung there; the heat shimmered over the buildings and the streets
of the town. Every afternoon at two Elizabeth Percy came down the
steps of the house that was made into apartments for nurses. She walked
along the burning pavements, around the corner, past the newsstand
where the magazines hung fluttering on lines of wire, to Massey's Drug-
store.

Her hair was very dark and as smooth as dark brown satin; it was
combed back from her calm forehead and fell curving under at the back
behind her ears. She wore plain uniforms with small round collars close
about her neck, and she was all white and fresh and slender and strong.

From the heat outside she would walk into the dim coolness of the
drugstore that smelled of soda and candy. There was a faint sweat upon
the marble of the soda fountain; Mr. Massey and the other clerks stood
about in their light tan linen coats, and they smiled at her without speaking. Dave was behind the prescription counter wrapping up a small
package; first the white paper and then slowly the thin bright red string.
He lifted his head as she walked down the center of the store to where
the tables were, and his eyes met Elizabeth's. She sat down at the small
black table and one of the boys from the fountain came and took her
order of Coca-Cola. Several electric fans whirred remotely, high on the
ceiling. The door opened again at the front, and three internes from the
hospital came in. They leaned together on the marble counter in their

129

whites. Their faces were young and pale with heat.

Dave came around the corner of the counter, and sat down beside Elizabeth. Mr. Massey walked slowly up toward the front of the store; he smiled absently at them; he always smiled at them as they sat together between two and three.

They never talked much. Elizabeth sucked the drink slowly through a straw, and lifted the glass and let bits of crushed ice drop into her mouth; they melted on her tongue. She loved to look at Dave. He was very thin and tall and he had straight yellow hair that fell forward in a lock on his forehead. His eyes were restless. He would glance at her suddenly and smile.

"How you doing over there?"

"She's just the same."

"Long case."

"Unh-hunh. Going to be longer."

"Tough you have to nurse one of those cases. Beckwith have any idea how long it'll be?"

One afternoon Elizabeth said, "Grainger told me yesterday he said he was going to use shock. Maybe."

"Insulin?"

"No, I don't think so."

Dave raised his eyebrows and shook his head. The damp yellow lock trembled against his forehead. He had finished the second year of medical school and was working at Massey's during the summer months.

"Oh-oh. That won't be so good."

"Grainger'll have it, in the mornings."

"No, no fun," he said.

"I'm so sorry for Mrs. Myles."

Dave shrugged his shoulders.

"Don't get tough," she said. "You're not a doctor yet. Beckwith's sorry for her, too. It's not the usual thing. She's gone through plenty."

"Sure," he said.

"Oh, real doctors have pity, you know; it's just you little boys."

She smiled at him, and he smiled back after a minute. He looked restless and impatient. He reached one hand under the table and put it on her knee, and looked into her long, calm, dark blue eyes.

"Meet you at eleven?" he said. Elizabeth nodded. He took his hand away.

"She wants to see you again."

"Oh, God."

"It doesn't hurt you any. Just go up there to her room for a minute and say good night. She gets so much out of it."

He gave a sort of groan, and shifted in his chair.

"She's got those damned eyes. I don't *mean* anything, I don't like her looking like that."

"It's just because we're going together," Elizabeth said. "It's the only thing outside herself, you see, like the only thing that's outside and ahead, and she likes to think about our going together."

"Oh, God."

"She asks me about you every day. Lots of times. I don't know whether she forgets she's asked before or whether . . . Come on, do it again once. It doesn't hurt you."

"All right. All right. Eleven."

"Eleven."

She got up and walked to the counter and laid the check down with a nickel. She went out into the heat, crossed the street, and walked up the wide steps of the hospital entrance.

In Copperthwaite Two the corridor was dim and hot. Elizabeth stopped at the desk and turned over the leaves of the order book. Doctor Beckwith had ordered the shock treatment for the morning; no breakfast. Elizabeth drew in her breath. Miss Grainger came out of the door of 53 and down the hall, without her cap.

"Hi," Elizabeth said.

"Hi."

"See you've got it ordered for tomorrow."

"Yeah, man."

"Does she know about it?"

"I'm not sure. He came up and went over her this morning, heart and all, before we went out. Told her, but not exactly; said they were going to give her a treatment and there'd be acute physical discomfort. I love Doctor Beckwith. Discomfort. I don't look forward to it, I tell you. Seems like there's some things you don't get used to, and I don't like shock."

"What have you all done?"

"About the same. Walked. This walking miles in this weather does me in. I'm going home and go to sleep."

Elizabeth flipped back the pages of the order book.

"What is this stuff, anyhow? We didn't have it, then."

"Oh . . . camphor derivative? . . . something. Reckon I'll know plenty in the morning. How's Dave?"

"Fine," Elizabeth said. They parted and went along the long corridor in opposite directions. Elizabeth pushed open the heavy door of 53.

Mrs. Myles sat beside the open window and in the vicious heat observed passing back and forth outside (along the pavement?) back and forth from hell the doughy and grimacing faces of the damned. And a little part of the rotted grapes that rolled about within her brain watched the faces with an abstracted care; each of the faces was forever familiar, a face seen before (where?), seen before and seen again, and where, where had been the face before? In her brain the fruit gave out a stench that she could taste in her mouth, and with it came the horror; no, no, those faces she had never seen before; it only seemed that she had; and the seeming was wrong and she could not send it away, the seeming stayed, shaking its tattered locks and grinning; yes, these faces had been seen before. The faces passed, and none of them was his. Watch, watch, observe with shrinking but insistent care each hideous face that comes nearer and nearer with death in its eyes and the unbelievable humanity, the bigness, in the coming-nearer mouths, until each face passed and was not his, was never his.

Her heart that was no longer her friend beat frantically one two three four five six seven eight eighty is a normal pulse for a woman seventy for a man but this was—hundred and forty . . . MAD

The heavy-strained tension split with the scream of silk. The door opened and Miss Percy came in. So cool so calm so bright. With calm brow, with dark hair, and eyes like dark blue water. Cool as the little leaves that tremble in the tree. What thou among the leaves hast never known. This she has never known, with her calm eyes. Oh reach to me, thou among the leaves, reach down to me in hell with your cool hands, reach down to me.

She sees it all clean. The same world, clean. It is just me. I must remember that, it is just me; the world is cool and calm and bright. Not this. It is just me. Not mad, he said, just an exaggeration of your understandable state of tension, just an exaggeration of a normal point of view, just an exaggeration but not mad.

"Poor old Mr. Duggan next door's making quite a lot of noise," Miss Percy said, smiling. She stood before the mirror of the yellow-oak bureau and took her cap from the bureau post and pinned it to the back of her dark head. "I hope it doesn't bother you too much. Anyway, we'll go right out."

"Poor Mr. Duggan," Mrs. Myles said. "Is he getting any better at all?"

"I think they're going to give him some treatments that will make him all well."

The nurse glanced quickly at the patient.

She didn't mean to say that. She doesn't know if I know it, too. They are coming.

"You'd better wear your wide hat," Miss Percy said. "The sun's real hot this afternoon."

Obediently she put the hat upon her head and tied the ribbons that held it on under her chin.

"Put a little lipstick on," the nurse said. "It's so becoming to you to have a little color in your lips. Don't you remember what Doctor Beckwith said when he met us outside the steps yesterday, how pretty you looked? You've put on a pound and a half in two weeks. It won't be long before we have you weighing what you ought to. Before you know it you're going to be right strong."

Now to smile. Now widen the corners of the mouth and look straight into Miss Percy's eyes and hold it for a moment. But no! This is no smile. This is the terrible and tragic shape of a comic mask. Thus grimace the damned, who burn in the fires, and looking upward to the cool hand that is stretched in kindness and impotence to meet their torment, try one last time and achieve the horrible stretch, the grin, of the comic mask.

They walked down the hot dim corridor and turned to the right.

"Can't we please go down in the elevator?" Mrs. Myles said.

Miss Percy's face looked troubled.

"I know," she said. "Only he wants you to walk through the hospital."

"All right."

So once again. Endure, endure. Endure to the end.

First they walked through the children's ward. Once it had not been bad; the universal slime had not had time to foul this too; she had seen them as children, delicate and pale and sweet. But then the tide of the slime had mounted here too, and ever since it had been this way. Student nurses, nurses, internes passed them. "Afternoon, Mrs. Myles." They all know me. Can they see it in my face? . . . In the little beds the children lay or sat, with their sick faces. Sickness was everywhere. This is the great house of sickness. The children's faces were greenish with the heat. Which among them is mine? He is dead. He is not dead; which among them is mine, not well and laughing, but sick, which among them is my sick, corrupted child, infected from me all its tiny beginnings with the worm of sick sick sick? I am sick and all of mine is sick.

And she smelled the sharp recurrent fear. Fear, that clawed at the ruin of her mind; fear that rattled in her chest about the flabby palpitating boundaries of her heart. This fear is wicked, she thought: I am not afraid *for* the children, I am afraid *of* them. I am afraid of everything. I am full of poison of wickedness and fear; cold poison.

"He wants you to face things," Miss Percy said as they passed through and beyond the men's ward. "You know. Not get so you think you couldn't do something, special."

"I know."

In the beds the men lay, with sickness floating in the pools of their eyes. They passed on through the women's ward. A woman looked up. One side of her face was swollen out to huge proportions, and covered with bandages through which leaked sticky, yellow stuff. There was the long ominous smell of sweet ether and they passed suddenly across the hall of the hospital and their feet sounded sharp and loud on the stone flagging, and they went out into the loud sad heat. They descended the steps and started to walk down the road away from the town.

Suddenly from behind in the sunshine blared a loud-speaker, carried on a truck painted silver, with huge letters advertising an air-cooled movie house downtown. Slowly, slowly, the truck crept along the hot street. The enormous screaming music shook the atmosphere:

> "Fall in love, fall in love, says my heart . . .
> *Fall in love,* FALL IN LOVE . . ."

It swung slowly around a corner out of sight. From far away in the afternoon the idiot voice still screamed:

"Fall in love, fall in love, says my heart . . ."

They walked steadily on, the nurse with a secret little smile; the woman, with a stiff and empty face.

The hours passed in gross and threatening procession. And with the hours the woman felt the always coming on, the rising walls, of the enclosing fear, like sound-proof glass, shutting her away; the terrible pawlike hand fumbling with the cork to stopper her finally into this bottle of aloneness.

She sat beside the window in the decline of the afternoon, and her hand was too sick with fear to stretch out to the shade and pull it down against the sun. She did not dare to move her hand. And soon the sun had bobbled behind the dreadful mountains of the west.

The nurse spoke to her several times and at last in her closing bottle she heard the voice from far away and turned and it was supper being put before her on a tray. In the bowls of all the spoons were faces, that grinned at her and twisted their mouths into screams.

She ate, and then she was sick and the good food left her body in protest and she sat again by the window where the evening light now ran in around the edges of the shade like liquid poison, wet and lying on the floor and on the furniture of the room. The nurse put a table before her and laid out cards for a game upon its surface.

She looked down and saw the ferret faces of the kings and queens, the knaves; pinched and animal-like faces that whispered until the whispering was like a whistling in the room; and she turned her face away, but there was only the faraway flapping shade with the night running in around the edges, and she looked again at her hands but they were vast and swollen and she turned away and closed her eyes but within her was nothing but fear.

"How do you feel?" the nurse said in the evening room.

"How do you feel?" the nurse said.

"How do you feel?" the nurse said.

"HOW DO YOU FEEL?" the nurse said.

The nurse said, "Mrs. Myles, is there anything the matter?"

"It's as if," she said, "all the human things had been taken out of me and it left holes, like a cheese with great empty holes. And the holes have to be filled with something and they are all filled up with fear. So that where I had all sorts of things now I haven't got anything but fear in all the holes."

But that wasn't it at all, not only that; there was the bottle, how to tell someone of the bottle, glass, and sound-proof, where the stopper was being pushed tight home with her inside; not like a moth, no, not so clean, not like the souls in bottles, *animula, vagula, blandula*. No, like a festering purple lump of tissue.

Hell is not heat or cold, it is banishment to the ultimate ego. And in a few hours I shall be stoppered forever, she thought. I will not be able to speak, I will not be able to hear. I will be *mad*.

She asked for a pencil and paper. She wrote, and her handwriting was not her own; it was strange and inchoate like the sawings of the line of a fever chart. She looked at it with desperation. Will I scream? Will I groan? Will I grimace and mouth meaningless words? What will I do, with all of them watching me, crawling loathsomely inside the bottle, the face plastered on the purple stinking tissue like the fearful little faces in the spoons; while they watch, with their cool, well eyes, dressed all in white.

She tried to explain about the bottle on the paper with her failing handwriting, and then she folded it and wrote the doctor's name outside.

"Put it somewhere," she said urgently. "I want you to give it to Doctor Beckwith tomorrow if . . . if I . . ."

If I can no longer communicate what I feel, if I am mad.

"You're going to be fine," the nurse said. "You're going to be fine. Nothing's going to happen to you. Don't be afraid."

She thinks I mean die. No. Only the bottle. Or die?

Or die? For they are coming in the morning with something in their hands. For they are coming in the morning, footsteps measured, slow, down the corridor to me, bearing . . . the cross? . . . in their arms. No. No. You can still endure a little, do not think of Christ, that's the beginning. When the stopper is jammed at last deep into the neck of the bottle, then it will all be thoughts of Christ. Just with the last resisting inch, I can avoid the thought of Christ. . . .

But Christ. So cool, so calm, so bright. O Jesus thou art standing outside the fast-closed door. Jesus with his mild face, his mournful eyes, the bright brown beard, the suffering. Oh, no!

The minutes, the hours passed in ever-gathering procession. Miss Percy ran water and opened the high, narrow bed and helped the woman into it.

"Dave is coming to say good night to you," she said above the bed.

"Dave is coming to say GOOD NIGHT TO YOU," she said.

Oh . . . Dave is coming to say good night to me. . . . Dave? I don't know what is that word: Dave. Something; once; better; but not now. Only the bones of ego smelling of fear and dirt.

"Mrs. Myles."

"Mrs. Myles."

"Mrs. Myles."

"MRS. MYLES!"

She turned her head and in the doorway, unreal, remote, beyond hell, they stood, the nurse, white and slender, and the young man—he was Dave. They stood there, down a tiny vista beckoning, the last reminder. For they were love. It still endured, somewhere, upon the fading world. It was a flickering candle point upon the dark; flickering in the waves that even now, like the great winds of hell, blew the candle flame, tiny, tiny.

The woman on the bed strained toward what she saw. Upon these bones of ego hangs one last shred of flesh, and as long as it hesitates there, gnawed by the mouths of cockroaches, so long that shred of flesh shall reach, shall strain toward what it sees, toward love. The shred is hanging by a nerve, and the candle point flickers and grows far, far away at the end of the cone-shaped darkness.

"Good night, Mrs. Myles."

"Good night," she said. "Are you going out somewhere together?"

"Unh-hunh," Miss Percy said. "Reckon we'll go for a drive in the country to find a breeze."

"Yes," the woman said. "I hope it'll be cool, in the country. I hope you have a lovely time. I hope you're happy."

She turned her head away from the door and closed her eyes, struggling to maintain that point of light somewhere in the darkness that was growing. As long as I can see it the bones will not be wholly bare, and the world not gone. I hope they will be happy. They love each other. Here I lie: in my sepulcher, and the stopper hovers, and the smell of brimstone everywhere. But while the candle flickers I will remember. When it gutters and goes out, I will go out, and the shred of flesh shall drop at last and the paw that reeks shall push the stopper down. . . .

"Well, if you need anything, you know you just have to ring and Miss Perley will get it for you, dear. Good night," the nurse said.

But that, the woman did not hear.

After eleven the hospital was quiet and the lights along the corridors were turned out, so that only the lights over the desks of the nurses in charge shone. The wards were dark and still; along some corridor could be heard occasionally the rattling trundle of a stretcher being pushed in a hurry, the stifled coming and going of a night emergency.

Elizabeth Percy went out through the hospital to the main entrance with Dave. A yawning nurse behind a desk raised her eyes and said "Hi!"; a doctor came hurriedly along the passage, wriggling his arms into a hospital coat as he went; his head was down and as Elizabeth passed he glanced upward from under his brows, nodded, and said, "Miss Percy. . . ." They came out onto the open stone flagging of the entrance hall where lights burned behind the admittance desk, and went down into the melting, melancholy night.

Elizabeth put her hand through Dave's arm and squeezed it; he glanced down at her and smiled.

"How you, babe?" he said.

"A little whipped. . . . That case is so hard, you can't do anything for her much and she's going through something awful."

"Forget it," he said. "You're off now. Climb in. Reckon it'll hold together a little longer."

She got into the old Chevrolet parked by the curb in the darkness.

They drove through the subsiding lights of the town, past the movie theatres with their electric signs turned off, now; the few people in light clothes dawdling before the doors of ice-cream parlors; there was the faint occasional hoot of a motor horn, the slam of a front door. As they passed into the outskirts of the town, the smell of the honeysuckle met them, drifting in from the country, and from far away the small sweet sawing of the crickets in the fields. They crossed a bridge and drove out along the country road, like a tunnel of darkness covered over with the branches of the trees. Their headlights made a white passage down the center of the tunnel. The smell of honeysuckle grew stronger, filling the whole night air, and sometimes they would pass a spot where the honeysuckle smell grew suddenly sharper, sweeter, bursting like fresh fountains into scent.

"My, this is nice," Elizabeth said. Her head was leaned back against the back of the seat.

He pressed her knee with his right hand and drew it toward his.

"Heat like we've been having can't last much longer," he said. "Registered over a hundred outside the store this afternoon. Got to crack sometime. May Leeds says her father and all the farmers are praying for rain."

"How's May?" Elizabeth asked in her low, quiet voice.

"Oh . . . I just took her to a movie while I was waiting around for you. She just dropped in while I was finishing up. . . . I've got to do something with the evenings, haven't I?"

"Of course, darling."

"It was a lousy movie."

She said nothing.

Far out along the road Dave stopped the car off to one side, under the boughs of the trees, and switched out the lights so that nothing could be seen; only the wide dark; the smell of the honeysuckle quivered through the darkness, and in the field beside them a whippoorwill called. Dave lit a cigarette and put his arm around Elizabeth.

"God, it's good to get out of that hellhole," he said.

After a moment Elizabeth spoke.

"I can't get Mrs. Myles out of my head," she said. "She just doesn't get any relief at all."

"Oh, skip the hospital when you're out of it."

"I know. Only I keep thinking that's what love can do to you."

"Inability to adjust."

"Yes, I know. But I guess it isn't so easy to adjust when you're too much in love, and then everything sort of came on her. I can't help picking things up. She was just mad about him and apparently he never cared much about her and she knew it, and that must be just . . . awful. And then when she got pregnant he went off with this other woman, and when she had her baby it died right away. Placenta previa. It would take quite a lot of adjusting."

"Well . . . Skip it. You can't go stewing about patients' problems. Leave that to Beckwith. How about kissing me?"

"You'd think she'd be through with love, wouldn't you? But she sort of hangs on to the idea of it. Like about . . . us."

"Yeah. Listen, I'm sorry, but I can't go up there any more and represent something for your patient. It just makes me feel too God-damn gummy."

"You don't have to. You never had to, only she seemed to get so much out of seeing you and it's awful seeing her every day, so lost. Anyway, she's getting shock in the morning."

"She is?"

"Yes. I hope it'll do the trick."

"How about skipping the hospital, baby? You're supposed to be a nurse, not an angel of mercy. Quit brooding about work out of hours. Kiss me."

She put both arms around him and kissed his mouth. His arms came around her and she felt the restlessness, the impatience in his body, and the eagerness, the searching.

"Oh, darling," she said. "I guess I'm pretty much in love with you."

"I don't mind you one bit myself," he murmured.

She started to speak, checked herself, and then spoke.

"Dave, darling, you wouldn't hurt me, would you?"

"Mmh-mmh."

"You could hurt me so easily. I'm so wide open to you."

"That's just the way I like you," he said, and he put his mouth down on hers, and his hands passed down her arms. Now they were close together, closer and closer in the satin darkness, and in the field the bird called at intervals and the smell of the honeysuckle came down in waves of shuddering sweetness. Over the country where they were the night sky seemed to brood, hanging soft and thick and vast over the land. Far away a train passed in the darkness and across the fields Elizabeth heard its whistle cry three times, three times—ah, ah, aaaah.

When they drove back into town it was very late and the air had a false coolness; there was a little breeze that would go away with the dawn. Elizabeth leaned silent against the seatback. Dave sat up straight and drove, and talked about the coming year of work.

"We get Parsons in surgery and will that be something. You remember Jim Jencks from down Eliza County, he was a real nice guy, I used to see a whole lot of him; he just had one run-in with Parsons after another, and that's one reason, I guess, he isn't going to be able to come back this year. Hope I don't get fixed up wrong with the old bastard."

"What's Jim Jencks doing now?" Elizabeth said.

"He just went on home. The damn fool, he got married. That finished him. Reckon he'll be raising pigs the rest of his life."

"I didn't know he got married."

"Yeah. Lehman, Lemmon . . . ? Married a nurse, anyway. Never had good sense."

Elizabeth made a small noise with her lips.

"Oh! . . . Beg your pardon! Only *you* know, the business of guys marrying nurses, the way they do. . . . You know just as well as I do."

"Yes."

He left her in the dark and empty street before the apartment house where she lived. In the silence of the town the car sounded noisily as he drove away. Elizabeth looked after the car for a moment and then she walked slowly up the brick steps to the house full of nurses asleep.

The woman in Room 53 was awake, passing from unconscious to conscious horror, as soon the the phlegm-gray dawn had filled the corners of the room. There was the relentless metronome beat of doom rapping everywhere. It could not be slowed, nor stopped, nor avoided, but beat faster minute by minute until at last the beat would fuse, would *be,* the footsteps coming down the corridor outside, bearing the thing that would be borne. The woman turned her head in an old and useless reflex against horror and stared out of the window into the gray light.

On the bank opposite the hospital window there were a number of little things, moving about and pecking, and she knew that they were birds; but they were not birds, they were frightful lumps of mud, mud-birds, that jerked about the dirt. She turned her eyes away from them in loathing, but there was nowhere else to look. She closed her eyes upon the horror of outside, to meet the inside horror.

The chorus sang the evil hymns. O Jesus, thou art standing outside the fast-closed door. O Jesus, thou . . . the bright brown beard, the promise that is stained and filthied with corruption, and where is there to fly to lose this wickedness? Abide with me; fast falls the eventide. The awful sweetish dripping of the notes in chorus; that seems to be a promise, that asks for comfort.

The panic grew and the metronome beat, a little faster; the tentacles within reached out in frenzy and there was nothing there to grasp, only abide with me; fast falls the eventide; the dim valley of sin, echoing in the shadows. Though I walk through the valley of the shadow of death, I shall fear no evil; for thou art with me; thy rod and thy staff. . . . Were those what they would bear? The rod and the staff? Though I walk through the valley of the shadow of death. . . . I shall fear this evil, spreading like phlegm along the valley, everywhere, and all is evil, abiding with me. . . .

Oh, no! she cried inside herself with one last straining, no! But where was there to look? And in the ultimate necessity there flickered far off the pale point of the candle flame.

And then the footsteps down the corridor. And then the footsteps, am I dreaming them? The door opened and the priests and the acolytes came in—no, the doctor and the resident and the internes and the nurse— no, the white-robed priests of this obscene observance, this sacrifice, and I am the sacrifice that lies quite still upon the altar, and they bear the weapon in their hands: the huge, brutal, long syringe lying upon a bed of gauze, and I am Christ to meet their sacrifice, to give my life. Six people in the room, and the sacrifice.

"Good morning, gentlemen," the woman said.

The nurse, by the head of the bed, laid her hand upon the patient's hand. The three internes stood grouped at the foot of the bed. The doctor stood on the right of the bed and looked down into the patient's face.

The resident stood halfway down the left side of the bed, and in his hands he held the syringe.

She looked up into the doctor's face and upon it lay his eyes, flat, like gray, wet, cold oysters laid upon a plate.

"Listen," the woman said hurriedly. "Tell me quick. Does it matter what thoughts I am thinking? I mean will this fasten them permanently this way? Because my thoughts are so bad, and I can't seem to think any good thoughts. . . ."

"It doesn't matter, kiddy," said the doctor. The eyes like oysters swam at her, and spun a little round and round. He laid his fingers on her wrist. The resident took her left arm and felt with his fingers along the veins on the inside of her elbow. She closed her eyes. Now let me think one good thought, that my brain may be embalmed in this sacrifice with a good thought held in it like a fly in amber. Oh, stay with me, flame, the point before the eyes, the one last point. . . .

A wave from the outside of sick; of liquid; of shuddering horror ran up her veins.

"Thrombosed," the resident said. "We'll have to try another."

"Steady, kiddy," the doctor said.

Oh, flame, abide with me in the moment of dissolution. .

Then crashingly a thousand carmine circles spun in her brain and there were crashes and mad carmine and the dark.

"Look at that," the leftmost interne said as the figure on the bed sat straight up, clenched in convulsion.

"Patient down on G Ward fractured three vertebrae in one of those," the resident said, watching.

"You'll have your good days and your bad days." The nurse's voice came to her. "You'll have your good days and your bad days, Mrs. Myles."

She was eating lunch off a tray and it was lettuce that she was putting in her mouth. It was thin and crisp and very cold. The world around her was hot and the sun beat through the window beside her. Everything was fatigue, and pain in her back, but the lettuce on her tongue was cool, and the nurse's voice; her name was Miss Percy and she was always there, in the revolving mist, speaking to her out of the wilderness, cool and clear.

"You'll have your good days and your bad days, Mrs. Myles."

She was walking through the jungle of the world, and she was lost. She did not know where she was. It was an utterly strange, green jungle. Only the nurse, Miss Percy, was there beside her, and so she continued to walk through this land.

They came to a brook that ran through a shady hollow and they sat down on a large stone by the margin of the brook and the nurse took off the woman's shoes, and she put her tired feet in the brook. The water was warm and fresh and ran softly past her feet. Beside the brook stood tall green trees that she had never seen before. She kept her feet in the soft running water and listened to the rustling in the leaves of the strange trees.

"How did I get here?" she asked. "Where have I been?"

The nurse's voice came with the sound of the brook, cool and clear.

"You're taking a walk in the country. You're staying at the hospital for a while."

"I don't remember . . ."

"You'll have amnesia for a little bit. It's all right."

It's all right . . .

Miss Percy stopped the doctor in the corridor.

"Doctor Beckwith, may I speak to you for a minute?"

The doctor stopped on one foot in his hurrying walk. The two horns of the stethoscope stuck up from the pocket of his white coat.

"My patient is getting hardly any sleep, doctor. I wondered if you could order something."

"Can't give sedatives, you know, with the treatments. Has a counter-active effect."

"She just seems so terribly tired."

"Well, she didn't even feel tired before. . . . I'll order insulin tonight, Miss Percy. See whether that'll put her to sleep."

"Thank you, doctor."

"You don't look as if you'd got much sleep yourself," the doctor said.

"Oh . . . it's just this heat."

"Got to break soon."

"Yes."

They were in a bowling alley, that was what it was, although she did not know where the bowling alley was or how she had got there. But the nurse was sitting on one of the wooden theatre seats behind her. She herself was standing, facing the alley with a bowl in her hand.

She continued with the action that somehow she had begun. She neither felt the bowl with her hand nor felt the floor under her feet when she moved forward. It was like moving through air. She willed herself to make the gestures that somewhere inside she knew should be made now, and her body carried out the commands, but without sensation, without seeming to touch anything at all.

It just shows what you can do by will power, she thought, surprised. I can do anything I will myself to do, even though I am moving in air.

She let go the bowl and watched down the long straight alley where the bowl rolled, and heard the rumble of the falling pins.

She watched as the three black bowls came rolling up the wooden trolley to the side, and came to a stop. She picked up one of them and although she had picked it up she felt nothing against her palm.

It's almost fun, she thought, seeing what you can do by will power.

It was night, and suddenly she could not bear to lie in bed any longer. Since the nurse had stuck the needle in her arm the strangest energy and slow hope had begun in her.

In the dim spaces of this room the nurse was moving about. She was taking off her cap.

"I want to get up," the woman said. "Can I get up? I want to talk."

The nurse turned and smiled.

"All right," she said. She pulled forward the big chair that was by the window, and helped the woman into it. The nurse sat down on a small straight chair and smiled at the woman.

"But were you going away . . ." the woman said, puzzled. Something stirred in her head, faintly remembered.

"No," the nurse said. "I haven't anywhere special to go. I'd be glad to stay a little later, Mrs. Myles."

"You don't know," she said, "what hope can feel like. It's like running water. I mean freedom. Oh, you don't know what it's like! To be able to see freedom. Even just a little bit."

"You're going to have all the freedom in the world."

"I keep thinking of the loveliest things—long straight roads and driving along them fast in an open car. You don't know what hope can feel like. It's like the wind beginning to blow. Am I really going to be free?"

Suddenly the words of something whose origin she could not remember came into her head and she began to repeat them aloud: "That this nation, under God, shall have a new birth in freedom, and that government of the people, by the people, for the people, shall not perish from the earth."

Shall not perish . . .

"That's what I mean," she said. "That's the way it feels. I can't remember but it wasn't that way before, it wasn't by the people, for the people, I mean as if I were the people, as if I were a nation. A woman like a nation."

"Yes," the nurse said. "I know. Instead of under a dictator, you mean. It's awful to live under a dictator and not belong to yourself any more, isn't it?"

"Yes," she said impatiently, pushing that part away from her, for now there was hope, forming like a five-petaled flower, like a star. Sitting forward on the edge of the chair in her excitement, she repeated the words again, whatever they were: "This nation, under God, shall have ŗ new birth in freedom—and that government of the people . . ."

And after some time the nurse went away and came back with a tall glass that was filled with sugared water, flavored deliciously with lemon, and the woman drank it.

And on some mornings the doctor and the resident and three internes came into her room, and the resident carried the large syringe. He was always the one who inserted the needle into her vein. It was a thing that came suddenly on some mornings and it had to be faced, once more; endure, she thought, endure to the end. And always at the last she summoned to her the vision, with her eyes closed, of the candle flame, that companioned her through the darkness, through the bad days, through it all. It did not leave her, it remained to fortify her in the last extremity, when they came and the needle went into her arm and in her head spun the carmine circles and the world crashed, and then the dark. . . .

"Don't think she'll have to have another," the doctor said, as they watched the figure in convulsion on the bed. "This stuff certainly is magic in some cases."

On an afternoon in the yellow sunshine, suddenly she was sitting under an apple tree in the yard beside the hospital, and the nurse, Miss Percy, was sitting on the grass beside her. Mrs. Myles turned her head slowly and smiled. The heat had gone; it was a cool and lovely afternoon; the leaves rustled in the tree above her and from its branches came the smell of apples.

On the grass farther away some internes were playing baseball. Their voices shouted to one another, and the ball could be heard smacking their cupped palms. A breeze trickled along the air. The shadows were beginning to lengthen from the wall of the hospital, and in that light the internes, in their white clothes, ran and shouted. From a grass bank on the other side of the road from the hospital a bird called, suddenly, sweetly.

"Hello," Mrs. Myles said.

"Hello, dear. You're feeling much better, aren't you?"

"Yes," she said. Things were swimming back into her memory, the buildings here were taking their places in the world. And everything was very calm, very peaceful; there was no hurry. It doesn't matter.

She looked at the nurse, who had been there all the time. In the darkness and the long confusion, in that strange land where she had been, the nurse had been with her all the time. She studied the dark, smooth hair, the oval face, and the long, dark blue, quiet eyes.

"How is Dave?" Mrs. Myles said.

"You're remembering, aren't you?" the nurse said, without looking at the patient. "I think he's fine. I haven't seen him for a while."

"But . . ."

That did not fit. She stayed silent for a little time, while the remembrances slowly rearranged themselves within her head.

"But, you're in love with him," she said slowly. "It was you both. You are in love with each other."

"Well . . . You see, we aren't going together any more."

Something was wrong. Wait while the sifting memory slowly settled. Her own life was dead, somehow she had learned that, someone had taught her that in the strange, twilight land. She knew that she had been reborn and that this was a new life. She could never have the things of her own old life, for they had gone and they were dead. But one thing only . . . a candle burning down a vista, some constant star that had companioned her through the dark valleys of the land she had left. . . . She remembered two figures standing in a doorway.

"You're not?"

"No," the nurse said. She looked tired. They stared at each other and then a new and curious thing happened, a wave swept upward and from her eyes the woman felt tears falling. It was not despair. It was only deepest sadness. The last thing had gone out of the old life. Now the past was wiped black and she was all alone and beginning a new life, reborn alone. The purest, quietest sadness swept her and she could not halt the tears that fell and fell.

"You mustn't mind at all, dear," the nurse said. But their eyes kept meeting: the nurse's quiet and dry, the woman's full of tears.

The baseball game had broken up and a young interne came strolling by the apple tree, and looked down at the two who sat upon the grass. His face Mrs. Myles knew. It had looked at her on many mornings.

"Afternoon, Mrs. Myles, Miss Percy," the interne said, and then stopped in embarrassment at the tears on the woman's face.

"Well . . ." he said. "Seems fine to have a good cry, doesn't it?"

"Yes," she said, crying quietly, for all that was dead, now, forever, and could never be brought back. And it was fading fast. Fade far away, dissolve, and quite forget what thou among the leaves hast never known. It was all over; it was finished; the fight with death and sin, the wandering in the strange lost land. It was all gone, and love was gone too, and the candle flame had silently gone out. Above their heads where they sat upon the grass the little leaves in the apple tree whispered. It was all gone, and from now on the world was new, a page unwritten.

Dr. Mahony

HENRY HANDEL RICHARDSON

THAT night a great storm rose. Mahony, sitting reading after every one else had retired, saw it coming, and, lamp in hand, went round the house to secure hasps and catches: in a recent deluge the girl Ellen had been almost drowned in her bed, through neglecting to fasten her door. This done, he stood at the window and watched the storm's approach. In one half of the sky the stars were still peacefully alight; the other was hidden by a dense cloud; and this came racing along, like a giant bat with outspread wings, and devoured the stars in its flight. The storm broke; there was a sudden shrill screeching, a grinding, piping, whistling, and the wind hurled itself against the house, as if to level it with the ground; failing in this, it banged and battered, making windows and doors shake like loose teeth in their sockets. Then it swept by to wreak its fury elsewhere, and there was a grateful lull, out of which burst a peal of thunder. And now peal followed peal, and the face of the sky, with its masses of swirling, frothy cloud, resembled an angry sea. The lightning ripped it in fierce zigzags, darting out hundreds of spectral fangs, in its craving to reach earth.—It was a magnificent sight.

Polly came running to see where he was, the child cried, Miss Tilly opened her door by a hand's-breadth, and thrust a red puffy face, framed in curl-twists, through the crack. Nobody thought of sleep while the commotion lasted, for fear of fire: once alight, these exposed little wooden houses blazed up like heaps of shavings. The clock-hands pointed to one, before the storm showed signs of abating. Now, the rain was pouring down, making an ear-splitting din on the iron roof,

151

and leaping from every gutter and spout. It had turned very cold. Mahony shivered as he got into bed.

He seemed hardly to have closed an eye when he was wakened by a loud knocking; at the same time, the wire of the night-bell was almost pulled in two. He sat up and looked at his watch. It wanted a few minutes to three; the rain was still falling in torrents, the wind sighed and moaned. Wild horses should not drag him out on such a night! Thrusting his arms into the sleeves of his dressing-gown, he threw up the parlour window.—"Who's there?"—The hiss of the rain cut his words through.

A figure on the doorstep turned at the sound. "Is this a doctor's? I wuz sent here. Doctor! for God's sake . . ."

"What is it?—Stop a minute! I'll open the door."

He did so, letting in a blast of wind, and a rush of rain that flooded the oilcloth. The intruder, off whom the water streamed, had to shout to make himself audible.

"It's me—Mat Doyle's me name! It's me wife, doctor; she's dying. I've bin all night on the road. Now, for the love of—"

"Where is it?" Mahony put his hand to the side of his mouth, to keep his words from flying adrift in the wind.

"Paddy's Rest. You're the third I've bin to. Not one of the dirty dogs'ull stir a leg! Me girl may die like a rabbit for all they care."—The man's voice broke, as he halloed further particulars.

"Paddy's Rest? On a night like this? Why, the creek will be out."

"Doctor! you're from th' ould country, I can hear it in your lip. Haven't you a wife, too, doctor? Wud you want to see her die? Then have a bit o' mercy on mine!"

"Tut, tut, man, none of that!" said Mahony curtly. "You should have bespoken me at the proper time to attend your wife.— Besides, there'll be no getting along the road to-night."

The other caught the note of yielding. "Sure an' you'd go out, doctor dear, without thinkin' to save your dog if he was drownin'. I've got me buggy down there; I'll take you safe. And you shan't regret it; I'll make it worth your while, by the Lord Harry, I will!"

"Pshaw!"—Mahony opened the door of the' surgery, and struck a match. It was a rough grizzled fellow—a "cockatooer," on his own showing—who presented himself in the lamplight, and told his tale. His poor wife had fallen ill that afternoon. At first, everything seemed to be going well; then she was seized with fits, had one fit after another, and all but bit her tongue in two. There was nobody with her but a young girl, whom he had fetched from a mile away. He had intended, when her time came, to bring her to the District Hospital. But they had been taken unawares.—While he waited, he sat with his elbows on his knees, his face between his clenched fists.

In dressing Mahony reassured Polly, and instructed her what to say to people who came inquiring after him; for it was unlikely he would be back before afternoon. Most of the regular patients could be left till then. The one exception, a case of typhoid in its second week, a young Scotch surgeon, Brace, whom he had obliged in a similar emergency, would no doubt see for him—she should send Ellen down with a note, the first thing.—And now, having poured Doyle out a nobbler, and put a flask in his own pocket, Mahony reopened the front door to the howl of the wind.

The lantern his guide carried shed only a tiny circlet of light on the blackness; and the two men picked their steps gingerly along the flooded road. The rain ran in jets off the brim of Mahony's hat, and trickled down the back of his neck. Did he inadvertently put his foot in a hole or a deep wheel-rut, the water splashed up over his jackboots.

Having climbed into the buggy, they advanced at a funeral pace, leaving it to the sagacity of the horse to keep the track. At the creek, sure enough, the water was out, the bridge gone. To reach the next one, five miles off, a crazy cross-country drive would have been necessary; and Mahony was for giving up the job. But Doyle would not acknowledge defeat. He unharnessed the horse, set Mahony on its back, and himself holding to its tail, forced the beast, by dint of kicking and lashing, into the water; and not only got them safely across, but also up the steep sticky clay of the opposite bank.—It was six o'clock and a cloudless morning, when, numb with cold, his clothing clinging to him like wet seaweed, Mahony entered the wooden hut, where the real work he had come out to do began. . . .

Later in the day, clad in an odd collection of baggy garments, he sat and warmed himself in the sun, which was fast drawing up, in the form of a blankety mist, the moisture from the ground. He had successfully performed, under the worst possible conditions, a ticklish operation; and was now so tired that, his chin sinking to his chest, he fell fast asleep.

Doyle wakened him by announcing the arrival of the buggy. The good man, who had had more than one nobbler during the morning, could not hold his tongue, but made still another wordy attempt to express his gratitude.—"Whither me girl lives or dies, it'll not be Mat Doyle who forgits what you did for him this night, doctor!" he declared, as he slashed out unavailingly at one of the many "skeeters" that annoyed him. "An' if ever you want a bit o' work done, or some one to do your lyin' awake at night for you, just you gimme the tip. I don't mind tellin' you now, I'd me shootin'-iron in here"— he touched his right hip— "an' if you'd refused—you was the third, mind you!—I'd have drilled you where you stood, God damn me if I wouldn't!"

Mahoney eyed the speaker with derision. "Much good that would done your wife, you fathead. . . . Well, well, we'll say nothing to *mine,* if you please, about anything of that sort."

"No, may all the saints bless 'er and give 'er health! An', as I say, doctor. . . ." In speaking, he had drawn a roll of banknotes from his pocket, and now he tried to stuff them between Mahony's fingers.

"What's this?—My good man, keep your money till it's asked for!" and Mahony unclasped his hands, so that the notes fluttered to the ground.

"Then there let 'em lay!"

But when, in clothes dried stiff as cardboard, Mahony was rolling townwards—his coachman a lad of some ten or twelve, who handled the reins to the manner born—as they went, he chanced to feel in his coat pocket, and there found five ten-pound notes, rolled up in a neat bundle.

The main part of the road was dry and hard again; but all dips and holes were wells of liquid mud, which bespattered the two of them from top to toe as the buggy bumped carelessly in and out. Mahony diverted himself by thinking of the handsome present he could give Polly with this sum. It would serve to buy that pair of gilt cornices, or the heavy gilt-framed pierglass, on which she had set her heart. He could see her, pink with pleasure, expostulating: "Richard! What *wicked* extravagance!" and hear himself reply: "And pray may my wife not have as pretty a parlour as her neighbours?" He even cast a thought, in passing, on the pianoforte, with which Polly longed to crown the furnishings of her room—though, of course, at least treble this amount would be needed to cover its cost.—But a fig for such nonsense! He knew of but one legitimate use to make of the unexpected little windfall, and that was, to put it by for a rainy day. "At my age, in my position, I *ought* to have fifty pounds in the bank!"—times without number he had said this to himself, with a growing impatience. But he had never managed to save a halfpenny. Thrive as the practice might, the expenses of living held even pace with it. He had to keep up appearances, too, nowadays; his debts of hospitality had doubled; nor did it do for his name to be absent from charities and subscription-lists. It was a guinea here, two guineas there, while the new saddle and the medical books he needed, were struck off the list.—And now his brain, having got its cue, started off again on the old treadmill, reckoning, totting up, finding totals, or more often failing to find them, till his head was as hot as his feet were cold. To-day, he could not think clearly at all.

Nor the next day either. By the time he reached home, he was conscious of feeling very ill: he had lancinating pains in his limbs, a chill down his spine, an outrageous temperature. To set out again on a round of visits was impossible. He had to tumble into bed, where he lay helpless.

He got between the sheets with that sense of utter well-being, of almost sensual satisfaction, which only one who is shivering with fever knows. And, at first, very small things were enough to fill him with content: the smoothness of the pillow's sleek linen; the shadowy light of the room, after long days spent in the dusty glare outside; the possibility of resting—the knowledge that it was his duty to rest; Polly's soft, firm hands, which, as she sponged his forehead or administered his self-prescribed doses, were always of the right temperature—warm in the cold stage, cool when the fever scorched him, and neither hot nor cold when the dripping sweats came on. In the beginning, he lay behind the dimity-curtains of the four-poster, feeling as though he had done for ever with the world and its cares. In this white, still haven, the noise of life came to him like the beating of a muffled drum, and soon died away altogether. And the thought crossed his mind that death itself would not be hard to face, if, when one's hour struck, this sense of aloofness, of detachment from earthly things, prevailed. Wrapped in a dreamless ease, the homing mortal would glide gently down the great River, back into the twilight from which he had sprung.—A further discovery was that only the busy doctor, eternally on the go, eternally, no matter what his own condition, at the beck and call of others, could truly appreciate the luxury of being ill.—But, as the fever declined, and the sweats lengthened, these slight pleasures lost their hold. Then, lying weak and helpless, he was ridden to death by black thoughts. Not only was day being added to day, he meanwhile not turning over a penny; but ideas which he knew to be preposterous insinuated themselves in his brain, and there spread and grew till they had ousted sanity. Thus, for hours on end, he writhed under the belief that his present illness was due solely to the proximity of the Great Swamp; and all that day he lay and cursed his folly, in having chosen just this neighbourhood to build in. Low fever, having once got a grip of its victim, did not readily let go; and he saw his practice cut up, ruined, by continual bouts of ill-health. Had he had the strength to rise, he would then and there have ordered in an army of workmen, bodily to shift the house to another site.— Again, there was the case of typhoid he had been anxious about, prior to his own breakdown: under his *locum tenens,* peritonitis had set in, and carried off the patient. At the time, he had accepted the news from Polly's lips with indifference—too ill to care. But, a little later, the knowledge of what it meant broke over him one morning; and, after that, he suffered the tortures of the damned. Not Brace; he alone would be held responsible for the death; and once more he saw his hopeful practice damaged—destroyed. Perhaps not altogether unjustly, either. Lying there, an easy prey to morbid apprehensions, he began to tax himself with a possible error of judgment. He rebuilt the case in memory, struggled to recall each slight variation in temperature, each swift change for better or worse; but, as fast as he captured one such detail, his drowsy brain let the last but one go, and he had to beat it up anew. During the night, he grew confident that the relatives of the dead woman intended to take action against him, for negligence or improper attendance. In all probability, they waited only for him to be on his feet again, to drag him out into the light of scandal and disgrace.

An attempt he made to speak of these devilish imaginings to wife and friend was a failure. He undertook it in a fit of desperation, when it seemed as if only a strong and well-grounded opposition would save his reason. But this was just what he could not get. Purdy, whom he tried first, held the crude notion that a sick person should never be gainsaid; and soothingly nodded, and sympathised, and agreed, till Mahony could have cried aloud at such blundering stupidity. Polly did better; she contradicted him. But not in the right way. She certainly pooh-poohed his fixed idea of the nearness of Yuille's Swamp making the house unhealthy; but she did not argue the matter out, step by step, and *convince* him that he was wrong. She just laughed at him, as at a foolish child, and kissed him, and tucked him in anew. And when it came to the typhoid's fatal issue, she had not the knowledge needed to combat him with any chance of success. She heard him anxiously out, and allowed herself to be made quite nervous over a possible fault on his part, so jealous was she for his growing reputation.

So that, in the end, it was he who had to comfort her.

"Don't take any notice of what I say to-day, wife! It's this blessed fever. . . . I'm light-headed, I think."

But he could hear her uneasily consulting with Purdy in the passage.

It was not till his pulse beat normally again, and he had spirit enough to open a book, that he could smile at such exaggerated fears. And now, too, reviving health brought back a wholesome interest in everyday affairs. He listened, with amusement, to Polly's account of the shifts Purdy was reduced to, to enter the house unseen by Miss Tilly. On his faithful daily call, the young man would creep round by the back door, and Tilly was growing more and more irate at her inability to waylay him. Yes, Polly was rather readily forced to admit, she *had* abetted him in his evasions.—("You know, Poll, I might just as well tie myself up to old Mother B. herself and be done with it!")—Out of sheer pique, Tilly had twice now accepted old Mr. Ocock's invitation to drive with him. Once, she had returned with a huge bag of lollies; and once, with a face like a turkey-cock. Polly couldn't help thinking . . . no, really, Richard, she could not! . . . that, perhaps, something might *come* of it. He should not laugh; but wait and see.

But, as he grew stronger, books and gossip alike palled on him; and the last days of his imprisonment had feet of lead. Many inquiries had been made after him; he could appreciate them now. People had missed their doctor, it seemed, and wanted him back. The wish was mutual; he hankered to see how this case had developed in his absence, and what Brace had made of that. It was a real red-letter day when he could snap to the catches of his gloves again, and mount the step of a buggy.

He had instructed Purdy to arrange for the hire of this vehicle, saddle-work being out of the question for him, in the meantime. And, on his first long journey—it led him past Doyle's hut, now, he was sorry to see, in the hands of strangers; for the wife, on the way to making a fair recovery, had got up too soon, overtaxed her strength and died, and the broken-hearted husband was gone off no one knew where—on this drive, as mile after mile slid from under the wheels, Mahony felt how grateful was the screen of a hood between him and the sun.

While he was laid up, the eternal question of how to live on his income had left him, relatively speaking, in peace. He had of late adopted the habit of doing his scraping and saving, of denying himself wholesale, at the outset of each quarter, so as to get the money due to Ocock put by betimes; while, for current expenses, Doyle's gift had been there to fall back on. His illness had naturally made a hole in this; and now the living momentarily from hand to mouth must begin anew.

With what remained of the sum, he proposed to settle his account at the livery stable. Then, the unexpected happened. His reappearance—he looked very thin and washed-out—evidently jogged a couple of sleepy memories; for, simultaneously, two big bills were paid, one of which he had entirely given up. In consequence, he again found himself fifty pounds to the good. And, driving to Ocock's office, on term day, he resolved to go on afterwards to the Bank of Australasia, and there deposit the money.

Grindle, now set off by a pair of flaming "sideboards," and a manner that aped Ocock's own, himself ushered Mahony into the sanctum. The latter's little affair was disposed of in a trice. Ocock was one of the busiest of men nowadays—he no longer needed to invent sham clients and fictitious interviews—and utilised the few odd minutes it took to procure a signature, jot down a note, open a drawer, unlock a tin box, to remark abstractedly on the weather, and put a polite inquiry: "And your good lady? In the best of health, I trust?"

On emerging from the inner room, Mahony saw that the places formerly filled by Tom and Johnny, were occupied by strangers; and he was wondering whether it would be indiscreet to ask what had become of the brothers, when Ocock cut across his intention.—"By the way, Jenkins, has that memorandum I spoke of been drawn up?" he turned to a clerk.

With a sheet of foolscap in his hand, he invited Mahony with a beck of the chin to re-enter his room, where he closed the door. "Half a moment! Now, doctor, if you happen to have a little money lying idle, I can put you on to a good thing—a very good thing indeed. I don't know, I'm sure, whether you keep an eye on the fluctuations of the share-market. If so, you'll no doubt have noticed the . . . let me say the extreme instability of those shares known as 'Porepunkahs.' After making an excellent start, they have drooped till they are now to be had at one-twentieth of their original value."

As a rule, he did not take much interest in mining matters, was Mahony's reply. However, he knew something of the claim in question, if only because several of his acquaintances had abandoned their shares, in disgust at the repeated calls and the lack of dividends.

"Exactly. Well now, doctor, I'm in a position to inform you that 'Pore-punkahs' will very shortly be prime favourites on the market, selling at from double to treble their original figure—their *original* figure, sir! No one with a few hundreds to spare could find a better investment. Now is the time to buy."

A few hundreds! . . . what does he take me for? thought Mahony; and declined the transaction off-hand. It was very good of Mr. Ocock to think of him; but he preferred to keep clear of all that kind of thing.

"Quite so, quite so!" returned Ocock suavely, hitting the note at once; and he dry-washed his hands, with the smile Mahony had never learnt to fathom. "Just as you please, of course.—I'll only ask you, doctor, to treat the matter as strictly confidential."

"I supose he says the same to every one he tells," was Mahony's comment as he flicked up his horse; and he wondered what the extent might be of the lawyer's personal interest in the "Porepunkah Company." It was quite likely that the number of shareholders was not large enough to take up the capital.

Still, the incident gave him food for thought, and only when it was after hours did he remember his intention of driving home by way of the Bank.

Later in the day, he came back on the incident, and pondered over his abrupt refusal of Ocock's offer. There was nothing out of the way in this: he never took advice well; and, was it forced upon him, a certain inborn contrariness drove him, nine times out of ten, to go and do just the opposite. Besides, he had not yet learned to look with lenience on the rage for speculation that had seized the inhabitants of Ballarat; and he held that it would be culpable for a man of his slender means to risk money in the great game.—But was there any hint of risk in the present instance? To judge from Ocock's manner, the investment was as safe as a house, and lucrative to a degree that made one's head swim. "Double to treble their original figure" the lawyer had predicted of the shares. An Arab-ian-nights fashion of growing rich, and no mistake! Very different from the laborious grind of *his* days, in which, moreover, he had always to reckon with the chance of not being paid for his services at all. That very afternoon had brought him a fresh example of this. He was returning from the Old Magpie Lead, where he had been called to a case of scarlet fever; and he saw himself covering the same road daily, for some time to come. But he had learned to adjudge his patients in a winking; and these, he could swear to it, would prove to be non-payers; of a kind even to cut and run, once the child was out of danger. Was he really justified, cramped for money as he was, in rejecting the straight tip Ocock had given him? And he debated this moot point—argued his need against his principles—the whole way home.

As soon as he had changed, and seen his suspect clothing hung out to air, he went impetuously back to Ocock's office. He had altered his mind. A small gift from a grateful patient: yes, fifty, please; they might bring him luck.—And he saw his name written down as the owner of half a hundred shares.

After this, he took a new interest in the mining sheet of the *Star;* turned to it, indeed, first of all. For a week, a fortnight, "Porepunkahs" remained stationary; then they made a call, and, if he did not wish to forfeit, he had to pay out as many shillings as he held shares. A day or two later, they sank a trifle, and Mahony's hopes with them. There even came a day when they were not mentioned; and he gave up his money for lost. But, of a sudden, they woke to life again, took an upward bound, and, within a month, were quoted at five pounds—on rumour alone. "Very sensitive indeed," said the *Star.* Purdy, his only confidant, went about swearing at himself for having let the few he owned lapse; and Mahony itched to sell. He could now have banked two hundred and fifty pounds.

But Ocock laughed him out of countenance—even went so far as to pat him on the shoulder. On no account was he to think of selling. "Sit tight, doctor . . . sit tight! Till I say the word."

And Mahony reluctantly obeyed.

Silent Snow, Secret Snow

CONRAD AIKEN

Just why it should have happened, or why it should have happened just when it did, he could not, of course, possibly have said; nor perhaps could it even have occurred to him to ask. The thing was above all a secret, something to be preciously concealed from Mother and Father; and to that very fact it owed an enormous part of its deliciousness. It was like a peculiarly beautiful trinket to be carried unmentioned in one's trouser-pocket—a rare stamp, an old coin, a few tiny gold links found trodden out of shape on the path in the park, a pebble of carnelian, a sea shell distinguishable from all others by an unusual spot or stripe— and, as if it were anyone of these, he carried around with him everywhere a warm and persistent and increasingly beautiful sense of possession. Nor was it only a sense of possession—it was also a sense of protection. It was as if, in some delightful way, his secret gave him a fortress, a wall behind which he could retreat into heavenly seclusion. This was almost the first thing he had noticed about it—apart from the oddness of the thing itself—and it was this that now again, for the fiftieth time, occurred to him, as he sat in the little schoolroom. It was the half hour for geography. Miss Buell was revolving with one finger, slowly, a huge terrestrial globe which had been placed on her desk. The green and yellow continents passed and repassed, questions were asked and answered, and now the little girl in front of him, Deirdre, who had a funny little constellation of freckles on the back of her neck, exactly like the Big Dipper, was standing up and telling Miss Buell that the equator was the line that ran around the middle.

162

Miss Buell's face, which was old and grayish and kindly, with gray stiff curls beside the cheeks, and eyes that swam very brightly, like little minnows, behind thick glasses, wrinkled itself into a complication of amusements.

"Ah! I see. The earth is wearing a belt, or a sash. Or someone drew a line round it!"

"Oh, no—not that—I mean—"

In the general laughter, he did not share, or only a very little. He was thinking about the Arctic and Antarctic regions, which of course, on the globe, were white. Miss Buell was now telling them about the tropics, the jungles, the steamy heat of equatorial swamps, where the birds and butterflies, and even the snakes, were like living jewels. As he listened to these things, he was already, with a pleasant sense of half-effort, putting his secret between himself and the words. Was it really an effort at all? For effort implied something voluntary, and perhaps even something one did not especially want; whereas this was distinctly pleasant, and came almost of its own accord. All he needed to do was to think of that morning, the first one, and then of all the others—

But it was all so absurdly simple! It had amounted to so little. It was nothing, just an idea—and just why it should have become so wonderful, so permanent, was a mystery—a very pleasant one, to be sure, but also, in an amusing way, foolish. However, without ceasing to listen to Miss Buell, who had now moved up to the north temperate zone, he deliberately invited his memory of the first morning. It was only a moment or two after he had waked up—or perhaps the moment itself. But was there, to be exact, an exact moment? Was one awake all at once? or was it gradual? Anyway, it was after he had stretched a lazy hand up toward the headrail, and yawned, and then relaxed again among his warm covers, all the more grateful on a December morning, that the thing had happened. Suddenly, for no reason, he had thought of the postman, he remembered the postman. Perhaps there was nothing so odd in that. After all, he heard the postman almost every morning in his life—his heavy boots could be heard clumping round the corner at the top of the little cobbled hill-street, and then, progressively nearer, progressively louder, the double knock at each door, the crossings and re-crossings of the street, till finally the clumsy steps came stumbling across to the very door, and the tremendous knock came which shook the house itself.

(Miss Buell was saying "Vast wheat-growing areas in North America and Siberia."

Deirdre had for the moment placed her left hand across the back of her neck.)

But on this particular morning, the first morning, as he lay there with his eyes closed, he had for some reason *waited* for the postman. He wanted to hear him come round the corner. And that was precisely the joke—he never did. He never came. He never had come—*round the corner*—again. For when at last the steps *were* heard, they had already, he was quite sure, come a little down the hill, to the first house; and even so, the steps were curiously different—they were softer, they had a new secrecy about them, they were muffled and indistinct; and while the rhythm of them was the same, it now said a new thing —it said peace, it said remoteness, it said cold, it said sleep. And he had understood the situation at once—nothing could have seemed simpler—there had been snow in the night, such as all winter he had been longing for; and it was this which had rendered the postman's first footsteps inaudible, and the later ones faint. Of course! How lovely! And even now it must be snowing—it was going to be a snowy day— the long white ragged lines were drifting and sifting across the street, across the faces of the old houses, whispering and hushing, making little triangles of white in the corners between cobblestones, seething a little when the wind blew them over the ground to a drifted corner; and so it would be all day, getting deeper and deeper and silenter and silenter.

(Miss Buell was saying "Land of perpetual snow.")

All this time, of course (while he lay in bed), he had kept his eyes closed, listening to the nearer progress of the postman, the muffled footsteps thumping and slipping on the snow-sheathed cobbles; and all the other sounds—the double knocks, a frosty far-off voice or two, a bell ringing thinly and softly as if under a sheet of ice—had the same slightly abstracted quality, as if removed by one degree from actuality —as if everything in the world had been insulated by snow. But when at last, pleased, he opened his eyes, and turned them towards the window, to see for himself this long-desired and now so clearly imagined miracle—what he saw instead was brilliant sunlight on a roof; and when, astonished, he jumped out of bed and stared down into the street, expecting to see the cobbles obliterated by the snow, he saw nothing but the bare bright cobbles themselves.

Queer, the effect this extraordinary surprise had had upon him—all the following morning he had kept with him a sense as of snow falling about him, a secret screen of new snow between himself and the world. If he had not dreamed such a thing—and how could he have dreamed it while awake?—how else could one explain it? In any case, the delusion had been so vivid as to affect his entire behavior. He could not now remember whether it was on the first or the second morning—or was it even the third?—that his mother had drawn attention to some oddness in his manner.

"But my darling—" she had said at the breakfast table—"what has come over you? You don't seem to be listening. . . ."

(Miss Buell was now asking if anyone knew the difference between the North Pole and the Magnetic Pole. Deirdre was holding up her flickering brown hand, and he could see the four white dimples that marked the knuckles.)

Perhaps it hadn't been either the second or third morning—or even the fourth or fifth. How could he be sure? How could he be sure just when the delicious *progress* had become clear? Just when it had really *begun?* The intervals weren't very precise. . . . All he now knew was, that at some point or other—perhaps the second day, perhaps the sixth— he had noticed that the presence of the snow was a little more insistent, the sound of it clearer; and, conversely, the sound of the postman's footsteps more indistinct. Not only could he not hear the steps come round the corner, he could not even hear them at the first house.

It was below the first house that he heard them; and then, a few days later, it was below the second house that he heard them; and a few days later again, below the third. Gradually, gradually, the snow was becoming heavier, the sound of its seething louder, the cobblestones more and more muffled. When he found, each morning, on going to the window, after the ritual of listening, that the roofs and cobbles were as bare as ever, it made no difference. This was, after all, only what he had expected. It was even what pleased him, what rewarded him: the thing was his own, belonged to no one else. No one else knew about it, not even his mother and father. There, outside, were the bare cobbles; and here, inside, was the snow. Snow growing heavier each day, muffling the world, hiding the ugly, and deadening increasingly—above all—the steps of the postman.

"But my darling—" she had said at the luncheon table—"what has come over you? You don't seem to listen when people speak to you. That's the third time I've asked you to pass your plate. . . ."

How was one to explain this to Mother? or to Father? There was, of course, nothing to be done about it: nothing. All one could do was to laugh embarrassedly, pretend to be a little ashamed, apologize, and take a sudden and somewhat disingenuous interest in what was being done or said. The cat had stayed out all night. He had a curious swelling on his left cheek—perhaps somebody had kicked him, or a stone had struck him. Mrs. Kempton was or was not coming to tea. The house was going to be house cleaned, or "turned out," on Wednesday instead of Friday. A new lamp was provided, for his evening work—perhaps it was eye-strain which accounted for this new and so peculiar vagueness of his—Mother was looking at him with amusement as she said this, but with something else as well. A new lamp? A new lamp. Yes Mother, No Mother, Yes Mother. School is going very well. The geometry is very easy. The history is very dull. The geography is very interesting—particularly when it takes one to the North Pole. Why the North Pole? Oh, well, it would be fun to be an explorer. Another Peary or Scott or Shackleton. And then abruptly he found his interest in the talk at an end, stared at the pudding on his plate, listened, waited,

and began once more—ah how heavenly, too, the first beginnings—
to hear or feel—for could he actually hear it?—the silent snow, the
secret snow.

(Miss Buell was telling them about the search for the Northwest
Passage, about Hendrik Hudson, the Half Moon.)

This had been, indeed, the only distressing feature of the new experience: the fact that it so increasingly had brought him into a kind of
mute misunderstanding, or even conflict, with his father and mother.
It was as if he were trying to lead a double life. On the one hand he
had to be Paul Hasleman, and keep up the appearance of being that
person—dress, wash, and answer intelligently when spoken to—; on
the other, he had to explore this new world which had been opened
to him. Nor could there be the slightest doubt—not the slightest—that
the new world was the profounder and more wonderful of the two.
It was irresistible. It was miraculous. Its beauty was simply beyond
anything—beyond speech as beyond thought—utterly incommunicable.
But how then, between the two worlds, of which he was thus constantly aware, was he to keep a balance? One must get up, one must
go to breakfast, one must talk with Mother, go to school, do one's lessons—and, in all this, try not to appear too much of a fool. But if all
the while one was also trying to extract the full deliciousness of another
and quite separate existence, one which could not easily (if at all) be
spoken of—how was one to manage? How was one to explain? Would
it be safe to explain? Would it be absurd? Would it merely mean that
he would get into some obscure kind of trouble?

These thoughts came and went, came and went, as softly and secretly as the snow; they were not precisely a disturbance, perhaps they
were even a pleasure; he liked to have them; their presence was something almost palpable, something he could stroke with his hand, without closing his eyes, and without ceasing to see Miss Buell and the
school-room and the globe and the freckles on Deirdre's neck; nevertheless he did in a sense cease to see, or to see the obvious external
world, and substituted for this vision the vision of snow, the sound
of snow, and the slow, almost soundless, approach of the postman.

Yesterday, it had been only at the sixth house that the postman had become audible; the snow was much deeper now, it was falling more swiftly and heavily, the sound of its seething was more distinct, more soothing, more persistent. And this morning, it had been—as nearly as he could figure—just above the seventh house—perhaps only a step or two above: at most, he had heard two or three footsteps before the knock had sounded. . . . And with each such narrowing of the sphere, each nearer approach of the limit at which the postman was first audible, it was odd how sharply was increased the amount of illusion which had to be carried into the ordinary business of daily life. Each day, it was harder to get out of bed, to go to the window, to look out at the— as always—perfectly empty and snowless street. Each day it was more difficult to go through the perfunctory motions of greeting Mother and Father at breakfast, to reply to their questions, to put his books together and go to school. And at school, how extraordinarily hard to conduct with success simultaneously the public life and the life that was secret. There were times when he longed—positively ached—to tell everyone about it—to burst out•with it—only to be checked almost at once by a far-off feeling as of some faint absurdity which was inherent in it—but *was* it absurd?—and more importantly by a sense of mysterious power in his very secrecy. Yes: it must be kept secret. That, more and more, became clear. At whatever cost to himself, whatever pain to others—

(Miss Buell looked straight at him, smiling, and said, "Perhaps we'll ask Paul. I'm sure Paul will come out of his day-dream long enough to be able to tell us. Won't you, Paul?" He rose slowly from his chair, resting one hand on the brightly varnished desk, and deliberately stared through the snow towards the blackboard. It was an effort, but it was amusing to make it. "Yes," he said slowly, "it was what we now call the Hudson River. This he thought to be the Northwest Passage. He was disappointed." He sat down again, and as he did so Deirdre half turned in her chair and gave him a shy smile, of approval and admiration.)

At whatever pain to others.

This part of it was very puzzling, very puzzling. Mother was very nice, and so was Father. Yes, that was all true enough. He wanted to be nice to them, to tell them everything—and yet, was it really wrong of him to want to have a secret place of his own?

At bedtime, the night before, Mother had said, "If this goes on, my lad, we'll have to see a doctor, we will! We can't have our boy—" But what was it she had said? "Live in another world"? "Live so far away"? The word "far" had been in it, he was sure, and then Mother had taken up a magazine again and laughed a little, but with an expression which wasn't mirthful. He had felt sorry for her. . . .

The bell rang for dismissal. The sound came to him through long curved parallels of falling snow. He saw Deirdre rise, and had himself risen almost as soon—but not quite as soon—as she.

II

On the walk homeward, which was timeless, it pleased him to see through the accompaniment, or counterpoint, of snow, the items of mere externality on his way. There were many kinds of bricks in the sidewalks, and laid in many kinds of pattern. The garden walls too were various, some of wooden palings, some of plaster, some of stone. Twigs of bushes leaned over the walls; the little hard green winter-buds of lilac, on gray stems, sheathed and fat; other branches very thin and fine and black and desiccated. Dirty sparrows huddled in the bushes, as dull in color as dead fruit left in leafless trees. A single starling creaked on a weather vane. In the gutter, beside a drain, was a scrap of torn and dirty newspaper, caught in a little delta of filth: the word ECZEMA appeared in large capitals, and below it was a letter from Mrs. Amelia D. Cravath, 2100 Pine Street, Fort Worth, Texas, to the effect that after being a sufferer for years she had been cured by Caley's Ointment. In the little delta, beside the fan-shaped and deeply runneled continent of brown mud, were lost twigs, descended from their parent trees, dead matches, a rusty horse-chestnut burr, a small concentration of sparkling gravel on the lip of the sewer, a fragment of eggshell, a streak of yellow sawdust which had been wet and was now dry and congealed, a brown pebble, and a broken feather. Further on was a cement sidewalk, ruled into geometrical parallelograms, with a brass inlay at one end commemorating the contractors who had laid it, and, halfway across, an irregular and random series of dog-tracks, immortalized in synthetic stone. He knew these well, and always stepped on them; to cover the little hollows with his own foot had always been a queer pleasure; today he did it once more, but perfunctorily and detachedly, all the while thinking of something else. That was a dog, a long time ago, who had made a mistake and walked on the cement while it was still wet. He had probably wagged his tail, but that hadn't been recorded. Now, Paul Hasleman, aged twelve, on his way home from school, crossed the same river, which in the meantime had frozen into rock. Homeward through the snow, the snow falling in bright sunshine. Homeward?

Then came the gateway with the two posts surmounted by egg-shaped stones which had been cunningly balanced on their ends, as if by Columbus, and mortared in the very act of balance: a source of perpetual wonder. On the brick wall just beyond, the letter H had been stenciled, presumably for some purpose. H? H.

The green hydrant, with a little green-painted chain attached to the brass screw-cap.

The elm tree, with the great gray wound in the bark, kidney-shaped, into which he always put his hand—to feel the cold but living wood. The injury, he had been sure, was due to the gnawings of a tethered horse. But now it deserved only a passing palm, a merely tolerant eye. There were more important things. Miracles. Beyond the thoughts of trees, mere elms. Beyond the thoughts of sidewalks, mere stone, mere brick, mere cement. Beyond the thoughts even of his own shoes, which trod these sidewalks obediently, bearing a burden—far above—of elaborate mystery. He watched them. They were not very well polished; he had neglected them, for a very good reason: they were one of the many parts of the increasing difficulty of the daily return to daily life, the morning struggle. To get up, having at last opened one's eyes, to go to the window, and discover no snow, to wash, to dress, to descend the curving stairs to breakfast—

At whatever pain to others, nevertheless, one must persevere in severance, since the incommunicability of the experience demanded it. It was desirable of course to be kind to Mother and Father, especially as they seemed to be worried, but it was also desirable to be resolute. If they should decide—as appeared likely—to consult the doctor, Doctor Howells, and have Paul inspected, his heart listened to through a kind of dictaphone, his lungs, his stomach—well, that was all right. He would go through with it. He would give them answer for question, too— perhaps such answers as they hadn't expected? No. That would never do. For the secret world must, at all costs, be preserved.

The bird-house in the apple-tree was empty—it was the wrong time of year for wrens. The little round black door had lost its pleasure. The wrens were enjoying other houses, other nests, remoter trees. But this too was a notion which he only vaguely and grazingly entertained— as if, for the moment, he merely touched an edge of it; there was something further on, which was already assuming a sharper importance; something which already teased at the corners of his eyes, teasing also at the corner of his mind. It was funny to think that he so wanted this, so awaited it—and yet found himself enjoying this momentary dalliance with the bird-house, as if for a quite deliberate postponement and enhancement of the approaching pleasure. He was aware of his delay, of his smiling and detached and now almost uncomprehending gaze at the little bird-house; he knew what he was going to look at next: it was his own little cobbled hill-street, his own house, the little river at the bottom of the hill, the grocer's shop with the cardboard man in the window—and now, thinking of all this, he turned his head, still smiling, and looking quickly right and left through the snow-laden sunlight.

And the mist of snow, as he had foreseen, was still on it—a ghost of snow falling in the bright sunlight, softly and steadily floating and turning and pausing, soundlessly meeting the snow that covered, as with a transparent mirage, the bare bright cobbles. He loved it—he stood still and loved it. Its beauty was paralyzing—beyond all words, all experience, all dream. No fairy-story he had ever read could be compared with it—none had ever given him this extraordinary com-bination of ethereal loveliness with a something else, unnameable, which was just faintly and deliciously terrifying. What was this thing? As he thought of it, he looked upward toward his own bedroom win-dow, which was open—and it was as if he looked straight into the room and saw himself lying half awake in his bed. There he was—at this very instant he was still perhaps actually there—more truly there than standing here at the edge of the cobbled hill-street, with one hand lifted to shade his eyes against the snow-sun. Had he indeed ever left his room, in all this time? since that very first morning? Was the whole progress still being enacted there, was it still the same morning, and himself not yet wholly awake? And even now, had the postman not yet come round the corner? . . .

This idea amused him, and automatically, as he thought of it, he turned his head and looked toward the top of the hill. There was, of course, nothing there—nothing and no one. The street was empty and quiet. And all the more because of its emptiness it occurred to him to count the houses—a thing which, oddly enough, he hadn't before thought of doing. Of course, he had known there weren't many—many, that is, on his own side of the street, which were the ones that figured in the postman's progress—but nevertheless it came to him as something of a shock to find that there were precisely *six,* above his own house— his own house was the seventh.

Six!

Astonished, he looked at his own house—looked at the door, on which was the number thirteen—and then realized that the whole thing was exactly and logically and absurdly what he ought to have known. Just the same, the realization gave him abruptly, and even a little frighten-ingly, a sense of hurry. He was being hurried—he was being rushed. For—he knit his brows—he couldn't be mistaken—it was just above the *seventh* house, his *own* house, that the postman had first been audible this very morning. But in that case—in that case—did it mean that tomorrow he would hear nothing? The knock he had heard must have been the knock of their own door. Did it mean—and this was an idea which gave him a really extraordinary feeling of surprise—that he would never hear the postman again?—that tomorrow morning the postman would already have passed the house, in a snow by then so deep as to render his footsteps completely inaudible? That he would have made his approach down the snow-filled street so soundlessly, so secretly, that he, Paul Hasleman, there lying in bed, would not have waked in time, or, waking, would have heard nothing?

But how could that be? Unless even the knocker should be muffled in the snow—frozen tight, perhaps? . . . But in that case—

A vague feeling of disappointment came over him; a vague sadness, as if he felt himself deprived of something which he had long looked forward to, something much prized. After all this, all this beautiful progress, the slow delicious advance of the postman through the silent and secret snow, the knock creeping closer each day, and the footsteps nearer, the audible compass of the world thus daily narrowed, narrowed, narrowed, as the snow soothingly and beautifully encroached and deepened, after all this, was he to be defrauded of the one thing he had so wanted—to be able to count, as it were, the last two or three solemn footsteps, as they finally approached his own door? Was it all going to happen, at the end, so suddenly? or indeed, had it already happened? with no slow and subtle gradations of menace, in which he could luxuriate?

He gazed upward again, toward his own window which flashed in the sun: and this time almost with a feeling that it would be better if he *were* still in bed, in that room; for in that case this must still be the first morning, and there would be six more mornings to come—or, for that matter, seven or eight or nine—how could he be sure?—or even more.

III

After supper, the inquisition began. He stood before the doctor, under the lamp, and submitted silently to the usual thumpings and tappings.

"Now will you please say 'Ah!'?"

"Ah!"

"Now again please, if you don't mind."

"Ah."

"Say it slowly, and hold it if you can—"

"Ah-h-h-h-h-h—"

"Good."

How silly all this was. As if it had anything to do with his throat! Or his heart or lungs!

Relaxing his mouth, of which the corners, after all this absurd stretching, felt uncomfortable, he avoided the doctor's eyes, and stared towards the fireplace, past his mother's feet (in gray slippers) which projected from the green chair, and his father's feet (in brown slippers) which stood neatly side by side on the hearth rug.

"Hm. There is certainly nothing wrong there . . ."

He felt the doctor's eyes fixed upon him, and, as if merely to be polite, returned the look, but with a feeling of justifiable evasiveness.

"Now, young man, tell me—do you feel all right?"

"Yes, sir, quite all right."

"No headaches? no dizziness?"

"No, I don't think so."

"Let me see. Let's get a book, if you don't mind—yes, thank you, that will do splendidly—and now, Paul, if you'll just read it, holding it as you would normally hold it—"

He took the book and read:

"And another praise have I to tell for this the city our mother, the gift of a great god, a glory of the land most high; the might of horses, the might of young horses, the might of the sea. . . . For thou, son of Cronus, our lord Poseidon, hast throned herein this pride, since in these roads first thou didst show forth the curb that cures the rage of steeds. And the shapely oar, apt to men's hands, hath a wondrous speed on the brine, following the hundred-footed Nereids. . . . O land that art praised above all lands, now is it for thee to make those bright praises seen in deeds."

He stopped, tentatively, and lowered the heavy book.

"No—as I thought—there is certainly no superficial sign of eye-strain."

Silence thronged the room, and he was aware of the focused scrutiny of the three people who confronted him. . . .

"We could have his eyes examined—but I believe it is something else."

"What could it be?" This was his father's voice.

"It's only this curious absent-minded—" This was his mother's voice.

In the presence of the doctor, they both seemed irritatingly apologetic.

"I believe it is something else. Now Paul—I would like very much to ask you a question or two. You will answer them, won't you—you know I'm an old, old friend of yours, eh? That's right! . . ."

His back was thumped twice by the doctor's fat fist—then the doctor was grinning at him with false amiability, while with one fingernail he was scratching the top button of his waistcoat. Beyond the doctor's shoulder was the fire, the fingers of flame making light prestidigitation against the sooty fireback, the soft sound of their random flutter the only sound.

"I would like to know—is there anything that worries you?"

The doctor was again smiling, his eyelids low against the little black pupils, in each of which was a tiny white bead of light. Why answer him? why answer him at all? "At whatever pain to others"—but it was all a nuisance, this necessity for resistance, this necessity for attention: it was as if one had been stood up on a brilliantly lighted stage, under a great round blaze of spotlight; as if one were merely a trained seal, or a performing dog, or a fish, dipped out of an aquarium and held up by the tail. It would serve them right if he were merely to bark or growl. And meanwhile, to miss these last few precious hours, these hours of which every minute was more beautiful than the last, more menacing—? He still looked, as if from a great distance, at the beads of light in the doctor's eyes, at the fixed false smile, and then, beyond, once more at his mother's slippers, his father's slippers, the soft flutter of the fire. Even here, even amongst these hostile presences, and in this arranged light, he could see the snow, he could hear it—it was in the corners of the room, where the shadow was deepest, under the sofa, behind the half-opened door which led to the dining room. It was gentler here, softer, its seethe the quietest of whispers, as if, in deference to a drawing room, it had quite deliberately put on its "manners"; it kept itself out of sight, obliterated itself, but distinctly with an air of saying, "Ah, but just wait! Wait till we are alone together! Then I will begin to tell you something new! Something white! something cold! something sleepy! something of cease, and peace, and the long bright curve of space! Tell them to go away. Banish them. Refuse to speak. Leave them, go upstairs to your room, turn out the light and get into bed—I will go with you, I will be waiting for you, I will tell you a better story than Little Kay of the Skates, or The Snow Ghost— I will surround your bed, I will close the windows, pile a deep drift against the door, so that none will ever again be able to enter. Speak to them! . . ." It seemed as if the little hissing voice came from a slow white spiral of falling flakes in the corner by the front window—but he could not be sure. He felt himself smiling, then, and said to the doctor, but without looking at him, looking beyond him still—

"Oh, no, I think not—"

"But are you sure, my boy?"

His father's voice came softly and coldly then—the familiar voice of silken warning. . . .

"You needn't answer at once, Paul—remember we're trying to help you—think it over and be quite sure, won't you?"

He felt himself smiling again, at the notion of being quite sure. What a joke! As if he weren't so sure that reassurance was no longer necessary, and all this cross-examination a ridiculous farce, a grotesque parody! What could they know about it? These gross intelligences, these humdrum minds so bound to the usual, the ordinary? Impossible to tell them about it! Why, even now, even now, with the proof so abundant, so formidable, so imminent, so appallingly present here in this very room, could they believe it?—could even his mother believe it? No—it was only too plain that if anything were said about it, the merest hint given, they would be incredulous—they would laugh—they would say "Absurd!" think things about him which weren't true. . . .

"Why no, I'm not worried—why should I be?"

He looked then straight at the doctor's low-lidded eyes, looked from one of them to the other, from one bead of light to the other, and gave a little laugh.

The doctor seemed to be disconcerted by this. He drew back in his chair, resting a fat white hand on either knee. The smile faded slowly from his face.

"Well, Paul!" he said, and paused gravely, "I'm afraid you don't take this quite seriously enough. I think you perhaps don't quite realize— don't quite realize—" He took a deep quick breath, and turned, as if helplessly, at a loss for words, to the others. But Mother and Father were both silent—no help was forthcoming.

"You must surely know, be aware, that you have not been quite yourself, of late? don't you know that? . . ."

It was amusing to watch the doctor's renewed attempt at a smile, a queer disorganized look, as of confidential embarrassment.

"I feel all right, sir," he said, and again gave the little laugh.

"And we're trying to help you." The doctor's tone sharpened.

"Yes sir, I know. But why? I'm all right. I'm just *thinking,* that's all."

His mother made a quick movement forward, resting a hand on the back of the doctor's chair.

"Thinking?" she said. "But my dear, about what?"

This was a direct challenge—and would have to be directly met. But before he met it, he looked again into the corner by the door, as if for reassurance. He smiled again at what he saw, at what he heard. The little spiral was still there, still softly whirling, like the ghost of a white kitten chasing the ghost of a white tail, and making as it did so the faintest of whispers. It was all right! If only he could remain firm, everything was going to be all right.

"Oh, about anything, about nothing—*you* know the way you do!"

"You mean—day-dreaming?"

"Oh, no—thinking!"

"But thinking about *what?*"

"Anything."

. He laughed a third time—but this time, happening to glance upward towards his mother's face, he was appalled at the effect his laughter seemed to have upon her. Her mouth had opened in an expression of horror. . . . This was too bad! Unfortunate! He had known it would cause pain, of course—but he hadn't expected it to be quite as bad as this. Perhaps—perhaps if he just gave them a tiny gleaming hint—?

"About the snow," he said.

"What on earth!" This was his father's voice. The brown slippers came a step nearer on the hearth rug.

"But my dear, what do you mean?" This was his mother's voice.

The doctor merely stared.

"Just *snow,* that's all. I like to think about it."

"Tell us about it, my boy."

"But that's all it is. There's nothing to tell. *You* know what snow is?"

This he said almost angrily, for he felt they were trying to corner him. He turned sideways so as no longer to face the doctor, and the better to see the inch of blackness between the window-sill and the lowered curtain—the cold inch of beckoning and delicious night. At once he felt better, more assured.

"Mother—can I go to bed, now, please? I've got a headache."

"But I thought you said—"

"It's just come. It's all these questions—! Can I, Mother?"

"You can go as soon as the doctor has finished."

"Don't you think this thing ought to be gone into thoroughly, and *now?*" This was Father's voice. The brown slippers again came a step nearer, the voice was the well-known "punishment" voice, resonant and cruel.

"Oh, what's the use, Norman—"

Quite suddenly, everyone was silent. And without precisely facing them, nevertheless he was aware that all three of them were watching him with an extraordinary intensity—staring hard at him—as if he had done something monstrous, or was himself some kind of monster. He could hear the soft irregular flutter of the flame; the cluck-click-cluck-click of the clock; far and faint, two sudden spurts of laughter from the kitchen, as quickly cut off as begun; a murmur of water in the pipes; and then, the silence seemed to deepen, to spread out, to become worldlong and worldwide, to become timeless and shapeless, and to center inevitably and rightly, with a slow and sleepy but enormous concentration of all power, on the beginning of a new sound. What this new sound was going to be, he knew perfectly well. It might begin with a hiss, but it would end with a roar—there was no time to lose— he must escape. It mustn't happen here—

Without another word, he turned and ran up the stairs.

IV

Not a moment too soon. The darkness was coming in long white waves. A prolonged sibilance filled the night—a great seamless seethe of wild influence went abruptly across it—a cold low humming shook the windows. He shut the door and flung off his clothes in the dark. The bare black floor was like a little raft tossed in waves of snow, almost overwhelmed, washed under whitely, up again, smothered in curled billows of feather. The snow was laughing: it spoke from all sides at once: it pressed closer to him as he ran and jumped exulting into his bed.

"Listen to us!" it said. "Listen. We have come to tell you the story we told you about. You remember? Lie down. Shut your eyes, now— you will no longer see much—in this white darkness who could see, or want to see? We will take the place of everything. . . . Listen—"

A beautiful varying dance of snow began at the front of the room, came forward and then retreated, flattened out toward the floor, then rose fountain-like to the ceiling, swayed, recruited itself from a new stream of flakes which poured laughing in through the humming window, advanced again, lifted long white arms. It said peace, it said remoteness, it said cold—it said—

But then a gash of horrible light fell brutally across the room from the opening door—the snow drew back hissing—something alien had come into the room—something hostile. This thing rushed at him, clutched at him, shook him—and he was not merely horrified, he was filled with such a loathing as he had never known. What was this? this cruel disturbance? this act of anger and hate? It was as if he had to reach up a hand toward another world for any understanding of it— an effort of which he was only barely capable. But of that other world he still remembered just enough to know the exorcising words. They tore themselves from his other life suddenly—

"Mother! Mother! Go away! I hate you!"

And with that effort, everything was solved, everything became all right: the seamless hiss advanced once more, the long white wavering lines rose and fell like enormous whispering sea-waves, the whisper becoming louder, the laughter more numerous.

"Listen!" it said. "We'll tell you the last, the most beautiful and secret story—shut your eyes—it is a very small story—a story that gets smaller and smaller—it comes inward instead of opening like a flower—it is a flower becoming a seed—a little cold seed—do you hear? we are leaning closer to you—"

The hiss was now becoming a roar—the whole world was a vast moving screen of snow—but even now it said peace, it said remoteness, it said cold, it said sleep.

Indian Camp

ERNEST HEMINGWAY

At the lake shore there was another rowboat drawn up. The two Indians stood waiting.

Nick and his father got in the stern of the boat and the Indians shoved it off and one of them got in to row. Uncle George sat in the stern of the camp rowboat. The young Indian shoved the camp boat off and got in to row Uncle George.

The two boats started off in the dark. Nick heard the oar-locks of the other boat quite a way ahead of them in the mist. The Indians rowed with quick choppy strokes. Nick lay back with his father's arm around him. It was cold on the water. The Indian who was rowing them was working very hard, but the other boat moved further ahead in the mist all the time.

"Where are we going, Dad?" Nick asked.

"Over to the Indian camp. There is an Indian lady very sick."

"Oh," said Nick.

Across the bay they found the other boat beached. Uncle George was smoking a cigar in the dark. The young Indian pulled the boat way up the beach. Uncle George gave both the Indians cigars.

They walked up from the beach through a meadow that was soaking wet with dew, following the young Indian who carried a lantern. Then they went into the woods and followed a trail that led to the logging road that ran back into the hills. It was much lighter on the logging road as the timber was cut away on both sides. The young Indian stopped and blew out his lantern and they all walked on along the road.

They came around a bend and a dog came out barking. Ahead were the lights of the shanties where the Indian bark-peelers lived. More dogs rushed out at them. The two Indians sent them back to the shanties. In the shanty nearest the road there was a light in the window. An old woman stood in the doorway holding a lamp.

Inside on a wooden bunk lay a young Indian woman. She had been trying to have her baby for two days. All the old women in the camp had been helping her. The men had moved off up the road to sit in the dark and smoke out of range of the noise she made. She screamed just as Nick and the two Indians followed his father and Uncle George into the shanty. She lay in the lower bunk, very big under a quilt. Her head was turned to one side. In the upper bunk was her husband. He had cut his foot very badly with an ax three days before. He was smoking a pipe. The room smelled very bad.

Nick's father ordered some water to be put on the stove, and while it was heating he spoke to Nick.

"This lady is going to have a baby, Nick," he said.

"I know," said Nick.

"You don't know," said his father. "Listen to me. What she is going through is called being in labor. The baby wants to be born and she wants it to be born. All her muscles are trying to get the baby born. That is what is happening when she screams."

"I see," Nick said.

Just then the woman cried out.

"Oh, Daddy, can't you give her something to make her stop screaming?" asked Nick.

"No. I haven't any anæsthetic," his father said. "But her screams are not important. I don't hear them because they are not important."

The husband in the upper bunk rolled over against the wall.

The woman in the kitchen motioned to the doctor that the water was hot. Nick's father went into the kitchen and poured about half of the water out of the big kettle into a basin. Into the water left in the kettle he put several things he unwrapped from a handkerchief.

"Those must boil," he said, and began to scrub his hands in the basin of hot water with a cake of soap he had brought from the camp. Nick watched his father's hands scrubbing each other with the soap. While his father washed his hands very carefully and thoroughly, he talked.

"You see, Nick, babies are supposed to be born head first but sometimes they're not. When they're not they make a lot of trouble for everybody. Maybe I'll have to operate on this lady. We'll know in a little while."

When he was satisfied with his hands he went in and went to work.

"Pull back that quilt, will you, George?" he said. "I'd rather not touch it."

Later when he started to operate Uncle George and three Indian men held the woman still. She bit Uncle George on the arm and Uncle George said, "Damn squaw bitch!" and the young Indian who had rowed Uncle George over laughed at him. Nick held the basin for his father. It all took a long time.

His father picked the baby up and slapped it to make it breathe and handed it to the old woman.

"See, it's a boy, Nick," he said. "How do you like being an interne?"

Nick said, "All right." He was looking away so as not to see what his father was doing.

"There. That gets it," said his father and put something into the basin.

Nick didn't look at it.

"Now," his father said, "there's some stitches to put in. You can watch this or not, Nick, just as you like. I'm going to sew up the incision I made."

Nick did not watch. His curiosity has been gone for a long time.

His father finished and stood up. Uncle George and the three Indian men stood up. Nick put the basin out in the kitchen.

Uncle George looked at his arm. The young Indian smiled reminiscently.

"I'll put some peroxide on that, George," the doctor said.

He bent over the Indian woman. She was quiet now and her eyes were closed. She looked very pale. She did not know what had become of the baby or anything.

"I'll be back in the morning," the doctor said, standing up. "The nurse should be here from St. Ignace by noon and she'll bring everything we need."

He was feeling exalted and talkative as football players are in the dressing room after a game.

"That's one for the medical journal, George," he said. "Doing a Cæsarean with a jack-knife and sewing it up with nine-foot, tapered gut leaders."

Uncle George was standing against the wall, looking at his arm.

"Oh, you're a great man, all right," he said.

"Ought to have a look at the proud father. They're usually the worst sufferers in these little affairs," the doctor said. "I must say he took it all pretty quietly."

He pulled back the blanket from the Indian's head. His hand came away wet. He mounted on the edge of the lower bunk with the lamp in one hand and looked in. The Indian lay with his face toward the wall. His throat had been cut from ear to ear. The blood had flowed down into a pool where his body sagged the bunk. His head rested on his left arm. The open razor lay, edge up, in the blankets.

"Take Nick out of the shanty, George," the doctor said.

There was no need of that. Nick, standing in the door of the kitchen, had a good view of the upper bunk when his father, the lamp in one hand, tipped the Indian's head back.

It was just beginning to be daylight when they walked along the logging road back toward the lake.

"I'm terribly sorry I brought you along, Nickie," said his father, all his post-operative exhilaration gone. "It was an awful mess to put you through."

"Do ladies always have such a hard time having babies?" Nick asked.

"No, that was very, very exceptional."

"Why did he kill himself, Daddy?"

"I don't know, Nick. He couldn't stand things, I guess."

"Do many men kill themselves, Daddy?"

"Not very many, Nick."

"Do many women?"

"Hardly ever."

"Don't they ever?"

"Oh, yes. They do sometimes."

"Daddy?"

"Yes."

"Where did Uncle George go?"

"He'll turn up all right."

"Is dying hard, Daddy?"

"No, I think it's pretty easy, Nick, It all depends."

They were seated in the boat, Nick in the stern, his father rowing. The sun was coming up over the hills. A bass jumped, making a circle in the water. Nick trailed his hand in the water. It felt warm in the sharp chill of the morning.

In the early morning on the lake sitting in the stern of the boat with his father rowing, he felt quite sure that he would never die.

Missis Flinders

TESS SLESINGER

"Home you go!" Miss Kane, nodding, in her white nurse's dress, stood for a moment—she would catch a breath of air—in the hospital door: "and thank you again for the stockings, you needn't have bothered"— drew a sharp breath and turning, dismissed Missis Flinders from the hospital, smiling, dismissed her forever from her mind.

So Margaret Flinders stood next to her basket of fruit on the hospital steps; both of them waiting, a little shame-faced in the sudden sunshine, and in no hurry to leave the hospital—no hurry at all. It would be nicer to be alone, Margaret thought, glancing at the basket of fruit which stood respectable and a little silly on the stone step (the candy-bright apples were blushing caricatures of Jean; Jean's explanation that he was a good boy: Jean's comfort, not hers). Flowers she could have left behind (for the nurses, in the room across the hall where they made tea at night); books she could have slipped into her suitcase; but fruit— Jean's gift, Jean's guilt, man's tribute to the Missis in the hospital—must be eaten; a half-eaten basket of fruit (she had tried to leave it: Missis Butter won't you . . . Missis Wiggam wouldn't you like. . . . But Missis Butter had aplenty of her own thank you, and Missis Wiggam said she couldn't hold acids after a baby)—a half-eaten basket of fruit, in times like these, cannot be left to rot.

Down the street Jean was running, running, after a taxi. He was going after the taxi for her; it was for her sake he ran; yet this minute that his back was turned he stole for his relief and spent in running away, his

186

buttocks crying guilt. And don't hurry, don't hurry, she said to them; I too am better off alone.

The street stretched in a long white line very finally away from the hospital, the hospital where Margaret Flinders (called there so solemnly Missis) had been lucky enough to spend only three nights. It would be four days before Missis Wiggam would be going home to Mister Wiggam with a baby; and ten possibly—the doctors were uncertain, Miss Kane prevaricated—before Missis Butter would be going home to Mister Butter without one. Zigzagging the street went the children; their cries and the sudden grinding of their skates she had listened to upstairs beside Missis Butter for three days. Some such child had she been—for the styles in children had not changed—a lean child gliding solemnly on skates and grinding them viciously at the nervous feet of grownups. Smile at these children she would not or could not; yet she felt on her face that smile fixed, painful and frozen that she had put there, on waking from ether three days back, to greet Jean. The smile spoke to the retreating buttocks of Jean: I don't need you; the smile spoke formally to life: thanks, I'm not having any. Not so the child putting the heels of his skates together Charlie Chaplin-wise and describing a scornful circle on the widest part of the sidewalk. Not so a certain little girl (twenty years back) skating past the wheels of autos, pursuing life in the form of a ball so red! so gay! better death than to turn one's back and smile over one's shoulder at life!

Upstairs Missis Butter must still be writhing with her poor caked breasts. The bed that had been hers beside Missis Butter's was empty now; Miss Kane would be stripping it and Joe would come in bringing fresh sheets. Whom would they put in beside Missis Butter, to whom would she moan and boast all night about the milk in her breasts that was turning, she said, into cheese?

Now Jean was coming back, jogging sheepishly on the running-board of a taxi, he had run away to the end of his rope and now was returning penitent, his eyes dog-like searching her out where she stood on the hospital steps (did they rest with complacence on the basket of fruit, his gift?), pleading with her, Didn't I get the taxi fast? like an anxious little boy. She stood with that smile on her face that hurt like too much ice-cream. Smile and smile; for she felt like a fool, she had walked open-eyed smiling into the trap (*Don't wriggle, Missis, I might injure you for life, Miss Kane had said cheerfully*) and felt the spring only when it was too late, when she waked from ether and knew like the thrust of a knife what she had ignored before. *Whatever did you do it for, Missis Flinders, Missis Butter was always saying; if there's nothing the matter with your insides—doesn't your husband . . . and Won't you have some fruit, Missis Butter, her calm reply: meaning, My husband gave me this fruit so what right have you to doubt that my husband. . . .* Her husband who now stumbled up the steps to meet her; his eyes he had sent ahead, but something in him wanted not to come, tripped his foot as he hurried up the steps.

"Take my arm, Margaret," he said. "Walk slowly," he said. The bitter pill of taking help, of feeling weakly grateful stuck in her throat. Jean's face behind his glasses was tense like the face of an amateur actor in the role of a strike-leader. That he was inadequate for the part he seemed to know. And if he felt shame, shame in his own eyes, she could forgive • him; but if it was only guilt felt man-like in her presence, a guilt which he could drop off like a damp shirt, if he was putting it all off on her for being a woman! "The fruit, Jean!" she said, "you've forgotten the fruit." "The fruit can wait," he said, magnanimously.

He handed her into the taxi as though she were a package marked glass—something, she thought, not merely troublesomely womanly, but ladylike. "Put your legs up on the seat," he said. "I don't want to, Jean." *Good-bye Missis Butter* Put your legs up on the seat. I don't want to—*better luck next time Missis Butter* Put your legs *I can't make out our window, Missis Butter* Put your "All right, it will be nice and uncomfortable." (She put her legs up on the seat.) *Good-bye Missis But. . . .* "Nothing I say is right," he said. "It's good with the legs up," she said brightly.

Then he was up the steps agile and sure after the fruit. And down again, the basket swinging with affected carelessness, arming him, till he relinquished it modestly to her outstretched hands. Then he seated himself on the little seat, the better to watch his woman and his woman's fruit; and screwing his head round on his neck said irritably to the man who had been all his life on the wrong side of the glass pane, "Charles Street!"

"Hadn't you better ask him to please drive slowly?" Margaret said.

"I was just going to," he said bitterly.

"And drive slowly," he shouted over his shoulder.

The driver's name was Carl C. Strite. She could see Carl Strite glance cannily back at the hospital; Greenway Maternity Home; pull his lever with extreme delicacy as though he were stroking the neck of a horse. There was a small roar—and the hospital glided backward: its windows ran together like the windows of a moving train; a spurt—watch out for those children on skates!—and the car was fairly started down the street.

Good-bye Missis Butter I hope you get a nice roommate in my place, I hope you won't find that Mister B let the ice-pan flow over again— and give my love to the babies when Miss Kane stops them in the door for you to wave at—good-bye Missis Butter, really good-bye.

Carl Strite (was he thinking maybe of his mother, an immigrant German woman she would have been, come over with a shawl on her head and worked herself to skin and bone so the kids could go to school and turn out good Americans—and what had it come to, here he was a taxi driver, and what taxi drivers didn't know! what in the course of their lackeys' lives they didn't put up with, fall in with! well, there was one decent thing left in Carl Strite, he knew how to carry a woman home from a maternity hospital) drove softly along the curb . . . and the eyes of his honest puzzled gangster's snout photographed as 'Your Driver' looked dimmed as though the glory of woman were too much for them, in a moment the weak cruel baby's mouth might blubber. Awful to lean forward and tell Mr. Strite he was laboring under a mistake. *Missis Wiggam's freckled face when she heard that Missis Butter's roommate . . . maybe Missis Butter's baby had been born dead but any-*

way she had had a baby . . . whatever did you do it for Missis Flind. . . .

"Well, patient," Jean began, tentative, jocular (bored? perturbed? behind his glasses?).

"How does it feel, Tidbit?" he said in a new, small voice.

Hurt and hurt this man, a feeling told her. He is a man, he could have made you a woman. "What's a D and C between friends?" she said. "Nobody at the hospital gave a damn about my little illegality."

"Well, but I do," he protested like a short man trying to be tall.

She turned on her smile; the bright silly smile that was eating up her face.

Missis Butter would be alone now with no one to boast to about her pains except Joe who cleaned the corridors and emptied bedpans—and thought Missis Butter was better than an angel because although she had incredible golden hair she could wisecrack like any brunette. Later in the day the eight-day mothers wobbling down the corridors for their pre-nursing constitutional would look in and talk to her; for wasn't Missis Butter their symbol and their pride, the one who had given up her baby that they might have theirs (for a little superstition is inevitable in new mothers, and it was generally felt that there must be one dead baby in a week's batch at any decent hospital) for whom they demanded homage from their visiting husbands? for whose health they asked the nurses each morning second only to asking for their own babies? That roommate of yours was a funny one, Missis Wiggam would say. Missis Wiggam was the woman who said big breasts weren't any good: here she was with a seven-pound baby and not a drop for it (here she would open the negligee Mister Wiggam had given her not to shame them before the nurses, and poke contemptuously at the floppy parts of herself within) while there was Missis Butter with no baby but a dead baby and her small breasts caking because there was so much milk in them for nothing but a. . . . Yes, that Missis Flinders was sure a funny one, Missis Butter would agree.

"Funny ones," she and Jean, riding home with numb faces and a basket of fruit between them—past a park, past a museum, past elevated pillars—intellectuals they were, bastards, changelings . . . giving up a baby for books they might never write, giving up a baby for economic freedom which meant that two of them would work in offices instead of one of them only, giving up a baby for intellectual freedom which meant that they smoked their cigarettes bitterly and looked out of the windows of a taxi onto streets and people and stores and hated them all. "We'd go soft," Jean had said; "we'd go bourgeois." Yes, with diapers drying on the radiators, bottles wrapped in flannel, the grocery man getting to know one too well—yes, they would go soft, they might slump and start liking people, they might weaken and forgive stupidity, they might yawn and forget to hate. "Funny ones," class-straddlers, intellectuals, tight-rope-walking somewhere in the middle (how long could they hang on without falling to one side or the other? one more war? one more depression?); intellectuals with habits generated from the right and tastes inclined to the left. Afraid to perpetuate themselves, were they? Afraid of anything that might loom so large in their personal lives as to outweigh other considerations? Afraid, maybe, of a personal life?

"Oh give me another cigarette," she said.

And still the taxi, with its burden of intellectuals and their inarticulate fruit-basket, its motherly, gangsterly, inarticulate driver, its license plates and its photographs all so very official, jogged on; past Harlem now; past fire escapes loaded with flower pots and flapping clothes; dingy windows opening to the soot-laden air blown in by the elevated roaring down its tracks. Past Harlem and through 125th Street: stores and wise-cracks, Painless Dentists, cheap florists; Eighth Avenue, boarded and plastered, concealing the subway that was reaching its laborious birth beneath. But Eighth Avenue was too jouncy for Mr. Strite's precious burden of womanhood (who was reaching passionately for a cigarette); he cut through the park, and they drove past quiet walks on which the sun had brought out babies as the fall rains give birth to worms.

"But ought you to smoke so much, so soon after—so soon?" Jean said, not liking to say so soon after what. His hand held the cigarettes out to her, back from her.

"They do say smoking's bad for childbirth," she said calmly, and with her finger tips drew a cigarette from his reluctant hand.

And tapping down the tobacco on the handle of the fruit-basket she said, "But we've got the joke on them there, we have." (Hurt and hurt this man, her feeling told her; he is a man and could have made you a woman.)

"Pretty nice girl, you are," Jean said, striking and striking at the box with his match.

"This damn taxi's shaking you too much," he said suddenly, bitter and contrite.

But Mr. Strite was driving like an angel. He handled his car as though it were a baby carriage. Did he think maybe it had turned out with her the way it had with Missis Butter? I could have stood it better, Missis Butter said, if they hadn't told me it was a boy. And me with my fourth little girl, Missis Wiggam had groaned (but proudly, proudly); why I didn't even want to see it when they told me. But Missis Butter stood it very well, and so did Missis Wiggam. They were a couple of good bitches; and what if Missis Butter had produced nothing but a dead baby this year, and what if Missis Wiggam would bring nothing to Mister Wiggam but a fourth little girl this year—why there was next year and the year after, there was the certain little world from grocery store to kitchen, there were still Mister Butter and Mister Wiggam who were both (Missis Wiggam and Missis Butter vied with each other) just *crazy* about babies. Well, Mister Flinders is different, she had lain there thinking (he cares as much for his unborn books as I for my unborn babies); and wished she could have the firm assurance they had in "husbands," coming as they did year after year away from them for a couple of weeks, just long enough to bear them babies either dead ones or girl ones . . . good bitches they were: there was something lustful beside smug in their pride in being "Missis." Let Missis Flinders so much as let out a groan because a sudden pain grew too big for her groins, let her so much as murmur because the sheets were hot beneath her—and Missis Butter and Missis Wiggam in the security of their maternity-sorority exchanged glances of amusement: she don't know what pain is, look at what's talking about PAIN. . . .

"Mr. Strite flatters us," she whispered, her eyes smiling straight and hard into Jean's. (Hurt and hurt. . . .)

"And why does that give you so much pleasure?" He dragged the words as though he were pounding them out with two fingers on the typewriter.

The name without the pain—she thought to say; and did not say. All at once she lost her desire to punish him; she no more wanted to "hurt this man" for he was no more man than she was woman. She would not do him the honor of hurting him. She must reduce him as she felt herself reduced. She must cut out from him what made him a man, as she had let be cut out from her what would have made her a woman. He was no man: he was a dried-up intellectual rabbit; he was sterile; empty and hollow as she was.

Missis Butter lying up on her pillow would count over to Missis Wiggam the fine points of her tragedy: how she had waited two days to be delivered of a dead baby; how it wouldn't have been so bad if the doctor hadn't said it was a beautiful baby with platinum-blond hair exactly like hers (and hers bleached unbelievably, but never mind, Missis Wiggam had come to believe in it like Joe and Mister Butter, another day and Missis Flinders herself, intellectual sceptic though she was, might have been convinced); and how they would pay the last instalment on— what a baby carriage, Missis Wiggam, you'd never believe me!—and sell it second-hand for half its worth. I know when I was caught with my first, Missis Wiggam would take up the story her mouth had been open for. And that Missis Flinders was sure a funny one. . . .

But I am not such a funny one, Margaret wanted, beneath her bright and silly smile, behind her cloud of cigarette smoke (for Jean had given in; the whole package sat gloomily on Margaret's lap) to say to them; even though in my "crowd" the girls keep the names they were born with, even though we sleep for a little variety with one another's husbands, even though I forget as often as Jean—Mister Flinders to you— to empty the pan under the icebox. Still I too have known my breasts to swell and harden, I too have been unable to sleep on them for their tenderness to weight and touch, I too have known what it is to undress slowly and imagine myself growing night to night. . . . I knew this for two months, my dear Missis Wiggam; I had this strange joy for two months, my dear Missis Butter. But there was a night last week, my good ladies, which Mister Flinders and I spent in talk—and damn fine talk, if you want to know, talk of which I am proud, and talk not one word of which you with your grocery-and-baby minds, could have understood; in a regime like this, Jean said, it is a terrible thing to have a baby—it means the end of independent thought and the turning of everything into a scheme for making money; and there must be institutions such as there are in Russia, I said, for taking care of the babies and their mothers; why in a time like this, we both said, to have a baby would be suicide—good-bye to our plans, good-bye to our working out of schemes for each other and the world—our courage would die, our hopes concentrate on the sordid business of keeping three people alive, one of whom would be a burden and an expense for twenty years. . . . And then we grew drunk for a minute making up the silliest names that we could call it if we had it—and what a tough little thing it is, I said, look, look, how it hangs on in spite of its loving mother jumping off tables and broiling herself in hot water . . . until Jean, frightened at himself, washed his hands of it: we mustn't waste any more time, the sooner these things are done the better. And I, as though the ether cap had already been clapped to my nose, agreed off-handedly. That night I did not pass my hands contentedly over my hard breasts; that night I gave no thought to the nipples grown suddenly brown and competent; I packed, instead, my suitcase: I filled it with all the white clothes I own. Why are you taking white clothes to the hospital, Jean said to me. I laughed. Why did I? White, for a bride; white, for a corpse; white, for a woman who refuses to be a woman. . . .

"Are you all right, Margaret?" (They were out now, safely out on Fifth Avenue, driving placidly past the Plaza where ancient coachmen dozed on the high seats of the last hansoms left in New York).

"Yes, dear," she said mechanically, and forgot to turn on her smile. Pity for him sitting there in stolid inadequacy filled her. He was a man, and he could have made her a woman. She was a woman, and could have made him a man. He was not a man; she was not a woman. In each of them the life-stream flowed to a dead end.

And all this time that the blood, which Missis Wiggam and Missis Butter stored up preciously in themselves every year to make a baby for their husbands, was flowing freely and wastefully out of Missis Flinders—toward what? would it pile up some day and make a brook? would it congeal within her and make a crazy woman?—all this time Mr. Strite, remembering, with his pudgy face, his mother, drove his taxi softly along the curb; no weaving in and out of traffic for Mr. Strite, no spurting at the corners and cheating the side-street traffic, no fine heedless rounding of rival cars for Mr. Strite; he kept his car going at a slow and steady roll, its nose poked blunt ahead, following the straight and narrow—Mr. Strite knew what it was to carry a woman home from the hospital.

But what in their past had warranted this? She could remember a small girl going from dolls to books, from books with colored pictures to books with frequent conversations; from such books to the books at last that one borrowed from libraries, books built up of solemn text from which you took notes; books which were gray to begin with, but which opened out to your eyes subtle layers of gently shaded colors. (And where in these texts did it say that one should turn one's back on life? Had the coolness of the stone library at college made one afraid? Had the ivy nodding in the open dormitory windows taught one too much to curl and squat looking out?) And Jean? What book, what professor, what strange idea, had taught him to hunch his shoulders and stay indoors, had taught him to hide behind his glasses? Whence the fear that made him put, in cold block letters, implacably above his desk the sign announcing him "Not at Home" to life?

Missis Flinders, my husband scaled the hospital wall at four o'clock in the morning, frantic I tell you. . . . But I just don't understand you,

To be driving like this at midday through New York; with Jean do you understand her, Missis Wiggam, would your husband. . . ? Why goodness, no, Mister Wiggam would sooner. . . ! And there he was, and they asked him, Shall we try an operation, Mister Butter? scaled the wall . . . shall we try an operation? (Well, you see, we are both writers, my husband and I . . . well, not exactly *stories*) if there's any risk to Shirley, he said, there mustn't be any risk to Shirley . . . Missis Wiggam's petulant, childish face, with its sly contentment veiled by what she must have thought a grown-up expression: Mister Wiggam bought me this negligee new, surprised me with it, you know—and generally a saving man, Mister Wiggam, not tight, but with three children—four now! Hetty, he says, I'm not going to have you disgracing us at the hospital this year, he says. Why the nurses will all remember that flannel thing you had Mabel and Suzy and Antoinette in, they'll talk about us behind our backs. (It wasn't that I couldn't make the flannel do again, Missis Butter, it wasn't that at all.) But he says, Hetty, you'll just have a new one this year, he says, and maybe it'll bring us luck, he says—you know, he was thinking maybe this time we'd have a boy . . . Well, I just have to laugh at you, Missis Flinders, not *wanting* one, why my sister went to doctors for five years and spent her good money just *trying* to have one. . . . Well, poor Mister Wiggam, so the negligee didn't work, I brought him another little girl—but he didn't say boo to me, though I could see he was disappointed. Hetty, he says, we'll just have another try! Oh I thought I'd die, with Miss Kane standing right there you know (though they do say these nurses . . .); but that's Mister Wiggam all over; he wouldn't stop a joke for a policeman. . . . No, I just can't get over you, Missis Flinders, if Gawd was willing to let you have a baby—and there really isn't anything wrong with your insides?

Jean's basket of fruit standing on the bed table, trying its level inadequate best, poor pathetic inarticulate intellectual basket of fruit, to comfort, to bloom, to take the place of Jean himself who would come in later with Sam Butter for visiting hour. Jean's too-big basket of fruit standing there, embarrassed. Won't you have a peach, Missis Wiggam (I'm sure they have less acid)? Just try an apple, Missis Butter? Weigh Jean's basket of fruit against Mister Wiggam's negligee for luck, against Mister Butter scaling the wall at four in the morning for the mother of his dead baby. *Please* have a pear, Miss Kane; a banana, Joe? How they spat the seeds from Jean's fruit! How it hurt her when, unknowing,

Missis Butter cut away the brown bruised cheek of Jean's bright-eyed, weeping apple! Jean! they scorn me, these ladies. They laugh at me, dear, almost as though I had no "husband," as though I were a "fallen woman." Jean, would you buy me a new negligee if I bore you three daughters? Jean, would you scale the wall if I bore you a dead baby? . . . Jean, I have an inferiority complex because I am an intellectual. . . . But a peach, Missis Wiggam! can't I possibly tempt you?

To be driving like this at mid-day through New York; with Jean bobbing like an empty ghost (for she could see he was unhappy, as miserable as she, he too had had an abortion) on the side-seat; with a taxi driver, solicitous, respectful to an ideal, in front; was this the logical end of that little girl she remembered, of that girl swinging hatless across a campus as though that campus were the top of the earth? And was this all they could give birth to, she and Jean, who had closed up their books one day and kissed each other on the lips and decided to marry?

And now Mr. Strite, with his hand out, was making a gentle right-hand turn. Back to Fifth Avenue they would go, gently rolling, in Mr. Strite's considerate charge. Down Fourteenth Street they would go, past the stores unlike any stores in the world; packed to the windows with imitation gold and imitation embroidery, with imitation men and women coming to stand in the doorways and beckon with imitation smiles; while on the sidewalks streamed the people unlike any other people in the world, drawn from every country, from every stratum, intellectual and social—carrying babies (the real thing, with pinched anaemic faces) and parcels (imitation finery priced low in the glittering stores). There goes a woman, with a flat, fat face, will produce five others just like herself, to dine off one-fifth the inadequate quantity her Mister earns today. These are the people not afraid to perpetuate themselves (forbidden to stop, indeed) and they will go on and on (humming "The best things in life are free") until the bottom of the world is filled with them; and suddenly there will be enough of them to combine their cock-eyed notions and take over the world to suit themselves. While I, while I and my Jean, with our good clear heads will one day go spinning out of the world and leave nothing behind . . . only diplomas crumbling in the museums. . . .

The mad street ended with Fifth Avenue; was left behind.

They were nearing home. Mr. Strite, who had never seen them before (who would never again, in all likelihood, for his territory was far uptown) was seeing them politely to the door. As they came near home all of Margaret's fear and pain gathered in a knot in her stomach. There would be nothing new in their house; there was nothing to expect; yet she wanted to find something there that she knew she could not find, and surely the house (once so gay, with copies of old paintings, with books which lined the walls from floor to ceiling, with papers and cushions and typewriters) would be suddenly empty and dead, suddenly, for the first time, a group of rooms unalive as rooms with "For Rent" still pasted on the windows. And Jean? did he know he was coming home to a place which had suffered no change, but which would be different forever afterward? Jean had taken off his glasses; passed his hand tiredly across his eyes; was sucking now as though he expected relief, some answer, on the tortoise-shell curve which wound around his ear.

Mr. Strite would not allow his cab to cease motion with a jerk. Mr. Strite allowed his cab to slow down even at the corner (where was the delicatessen that sold the only loose ripe olives in the Village), so they rolled softly past No. 14 (where lived Kilgreen who wrote plays which would never be produced and dropped in at breakfast time for a hair of the dog that bit him the night before); on past the tenement which would eventually be razed to give place to modern three-room apartments with In-a-Dor beds; and then slowly, so slowly that Mr. Strite must surely be an artist as well as man who had had a mother, drew up and slid to a full stop before No. 20, where two people named Mister and Missis Flinders rented themselves a place to hide from life (both life of the Fifth Avenue variety, and life of the common, or Fourteenth Street, variety: in short, life).

So Jean, with his glasses on his nose once more, descended; held out his hand; Mr. Strite held the door open and his face most modestly averted; and Margaret Flinders painfully and carefully swung her legs down again from the seat and alighted, step by step, with care and confusion. The house was before them; it must be entered. Into the house they must go, say farewell to the streets, to Mr. Strite who had guided them through a tour of the city, to life itself; into the house they must go and hide. It was a fact that Mister Flinders (was he reluctant to come home?) had forgotten his key; that Missis Flinders must delve under the white clothes in her suitcase and find hers; that Mr. Strite, not yet satisfied that his charges were safe, sat watchful and waiting in the front of his cab. Then the door gave. Then Jean, bracing it with his foot, held out his hand to Margaret. Then Mr. Strite came rushing up the steps (something had told him his help would be needed again!), rushing up the steps with the basket of fruit hanging on his arm, held out from his body as though what was the likes of him doing holding a woman's basket just home from the hospital. "You've forgot your fruit, Missis!"

Weakly they glared at the fruit come to pursue them; come to follow them up the stairs to their empty rooms; but that was not fair; come, after all, to comfort them. "You must have a peach," Margaret said.

No, Mr. Strite had never cared for peaches; the skin got in his teeth.

"You must have an apple," Margaret said.

Well, no, he must be getting on uptown. A cigarette (he waved it, deprecated the smoke it blew in the lady's face) was good enough for him.

"But a pear, just a pear," Margaret said passionately.

Mr. Straite wavered, standing on one foot. "Maybe he doesn't want any fruit," said Jean harshly.

"Not want any *fruit!*" cried Margaret gayly, indignantly. Not want any fruit?—ridiculous. Not want the fruit my poor Jean bought for his wife in the hospital? Three days I spent in a Maternity Home, and I produced, with the help of my husband, one basket of fruit (tied with ribbon, pink—for boys). Not want any of our fruit? I couldn't bear it, I couldn't bear it. . . .

Mr. Strite leaned over; put out a hand and gingerly selected a pear—

"For luck," he said, managing an excellent American smile. They watched him trot down the steps to his cab, all the time holding his pear as though it were something he would put in a memory book. And still they stayed, because Margaret said foolishly, "Let's see him off"; because she was ashamed, suddenly, before Jean; as though she had cut her hair unbecomingly, as though she had wounded herself in some unsightly way—as though (summing up her thoughts as precisely, as decisively as though it had been done on an adding-machine) she had stripped and revealed herself not as a woman at all, but as a creature who would not be a woman and could not be a man. And then they turned (for there was nothing else to stay for, and on the street and in the sun they were ashamed as though they had been naked)—and went in the door and heard it swing to, pause on its rubbery hinge, and finally click behind them.

The District Doctor

IVAN TURGENIEV

O NE day in autumn on my way back from a remote part of the country I caught cold and fell ill. Fortunately the fever attacked me in the district town at the inn; I sent for the doctor. In half-an-hour the district doctor appeared, a thin, dark-haired man of middle height. He prescribed me the usual sudorific, ordered a mustard-plaster to be put on, very deftly slid a five-ruble note up his sleeve, coughing drily and looking away as he did so, and then was getting up to go home, but somehow fell into talk and remained. I was exhausted with feverishness; I foresaw a sleepless night, and was glad of a little chat with a pleasant companion. Tea was served. My doctor began to converse freely. He was a sensible fellow, and expressed himself with vigour and some humour. Queer things happen in the world: you may live a long while with some people, and be on friendly terms with them, and never once speak openly with them from your soul; with others you have scarcely time to get acquainted, and all at once you are pouring out to him—or he to you—all your secrets, as though you were at confession. I don't know how I gained the confidence of my new friend—anyway, with nothing to lead up to it, he told me a rather curious incident; and here I will report his tale for the information of the indulgent reader. I will try to tell it in the doctor's own words.

"You don't happen to know," he began in a weak and quavering voice (the common result of the use of unmixed Berezov snuff); "you don't happen to know the judge here, Mylov, Pavel Lukich? . . . You don't know him? . . . Well, it's all the same." (He cleared his throat

201

and rubbed his eyes.) "Well, you see, the thing happened, to tell you exactly without mistake, in Lent, at the very time of the thaws. I was sitting at his house—our judge's you know—playing preference. Our judge is a good fellow, and fond of playing preference. Suddenly" (the doctor made frequent use of this word, suddenly) "they tell me, 'There's a servant asking for you.' I say, 'What does he want?' They say, 'He has brought a note—it must be from a patient.' 'Give me the note,' I say. So it is from a patient—well and good—you understand—it's our bread and butter. . . . But this is how it was: a lady, a widow, writes to me; she says, 'My daughter is dying. Come, for God's sake!' she says, 'and the horses have been sent for you.' . . . Well, that's all right. But she was twenty miles from the town, and it was midnight out of doors, and the roads in such a state, my word! And as she was poor herself, one could not expect more than two silver rubles, and even that problematic; and perhaps it might only be a matter of a roll of linen and a sack of oatmeal in payment. However, duty, you know, before everything: a fellow-creature may be dying. I hand over my cards at once to Kalliopin, the member of the provincial commission, and return home. I look; a wretched little trap was standing at the steps, with peasant's horses, fat—too fat—and their coat as shaggy as felt; and the coachman sitting with his cap off out of respect. Well, I think to myself, 'It's clear, my friend, these patients aren't rolling in riches.' . . . You smile; but I tell you, a poor man like me has to take everything into consideration. . . . If the coachman sits like a prince, and doesn't touch his cap, and even sneers at you behind his beard, and flicks his whip—then you may bet on six rubles. But this case, I saw, had a very different air. However, I think there's no help for it; duty before everything. I snatch up the most necessary drugs, and set off. Will you believe it? I only just managed to get there at all. The road was infernal: streams, snow, watercourses, and the dyke had suddenly burst there—that was the worst of it! However, I arrived at last. It was a little thatched house. There was a light in the windows; that meant they expected me. I was met by an old lady, very venerable, in a cap. 'Save her!' she says; 'she is dying.' I say, 'Pray don't distress yourself—Where is the invalid?' 'Come this way.' I see a clean little room, a lamp in the corner; on the bed a girl of twenty, unconscious. She was in a burning heat, and breathing heavily—it was fever. There were two other girls, her sisters, scared and in tears. 'Yesterday,' they tell me, 'she was perfectly well and had a good appetite; this morning she complained of her head, and this evening, suddenly, you see, like this.' I say again: 'Pray don't be uneasy.' It's a doctor's duty, you know—and I went up to her and bled her, told them to put on a mustard-plaster, and prescribed a mixture. Meantime I looked at her; I looked at her, you know—there, by God! I had never seen such a face!—she was a beauty, in a word! I felt quite shaken with pity. Such lovely features; such eyes! . . . But, thank God! she became easier; she fell into a perspiration, seemed to come to her senses, looked round, smiled, and passed her hand over her face. . . . Her sisters bent over her. They ask, 'How are you?' 'All right,' she says, and turns away. I looked at her; she had fallen asleep. 'Well,' I say, 'now the patient should be left alone.' So we all went out on tiptoe; only a maid remained, in case she was wanted. In the parlour there was a samovar standing on the table, and a bottle of rum; in our profession one can't get on without it. They gave me tea; asked me to stop the night. . . . I consented: where could I go, indeed, at that time of night? The old lady kept groaning. 'What is it?' I say; 'she will live; don't worry yourself; you had better take a little rest yourself; it is about two o'clock.' 'But will you send to wake me if anything happens?' 'Yes, yes.' The old lady went away, and the girls too went to their own room; they made up a bed for me in the parlour. Well, I went to bed—but I could not get to sleep, for a wonder; for in reality I was very tired. I could not get my patient out of my head. At last I could not put up with it any longer; I got up suddenly; I think to myself, 'I will go and see how the patient is getting on.' Her bedroom was next to the parlour. Well, I got up, and gently opened the door—how my heart beat! I looked in: the servant was asleep, her mouth wide open, and even snoring, the wretch! but the patient lay with her face towards me, and her arms flung wide apart, poor girl! I went up to her . . . when suddenly she opened her eyes and stared at me! 'Who is it? who is it?' I was in confusion. 'Don't be alarmed, madam,' I say; 'I am the doctor; I have come to see how you feel.' 'You the doctor?' 'Yes, the doctor; your mother sent for me from the town; we have bled you, madam; now pray go to sleep, and in a day or two, please God! we will set you on your feet again.' 'Ah, yes, yes, doctor, don't let me die. . . . please, please.' 'Why do you talk like that? God bless you!' She is in a fever again, I think to myself; I felt her pulse; yes, she was feverish. She looked at me, and then took me by the hand. 'I will tell you why I don't want to die; I will tell you. . . . Now we are alone; and only, please don't you . . . not to any one . . . Listen. . . .' I bent down; she moved her lips quite to my ear; she touched my cheek with her hair—I confess my head went round—and began to whisper. . . . I could make out nothing of it. . . . Ah, she was delirious! . . . She whispered and whispered, but so quickly, and as if it were not in Russian; at last she finished, and shivering dropped her head on the pillow, and threatened me with her finger: 'Remember, doctor, to no one.' I calmed her somehow, gave her something to drink, waked the servant, and went away."

At this point the doctor again took snuff with exasperated energy, and for a moment seemed stupefied by its effects.

"However," he continued, "the next day, contrary to my expectations, the patient was no better. I thought and thought, and suddenly decided to remain there, even though any other patients were expecting me. . . . And you know one can't afford to disregard that; one's practice suffers if one does. But, in the first place, the patient was really in danger; and secondly, to tell the truth, I felt strongly drawn to her. Besides, I liked the whole family. Though they were really badly off, they were singularly, I may say, cultivated people. . . . Their father had been a learned man, an author; he died, of course, in poverty, but he had managed before he died to give his children an excellent education; he left a lot of books too. Either because I looked after the invalid very carefully, or for some other reason; anyway, I can venture to say all the household loved me as if I were one of the family. . . . Meantime the roads were in a worse state than ever; all communications, so to say, were cut off completely; even medicine could with difficulty be got from the town. . . . The sick girl was not getting better. . . . Day after day, and day after day . . . but . . . here. . . ." (The doctor made a brief pause.) "I declare I don't know how to tell you. . . ." (He again took snuff, coughed, and swallowed a little tea.) "I will tell you without beating about the bush. My patient . . . how should I say? . . . Well, she had fallen in love with me . . . or, no, it was not that she was in love . . . however . . . really, how should one say?" (The doctor looked down and grew red.) "No," he went on quickly, "in love, indeed! A man should not over-estimate himself. She was an educated girl, clever and well-read, and I had even forgotten my Latin, one may say, completely. As to appearance" (the doctor looked himself over with a smile) "I am nothing to boast of there either. But God Almighty did not make me a fool; I don't take black for white; I know a thing or two; I could see very clearly, for instance that Aleksandra Andreyevna—that was her name—did not feel love for me, but had a friendly, so to say, inclination—a respect or something for me. Though she herself perhaps mistook this sentiment, anyway this was her attitude; you may form your own judgment of it. But," added the doctor, who had brought out all these disconnected sentences without taking breath, and with obvious embarrassment, "I seem to be wandering rather—you won't understand anything like this . . . There, with your leave, I will relate it all in order."

He drank off a glass of tea, and began in a calmer voiec.

"Well, then. My patient kept getting worse and worse. You are not a doctor, my good sir; you cannot understand what passes in a poor fellow's heart, especially at first, when he begins to suspect that the disease is getting the upper hand of him. What becomes of his belief in himself? You suddenly grow so timid; it's indescribable. You fancy then that you have forgotten everything you knew, and that the patient has no faith in you, and that other people begin to notice how distracted you are, and tell you the symptoms with reluctance; that they are looking at you suspiciously, whispering . . . Ah! it's horrid! There must be a remedy, you think, for this disease, if one could find it. Isn't this it? You try—no, that's not it! You don't allow the medicine the necessary time to do good . . . You clutch at one thing, then at another. Sometimes you take up a book of medical prescriptions—here it is, you think! Sometimes, by Jove, you pick one out by chance, thinking to leave it to fate. . . . But meantime a fellow-creature's dying, and another doctor would have saved him. 'We must have a consultation,' you say; 'I will not take the responsibility on myself.' And what a fool you look at such times! Well, in time you learn to bear it; it's nothing to you. A man has died—but it's not your fault; you treated him by the rules. But what's still more torture to you is to see blind faith in you, and to feel yourself that you are not able to be of use. Well, it was just this blind faith that the whole of Aleksandra Andreyevna's family had in me; they had forgotten to think that their daughter was in danger. I, too, on my side assure them that it's nothing, but meantime my heart sinks into my boots. To add to our troubles, the roads were in such a state that the coachman was gone for whole days together to get medicine. And I never left the patient's room; I could not tear myself away; I tell her amusing stories, you know, and play cards with her. I watch by her side at night. The old mother thanks me with tears in her eyes; but I think to myself, 'I don't deserve your gratitude.' I frankly confess to you—there is no object in concealing it now—I was in love with my patient. And Aleksandra Andreyevna had grown fond of me; she would not sometimes let any one be in her room but me. She began to talk to me, to ask me questions; where I had studied, how I lived, who are my people, whom I go to see. I feel that she ought not to talk; but to forbid her to—to forbid her resolutely, you know—I could not. Sometimes I held my head in my hands, and asked myself, "What are you doing, villain?" . . . And she would take my hand and hold it, give me a long, long look, and turn away, sigh, and say, 'How good you are!' Her hands were so feverish, her eyes so large and languid. . . . 'Yes,' she says, 'you are a good, kind man; you are not like our neighbours. . . . No, you are not like that. . . . Why did I not know you till now!' 'Aleksandra Andreyevna, calm yourself,' I say. . . . 'I feel, believe me, I don't know how I have gained . . . but there, calm yourself. . . . All will be right; you will be well again.' And meanwhile I must tell you," continued the doctor, bending forward and raising his eyebrows, "that they associated very little with the neighbours, because the smaller people were not on their level, and pride hindered them from being friendly with the rich. I tell you, they were an exceptionally cultivated family; so you know it was gratifying for me. She would only take her medicine from my hands ... she would lift herself up, poor girl, with my aid, take it, and gaze at me. ... My heart felt as if it were bursting. And meanwhile she was growing worse and worse, worse and worse, all the time; she will die, I think to myself; she must die. Believe me, I would sooner have gone to the grave myself; and here were her mother and sisters watching me, looking into my eyes ... and their faith in me was wearing away. 'Well? how is she?' 'Oh, all right, all right!' All right, indeed! My mind was failing me. Well, I was sitting one night alone again by my patient. The maid was sitting there too, and snoring away in full swing; I can't find fault with the poor girl, though; she was worn out too. Aleksandra Andreyevna had felt very unwell all the evening; she was very feverish. Until midnight she kept tossing about; at last she seemed to fall asleep; at least, she lay still without stirring. The lamp was burning in the corner before the holy image. I sat there, you know, with my head bent; I even dozed a little. Suddenly it seemed as though some one touched me in the side; I turned round. ... Good God! Aleksandra Andreyevna was gazing with intent eyes at me ... her lips parted, her cheeks seemed burning. 'What is it?' 'Doctor, shall I die?' 'Merciful Heavens!' 'No, doctor, no; please don't tell me I shall live ... don't say so. ... If you knew. ... Listen! for God's sake don't conceal my real position, and her breath came so fast. 'If I can know for certain that I must die ... then I will tell you all—all!' 'Aleksandra Andreyevna, I beg!!' 'Listen; I have not been asleep at all ... I have been looking at you a long while. ... For God's sake! ... I believe in you; you are a good man, an honest man; I entreat you by all that is sacred in the world—tell me the truth! If you knew how important it is for me. ... Doctor, for God's sake tell me. ... Am I in danger?' 'What can I tell you, Aleksandra Andreyevna, pray?' 'For God's sake, I beseech you!' 'I can't disguise from you,' I say, 'Aleksandra Andreyevna; you are certainly in danger; but God is merciful.' 'I shall die, I shall die.' And it seemed as though she were pleased; her face grew so bright; I was alarmed. 'Don't be afraid, don't be afraid! I am not frightened of death at all.' She suddenly sat up and leaned on her elbow. 'Now . . . yes, now I can tell you that I thank you with my whole heart . . . that you are kind and good—that I love you!' I stare at her, like one possessed; it was terrible for me, you know. 'Do you hear, I love you!' 'Aleksandra Andreyevna, how have I deserved——' 'No, no, you don't—you don't understand me.' . . . And suddenly she stretched out her arms, and taking my head in her hands, she kissed it. . . . Believe me, I almost screamed aloud. . . . I threw myself on my knees, and buried my head in the pillow. She did not speak; her fingers trembled in my hair; I listen; she is weeping. I began to soothe her, to assure her. . . . I really don't know what I did say to her. 'You will wake up the girl,' I say to her; 'Aleksandra Andreyevna, I thank you . . . believe me . . . calm yourself.' 'Enough, enough!' she persisted; 'never mind all of them; let them wake, then; let them come in—it does not matter; I am dying, you see. . . . And what do you fear? why are you afraid? Lift up your head. . . . Or, perhaps, you don't love me; perhaps I am wrong. . . . In that case, forgive me.' 'Aleksandra Andreyevna, what are you saying! . . . I love you, Aleksandra Andreyevna.' She looked straight into my eyes, and opened her arms wide. 'Then take me in your arms.' I tell you frankly, I don't know how it was I did not go mad that night. I feel that my patient is killing herself; I see that she is not fully herself; I understand, too, that if she did not consider herself on the point of death, she would never have thought of me; and, indeed, say what you will, it's hard to die at twenty without having known love; this was what was torturing her; this was why, in despair, she caught at me—do you understand now? But she held me in her arms, and would not let me go. 'Have pity on me, Aleksandra Andreyevna, and have pity on yourself,' I say. 'Why, she says; 'what is there to think of? You know I must die.' . . . This she repeated incessantly. . . . 'If I knew that I should return to life, and be a proper young lady again, I should be ashamed . . . of course, ashamed . . . but why now?' 'But who has said you will die?' 'Oh, no, leave off!

you will not deceive me; you don't know how to lie—look at your face.' . . . 'You shall live, Aleksandra Andreyevna; I will cure you; we will ask your mother's blessing . . . we will be united—we will be happy.' 'No, no, I have your word; I must die . . . you have promised me . . . you have told me.' . . . It was cruel for me—cruel for many reasons. And see what trifling things can do sometimes; it seems nothing at all, but it's painful. It occurred to her to ask me, what is my name; not my surname, but my first name. I must needs be so unlucky as to be called Trifon. Yes, indeed; Trifon Ivanich. Every one in the house called me doctor. However, there's no help for it. I say, 'Trifon, madam.' She frowned, shook her head, and muttered something in French—ah, something unpleasant, of course!—and then she laughed—disagreeably too. Well, I spent the whole night with her in this way. Before morning I went away, feeling as though I were mad. When I went again into her room it was daytime, after morning tea. Good God! I could scarcely recognise her; people are laid in their grave looking better than that. I swear to you, on my honour, I don't understand—I absolutely don't understand—now, how I lived through that experience. Three days and nights my patient still lingered on. And what nights! What things she said to me! And on the last night—only imagine to yourself—I was sitting near her, and kept praying to God for one thing only: 'Take her,' I said, 'quickly, and me with her.' Suddenly the old mother comes unexpectedly into the room. I had already the evening before told her—the mother—there was little hope, and it would be well to send for a priest. When the sick girl saw her mother she said: 'It's very well you have come; look at us, we love one another—we have given each other our word.' 'What does she say, doctor? what does she say?' I turned livid. 'She is wandering,' I say; 'the fever.' But she: 'Hush, hush; you told me something quite different just now, and have taken my ring. Why do you pretend? My mother is good—she will forgive—she will understand—and I am dying. . . . I have no need to tell lies; give me your hand.' I jumped up and ran out of the room. The old lady, of course, guessed how it was.

"I will not, however, weary you any longer, and to me too, of course,

it's painful to recall all this. My patient passed away the next day. God
rest her soul!" the doctor added, speaking quickly and with a sigh.
"Before her death she asked her family to go out and leave me alone
with her."

" 'Forgive me,' she said; 'I am perhaps to blame towards you . . . my
illness . . . but believe me, I have loved no one more than you . . . do
not forget me . . . keep my ring.' "

The doctor turned away; I took his hand.

"Ah!" he said, "let us talk of something else, or would you care to
play preference for a small stake? It is not for people like me to give
way to exalted emotions. There's only one thing for me to think of;
how to keep the children from crying and the wife from scolding. Since
then, you know, I have had time to enter into lawful wedlock, as they
say. . . . Oh . . . I took a merchan't daughter—seven thousand for her
dowry. Her name's Akulina; it goes well with Trifon. She is an ill-
tempered woman, I must tell you, but luckily she's asleep all day. . . .
Well, shall it be preference?"

We sat down to preference for halfpenny points. Trifon Ivanich won
two rubles and a half from me, and went home late, well pleased with
his success.

The Witch Doctor of Rosy Ridge

MacKINLAY KANTOR

THE old-timers used to tell tales about Granny Blackshears and the boy she raised up, Thin Jimmy, and of the mighty tussle he had with a gang of Bobcats who came through the woods to do him harm. I reckon they would tell those same tales today; but now all the old-timers lie quiet amongst the moss.

And so I will speak a history which they might utter if they were flesh again. It is true as any tale can be, because I got it from my mother's own lips.

Before a man can fathom the ways of Thin Jimmy Blackshears and why he wore amulets around his neck, and carried his pockets full of charms, he must listen to another account sadder by far; and the waters at Lorn Widow Crossing still talk about it.

Because Granny Blackshears herself was the widow of the legend. Her husband it was whose team lost footing in a springtime flood, and went twisting and fighting through the angry riffles until they were drownded, and their master along with them.

Yes, and more than that: for the Blackshears' daughter was smothered in the currents at the same time, and the Blackshears' daughter's husband too. But the elder woman held their baby safe in her arms, after her nearer relations were drowned.

Then, according to the story, Mrs. Virginia Blackshears made herself a camp nigh to the water's edge, and there she was abiding with her grandchild when people chanced to find her; and it was weeks before the soundness of her mind returned.

211

Some say the soundness never did return, and that only a smidgin of her wits resumed their proper place—which would account for the strange life she began to lead. But wiser folks declare that no great innocence clouded her memory; they say that beneath the hard lines of her little face and under the fresh-turned graying of her hair, she was wiser and kinder than many a woman whose husband is alive and hearty and willing to eat the best she can bake, and to pet her or squabble with her as the spirit moves him.

That was in the earliest times, when Mr. Blackshears and his horses and relations were washed to their death. Indian trails still ran crooked through the woods, and the timber was thick and untrodden enough to hide miraculous things. There were catamounts still claiming this new country—or painters, as some folks described them—and bear marks still showed upon trees where the animals had scratched them. Fresh-arrived citizens would wake up sometimes to see Indians pacing past in the moonlight.

No matter how fierce and cruel the high, dark ridges seemed to other folks, poor Mrs. Blackshears declared that the thickets and the creatures prowling therein were the only friends she had left in this world. She had come from Kentucky, Mrs. Blackshears had, and her father was a reckless man who crossed over from Eastern states in the time of Daniel Boone. She was brought up to poverty and dangers of all kinds; she had a plumb courageous eye, and it would have taken more than a mouse to send her squealing.

Though poor, she swore that she was rich, and maybe that was the reason some people opined that her ways of thinking were addled beyond recall. She said that she owned every morsel of root and nut that grew in the timber—that snake-root and vervain and blood-root and mandrake all were hers. She believed that she had especial claim on every bluebird's wing, and that the feathers of the orioles were a kind of gilt that nobody else could purchase. She understood the activities of shooting stars and lightning blaze, and she was never known to be afraid of fox-fire.

And when thunder rattled and laughed beyond the western limits or

Rosy Ridge, she said it spoke a language that few other mortals could interpret; and that some people's milk might be turned to sourness by the thunder's booming, but never hers.

Deprived of husband and daughter, desolate of household goods and skillet and spinning wheel and bed covers to wrap her in, she whispered that the riches of the woods were meant for her and her grand-boy, and she would take them. Her money would be a peculiar kind of yellow leaf which she dried and kept in a bag, and her fat would be the fat of pines, and rattlesnakes would leave her path when she walked abroad.

Oh, there were kind people even when they dwelt so far apart and when every cabin had a hog-pen finish. They tried to do the best they could by her. I reckon there were half a dozen families in the region who would have taken the Blackshears woman to board and sleep and toil with them—to treat her like a maiden aunt, perhaps, and let her share their pone and hominy, and eat the meat their men brought home —since she had no man to fetch a haunch of venison to her.

But she was independent-minded. Maybe violent misfortunes had strengthened her independence and taught her to build little trust in human love, since it could easily be swept away when the waters rose.

Sole alone she dwelt, and she became a doctor to be summoned in time of need. Many were the horses' hoofs that cut the trail towards her door in the night-time. Granny Blackshears' fame went abroad, far over past Billingsgate and up into mountains that block the sky a day's journey to the south.

The panthers were killed and the brush thinned down somewhat, and the last Indians came bedraggled to the doors and begged for whiskey. And the hair on Granny Blackshears turned yellow-white and stringy; and some said that she was a witch.

But no witch who ever rode upon a broomstick had such soothing ways with a baby that was puny. And some folks do recite that Granny Blackshears sighed a compact with the Devil himself; but if that is true, the Devil taught her what to do when young mothers lay gasping for breath, or when strong men had flayed themselves with mishandled axes and the proud flesh started to grow. I reckon his name wasn't the Devil at all—not Him who taught her year by year the wondrous things she managed to do. For if her riches lived yonder among the pale clumps of liverwort, her God lived up those gullies too.

Her cabin was a lonely one, and I have heard that in early days she made her bed in a cave. But finally she managed a log house.

Granny Blackshears was no spring lamb when first she met her tragedy at Lorn Widow Crossing; she aged more rapidly than even a hard-working housewife of that time, and people called her Granny from the start. But she didn't mind. She was intent on raising her orphaned grandchild, and raise him she did.

The child grew wild as a ground-hog, and able to move faster on his feet. Jimmy was his name; by the time the boy had seen five summers he was called Thin Jimmy, because of the way the bones showed in his face.

It is told that she fed him on fox food and wolf food and coon food, but you can take a lick of salt along with that. Still, victuals were scarce in Granny's cabin during plenty of winters, and frosty air and a corn-shuck bed never put meat on anybody's bones, no matter how health-giving such a life may be.

Thin Jimmy was ungainly looking as he grew older, but he could climb a tree in a way to make any squirrel look sick. I reckon if he had had a tail, he could have hung by it, possum fashion, for he got his first training hanging onto Granny Blackshears' shoulders; and she had a kind of papoose arrangement to tie him in, when she went abroad on her doctoring business.

When he got old enough, Thin Jimmy kept house for Granny whilst she was gone, and other children believed that he entertained spooks and lizards and wildcats all together. To joke about Thin Jimmy—to make outrageous sport of his long arms and legs and his fierce, hard face was one kind of occupation; but to meet him in the berry bushes was an-other. Many was the youngun who came hightailing home with eyes popping and wind clean gone, gasping out the fearsome news that he had met Thin Jimmy amongst the brambles.

And children believed that Thin Jim could walk abroad at night even
when the moon and stars were concealed by clouds, and that he had cat
eyes to see around the tree trunks. He wore buckskin and linsey-woolsey;
he had a coonskin cap all rough and scraggly atop his unshorn head.

Many's the time that he was seen loping through the woods like a
scairt deer, when people came nigh. For he didn't understand that most
of the younguns would have cut and run if he had said Boo; and he was
shy and secretive and retiring through all the years of his growth.

He was found, sometimes, laying quiet beside the pools that formed
behind fallen trees on the edges of Agony Creek. His moccasins made
tracks in strange places when snow was on the ground. As he grew
older, he acquired himself a rifle-gun and was said to be skillful with it.
Wild turkeys now cooked on Granny's fire, and rabbits stewed in their
gravy whenever the old lady had a mind for such fare.

Far above six feet Thin Jimmy grew, before he was seventeen. His
legs and arms and chest were thin, but they were hard as old hides at the
tanner's. His hair hung dense and stringy to his shoulders, and the first
fluff of manhood's beard showed like a gray lichen on his face.

He accumulated money too—at least in such amount as Granny Blackshears needed to purchase herself things of comfort. For he dug gentian
roots and dried them, and carried quantities down to the trading store
at Delight. It was a moment of wonderment when Thin Jimmy dropped
his little pack upon the counter, and told the man to weigh what he had
brought.

Yes, he must have been a comfort to poor old Granny Blackshears'
heart; she led a meager life, except for him. Her only relation with
other folks was when they were sick or when plentiful troubles roosted
on their doorsills. She saw miseries through all her years, and devoted
herself only to finding out the remedies if she could. And sometimes I
wonder what she and the boy talked about, in the mysteriousness of
nights when they sat within their home, and when there was no necessary curing to be done elsewhere. But it's certain fact that she taught
Thin Jimmy how to read and how to write his name, and more than
that.

The Rosy Ridge medical doctor in those days, and the only doctor for miles around, was named Doctor Hardaway Mercer; you could make no joke about his name, for his way of life was never hard. He was a genial and good-tempered man unless badly roused, and when highty-tighty folks used to assail the notion of what they called granny-izing and witch-doctoring, Doctor Hardaway Mercer would merely chuckle.

He's say that where there was so much smoke, there must be some flame; he held opinion that Granny Blackshears did more good than harm, with all her roots and dried leaves and queer understandings.

"I reckon she hain't got a license," Doctor Mercer would say. "I reckon she doesn't know the oath of Hippocrates—but it's my belief that she observes it." And then he'd laugh deep within his heavy chest and tug knowingly at his whiskers, and go striding up Agony Creek with a pole over his shoulder.

For he enjoyed angling after the tender little fish that flickered themselves amongst the colored riffles, better than he did fishing for ailments in mankind's inner regions, though I reckon he was successful at both. He was a widower-man, and his pride and joy was in his little daughter Adela; and when she was grown up enough to trot along with him on his fishing, he had her trot.

There she stood one day, in the shallower flows of Agony Creek, and it was the same summer that Thin Jimmy Blackshears had come to be seventeen. Adela Mercer was only twelve, but her feet were the prettiest sight that the sleek little leeches and water skaters ever saw.

Her father had gone upstream to whip the quieter pools with his fly, and Adela had decided to catch herself some craw-daddies. She stood there with the water talking around her legs, and her long black hair hanging thick to her waist. Her hair was so black that the sun seemed to find silver shadows amidst its softness.

Her luck at craw-dad catching was bad, because she was fearful lest the craw-daddies nip her fingers. Then Thin Jimmy Blackshears came from the willows, quieter than any water snake, and showed her how to catch them.

"Craw-dad nippers," he said. "They're mighty good. You keep them in your pocket, little girl, and you'll never suffer miseries of the stomach."

Perhaps because she was so small and gentle and trusting, he took the little girl to a grassy place above the bank, and there he said he'd show her things. And he opened up a kind of pouch he carried within his clothes, and it was full of mixed-up wonders. There was a mad-stone and a snake-stone and a blood-stone, and there was a piece of turtle shell and some dried toenails, and ever the white tooth of a bull.

And then he showed her what he wore around his neck upon a piece of greasy string: a squirrel's tooth to make him forecast the things to come, and a wolf's fang to make him brave. And sewed tight against his coonskin cap, he had a string of snake rattles; as long as he wore them, Thin Jimmy declared, his head would never ache. He had a dead spider, too, and pink pearls that came in clams. And the queerest thing of all was the stone which he called a toad-stone because it was shaped that way, and when he had it no poison could affect him.

Along with these preventions that he toted wherever he went, he understood that humankind is weak and subject to a million ills. He had learned a sight from Granny Blackshears about plants and herbs and Indian tonics, and he poured his wisdom out into the little girl's ears, as if he were glad to have someone to talk to.

But when her father came downstream and hailed the child, Thin Jimmy went slithering away into the thickets so fast that the little girl rubbed her eyes.

"Adela," inquired Doctor Hardaway Mercer, "were you scairt of Thin Jimmy?"

She shook her head and said she wasn't scairt no way. But she clung close against her father's side as they went home; and after that she would never squint at a new moon through window glass without turning something over in her pocket; she dreamed about mad-stones on more nights than one.

And maybe Thin Jimmy Blackshears' dreams had been occupied solely with mad-stones and such implements, up until that time. But from then on, a small and skinny girl with calm brown eyes must have walked in them.

Naturally she was far too young for romancing, and in any case Thin Jimmy was far too savage and shy to think of courting any female mortal that ever breathed. Still, it can be imagined that he considered her hair glossier than the soft feathers of a blackbird, and her voice as trusting and full of wonderment as the green peepers of spring when they played their fiddles in the grass.

A fat partridge found its way somehow to Doctor Mercer's front stoop, and there it lay when the doctor's sister by marriage, Miss Eulalie Kershaw, went out to sweep the step one fine morning. And later in the season there was a brace of plump squirrels, and people wondered that Thin Jimmy would have the courage to creep so close to civilization as the outskirts of Delight, to leave these gifts for the child who had touched his fancy.

And when spring moved over the land again, it was Adela Mercer herself who went frequent to the stoop to see if Thin Jimmy had fetched a present out of the forest. Sometimes there were violets and sometimes the little thread-flowers, paler and more delicate than any other wild thing a-growing; and once there were pearls from clam-shells taken out of the river far away. Things like this Adela kept as a kind of treasure. She had a colored Christmas box in which she stored her ribbons and other girlish truck: the dried flowers given her by Thin Jimmy, and the pearls too, were cherished there.

Her aunt used to rare around at such doings—as season after season went by, with uncommon tributes laid before Adela's door.

"He's wild as a civet-cat," she would cry in dudgeon to Doctor Mercer. "He's the offspring of an old-witch-granny, and I doubt the wisdom of Adela's accepting presents from a timber-bred critter like him."

But Doctor Mercer just laughed. He wanted to know if her aunt would have Adela kick the bouquets off the porch, and feed the game to the hog he was fattening.

"Never you mind," cried Miss Eulalie. "Adela is growing tall and comely all of a sudden, and it's time you gave serious thought to the matter. Why," Miss Eulalie clattered away, "there were a dozen young bucks rolling eyes at her, when we attended the last play-party at the Baggetts'. I'd sooner see her coloring up when one of the Billins boys looked at her."

And it wasn't asking much to have that occur. For by the time Adela Mercer was in her earliest womanhood, the men of the neighborhood would go far out of their way to pass her house and catch a glimpse of her behind the vines. And foremost in the crew rode young Letcher, second son of the Billinses.

There was a scad of Billins boys—twelve in all, when the record was complete—though some died when they were babes. But in those days there were Zeke and Letcher and Jack, grown more or less to man's estate, with three younguns trailing them. Their father was a substantial person who farmed good acres in good fashion, and conducted a saw-mill into the bargain. But he ruled his boys with an easy hand, and most citizens agreed that he didn't rule them hard enough.

Certain it is that Letcher was a tribulation to the schoolmaster and a sore trial to other people in the community, when he outgrew his shirt-tail days. He had a claybank horse that he rode like greased lightning, and at the Christmas season Letcher and his ornery friends would get full of Christmas cheer and go whooping and shooting around the neighborhood. They had a kind of band or army, those boys did, and called themselves the Bobcats, and every Bobcat wore a fur tail of that variety sewed to his hat.

They were nothing like so mean as the Dessark boys who galloped those hills in later periods; their inclinations were not towards robbery and murder, like the night-riders who followed them. But they han-kered to make a noise in the world, and do frantic stunts, and perform pranks that quieter boys might shun. They were known to shoot gourds off each other's heads, and to frighten old ladies with ticktacks against their windows; and once five cats came into prayer-meeting, stepping high with paper boots tied on their feet, and it was the Bobcats who sent them there.

Old Doctor Mercer didn't mind their dangerous ways or their foolishness. "Boys will be boys," he said, although several of these were rapidly lengthening into manhood, and should have devoted themselves to soberer ambitions. And Doc wasn't annoyed when Letcher Billins started tying his claybank in front of the Mercer house, and coming in to amuse Adela with sprightly talk and circus tricks.

Miss Eulalie was in no way annoyed either: Abraham Billins was believed to be worth eight thousand in cold cash, and the saws in his mill hummed hourly as more and more people moved into the vicinity and felt the need of lumber. Zeke Billins was a sickly young man, and who knew how long he might last if a fever got hold of him? Letcher Billins was next-to-the-eldest, and doubtless he would settle into some kind of decency if he inherited the family fortunes.

Miss Eulalie had an eye to future comfort; she had an ear that could catch the ring of a thin dime clear across the neighborhood. So she smiled when she saw that pale horse gnawing the fence palings, and she reckoned Letcher wasn't half so untamed as a certain thin person in buckskins who came creeping through the thickets to drop his wildflowers at the doorstep, and vanish away again without ever a soul laying eyes on him.

The gentian roots grew and the wild turkeys gobbled; fish still flicked themselves in the waters where Doc Mercer commonly sought them.

As for Thin Jimmy Blackshears, he spent his time in bottling hen's oil for Granny, and stewing up tobacco and mutton tallow as she needed them; and he was stripping out the inner bark of butternut trees and tincturing the blood-root, and counting crows upon the wing for weather prophecy, just as he always did.

And as for Adela Mercer, she had grown pretty and mildly plump; there was pink within her skin, and her eyes laughed when they looked at you. I don't know whether they laughed when she looked at Letcher Billins or not, but he was around there most of the time for her to look at. People said that Letcher was an eligible young man despite his crazy activities and his ornery ways with the Bobcats. What he needed in his life was a settling influence, and likely Adela Mercer would award it to him.

Bitter trials do not come singly as a rule, and now Doctor Hardaway Mercer had the first tribulation which had visited him since his wife died many years before. It came in the shape of a runaway back in Kentucky, where his only brother was mortally hurt, and the family wrote a letter to Doctor Mercer while the brother lay a-dying.

Mercer had to pack and go; it was a long journey; he had to tend his brother devotedly when he got there, and when the man died there were the children to see after, and a million business disturbances to straighten out for the widow.

And through all those weeks of worry, there was unhappiness occurring within Hardaway Mercer's own home, nigh to the town of Delight. His child Adela was stricken with a misery. She thinned down unreasonably, and she complained of anguish in her side and under her shoulder. Her skin no longer looked as if rose petals lay upon it.

There were some people inclined towards sentimentality who said that she needed her father's return, as a sole and certain cure: motherless daughters were apt to hold their fathers close to their hearts, and perhaps Adela was pining for the doctor. There were others, more literal-minded, who declared that Miss Eulalie Kershaw's cooking was the cause of it all.

Well, Adela was sick enough; she·wouldn't eat, and she experienced pain and fever. The only other doctor in the neighborhood lived at Billingsgate, and he was a harsh man who had quarreled with Hardaway Mercer on some matter of profession. Miss Eulalie Kershaw said she'd be blowed up with gunpowder before she'd summon the Billingsgate man, and that she knew enough to cure any two girls the size of Adela.

She brought bottles from the doctor's shelves, and I reckon she used them all. She poured everything from Indian Cathartic Syrup to Colby's Cholera Tincture down that poor girl's throat. She gave her Wahoo Tonic and Wilson's English Worm Cakes, and she rubbed her back with Kittredge's Salve. She gave her Alcoholic Extract of Ignatia Amara, too.

But the prime cure she offered was Mrs. Winslow's Soothing Syrup; Aunt Eulalie said if that didn't fetch Adela into bounding health, nothing else would. And the hollows under Adela Mercer's eyes grew deeper, and she lay listless upon her pillows.

No one of the neighbors dared to summon Granny Blackshears. Miss Eulalie Kershaw, with her specs and her big teeth and her loud voice, was now Adela's guardian, and Miss Eulalie held no brief for grannyizing.

"Mrs. Winslow's Soothing Syrup has cured folks afore this," said Miss Eulalie. "Take it, child! It's good enough for what ails you."

The neighbors grew alarmed. Mrs. Drummond it was who wrote to Doctor Mercer that he'd best hasten home from Kentucky and see to things, or else he'd have to stand beside a grave when he did come. It was miserable to observe the Mercer house, from whence good cheer and kindness and laughter had always come forth, now turned grim and silent—with the blinds pulled down and the daughter fever-ridden.

I reckon Letcher Billins was reasonably upset. He'd bounce in every day to see how Adela was faring, and once he brought her a bottle of scent, and another time a box of chocolate drops that he had rode all the way to Billingsgate to purchase for her. But it was whispered that other eyes than his watched the house on frequent occasions, and that a tall shape was heard to go rustling away through the leaves, close before dawn or after the dusk had fallen.

Sure enough, Jimmy Blackshears must have heard of Adela Mercer's ailment; and so had everybody else in the Rosy Ridge country. But Thin Jim was so withdrawn into his solitary pursuits that he dared not pull the Mercer latch-strings unbidden.

There came a night when Adela didn't know the neighbor women who waited nigh her bed, nor recognize her Aunt Eulalie. Her eyes stared through them as if they had been window-glass, and she quoted strange words aloud in her restlessness and in all the pain of her sickness.

She spoke up through layers of fever, and she said that shoemakers' children never had shoes; she said that she was a doctor's daughter—the child of a man who had cured many—but now there was no one to cure her.

Then Mrs. Andrew Drummond went a-flying home, to tell old Andrew of the weakness and danger that beset Adela, and how nigh she seemed coming to her end.

Andrew Drummond said angry words. He pulled on his boots and poured himself a drink from his flask.

"Aye," he said, "she's a winning lass, and I'll not be the man to stand idly by and see her come to harm! It's dark the night, and Eulalie Kershaw is an old rullion, but I'm away to fetch Granny Blackshears!"

Then up he rode, six miles along the chilly length of Rosy Ridge, and he was as angry and as frightened as any Scotchman could be—or any native Missourian either, for that matter. He knocked upon the door of Granny Blackshears' cabin, as so many other plaintive people had knocked before him. When the door opened, it was a man who lifted the latch, and Thin Jimmy was the man.

"No," said he, "Granny ain't to home, nor will she be. The Huckstep babe and mother are badly took, over at Lorn Widow, and she's there a-tending them."

Sweat stood out on Andrew Drummond's forehead.

"Look you here, Thin Jimmy," he cried, "there's naught to be done for Adela Mercer but what your granny can do! Aye, the lass is wandering in her wits the night."

Thin Jimmy stood there, tall and strange in his wool and buckskins, and he looked down at Mr. Drummond. "She's bad took?"

"Weeks agone!" exclaimed Andrew Drummond. "She's no better now. The fever was high within her when my woman left the house; and the poor bairn talks about her side, and she makes an ourie noise when she tries to breathe."

Candle-light shone again Andrew Drummond's eyes, and he couldn't examine Thin Jimmy's face. "Well, I can go down myself," Thin Jimmy whispered, for all his shyness. "It sounds as if it might be a liver inflammation."

Old Andrew Drummond drew his tartan shawl close around his

shoulders. "Has your granny taught you, lad, aught of what she knows?"

"I reckon," said Thin Jimmy, "that she's taught me all."

"Aye," Drummond told him. "I brought a led horse along. Fetch your paraphernalia, now, and come away with me."

Thin Jimmy went to the far end of the cabin, and there were stored, on shelves and hooks and pegs, a million pokes and bottles and little bundles of bark and dried weeds. Most carefully he selected several things and wrapped them together; and he fetched them all those miles down to the Mercer house, riding silent behind Andrew.

Adela was having a miserable time when they got there. Neighbor women had come into the room, and Mrs. Drummond had returned as well. Deliriousness no longer overcame Adela, though the appearance of her face was terrible to see, and her coughing too, and the pain with which she breathed. It was years since Thin Jimmy had stood nigh to her, for all the presents he had deposited on her stoop; she stared up, wondering out of her big brown eyes, and he looked just as wondering.

At last that wild young man did find his voice, and he asked her the questions he needed to ask, and he found just where the pain was plaguing her. The neighbor women got over their awe of him, and loosened up and told him things which Adela hadn't told about herself; although Miss Eulalie sat over by the lamp and glared and sniffed.

Then Thin Jimmy asked Andrew Drummond to lead him into the kitchen where the stove lids were red. He opened the bundles he had brought, and he took out handfuls of smartweed and wormwood and the bark of sumach roots, and these things Jimmy put into a pot to boil.

"They were gathered correct," he said. "They were gathered at the right time of the moon, and they were cured according to the ways that Granny knows. And now I'll do what I can. But in the meantime, here are some other medicines for you to put in her bed, and let her keep them nigh her all the time." And he gave to Andrew Drummond a small dried potato, and a knuckle from a pig's foot, and a pair of craw-dad claws.

Well, that was witchery all right, but old Andrew was willing to grasp at any hope offered. So he wrapped them according to instructions, and his wife put them close beside Adela's body beneath the bedclothes.

Out from the kitchen appeared Thin Jimmy, and he had boiled the strength from the weeds and bark that were stewing; and then he had strained and boiled them further. He added lard too, and turpentine; but because he was a man and because he was scairt of all the world, and perhaps most especially of young females, he had Mrs. Drummond proceed from there.

The woman rubbed that stuff around the painful portions of Adela Mercer, and pressed a flannel cloth above the mixture again and again, and passed a hot iron over the flannel.

"You got to heat it in," Thin Jimmy had cautioned her. "You got to keep heating it in, or it will bring no relief to her internals."

More kinds of doctoring he had ready to hand, and he employed them. He cooked up mandrakes and blue-flag roots, and another kind of root as well. That strange dose he made Adela swallow down soon after the salve was applied, and again before hc left the house at dawn. Everybody on the eastern limits of Rosy Ridge had heard of his visit by that time, for it was a wondrous thing to think of Thin Jimmy shedding his retiring habits, and playing doctor to a girl that her Aunt Eulalie couldn't help no way.

And other people than the householders had heard of Thin Jimmy's adventure: the Bobcats were waiting for him in full force, with Letcher Billins at their head. Andrew Drummond had offered Thin Jimmy his horse for riding back home, but Thin Jimmy was accustomed to shank's mare and said that he'd much prefer to leg it.

So he set off; and then as he passed the sycamores that grew beyond the turning of the road (and that still grow there in modern times) he came face to face with five young men who sat their horses and stared at him.

Letcher Billins didn't hold with witch-doctoring, and most especially Billins was always quick to pride himself because of his light heart and when he considered that the witch-doctor was rivaling him in Adela

Mercer's affections. Letcher and his associates had attended a dance at Mammy Park's place, far down the Billingsgate road, and more than a little corn liquor had flowed their way. Some young men wouldn't be eager for dancing when certain young ladies lay sick abed, but Letcher Billins was always quick to pride himself because of his light heart and risibilities.

And then he came back to Delight with the other Bobcats in tow. His insides were heated as if an iron had been passed across his skin instead of Adela's.

The Bobcats said, "Thin Jimmy, we're eager to have a word with you," and Jimmy Blackshears was plumb astonished when he glimpsed them.

"Talk away," he said. "I'd take it kindly if you didn't talk too long, for I've six miles ahead of me."

"You're more than that behind you, maybe," said Letcher Billins, and the other boys ho-hoed to hear him say it. "You've mad-stones and blood-stones and funny herbs, and all other kinds of rigmarole. You hain't no doctor; so I warn you to keep your spooky habits far removed from Miss Adela Mercer."

And Thin Jimmy up and answered him, "I'm trying to cure her of her misery."

"Well enough, witch man," said Letcher Billins. "I don't misdoubt your intentions. I just don't desire you casting any spells."

Thin Jimmy folded his arms across his flat chest and looked hard at them all. His eyes went back in his head. "If I can cast a spell that will heal her body," he said, "I'd count myself fortunate. And if it can be done with pigs knuckles or blue-flag or wormwood, I aim to do it."

Well, he looked mighty purposeful. The Bobcats hadn't yet lashed themselves into any devilment, so they pulled their horses aside and let Blackshears pass until he had vanished in the Rosy Ridge direction.

But then they got to talking amongst themselves, and they joked Letcher Billins unmercifully about such goings on.

"How would you like it," one of the Tinley boys inquired of Lane Cutts, "if your girl was being magicked away from you?" He said it sly, but loud enough for Letcher Billins to hear, and Letcher pulled his mouth down tight.

He invited his cronies over to the saw-mill shack to wet their whistles before they rode for home, and I reckon the whistles thought they needed a lot of wetting.

They sat around with a jug or two, for a couple of hours. Dell Tinley said that he had heard of a youngun who was cured of heart ailments by having a hole drilled into a blue beech tree and some of his hair stuffed into the hole; and Angie Steedman swore that there wasn't anything better to stop the flowing of a bloody wound than seven spider webs laid acrost it, especially if the webs had been spun in November.

Thus they kept on rallying Letcher Billins and reciting magic words and mumble-jumble, until about nine o'clock Letcher got up and heaved his empty jug against the stove.

He ripped out his knife and carved the air around his head, and he brayed, "Any man who says I'll stand by and let Adela be witch-doctored to her death, has got to give me the first bite! I'm going up there on Rosy Ridge and open that critter's carcass, and see if he's actually plagued with moonbeams!"

So the rest all swort that they would go along. They went squawling away up the hill road, past the Drummond house and the MacBean place and then west along the trail that we call Lovers' Walk.

The cold morning air soaked a little soberness into their arms and legs. They were steady enough, but they weren't yet kindly of heart; and when they grouped their horses around the Blackshears cabin they were still fighting mean.

Letcher Billins, most of all, was enraged at the meddling manners of Thin Jimmy.

"Unbar your door!" he yelled. "Lock up your spooks in their swill barrels, Jimmy Blackshears. Come outside and say us a miracle!"

Thin Jimmy was sound asleep when they began their outcry, but it didn't take him long to blink the sleep from his eyes. He put on some duds, though not many, and he opened the door most steady. He stood there with his bare chest shining in the morning sun.

"Well, well," Letcher Billins told him, "do my eyes deceive me? You look just like an ordinary human, without your shirt, although the hair doesn't grow as thick as it might."

And Jimmy Blackshears asked them quiet, "Why do you folks make so much rumpus? Is somebody sick?"

Billins leaned down over his horse's neck and he narrowed his gaze. "Adela Mercer is sick," he said. "She'll be sicker if you continue doctoring her. I've come up to warn you to keep your distance from that house, with all your toad-ears and skunk-musk and turtle-feet!"

Thin Jimmy turned pale; it was the paleness of eager rage, and the Bobcats had no sense to understand his feelings.

"I want to cure her," he said, "because she's mighty sweet and mighty pretty. And I reckon I'll cure her, too, for I know the medicine she needs."

Then Letcher Billins turned around on his horse and pleaded with the other Bobcats to observe how he held his temper. "And you, Thin Jimmy," he said. "I reckon I ought to shoot you in your tracks, or slice the ears from off your head. You set foot in the Mercer yard again and you'll need more than a blood-stone to cure you!"

It is hard to tell what went on in Thin Jimmy Blackshears' mind, for he had never exchanged angriness with anyone so far as known; never before had he been challenged or ordered about his business. He knew the milk-snakes of the gullies better than he knew the manners of human beings . . . he knew the kind of voices that none of the Bobcats could speak with. And he wore a wolf's fang, to make him brave.

He eased forward and he put his hand on Letcher Billins' bridle with all earnestness. "I've never had trouble with no man," he said. "I've never courted troublesome doings. But don't let none of your friends halt me on my path toward Adela Mercer's, for most surely I will kill any man who gets in my way."

There was something clabbering about the way he said it, and the other Bobcats kind of slunk behind Letcher. But the corn was still going around inside Letcher's head. So he reached for his knife, and let out a yell that should have frightened any ordinary mortal off the face of the earth.

Then Jimmy's long fingers closed around Billins' leg, and the next moment Letcher Billins hit the ground, and his horse went skipping off in fair astonishment. Tooth and claw and kick and jab, bite and bump and choke and squeeze—that was the way Thin Jimmy fought, and in another minute Letcher Billins' knife went sailing over the roof tree.

Now I'll never say where Jimmy Blackshears got his lessons in tussling, and certainly no other child had ever rolled and cuffed with him when he was growing up. Maybe he learned his strategies amidst the brush, as he watched the deer a-fighting in that season when their necks swelled. And maybe he had absorbed knowledge of scrimmages when he saw the dog mink go for one another, and the black-headed robins too.

He didn't spare a hold or restrain himself from any gouge. Still, that was more or less the fashion of fighting in those days. And the Bobcats were armed. . . .

Then he and Letcher were on their feet. Letcher lifted a kick that would have torn Thin Jimmy's jaw plumb out of his chin, if it had struck him. But the wild man caught Billins' boot when it came up, and he sent Letcher a-rolling. Now two more Bobcats were on him, and one of them was mean enough to have his knife out. It gashed Thin Jimmy's arm, but he took it away, and a bone snapped when he took it.

The other young bucks dove off their horses. They skirmished around, hunting for a chance. They found black eyes and bloody noses and torn lips instead, and they lost their air out of their lungs when Jimmy's heel came against them.

He fought his way backward to the cabin door; I reckon he had notion that his rifle was inside, and he would have used it too, for he considered that he was fighting for Adela Mercer's life as hard as ever he might. Oh, there would have been bloodshed of a more grievous kind, and somebody would have died; that much is sure.

But then there came the knocking of a horse's feet against the hard ground, and a tall man with white whiskers rode up abreast of the cabin door. He roared at the fighting men to hold themselves steady.

It was Doctor Hardaway Mercer, fresh come from Kentucky, and fresher come from his daughter's bedside. Like most men who rode abroad on lonely missions in the early days, he toted a pocket pistol; and now he leveled it, and desired all and sundry to hold their hands aloft.

They did it, too, though everybody was bleeding sore.

For a while the doctor sat glowering. The Bobcats were hanging their heads as if they realized already the wrong that they had committed.

"I heard it all," Doc Mercer told them, "and how you desired to come up here and show your wrath to a man who has done me the service of his life! You may not know it, Letcher Billins, but Adela was sitting up right peart by the time I arrived this morning, and she begged for chicken broth and biscuits. They say she was at death's door only last night, before Thin Jimmy tended her."

"Well," said Letcher Billins, lowering his hand long enough to wipe away the blood from his nose, "I don't hold with witch-doctoring. I didn't want him casting spells over Adela."

"He can cast any spells he wants to," said Doc Mercer, with his voice trembling. "I presume he knows that, now. I suggest that you Bobcats waltz for home and get yourselves cured up, if you can. This will make a tall tale in our community: one man against five, and damn near whipping the daylights out of you!"

But then he relented, for Doc Mercer's bark was always worse than his bite. He clumb down off his horse and put his pistol away and said that he'd patch them all up if he could. But before he would lay a finger on Letcher or the Tinleys or any of that crowd, he bandaged the gash in Thin Jimmy's arm.

And he talked all the time he was messing around with the wounded. He said, "Flag root and wormwood—that's what Andrew Drummond said was used. . . . Smartweed and wormwood and sumach roots, boiled down and mixed with turpentine and lard. Well, it would have its values; I can understand that. I say nothing whatsoever," he added cautiously, "about the therapeutic importance of pigs' knuckles and craw-dad claws."

At last the Bobcats traipsed for home, looking cheap and feeling cheaper. They went into retirement from their activities for quite a spell. It wasn't a brave story to be borne around the neighborhood—how the five of them had mighty nigh failed to lick one lone Thin Jimmy. And from that time on, Letcher Billins' claybank horse had to chaw other palings besides those at the Mercers'.

Back in the Blackshears cabin, old Doctor Mercer put his arm around Thin Jimmy. "She'll do well enough, boy," he said. "I'm here at last, thank God, to look after her. . . . Mandrakes and blue-flag roots! Well, apparently there's something to that dose, taken internally, and I'd better look into it right prompt. I want you to come down to the house and you can dwell there for a spell, with your cut arm and all, until Granny Blackshears gets home."

They traveled the trail that leads east down Rosy Ridge, with Doctor Mercer's horse a-carrying double.

He said to Thin Jimmy, "Craw-daddies and dead spiders and dried potatoes! That's magic, young man, and worthless, and not to be tampered with anyhow. . . . But you can read, and how would you like to ride around on professional calls with me and read *Materia Medica* while you do it?"

Well, Thin Jimmy thought he would like to try that well enough. And then he owned that he had a little money too, if his medical education would cause expense. For he had saved four hundred and seventy-three dollars from selling gentian roots and such natural valuables, and he had buried it under the floor.

They say that Miss Eulalie Kershaw adopted a different tone, when she heard about that money. Four hundred and seventy-three dollars was quite a sum in those days; and I'd like to have that much in my pocket now.

Thereupon happiness began for all concerned, although Granny Blackshears scowled to think of Thin Jimmy deciding with superior knowledge that there was no benefit in dried potatoes or craw-dad claws. She held that they possessed important virtues, to the end of her days.

And thus Thin Jimmy became a doctor, back in those early times before the War. And thus Adela became a doctor's wife; and almost the first patient Doctor Blackshears had was Letcher Billins, who had been up to some prank or other. He came seeking the extraction of bird-shot which an angry neighbor had fired into his southernmost portions.

Father is Firm with His Ailments

CLARENCE DAY

FATHER got annoyed at us when we didn't stay well. He usually stayed well himself and he expected us to be like him, and not faint and slump on his hands and thus add to his burdens.

He was fearless about disease. He despised it. All this talk about germs, he said, was merely new-fangled nonsense. He said that when he was a boy there had been no germs that he knew of. Perhaps invisible insects existed, but what of it? He was as healthy as they were. "If any damned germs want to have a try at me," he said, "bring 'em on."

From Father's point of view, Mother didn't know how to handle an ailment. He admired her most of the time and thought there was nobody like her; he often said to us boys, "Your mother is a wonderful woman"; but he always seemed to disapprove of her when she was ill.

Mother went to bed, for instance, at such times. Yet she didn't make noises. Father heard a little gasping moan sometimes, but she didn't want him to hear even that. Consequently he was sure she wasn't suffering. There was nothing to indicate it, he said.

The worse she felt, the less she ever said about it, and the harder it was for him to believe that there was anything really wrong with her. "He says he can't see why I stay in bed so long," she once wrote to me, when I was away, "but this colitis is a mean affair which keeps one perfectly flat. The doctor told him yesterday the meaning of colitis, but he said he 'had never heard of the damned thing, thank God.' He feels very abused that he should be 'so upset by people with queer things the matter with them and doctors all over the place.'" (Mother underlined the word "people.")

233

Even Mother's colds made him fretful. Whenever she had one, she kept going as long as she could, pottering about her room looking white and tired, with a shawl round her shoulders. But sometimes she had to give up and crawl into her bed.

Father pished and poohed to himself about this, and muttered that it was silly. He said Mother was perfectly healthy. When people thought they were ill, he declared, it didn't mean that there was anything the matter with them, it was merely a sign of weak character. He often told Mother how weak it was to give in to an ailment, but every time he tried to strengthen her character in this respect, he said she seemed to resent it. He never remembered to try except when she could hardly hold her head up. From his point of view, though, that was the very time that she needed his help.

He needed hers, too, or not exactly her help but her company, and he never hesitated to say so. When she was ill, he felt lost.

He usually came up from his office at about five or six. The first thing he did was to look around the house to find Mother. It made his home feel queer and empty to him when she wasn't there.

One night about six o'clock he opened the door of her bedroom. There was no light except for a struggling little fire which flickered and sank in the grate. A smell of witch-hazel was in the air, mixed with spirits of camphor. On the bed, huddled up under an afghan, Mother lay still, in the dark.

"Are you there, Vinnie?" Father said, in a voice even louder than usual because of his not being sure.

Mother moaned, "Go away."

"What?" he asked, in astonishment.

"Go away. Oh, go 'way."

"Damnation!" he said, marching out.

"Clare!"

"What is it?"

"Won't you *ple-e-ease* shut my door again!"

Father ground his teeth and shut it with such a bang that it made Mother jump.

He told himself she had nothing the matter with her. She'd be all right in the morning. He ate a good dinner. Being lonely, he added an extra glass of claret and some toasted crackers and cheese. He had such a long and dull evening that he smoked two extra cigars.

After breakfast the next morning, he went to her bedroom again. The fire was out. Two worn old slippers lay on a chair. The gray daylight was cheerless. Father stood at the foot of Mother's bed, looking disconsolately at her because she wasn't well yet. He had no one to laugh at or quarrel with; his features were lumpy with gloom.

"What is it?" Mother asked in a whisper, opening her weary eyes.

"Nothing," he said loudly. "Nothing."

"Well, for mercy's sake, don't come in here looking like that, Clare," Mother begged.

"What do you mean? Looking like what?"

"Oh, go away!" Mother shrieked. "When people are sick, they like to see a smile or something. I never will get well if you stand there and stare at me that way! And shut my door quietly this time. And let me alone."

Outside her door, when I asked him how Mother was, he said with a chuckle: "She's all right again. She isn't out of bed yet, but she sounds much better this morning."

Father's own experiences in a sick-room had been very few. When he was in his early thirties, he had an attack of gout which lasted three weeks. From that time until he was seventy-four and had pneumonia, he had no other serious illnesses. He said illnesses were mostly imaginary and he didn't believe in them.

He even declared that his pneumonia was imaginary. "It's only some idea of that doctor's," he said. "Nothing the matter with me but a cold." Our regular physician had died, and this new man and two trained nurses had all they could do, at first, to keep Father in bed.

The new doctor had pale-blue eyes, a slight build, and a way of inwardly smiling at the persons he talked to. He had a strong will in crises, and he was one of the ablest physicians in town. Mother had chosen him, however, chiefly because she liked one of his female cousins.

When Father got worse, the doctor kept warning him that it really *was* pneumonia, and that if he wouldn't be tractable, he might not get over it—especially at seventy-four.

Father lay in bed glowering at him and said: "I didn't send for you, sir. You needn't stand there and tell me what you want me to do. I know all about doctors. They think they know a damned lot. But they don't. Give your pills and things to Mrs. Day—she believes in them. That's all I have to say. There's no need to continue this discussion. There's the door, sir. Goodbye."

But somehow the discussion kept on, and much to his surprise Father at last became convinced he was ill. The doctor, leaving him alone in his bedroom to digest the bad news, came out in the hall, anxious and tired, to have a few words with Mother. As they stood outside Father's door whispering quietly, they heard his voice from within. Apparently, now that he knew he was in trouble, his thoughts had turned to his God. "Have mercy!" they heard him shouting indignantly. "I say have mercy, damn it!"

Any sufferings that Father ever had he attributed solely to God. Naturally, he never thought for a moment that God could mean him to suffer. He couldn't imagine God's wishing to punish him either, for his conscience was clear. His explanation seemed to be that God was clumsy, not to say muddle-headed.

However, in spite of God and the doctor, Father got over pneumonia, just as, some forty years before, he had got over his gout. Only, in conquering his gout, he had had the help of a cane and a masseur called Old Lowndes.

While the gout was besieging him, Father sat in a big chair by the fire with his bad foot on a stool, armed with a cane which he kept constantly ready. Not that he used the cane to walk with. When he walked, he hopped around on his other foot, uttering strong howls of fury. But he valued his cane highly, and needed it, too, as a war club. He threatened the whole family with it. When visitors entered the room he brandished it fiercely at them, to keep them away from his toe.

Old Lowndes was allowed to approach nearer than others, but he was warned that if he made any mistakes that cane would come down on his head. Father felt there was no knowing what harm Lowndes might have done if he hadn't shaken his cane at him and made him take care. As it was, owing largely to his useful stick, Father got well.

This experience convinced him that any disease could be conquered by firmness.

When he had a cold, his method of dealing with it was to try to clear it out by main force, either by violently blowing his nose or, still better, by sneezing. Mother didn't like him to sneeze, he did it with such a roar. She said she could feel it half across the room, and she was sure it was catching. Father said this was nonsense. He said his sneezes were healthy. And presently we'd hear a hearty, triumphant blast as he sneezed again.

Aside from colds, which he had very seldom, his only foes were sick headaches. He said headaches only came from eating, however. Hence a man who knew enough to stop eating could always get rid of one that way. It took time to starve it out thoroughly. It might take several hours. But as soon as it was gone, he could eat again and enjoy his cigar.

When one of these headaches started, Father lay down and shut his eyes tight and yelled. The severity of a headache could be judged by the volume of sound he put forth. His idea seemed to be to show the headache that he was just as strong as it was, and stronger. When a headache and he went to bed together, they were a noisy pair.

Father's code required him to be game, I suppose. He never spoke or thought of having a code; he wasn't that sort of person; but he denounced men whose standards were low, as to gameness or anything else. It didn't occur to him to conceal his sufferings, however; when he had any pains, he expressed them fully as he knew how. His way of being brave was not to keep still but to keep on fighting the headache.

Mother used to beg him to be quiet at night, even if he did have a neadache, and not wake up the whole house. He never paid the slightest attention to such a request. When she said, "Please don't groan so much, Clare," he'd look at her in disgust, as though he were a warrior being asked to stifle his battle-cries.

One evening he found Mother worrying because Aunt Emma was ill with some disease that was then epidemic.

"Oh, pooh!" Father said. "Nothing the matter with Emma. You can trust people to get any ailment whatever that's fashionable. They hear of a lot of other people having it, and the first thing you know they get scared and think they have it themselves. Then they go to bed, and send for the doctor. The doctor! All poppycock."

"Well, but Clare dear, if you were in charge of them, what would you do instead?"

"Cheer 'em up, that's the way to cure 'em."

"How would you cheer them up, darling?" Mother asked doubtfully.

"I? I'd tell 'em, *'Bah!'* "

The Death of a Bachelor

ARTHUR SCHNITZLER

Someone had knocked at the door, quite gently, but the doctor awoke at once, turned on the light, and sat up in bed. He glanced at his wife who was sleeping quietly, picked up his dressing-gown, and went into the hall. He did not at once recognise the old woman who stood there, with the grey shawl over her head.

"The master is suddenly taken very bad," she said; "would the doctor be kind enough to come at once?"

Now he recognised the voice: it was the housekeeper of that old friend of his who had never married. The doctor's first thought was, "My friend is fifty-five years old, his heart has been out of order for years—it might well be something serious," and he said, "I'll come at once—will you wait for me?"

"Excuse me, doctor, but I have to hurry around to two other gentlemen," and she mentioned the names of the merchant and the author.

"But what is your business with them?"

"My master wants to see them again."

"See them again?"

"Yes, sir."

"He is sending for his friends," thought the doctor, because he feels very near to death," . . . and he asked, "Is anyone with your master?"

"Of course," the old woman answered. "Johann is with him all the time." And she departed.

The doctor went back into his bedroom, and while he was dressing quickly and as noiselessly as possible, a feeling of bitterness came over him. It was not so much grief at the possibility of losing a good old

239

friend, but the painful consciousness that they were all so far on in years, though not so long ago they had been young.

The doctor drove in an open carriage through the soft, heavy air of that spring night, to the neighbouring suburb where his friend lived. He looked up at the bedroom window which stood wide open, and whence the pale lamplight glimmered into the night.

The doctor went up the stairs, the servant opened the door, greeted him gravely, and dropped his left arm in a gesture of grief.

"What?" asked the doctor, catching his breath. "Am I too late?"

"Yes, sir," answered the servant, "my master died a quarter of an hour ago."

The doctor heaved a deep sigh and went into the room. There lay his dead friend, with thin, bluish, half-open lips, his arms outstretched over the white coverlet; his meagre beard was in disorder, and a few grey wisps of hair had strayed over his pale damp forehead. The silk-shaded electric lamp that stood on the night table cast a reddish shadow over the pillows. The doctor looked at the dead man. "When was he last in our house?" he thought to himself. "I remember it was snowing that evening. It must have been last winter." They had not seen much of each other latterly.

From without came the sound of horses' hoofs pawing the road. The doctor turned away from the dead man and looked across at the slender branches of the trees swaying in the night air.

The servant came in and the doctor then enquired how it had all happened.

The servant told a familiar story of a sudden attack of vomiting and breathlessness. Then his master had leapt out of bed, paced up and down the room, rushed to his writing-table, tottered back to bed again, where he lay racked with thirst and groaning and after one last effort to raise himself he had sunk back upon the pillows. The doctor nodded and laid his hand on the dead man's forehead.

A carriage drew up. The doctor went over to the window. He saw the merchant get out and glance enquiringly up at the house. Unconsciously the doctor let his hand fall just as the servant had done who opened the door to him. The merchant threw back his head as if refusing to believe it, and the doctor shrugged his shoulders, left the window, and sat down, in sudden weariness, on a chair at the feet of the dead man. The merchant came in wearing a yellow overcoat unbuttoned, put his hat on a small table near the door, and shook the doctor by the hand. "How dreadful!" he said; "how did it happen?" And he stared dubiously at the dead man.

The doctor told him what he knew, and added: "Even if I had been able to come at once, I could have done nothing."

"Fancy," said the merchant, "it is exactly a week to-day since I last spoke to him at the theatre. I wanted to have supper with him afterwards, but he had one of his secret appointments."

"What, still?" said the doctor, with a gloomy smile.

Outside another carriage stopped. The merchant went to the window. When he saw the author getting out, he drew back, not wanting to announce the sad news by his expression. The doctor had taken a cigarette out of his case and was twisting it about in an embarrassed sort of way. "It's a habit I've had since my hospital days," he remarked apologetically. "When I left a sick-room at night, the first thing I always did was to light a cigarette, whether I had been to give an injection of morphia or to certify a death."

"Do you know," said the merchant, "how long it is since I saw a corpse? Fourteen years—not since my father lay in his coffin."

" But—your wife?"

"I saw my wife in her last moments, but not afterwards."

The author appeared, shook hands with the other two, and glanced doubtfully at the bed. Then he walked resolutely up to it and looked earnestly at the dead man, yet not without a contemptuous twitch of the lips. "So it was he," he said to himself. For he had played with the question which of his more intimate friends was to be the first to take the last journey.

The housekeeper came in. With tears in hers eyes she sank down by the bed, sobbed, and wrung her hands. The author laid his hand gently and soothingly on her shoulders.

The merchant and the doctor stood at the window, and the dank air of the spring night played upon their foreheads.

"It is really very odd," began the merchant, "that he has sent for all of us. Did he want to see us all gathered round his death-bed? Had he something important to say to us?"

"As far as I'm concerned," said the doctor, with a sad smile, "it would would not be odd, as I am a doctor. And you," he said, turning to the merchant, "you were at times his business adviser. So perhaps it was a matter of some last instructions that he wanted to give you personally."

"That is possible," said the merchant.

The housekeeper had left the room, and the friends could hear her talking to the other servants in the hall. The author was still standing by the bed carrying on a silent dialogue with the dead man.

"I think," whispered the merchant to the doctor, "that latterly he saw more of our friend. Perhaps he can throw some light on the question."

The author stood motionless, gazing steadily into the closed eyes of the dead man. His hands, which held his broad-brimmed grey hat, were crossed behind his back. The two others began to grow impatient, and the merchant went up to his and cleared his throat.

"Three days ago," observed the author, "I went for a two-hours' walk with him among the hills and vineyards. Would you like to know what he talked about? A trip to Sweden, that he had planned for the summer, a new Rembrandt portfolio just published by Watson's in London, and last of all about Santos Dumont. He went into all sorts of mathematical and scientific details about a dirigible airship, which, to be frank with you, I did not entirely grasp. He certainly was not thinking about death. It must indeed be true that at a certain age people again stop thinking about it."

The doctor had gone into the adjoining room. Here he might certainly venture to light his cigarette. The sight of white ashes in the bronze tray on the writing-table struck him as strange and almost uncanny. He wondered why he was still there at all, as he sat down on the chair by the writing-table. He had the right to go as soon as he liked, since he had obviously been sent for as a doctor. For their friendship had nearly come to an end. "At my time of life," he went on, pursuing his reflection, "it is quite impossible for a man like me to keep friends with someone who has no profession and never has had one. What would he have taken up if he had not been rich? He would probably have turned to literature: he was very clever." And he remembered many malicious but pointed remarks the dead man had made, more especially about the works of their common friend, the author.

The author and the merchant came in. The author assumed an expression of disapproval when he saw the doctor sitting at the deserted writing-table with a cigarette in his hand, which was, however, still unlit, and he closed the door behind him. Here, however, they were to some extent in another world.

"Have you any sort of idea? . . . " asked the merchant.

"About what?" asked the author absent-mindedly.

"What made him send for us, and just us?"

The author thought it unnecessary to look for any special reason. "Our friend," he explained, "felt death was upon him, and if he had lived a rather solitary life, at least, at such an hour people who are by nature socially inclined probably feel the need of seeing their friends about them."

"He had a mistress, though," remarked the merchant.

"Oh, a mistress," repeated the author, and contemptuously raised his eyebrows.

At this moment the doctor noticed that the middle drawer of writing-table was half open.

"I wonder if his will is here?" he asked.

"That's no concern of ours," observed the merchant, "at least at this moment. And in any case there is a married sister living in London."

The servant came in. He respectfully asked what arrangements he should make about having the body laid out, the funeral, and the mourning cards. He knew that a will was in the possession of his master's lawyer, but he was doubtful whether it contained instructions in these matters. The author found the room stuffy and close; he drew aside the heavy red curtains over one of the windows and threw open both casements, and a great waft of the dark blue spring night poured into the room. The doctor asked the servant whether he had any idea why the dead man had sent for him, because, if he remembered rightly, it was years since he had been summoned to that house in his capacity as doctor. The servant, who obviously expected the question, pulled a swollen-looking wallet from his jacket-pocket, took out a sheet of paper, and explained that seven years ago his master had written down the names of the friends whom he wanted sent for when he was dying. So that, even if the dead man had been unconscious at the time, he would have ventured to send for the gentlemen on his own responsibility.

The doctor took the sheet of paper from the servant's hand and found five names written on it: in addition to those present was the name of a friend who had died two years ago, and another that he did not know. The servant explained that the latter was a manufacturer whose house the dead man used to visit nine or ten years ago, and whose address had been lost and forgotten. The three looked at each other with uneasy curiosity. "What does that mean?" asked the merchant. "Did he intend to make a speech in his last hours?"

"A funeral oration on himself, no doubt," added the author.

The doctor had turned his eyes on the open drawer of the writing-table, and suddenly these words, in large Roman letters, stared at him from the cover of an envelope: "To my friends."

"Hullo!" he cried, took the envelope, held it up, and showed it to the others. "This is for us." He turned to the servant and, with a movement of the head, indicated that he was not wanted. The servant went.

"For us?" said the author, with wide-open eyes.

"There can be no doubt," said the doctor, "that we are justified in opening this."

"It's our duty," said the merchant, and buttoned up his overcoat.

The doctor had taken a paper-knife from a glass tray, opened his eye-glasses. The author took advantage of the brief interval to pick up the letter and unfold it. "As it is for all of us," he remarked casually, and bent over the writing-table so that the light from the shaded lamp should fall on the paper. Near him stood the merchant. The author remained seated.

"You might read it aloud," said the merchant, and the author began.

" 'To my friends,' "—he stopped with a smile—"yes, it's written here also," and he went on reading in a tone of admirable detachment. " 'About a quarter of an hour ago I breathed my last. You are assembled at my death-bed, and you are preparing to read this letter together—if it still exists in the hour of my death I ought to add. For it might so happen that I should come to a better frame of mind . . .' "

"What?" asked the doctor.

" 'A better frame of mind,' " repeated the author, and continued: " 'and decide to destroy this letter, for it can do not the slightest good to me, and, at the very least, may cause you some unpleasant hours, even if it does not absolutely poison the life of one or other of you.' "

"Poison our lives?" repeated the doctor, in a wondering tone, as he polished his eyeglasses.

"Quicker," said the merchant in a husky voice.

The author continued. " 'And I ask myself what kind of evil humour it is that sends me to the writing-table to-day and induces me to write down words whose effect I shall never be able to read upon your faces. And even if I could the pleasure I should get would be too trifling to serve an excuse for the incredible act I am now about to commit with feelings of the heartiest satisfaction.' "

"Ha!" cried the doctor in a voice he did not recognise as his own. The author threw a glance of irration at him, and read on, quicker and with less expression than before. " 'Yes, it is an evil humour, and nothing else, for I have really nothing whatever against any of you. I like you all very well in my own way, just as you like me in your way. I never despised you, and if I often laughed at you, I never mocked you. No, not once— and least of all in those hours of which you are so soon to call to mind such vivid and such painful images. Why, then, this evil humour? Perhaps it arose from a deep and not essentially ignoble desire not to leave the world with so many lies upon my soul. I might imagine so, if I had even once had the slightest notion of what men call remorse.' "

"Oh, get on to the end of it," said the doctor in a new and abrupt tone.

The merchant, without more ado, took the letter from the author, who felt a sort of paralysis creeping over his fingers, glanced down it quickly and read the words: " 'It was fate, my dear friends, and I could not alter it. I have had the wives of all of you: yes, every one.' "

The merchant stopped suddenly and turned back to the first sheet.

"The letter was written nine years ago," said the merchant.

"Go on," said the author sharply.

And the merchant proceeded. "Of course the circumstances were different in each case. With one of them I lived almost as though we had been married, for many months. The second was more or less what the world is accustomed to call a mad adventure. With the third, the affair went so far that I wanted us to kill ourselves together. The fourth I threw downstairs because she betrayed me with another. And the last was my mistress on one occasion only. Do you all breathe again—my goods friends? You should not. It was perhaps the loveliest hour of my life ... and hers. Well, my friends, I have nothing more to tell you. Now I am going to fold up this letter, put it away in my writing-desk—and there may it lie until my humour changes and I destroy it, or until it is given into your hands in that hour when I lie upon my death-bed. Farewell.' "

The doctor took the letter from the merchant's hands and read it with apparent care from the beginning to the end. Then he looked up at the merchant who stood by with folded arms and gazed down at him with something like derision.

"Although your wife died last year," said the doctor calmly, "it is none the less true."

The author paced up and down the room, jerked his head convulsively from side to side a few times, and suddenly hissed out through his clenched teeth, "the swine," and then stared in front of him as though looking for something that had dissolved into air. He was trying to recall the image of the youthful creature that he had once held in his arms as wife. Other women's faces appeared, often recalled but long since, he had thought, forgotten, but he could not bring before his mind the one he wanted. For his wife's body was withered and held no attraction for him, and it was so long since she had been his beloved. But she had become something nobler: a friend and a comrade; full of pride at his successes, full of sympathy with his disappointments, full of insight into his deepest nature. It seemed to him not impossible that the dead man had, in his wickedness, secretly envied him his comrade and tried to take her away. For all these others—what had they really meant to him? He called to mind certain adventures, some of old days and some more recent; there had been enough and to spare of them in his varied literary life, and his wife had smiled or wept over them as they went their course. Where was all this now? As faded as that far-off hour when his wife had flung herself into the arms of a man of no account, without reflection, perhaps without thought: almost as extinct as the recollection of that same hour in the dead skull that lay within on that pitifully crumpled pillow. But perhaps this last will and testament was a bundle of lies— the last revenge of a poor commonplace fellow who knew himself condemned to eternal oblivion, upon a distinguished man over whose works death has been given no power. This was not at all improbable. But even if it were true—it was a petty revenge and unsuccessful in either case.

The doctor stared at the sheet of paper that lay before him, and thought of his gentle, ever kindly wife, now growing old, who lay asleep at home. He thought also of his three children: of his eldest who was now doing his one year's military service, of his tall daughter, who was engaged to a lawyer, and of the youngest, who was so graceful and charming that a famous artist, who had lately met her at a ball, had asked if he might paint her. He thought of his comfortable home, and all this that surged up at him from the dead man's letter seemed to him not so much untrue as, in some mysterious way, almost sublimely insignificant. He scarcely felt that at this moment he had experienced anything new. A strange epoch in his existence came into his mind, fourteen or fifteen years before, when he had met with certain troubles over his profession, and, worn out and nearly crazy, had planned to leave the city, his wife and family. At the same time he had entered upon a kind of wild, reckless existence, in which a strange hysterical woman had played a part, who had subsequently committed suicide over another lover. How his life had gradually returned to its original course he could not now remember in the least. But it must have been in those bad times, which had passed away as they had come, like an illness, that his wife had betrayed him. Yes, it must so have happened, and it was clear to him that he had really always known it. Was she not once on the point of confessing it? Had she not given him hints? Thirteen or fourteen years ago. . . . When could it have been . . . ? Wasn't it one summer on a holiday trip—late in the evening on the terrace of some hotel? In vain he tried to recall those vanished words.

The merchant stood at the window and stared into the soft pale night. He was determined he would remember his dead wife. But however much he searched his inmost consciousness, at first he could only see himself in the light of a grey morning, standing in black clothes outside a curtained doorway, receiving and returning sympathetic handshakes, with a stale reek of carbolic and flowers in his nostrils. Slowly he succeeded in recalling to his mind the image of his dead wife. And yet at first it was but the image of an image for he could only see the large portrait in a gilt frame that hung over the piano in the drawing-room at home and displayed a haughty-looking lady of thirty in a ball dress. Then at last she herself appeared as a young girl, who, nearly twenty years before, pale and trembling, had accepted his proposal of marriage. Then there arose before him the appearance of a woman in all her splendour, enthroned beside him in a theatre-box, gazing at the stage, but inwardly far away. Then he remembered a passionate creature who welcomed him with unexpected warmth on his return from a long journey. Swiftly again his thoughts turned to a nervous tearful being, with greenish heavy eyes, who had poisoned his days with all manner of evil humours. Next he saw an alarmed, affectionate mother, in a light morning frock, watching by the bedside of a sick child, who none the less, died. Last of all, he saw a pale, outstretched creature in a room reeking of ether, her mouth so pitifully drawn down at the corners, and cold beads of sweat on her forehead, who had shaken his very soul with pity. He knew that all these pictures, and a hundred others, that flashed past his mind's eye with incredible speed, were of one and the same being who had been lowered into the grave two years ago, over whom he had wept, and after whose death he had felt freed from bondage. It seemed to him he must choose one out of all these pictures to reach some definite reaction; for at present he was tossed by shame and anger, groping in the void. He stood there irresolute, and gazed across at the houses in their gardens, shimmering faintly red and yellow in the moonlight and looking like pale painted walls with only air behind them.

"Good-night," said the doctor and got up.

The merchant turned toward him and said: "There's nothing more for me to do here either."

The author had picked up the letter, stuffed it unobtrusively into his coat pocket, and opened the door into the adjoining room. Slowly he walked up to the death-bed, and the others watched him looking down silently at the corpse, his hands behind his back. Then they turned away.

In the hall the merchant said to the servant: "As regards the funeral, it is possible that the will in possession of the lawyers may contain some further instructions."

"And don't forget," pursued the doctor, "to telegraph to your master's sister in London."

"To be sure, sir," replied the servant, as he opened the front door.

The author overtook them on the doorstep. "I can take you both with me," said the doctor, whose carriage was waiting.

"Thank you, no," said the merchant. "I shall walk."

He shook hands with both of them and walked down the road towards the city, glad to feel the soft night air upon his face.

The author got into the carriage with the doctor. The birds were beginning to sing in the garden. The carriage drove past the merchant, and the three men raised their hats, ironically polite, each with an identical expression on his face. "Shall we soon see another play of yours?" the doctor asked the author in his usual voice.

The latter launched into an account of the extraordinary difficulties involved in the production of his latest drama which, he had to confess, contained the most sweeping attacks on everything generally held to be sacred. The doctor nodded and did not listen. Nor did the author, for the familiar sentences fell from his lips as though he had learned them by heart.

Both men got out at the doctor's house, and the carriage drove away.

The doctor rang. They both stood and said nothing. As the footsteps of the porter approached, the author said, "Good-night, my dear doctor"; and he added slowly, with a twitch of his nostrils, "I shan't mention this to my wife, you know."

The doctor threw a sidelong glance at him and smiled his charming smile.

The door opened, they shook each other by the hand, the doctor disappeared into the passage, and the door slammed. The author went.

He felt in his breast pocket. Yes, the letter was there. His wife would find it sealed and secure among his papers. And with that strange power of imagination that was peculiarly his own, he could already hear her whispering over his grave, "Oh, how splendid of you . . . how noble!"

A Negro Doctor in the South

WALTER WHITE

HIS OFFICE completed, Kenneth began the making of those contacts he needed to secure the patients he knew were coming. In this his mother and Mamie were of invaluable assistance. Everybody knew the Harpers. It was a simple matter for Kenneth to renew acquaintances broken when he had left for school in the North. He joined local lodges of the Grand United Order of Heavenly Reapers and the Exalted Knights of Damon. The affected mysteriousness of his initiation into these fraternal orders, the secret grip, the passwords, the elaborately worded rituals, all of which the other members took so seriously, amused him, but he went through it all with an outwardly solemn demeanour. He knew it was good business to affiliate himself with these often absurd societies which played so large a part in the lives of these simple and illiterate coloured folk. Along with the strenuous emotionalism of their religion, it served as an outlet for their naturally deep feelings.

In spite of the renewal of acquaintances, the careful campaign of winning confidence in his ability as a physician, Kenneth found that the flood of patients did not come as he had hoped. The coloured people of Central City had had impressed upon them by three hundred years of slavery and that which was called freedom after the Emancipation Proclamation was signed, that no Negro doctor, however talented, was quite as good as a white one. This slave mentality, Kenneth now realized, inbred upon generation after generation of coloured folk, is the greatest handicap from which the Negro suffers, destroying as it does that confidence in his own ability which would enable him to meet without fear or apology the test of modern competition.

Kenneth's youthful appearance, too, militated against him. Though

251

twenty-nine years old, he looked not more than a mere twenty-four or twenty-five. "He may know his stuff and be as smart as all outdoors," ran the usual verdict, "but I don't want no boy treating me when I'm sick."

Perhaps the greatest factor contributing to the coloured folks' lack of confidence in physicians of their own race was the inefficiency of Dr. Williams, the only coloured doctor in Central City prior to Kenneth's return. Dr. Williams belonged to the old school and moved on the theory that when he graduated some eighteen years before from a medical school in Alabama, the development of medical knowledge had stopped. He fondly pictured himself as being the most prominent personage of Central City's Negro colony, was pompous, bulbous-eyed, and exceedingly fond of long words, especially of Latin derivation. He made it a rule of his life never to use a word of one syllable if one of two or more would serve as well. Active in fraternal order circles (he was a member of nine lodges), class-leader in Central City's largest Methodist church, arbiter supreme of local affairs in general, he filled the role with what he imagined was unsurpassable éclat. His idea of complimenting a hostess was ostentatiously to loosen his belt along about the middle of dinner. Once he had been introduced as the "black William Jennings Bryan," believed it thereafter, and thought it praise of a high order.

He was one of those who say on every possible occasion: "I am kept so terribly busy I never have a minute to myself." Like nine out of ten who say it, Dr. Williams always repeated this stock phrase of those who flatter themselves in this fashion—so necessary to those of small minds who would be thought great—not because it was true, but to enhance his pre-eminence in the eyes of his hearers—and in his own eyes as well.

He always wore coats which resembled morning coats, known in local parlance as "Jim-swingers." He kept his hair straightened, wore it brushed straight back from his forehead like highly polished steel wires, and, with promades and hair oils liberally applied, it glistened like the patent leather shoes which adorned his ample feet.

His stout form filled the Ford in which he made his professional calls, and it was a sight worth seeing as he majestically rolled through the streets of the town bowing graciously and calling out loud greetings to the acquaintances he espied by the way. Always his bows to white people were twice as low and obsequious as to those of darker skin. Until Kenneth returned, Dr. Williams had had his own way in Central City. Through his fraternal and church connections and lack of competition, he had made a little money, much of it through his position as medical examiner for the lodges to which he belonged. As long as he treated minor ailments—cuts, colic, childbirths, and the like—he had little trouble. But when more serious maladies attacked them, the coloured population sent for the old white physician, Dr. Bennett, instead of for Dr. Williams.

The great amount of time at his disposal irritated Kenneth. He was like a spirited horse, champing at the bit, eager to be off. The patronizing air of his people nettled him—caused him to reflect somewhat bitterly that "a prophet is not without honour save in his own country." And when one has not the gift of prophecy to foretell, or of clairvoyance to see, what the future holds in the way of success, one is not likely to develop a philosophic calm which enables him to await the coming of long-desired results.

He was seated one day in his office reading when his mother entered. Closing his book, he asked the reason for her frown.

"You remember Mrs. Bradley—Mrs. Emma Bradley down on Ashley Street—don't you, Kenneth?" Without waiting for a reply, Mrs. Harper went on: "Well, she's mighty sick. Jim Bradley has had Dr. Bennett in to see what's the matter with her but he doesn't seem to do her much good."

Kenneth remembered Mrs. Bradley well indeed. The most talkative woman in Central City. It was she who had come to his mother with a long face and dolorous manner when he as a youngster had misbehaved in church. He had learned instinctively to connect Mrs. Bradley's visits with excursions to the little back room accompanied by his mother and a switch from the peach-tree in the back yard—a sort of natural cause and effect. Visions of those days rose in his mind and he imagined he could feel the sting of those switches on his legs now.

"What seems to be the trouble with her?" he asked.

"It's some sort of stomach-trouble—she's got an awful pain in her side. She says it can't be her appendix because she had that removed up to Atlanta when she was operated on there for a tumor nearly four years ago. Dr. Bennett gave her some medicine but it doesn't help her any. Won't you run down there to see her?"

"I can't mama, until I am called in professionally. Dr. Bennett won't like it. It isn't ethical. Besides, didn't Mrs. Bradley say when I came back that she didn't want any coloured doctor fooling with her?"

"Yes she did, but you mustn't mind that. Just run in to see her on a social call."

Kenneth rose and instinctively took up his bag. Remembering, he put it down, put on his hat, kissed his mother, and walked down to Mrs. Bradley's. Outside the gate stood Dr. Bennett's mud-splashed buggy, sagging on one side through years of service in carrying its owner's great bulk. Between the shafts stood the old bay horse, its head hung dejectedly as though asleep.

Entering the gate held by one hinge, Kenneth made his way to the little three-room unpainted house which served as home for the Bradleys and their six children. On knocking, the door was opened by Dr. Bennett, who apparently was just leaving. He stood there, his hat on, stained by many storms, its black felt turning a greenish brown through years of service and countless rides through the red dust of the roads leading out of Central City. Dr. Bennett himself was large and flabby. His clothes hung on him in haphazard fashion and looked as though they had never been subjected to the indignity of a tailor's iron. A Sherlock Holmes, or even one less gifted, could read on his vest with little difficulty those things which its wearer had eaten for many meals past. Dr. Bennett's face was red through exposure to many suns, and covered with the bristle of a three days' growth of beard. Small eyes set close together, they belied a bluff good humour which Dr. Bennett could easily assume when there was occasion for it. The corners of the mouth were stained a deep brown where tobacco juice had run down the folds of the flesh.

Behind him stood Jim Bradley with worried face, his ashy black skin showing the effects of remaining all night by the bedside of his wife. Dr. Bennett looked at Kenneth inquiringly.

"Don't you remember me, Dr. Bennett? I'm Kenneth Harper."

"Bless my soul, so it is. How're you, Ken? Let's see—it's been nigh on to eight years since you went No'th, ain't it? Heard you was back in town. Hear you goin' to practice here. Come 'round to see me some time. Right glad you're here. I'll be kinder glad to get somebody t' help me treat these niggers for colic or when they get carved up in a crap game. Hope you ain't got none of the No'th'n ideas 'bout social equality while you was up there. Jus' do like your daddy did, and you'll get along all right down here. These niggers who went over to France and ran around with them French-women been causin' a lot of trouble 'round here, kickin' up a rumpus, and talkin' 'bout votin' and ridin' in the same car with white folks. But don't you let them get you mixed up in it, 'cause there'll be trouble sho's you born if they don't shut up and git to work. Jus' do like your daddy did, and you'll do a lot to keep the white folks' friendship."

Dr. Bennett poured forth all this gratuitous advice between asthmatic wheezes without waiting for Kenneth to reply. He then turned to Jim Bradley with a parting word of advice.

"Jim, keep that hot iron on Emma's stomach and give her those pills every hour. 'Tain't nothin' but the belly-ache. She'll be all right in an hour or two."

Turning without another word, he half ambled, half shuffled out to his buggy, pulled himself up into it with more puffing and wheezing, and drove away.

Jim Bradley took Kenneth's arm and led him back on to the little porch, closing the door behind him.

"I'm pow'ful glad t' see you, Ken. My, but you done growed sence you went up No'th! Befo' you go in dar, I want t' tell you somethin'. Emma's been right po'ly fuh two days. Her stomach's swelled up right sma't and she's been hollering all night. Dis mawning she don't seem jus' right in de haid. I tol' her I was gwine to ast you to come to see her, but she said she didn't want no young nigger doctah botherin' with her. But don't you min' her. I wants you to tell me what to do." Kenneth smiled.

"I'll do what I can for her, Jim. But what about Dr. Bennett?"

"Dat's a' right. He give her some med'cine but it ain't done her no good. She's too good a woman fuh me to lose her, even if she do talk a li'l too much. You make out like you jus' drap in to pass the time o' day with her."

Kenneth entered the dark and ill-smelling room. Opposite the door a fire smouldered in the fire-place, giving fitful spurts of flame that illumined the room and then died down again. There was no grate, the pieces of wood resting on crude andirons, blackened by the smoke of many fires. Over the mantel there hung a cheap charcoal reproduction of Jim and Emma in their wedding-clothes, made by some local "artist" from an old photograph. One or two nondescript chairs worn shiny through years of use stood before the fire. In one corner stood a dresser on which were various bottles of medicine and of "Madame Walker's Hair Grower." On the floor a rug, worn through in spots and patched with fragments of other rugs all apparently of different colours, covered the space in front of the bed. The rest of the floor was bare and showed evidences of a recent vigorous scrubbing. The one window was closed tightly and covered over with a cracked shade, long since divorced from its roller, tacked to the upper ledge of the window.

On the bed Mrs. Bradley was rolling and tossing in great pain. Her eyes opened slightly when Kenneth approached the bed and closed again immediately as a new spasm of pain passed through her body. She moaned piteously and held her hands on her side, pressing down hard one hand over the other.

At a sign from Jim, Kenneth started to take her pulse.

"Go way from her and leave me 'lone! Oh, Lawdy, why is I suff'rin' this way! I jus' wish I was daid! Oh—oh—oh!"

This last as she writhed in agony. Kenneth drew back the covers, examined Mrs. Bradley's abdomen, took her pulse. Every sign pointed to an attack of acute appendicitis. He informed Jim of his diagnosis.

"But, Doc, it ain't dat trouble, 'cause Emma says dat was taken out a long time ago."

"I can't help what she says. She's got appendicitis. You go get Dr. Bennett and tell him your wife has got to be operated on right away or she is going to die. Get a move on you now! If it was my case, I would operate within an hour. Stop by my house and tell Bob to bring me an ice bag as quick as he can."

Jim hurried away to catch Dr. Bennett. Kenneth meanwhile did what he could to relieve Mrs. Bradley's suffering. In a few minutes Bob came with the ice bag. Then Jim returned with his face even more doleful than it had been when Kenneth had told him how sick his wife was.

"Doc Bennett says he don't care what you do. He got kinder mad when I told him you said it was 'pendicitis, and tol' me dat if I couldn't take his word, he wouldn't have anything mo' to do with Emma. He seemed kinder mad 'cause you said it was mo' than a stomach-ache. Said he wa'n't goin' to let no young nigger doctor tell him his bus'ness. So, Doc, you'll have t' do what you thinks bes'."

"All right, I'll do it. First thing, I'm going to move your wife over to my office. We can put her up in the spare room. Bob will drive her over in the car. Get something around her and you'd better come on over with her. I'll get Dr. Williams to help me."

Kenneth was jubilant at securing his first surgical case since his return to Central City, though his pleasure was tinged with doubt as to the ethics of the manner in which it had come to him. He did not let that worry him very long, however, but began his preparations for the operation.

First he telephoned to Mrs. Johnson, who, before she married and settled down in Central City, had been a trained nurse at a coloured hospital at Atlanta. She hurried over at once. Neat, quiet, and efficient, she took charge immediately of preparations, sterilizing the array of shiny instruments, preparing wads of absorbent cotton, arranging bandages and catgut and haemostatics.

Kenneth left all this to Mrs. Johnson, for he knew in her hands it would be well done. He telephoned to Dr. Williams to ask that he give the anaesthesia. In his excitement Kenneth neglected to put in his voice the note of asking a great and unusual favor of Dr. Williams. That eminent physician, eminent in his own eyes, cleared his throat several times before replying, while Kenneth waited at the other end of the line. He realized his absolute dependence on Dr. Williams, for he knew no white doctor would assist a Negro surgeon or even operate with a coloured assistant. There was nòne other in Central City who could give the ether to Mrs. Bradley. It made him furious that Dr. Williams should hesitate so long. At the same time, he knew he must restrain the hot and burning words that he would have used. The pompous one hinted of the pressure of his own work—work that would keep him busy all day. Into his words he injected the note of affront at being asked—he, *the* coloured physician of Central City—to assist a younger man. Especially on that man's first case. Kenneth swallowed his anger and pride, and pleaded with Dr. Williams at least to come over. Finally, the older physician agreed in a condescending manner to do so.

Hurrying back to his office, Kenneth found Mrs. Bradley arranged on the table ready for the operation. Examining her, he found she was in delirium, her eyes glazed, her abdomen hard and distended, and she had a temperatiure of 105 degrees. He hastily sterilized his hands and put on his gown and cap. As he finished his preparations, Dr. Williams in leisurely manner strolled into the room with a benevolent and patronizing "Howdy, Kenneth, my boy. I won't be able to help you out after all. I've got to see patients of my own."

He emphasized "my own," for he had heard of the manner by which Kenneth had obtained the case of Mrs. Bradley. Kenneth, pale with anger, excited over his first real case in Central City, stared at Dr. Williams in amazement at his words.

"But, Dr. Williams, you can't do that! Mrs. Bradley here is dying!"

The older doctor looked around patronizingly at the circle of anxious faces. Jim Bradley, his face lined and seamed with toil, the lines deepened in distress at the agony of his wife and the imminence of losing her, gazed at him with dumb pleading in his eyes, pleading without spoken words with the look of an old, faithful dog beseeching its master. Bob looked with a malevolent glare at this pompous sleekness, as though he would like to spring upon him. Mrs. Johnson plainly showed her contempt of such callousness on the part of one who bore the title, however poorly, of physician. In Kenneth's eyes was a commingling of eagerness and rage and bitterness and anxiety. On Emma Bradley's face there was nothing but the pain and agony of her delirious ravings. Dr. Williams seemed to enjoy thoroughly his little moment of triumph. He delayed speaking in order that it might be prolonged as much as possible. The silence was broken by Jim Bradley.

"Doc, won't you please he'p?" he pleaded. "She's all I got!"

Kenneth could remain silent no longer. He longed to punch that fat face and erase from it the supercilious smirk that adorned it.

"Dr. Williams," he began with cold hatred in his voice, "either you are going to give this anaesthesia or else I'm going to go into every church in Central City and tell exactly what you've done here today."

Dr. Williams turned angrily on Kenneth.

"Young man, I don't allow anybody to talk to me like that—least of all, a young whippersnapper just out of school . . ." he shouted.

By this time Kenneth's patience was at an end. He seized the lapels of the other doctor's coat in one hand and thrust his clenched fist under the nose of the now thoroughly alarmed Dr. Williams.

"Are you going to help—or aren't you?" he demanded.

The situation was becoming too uncomfortable for the older man. He could stand Kenneth's opposition but not the ridicule which would inevitably follow the spreading of the news that he had been beaten up and made ridiculous by Kenneth. He swallowed—a look of indecision passed over his face as he visibly wondered if Kenneth really dared hit him—followed by a look of fear as Kenneth drew back his fist as though to strike. Discretion seemed the better course to pursue—he could wait until a later and more propitious date for his revenge—he agreed to help. A look of relief came over Jim Bradley's face. A grin covered Bob's as he saw his brother showing at last some signs of fighting spirit. Without further words Kenneth prepared to operate. . . .

Martha's Vacation

VARDIS FISHER

I

MARTHA stood by the great front door of the hospital, feeling very timid and alone. She pressed her homely face to a pane of glass and looked in; and then, seeing that her nose had stained the glass, she took a soiled handkerchief and tried to wipe the stain off. She was still briskly rubbing when the door was opened and a nurse in white stepped outside and looked at her.

"Oh!" cried Martha, abashed. Her fingers, working against her thigh, fed the handkerchief into a wad within her palm. She glanced guiltily at the pane of glass and then at the nurse. And the nurse looked at Martha's huge belly, at her worn shoes, at her round earnest face.

"You wish to see someone?"

"Uh-huh," Martha said. "I——"

"Will you come in?" The brisk manner of the nurse frightened Martha. She entered a gleaming hallway and looked about anxiously. The nurse said: "This way, please," and her voice was like the edge of a razor. She led Martha into an office that was one spotless gleam. "Wait here a moment."

The nurse left the office, her clothes alive with cleanliness, and Martha drew her breath on a great sigh. She looked at the chairs, but they were very clean and she dared not sit on them. She looked behind her to see if her shoes had tracked the floor. And she was standing here, trembling a little and feeling very lonely, when another nurse enterd. The nurse seated herself at a desk.

"Will you sit down?" she asked.

Martha sank weakly to a chair.

"When do you expect your child?"

"I——" Martha stared, helpless. "I feel pains," she said.

"You do?" The nurse frowned and Martha was paralyzed. "Have you made arrangements here?"

"Huh-unh," Martha said.

"Who sent you here?"

"No one. I just come."

For a long moment the nurse looked at her. Her eyes, it seemed to Martha, were not friendly. They were clean cold eyes like her dress and the walls.

"Wheres is your husband?"

Martha looked down at the short hands lying in her lap.

"What is your name?"

"Martha Scott."

"Where are your parents?"

"I—I don't have none."

"You mean you're an orphan? How old are you?"

"Twenty-two."

"Do you work?"

"Yes, when I'n get work."

"What kind of work?"

"Oh, just anything. Just—just anything."

"And the father of your child, won't he marry you?"

Martha again stared at her hands. She hesitated; when she looked up to meet the steady gaze of the nurse, there was terror in her eyes.

"Huh-unh," she said.

II

Martha felt better now. She was lying in a spotless bed and her pain was done. There was a strong smell in the room but everything else was very lovely and nice. Somewhere in this great building was her infant but she did not think of it; there was so much else to think of: the soft deep bed on which she lay, the clean fragrance of the bedding, the touch

Vardis Fisher

of cool linen on her hot flesh. There was a picture on the wall and she thought it was very nice, too: a young girl in a lovely place, with grass and running water and trees. In all her years she had never once seen running water.

When a nurse came, bringing her son, she took the tiny thing in her arms and laid it to her breast.

"How you feeling?"

"Just fine." Martha looked up and smiled. Never before had anyone asked how she felt. The people here were very nice. "I like it here," she said.

"Do you have enough to eat?"

The nurse left the room and Martha suckled her child. The tiny sucking mouth gave her a little pleasure but not the deep pleasure George had given her. George had lain against her, his hungry mouth to her breast, his curly hair in her face, smelling of something sweet. She had been very happy then. Well, she was very happy now, in a different way. She might be here a long time—she wondered how long—having food brought to her bedside, having people smile at her and ask how she felt. She brushed her teeth now. The nurse had given her a new brush, taking it out of a sealed package, and powder that was sweet in her mouth. Afternoons, she chose from a bowl of fruit, taking a very little, not caring to take much. . . .

"Is that all you want?"

"Yes, that's all."

"Honest?"

"Yes, honest," Martha looked up and smiled. "And thanks."

III

After a week passed she sat up in bed and tried to realize to its fullest the wonder of this place. There was no unpleasant smell in her room now. The nurse smelled as if she had just been starched and laundered; and so did the bed. She looked around her, thinking of her own dark hallway room. The pillows here were soft and she loved to bury her face in them and feel their cool cleanness; to move her head and feel the softness on the back of her neck. She loved to stretch out in this bed, thrusting with her naked legs into the cool recesses, remembering the hot world outside; reaching out with her arms and feeling the delicious chill; drawing the sheet, almost stiff with cleanliness and with a sweet smell, to her mouth and breathing of it.

The nurse had brought her some magazines. She did not read easily and she had to spell many of the words out and many of them she did not understand; but she felt her way through these love-tales and they thrilled her in a way George had thrilled her: a sudden rapture that came awake in her and moved in a flood to her heart. It was nice to lie here in a clean bed, with no work to do, and read of lovely things.

"Do you need more light?"

"No, ma'am. I'n see all right."

"Do you like these stories?"

"Yes, ma'am." Martha looked at her with eyes wide and bright. "They're awful nice, I think."

Every day a doctor came in. He was a tall man with a mustache and Martha thought he was very good-looking and very kind. He smiled at her and asked how she felt.

"Just fine," Martha said, her smile answering his.

"You look fit as a fiddle."

"I sure feel fine." Martha stretched luxuriously under the sheet. "I like it here," she said.

"You do? Most persons don't like a hospital."

"Oh, I do. I think it's awful nice. I could stay here a long time."

And when, one day, the nurse said: "You will leave tomorrow, you know," Martha stared at her and felt lost.

"Tomorrow?"

"Yes."

"Please, couldn't I stay a little while longer?"

"I'm afraid not. You see, other patients are coming all the time. You've been here two weeks, you know."

"I have! It seems like two days." She looked around her. "Like two hours," she said. "Couldn't I stay a little longer? ... Couldn't I?"

"I'm afraid not." The nurse did not look at her.

"Wouldn't the doctor let me?"

"The doctor doesn't have anything to do with it."

"Oh," Martha said. She lay in silence, wondering. "If I could just stay one more day," she said, "it would be awful nice."

The next morning with the babe in her arms she stood in a hallway and looked back at her room. She returned and looked in, and a nurse came and smiled and led her away.

IV

Fifteen months passed and Martha stood again at the great front door of the hospital. She did not press her face to the glass and look in. She opened the big door and entered, and nurses hurried by on slim-slippered feet and did not look at her. She advanced a little, seeking the office where she had been questions. The white nurse was there.

"Hello," Martha said.

"You wish to see someone?"

"Please. I'd like to see Miss Anderson. She's a nurse here."

The woman gave Martha a long and curious stare.

"Weren't you here once before?"

"Yes." Martha brightened and stepped into the office. "I'm Martha Scott," she said.

The nurse turned to records and searched among them. For a long moment she looked at one. She turned to Martha, her eyes unfriendly.

"And you're back again!"

Martha was radiant now. Her tired face smiled and her eyes filled with happiness that was clean and bright.

"And, please," she said, "could I have the same room I had last time?"

The Scarlet Plague

JACK LONDON

THE WAY led along upon what had once been the embankment of a railroad. But no train had run upon it for many years. The forest on either side swelled up the slopes of the embankment and crested across it in a green wave of trees and bushes. The trail was as narrow as a man's body, and was no more than a wild-animal runway. Occasionally, a piece of rusty iron, showing through the forest-mould, advertised that the rail and the ties still remained. In one place, a ten-inch tree, bursting through at a connection, had lifted the end of a rail clearly into view. The tie had evidently followed the rail, held to it by the spike long enough for its bed to be filled with gravel and rotten leaves, so that now the crumbling, rotten timber thrust itself up at a curious slant. Old as the road was, it was manifest that it had been the mono-rail type.

An old man and a boy travelled along this runway. They moved slowly, for the old man was very old, a touch of palsy made his movements tremulous, and he leaned heavily upon his staff. A rude skull-cap of goat-skin protected his head from the sun. From beneath this fell a scant fringe of stained and dirty-white hair. A visor, ingeniously made from a large leaf, shielded his eyes, and from under this he peered at the way of his feet on the trail. His beard, which should have been snow-white but which showed the same weather-wear and camp-stain as his hair, fell nearly to his waist in a great tangled mass. About his chest and shoulders hung a single, mangy garment of goat-skin. His arms and legs, withered and skinny, betokened extreme age, as well as did their

265

sunburn and scars and scratches betoken long years of exposure to the elements.

The boy, who led the way, checking the eagerness of his muscles to the slow progress of the elder, likewise wore a single garment—a ragged-edged piece of bear skin, with a hole in the middle through which he had thrust his head. He could not have been more than twelve years old. Tucked coquettishly over one ear was the freshly severed tail of a pig. In one hand he carried a medium-sized bow and an arrow. On his back was a quiverful of arrows. From a sheath hanging about his neck on a thong, projected the battered handle of a hunting knife. He was as brown as a berry, and walked softly, with almost a catlike tread. In marked contrast with his sunburned skin were his eyes—blue, deep blue, but keen and sharp as a pair of gimlets. They seemed to bore into all about him in a way that was habitual. As he went along he smelled things, as well, his distended, quivering nostrils carrying to his brain an endless series of messages from the outside world. Also, his hearing was acute, and had been so trained that it operated automatically. Without conscious effort, he heard all the slight sounds in the apparent quiet— heard, and differentiated, and classified these sounds—whether they were of the wind rustling the leaves, of the humming of bees and gnats, of the distant rumble of the sea that drifted to him only in lulls, or of the gospher, just under his foot, shoving a pouchful of earth into the entrance of his hole.

Suddenly he became alertly tense. Sound, sight, and odor had given him a simultaneous warning. His hand went back to the old man, touching him, and the pair stood still. Ahead, at one side of the top of the embankment, arose a crackling sound, and the boy's gaze was fixed on the tops of the agitated bushes. Then a large bear, a grizzly, crashed into view, and likewise stopped abruptly, at sight of the humans. He did not like them, and growled querulously. Slowly the boy fitted the arrow to the bow, and slowly he pulled the bowstring taut. But he never removed his eyes from the bear. The old man peered from under his green leaf at the danger, and stood as quietly as the boy. For a few seconds this mutual scrutinizing went on; then, the bear betraying a growing irritability, the boy, with a movement of his head, indicated that the old man must step aside from the trail and go down the embankment. The boy followed, going backward, still holding the bow taut and ready. They waited till a crashing among the bushes from the opposite side of the embankment told them the bear had gone on. The boy grinned as he led back to the trail.

"A big un, Granser," he chuckled.

The old man shook his head.

"They get thicker every day," he complained in a thin, undependable falsetto. "Who'd have thought I'd live to see the time when a man would be afraid of his life on the way to Cliff House. When I was a boy, Edwin, men and women and little babies used to come out here from San Francisco by tens of thousands on a nice day. And there weren't any bears then. No. sir. They used to pay money to look at them in cages, they were that rare."

"What is money, Granser?"

Before the old man could answer, the boy recollected and triumphantly shoved his hand into a pouch under his bear-skin and pulled forth a battered and tarnished silver dollar. The old man's eyes glistened, as he held the coin close to them.

"I can't see," he muttered. "You look and see if you can make out the date, Edwin."

The boy laughed.

"You're a great Granser," he cried delightedly, "always making believe them little marks mean something."

The old man manifested an accustomed chagrin as he brought the coin back again close to his own eyes.

"2012," he shrilled, and then fell to cackling grotesquely. "That was the year Morgan the Fifth was appointed President of the United States by the Board of Magnates. It must have been one of the last coins minted, for the Scarlet Death came in 2013. Lord! Lord!—think of it! Sixty years ago, and I am the only person alive today that lived in those times. Where did you find it, Edwin?"

The boy, who had been regarding him with the tolerant curiousness one accords to the prattlings of the feeble-minded, answered promptly.

"I got it off of Hoo-Hoo. He found it when we was herdin' goats down near San Jose last spring. Hoo-Hoo said it was *money*. Ain't you hungry, Granser?"

The ancient caught his staff in a tighter grip and urged along the trail, his old eyes shining greedily.

"I hope Hare-Lip's found a crab . . . or two," he mumbled. "They're good eating, crabs, mighty good eating when you've no more teeth and you've got grandsons that love their old grandsire and make a point of catching crabs for him. When I was a boy—"

But Edwin, suddenly stopped by what he saw, was drawing the bowstring on a fitted arrow. He had paused on the brink of a crevasse in the embankment. An ancient culvert had here washed out, and the stream, no longer confined, had cut a passage through the fill. On the opposite side the end of a rail projected and overhung. It showed rustily through the creeping vines which overran it. Beyond, crouching by a bush, a rabbit looked across at him in trembling hesitancy. Fully fifty feet was the distance, but the arrow flashed true; and the transfixed rabbit, crying out in sudden fright and hurt, struggled painfully away into the brush. The boy himself was a flash of brown skin and flying fur as he bounded down the steep wall of the gap and up the other side. His lean muscles were springs of steel that released into graceful and efficient action. A hundred feet beyond, in a tangle of bushes, he overtook the wounded creature, knocked its head on a convenient tree-trunk, and turned it over to Granser to carry.

"Rabbit is good, very good," the ancient quavered, "but when it come to a toothsome delicacy I prefer crab. When I was a boy—"

"Why do you say so much that ain't got no sense?" Edwin impatiently interrupted the other's threatened garrulousness.

The boy did not exactly utter these words, but something that remotely resembled them and that was more guttural and explosive and economical of qualifying phrases. His speech showed distant kinship with that of the old man, and the latter's speech was approximately an

English that had gone through a bath of corrupt usage.

"What I want to know," Edwin continued, "is why you call crab 'toothsome delicacy?' Crab is crab, ain't it? No one I never heard calls it such funny things."

The old man sighed but did not answer, and they moved on in silence. The surf grew suddenly louder, as they emerged from the forest upon a stretch of sand dunes bordering the sea. A few goats were browsing among the sandy hillocks, and a skin-clad boy, aided by a wolfish-looking dog that was only faintly reminiscent of a collie, was watching them. Mingled with the roar of the surf was a continuous, deep-throated barking or bellowing, which came from a cluster of jagged rocks a hundred yards out from shore. Here huge sea-lions hauled themselves up to lie in the sun or battle with one another. In the immediate foreground arose the smoke of a fire, tended by a third savage-looking boy. Crouched near him were several wolfish dogs similar to the one that guarded the goats.

The old man accelerated his pace, sniffing eagerly as he neared the fire.

"Mussels!" he muttered ecstatically. "Mussels! And ain't that a crab, Hoo-Hoo? Ain't that a crab? My, my, you boys are good to your old grandsire."

Hoo-Hoo, who was apparently of the same age as Edwin, grinned. "All you want, Granser. I got four."

The old man's palsied eagerness was pitiful. Sitting down in the sand as quickly as his stiff limbs would let him, he poked a large rock-mussel from out of the coals. The heat had forced its shells apart, and the meat, salmon-colored, was thoroughly cooked. Between thumb and forefinger, in trembling haste, he caught the morsel and carried it to his mouth. But it was too hot, and the next moment was violently ejected. The old man spluttered with the pain, and tears ran out of his eyes and down his cheeks.

The boys were true savages, possessing only the cruel humor of the savage. To them the incident was excruciatingly funny, and they burst into loud laughter. Hoo-Hoo danced up and down, while Edwin rolled gleefully on the ground. The boy with the goats came running to join in the fun.

"Set 'em to cool, Edwin, set 'em to cool," the old man besought, in the midst of his grief, making no attempt to wipe away the tears that still flowed from his eyes. "And cool a crab, Edwin, too. You know your grandsire likes crabs."

From the coals arose a great sizzling, which proceeded from the many mussels, bursting open their shells and exuding their moisture. They were large shellfish, running from three to six inches in length. The boys raked them out with sticks and placed them on a large piece of driftwood to cool.

"When I was a boy, we did not laugh at our elders; we respected them."

The boys took no notice, and Granser continued to babble an incoherent flow of complaint and censure. But this time he was more careful, and did not burn his mouth. All began to eat, using nothing but their hands and making loud mouth-noises and lip-smackings. The third boy, who was called Hare-Lip, slyly deposited a pinch of sand on a mussel the ancient was carrying to his mouth; and when the grit of it bit into the old fellow's mucous membrane and gums, the laughter was again uproarious. He was unaware that a joke had been played on him, and spluttered and spat until Edwin, relenting, gave him a gourd of fresh water with which to wash out his mouth.

"Where's them crabs, Hoo-Hoo?" Edwin demanded. "Granser's set upon having a snack."

Again Granser's eyes burned with greediness as a large crab was handed to him. It was a shell with legs and all complete, but the meat had long since departed. With shaky fingers and babblings of anticipation, the old man broke off a leg and found it filled with emptiness.

"The crabs, Hoo-Hoo?" he wailed. "The crabs?"

"I was foolin', Granser. They ain't no crabs. I never found one."

The boys were overwhelmed with delight at sight of the tears of senile disappointment that dribbled down the old man's cheeks. Then, unnoticed, Hoo-Hoo replaced the empty shell with a fresh-cooked crab. Already dismembered, from the cracked legs the white meat sent forth a small cloud of savory steam. This attracted the old man's nostrils, and he looked down in amazement. The change of his mood to one of joy was immediate. He snuffled and muttered and mumbled, making almost a croon of delight, as he began to eat. Of this the boys took little notice, for it was an accustomed spectacle. Nor did they notice his occasional exclamations and utterances of phrases which meant nothing to them, as, for instance, when he smacked his lips and champed his gums while muttering: "Mayonnaise! Just think—mayonnaise! And it's sixty years since the last was ever made! Two generations and never a smell of it! Why, in those days it was served in every restaurant with crab."

When he could eat no more, the old man sighed, wiped his hands on his naked legs, and gazed out over the sea. With the content of a full stomach, he waxed reminiscent.

"To think of it! I've seen this beach alive with men, women, and children on a pleasant Sunday. And there weren't any bears to eat them up, either. And right up there on the cliff was a big restaurant where you could get anything you wanted to eat. Four million people lived in San Francisco then. And now, in the whole city and county there aren't forty all told. And out there on the sea were ships and ships always to be seen, going in for the Golden Gate or coming out. And airships in the air—dirigibles and flying machines. They could travel two hundred miles an hour. The mail contracts with the New York and San Francisco Limited demanded that for the minimum. There was a chap, a Frenchman, I forget his name, who succeeded in making three hundred; but the thing was risky, too risky for conservative persons. But he was on the right clew, and he would have managed it if it hasn't been for the Great Plague. When I was a boy, there were men alive who remembered the coming of the first aeroplanes, and now I have lived to see the last of them, and that sixty years ago."

The old man babbled on, unheeded by the boys, who were long accustomed to his garrulousness, and whose vocabularies, besides, lacked the greater portion of the words he used. It was noticeable that in these rambling soliloquies his English seemed to recrudesce into better construction and phraseology. But when he talked directly with the boys it lapsed, largely into their own uncouth and simpler forms.

"But there weren't many crabs in those days," the old man wandered on. "They were fished out, and they were great delicacies. The open season was only a month long, too. And now crabs are accessible the whole year around. Think of it—catching all the crabs you want, any time you want, in the surf of the Cliff House beach!"

A sudden commotion among the goats brought the boys to their feet. The dogs about the fire rushed to join their snarling fellow who guarded the goats, while the goats themselves stampeded in the direction of their human protectors. A half dozen forms, lean and gray, glided about on the sand hillocks or faced the bristling dogs. Edwin arched an arrow that fell short. But Hare-Lip, with a sling such as David carried into battle against Goliath, hurled a stone through the air that whistled from the speed of its flight. It fell squarely among the wolves and caused them to slink away toward the dark depths of the eucalyptus forest.

The boys laughed and lay down again in the sand, while Granser sighed ponderously. He had eaten too much, and, with hands clasped on his paunch, the fingers interlaced, he resumed his maunderings.

" 'The fleeting systems lapse like foam,' " he mumbled what was evidently a quotation. "That's it—foam, and fleeting. All man's toil upon the planet was just so much foam. He domesticated the serviceable animals, destroyed the hostile ones, and cleared the land of its wild vegetation. And then he passed, and the flood of primordial life rolled back again, sweeping his handiwork away—the weeds and the forest inundated his fields, the beasts of prey swept over his flocks, and now there are wolves on the Cliff House beach." He was appalled by the thought. "Where four million people disported themselves, the wild wolves roam to-day, and the savage progeny of our loins, with prehistoric weapons, defend themselves against the fanged despoilers. Think of it! And all because of the Scarlet Death—"

The adjective had caught Hare-Lip's ear.

"He's always saying that," he said to Edwin. "What is *scarlet?*"

" 'The scarlet of the maples can shake me like the cry of bugles going by,' " the old man quoted.

"It's red," Edwin answered the question. "And you don't know it because you come from the Chauffeur Tribe. They never did know nothing, none of them. *Scarlet* is red—I know that."

"Red is red, ain't it?" Hare-Lip grumbled. "Then what's the good of gettin' cocky and calling it scarlet?"

"Granser, what for do you always say so much what nobody knows?" he asked. "Scarlet ain't anything, but red is red. Why don't you say red, then?"

"Red is not the right word," was the reply. "The plague was scarlet. The whole face and body turned scarlet in an hour's time. Don't I know? Didn't I see enough of it? And I am telling you it was scarlet because—well, because it *was* scarlet. There is no other word for it."

"Red is good enough for me," Hare-Lip muttered obstinately. "My dad calls red red, and he ought to know. He says everything died of the Red Death."

"Your dad is a common fellow, descended from a common fellow," Granser retorted heatedly. "Don't I know the beginnings of the Chauffeurs? Your grandsire was a chauffeur, a servant, and without education. He worked for other persons. But your grandmother was of good stock, only the children did not take after her. Don't I remember when I first met them, catching fish at Lake Temescal?"

"What is *education?*" Edwin asked.

"Calling red scarlet," Hare-Lip sneered, then returned to the attack on Granser. "My dad told me, an' he got it from his dad afore he croaked, that your wife was a Santa Rosan, an' that she was sure no account. He said she was a *hash-slinger* before the Red Death, though I don't know what a *hash-slinger* is. You can tell me, Edwin."

But Edwin shook his head in token of ignorance.

"It is true, she was a waitress," Granser acknowledged. "But she was a good woman, and your mother was her daughter. Women were very scarce in the days after the Plague. She was the only wife I could find, even if she was *a hash-slinger*, as your father calls it. But it is not nice to talk about our progenitors that way."

"Dad says that the wife of the first Chauffeur was a *lady*—"

"What's a *lady?*" Hoo-Hoo demanded.

"A *lady's* a Chauffeur squaw," was the quick reply of Hare-Lip.

"The first Chauffeur was Bill, a common fellow, as I said before," the old man expounded; "but his wife was a lady, a great lady. Before the Scarlet Death she was the wife of Van Worden. He was President of the Board of Industrial Magnates, and was one of the dozen men who ruled America. He was worth one billion, eight hundred millions of dollars—coins like you have there in your pouch, Edwin. And then came the Scarlet Death, and his wife became the wife of Bill, the first Chauffeur. He used to beat her, too. I have seen it myself."

Hoo-Hoo, lying on his stomach and idly digging his toes in the sand, cried out and investigated, first, his toenail, and next, the small hole he had dug. The other two boys joined him, excavating the sand rapidly with their hands till there lay three skeletons exposed. Two were of adults, the third being that of a part-grown child. The old man hudged along on the ground and peered at the find.

"Plague victims," he announced. "That's the way they died everywhere in the last days. This must have been a family, running away from the contagion and perishing here on the Cliff House beach. They—what are you doing, Edwin?"

This question was asked in sudden dismay, as Edwin, using the back of his hunting knife, began to knock out the teeth from the jaws of one of the skulls.

"Going to string 'em," was the response.

The three boys were now hard at it; and quite a knocking and hammering arose, in which Granser babbled on unnoticed.

"You are true savages. Already has begun the custom of wearing human teeth. In another generation you will be perforating your noses and ears and wearing ornaments of bone and shell. I know. The human race is doomed to sink back farther and farther into the primitive night ere again it begins its bloody climb upward to civilization. When we increase and feel the lack of room, we will proceed to kill one another. And then I suppose you will wear human scalp-locks at your waist, as well—as you, Edwin, who are the gentlest of my grandsons, have already begun with that vile pigtail. Throw it away, Edwin, boy; throw it away."

"What a gabble the old geezer makes," Hare-Lip remarked, when, the teeth all extracted, they began an attempt at equal division.

They were very quick and abrupt in their actions, and their speech, in moments of hot discussion over the allotment of the choicer teeth, was truly a gabble. They spoke in monosyllables and short jerky sentences that was more a gibberish than a language. And yet, through it ran hints of grammatical construction, and appeared vestiges of the conjugation of some superior culture. Even the speech of Granser was so corrupt that were it put down literally it would be almost so much nonsense to the reader. This, however, was when he talked with the boys. When he got into the full swing of babbling to himself, it slowly purged itself into pure English. The sentences grew longer and were enunciated with a rhythm and ease that was reminiscent of the lecture platform.

"Tell us about the Red Death, Granser," Hare-Lip demanded, when the teeth affair had been satisfactorily concluded.

"The Scarlet Death," Edwin corrected.

"An' don't work all that funny lingo on us," Hare-Lip went on. "Talk sensible, Granser, like a Santa Rosan ought to talk. Other Santa Rosans don't talk like you."

II

The old man showed pleasure in being thus called upon. He cleared his throat and began.

"Twenty or thirty years ago my story was in great demand. But in these days nobody seems interested—"

"There you go!" Hare-Lip cried hotly. "Cut out the funny stuff and talk sensible. What's *interested?* You talk like a baby that don't know how."

"Let him alone," Edwin urged, "or he'll get mad and won't talk at all. Skip the funny places. We'll catch on to some of what he tells us."

"Let her go, Granser," Hoo-Hoo encouraged; for the old man was already maundering about the disrespect for elders and the reversion to cruelty of all humans that fell from high culture to primitive conditions.

The tale began.

"There were very many people in the world in those days. San Francisco alone held four millions—"

"What is millions?" Edwin interrupted.

Granser looked at him kindly.

"I know you cannot count beyond ten, so I will tell you. Hold up your two hands. On both of them you have altogether ten fingers and thumbs. Very well. I now take this grain of sand—you hold it, Hoo-Hoo." He dropped the grain of sand into the lad's palm and went on. "Now that grain of sand stands for the ten fingers of Edwin. I add another grain. That's ten more fingers. And I add another, and another, and another, until I have added as many grains as Edwin has fingers and thumbs. That makes what I call one hundred. Remember that word—one hundred. Now I put this pebble in Hare-Lip's hand. It stands for ten grains of sand, or ten tens of fingers, or one hundred fingers. I put in ten pebbles. They stand for thousand fingers. I take a mussel-shell, and it stands for ten pebbles, or one hundred grains of sand, or one thousand fingers. . . ."

And so on, laboriously, and with much reiteration, he strove to build up in their minds a crude conception of numbers. As the quantities increased, he had the boys holding different magnitudes in each of their hands. For still higher sums, he laid the symbols on the log of driftwood; and for symbols he was hard put, being compelled to use the teeth from the skulls for millions, and the crabshells for billions. It was here that he stopped, for the boys were showing signs of becoming tired.

"There were four million people in San Francisco—four teeth.

The boys' eyes ranged along from the teeth and from hand to hand, down through the pebbles and sand-grains to Edwin's fingers. And back again they ranged along the ascending series in the effort to grasp such inconceivable numbers.

"That was a lot of folks, Granser," Edwin at last hazarded.

"Like sand on the beach here, like sand on the beach, each grain of sand a man, or woman, or child. Yes, my boy, all those people lived right here in San Francisco. And at one time or another all those people came out on this very beach—more people than there are grains of sand. More—more—more. And San Francisco was a noble city. And across the bay—where we camped last year, even more people lived, clear from Point Richmond, on the level ground and on the hills, all the way around to San Leandro—one great city of seven million people.—Seven teeth . . . there, that's it, seven millions."

Again the boys' eyes ranged up and down from Edwin's fingers to the teeth on the log.

"The world was full of people. The census of 2010 gave eight billions for the whole world—eight crab-shells, yes, eight billions. It was not like to-day. Mankind knew a great deal more about getting food. And the more food there was, the more people there were. In the year 1800, there were one hundred and seventy millions in Europe alone. One hundred years later—a grain of sand, Hoo-Hoo—one hundred years later, at 1900, there were five hundred millions in Europe—five grains of sand, Hoo-Hoo, and this one tooth. This shows how easy was the getting of food, and how men increased. And in the year 2000, there were fifteen hundred millions in Europe. And it was the same all over the rest of the world. Eight crab-shells there, yes, eight billion people were alive on the earth when the Scarlet Death began.

"I was a young man when the Plague came—twenty-seven years old; and I lived on the other side of San Francisco Bay, in Berkeley. You remember those great stone houses, Edwin, when we came down the hills from Contra Costa? That was where I lived, in those stone houses. I was a professor of English literature."

Much of this was over the heads of the boys, but they strove to comprehend dimly this tale of the past.

"What was them stone houses for?" Hare-Lip queried.

"You remember when your dad taught you to swim?" The boy nodded. "Well, in the University of California—that is the name we had for the houses—we taught young men and women how to think, just as I have taught you now, by sand and pebbles and shells, to know how many people lived in those days. There was very much to teach. The young men and women we taught were called students. We had large rooms in which we taught. I talked to them, forty or fifty at a time, just as I am talking to you now. I told them about the books other men had written before their time, and even, sometimes, in their time—"

"Was that all you did?—just talk, talk, talk?" Hoo-Hoo demanded. "Who hunted your meat for you? and milked the goats? and caught the fish?"

"A sensible question, Hoo-Hoo, a sensible question. As I have told you, in those days food-getting was easy. We were very wise. A few men got the food for many men. The other men did other things. As you say, I talked. I talked all the time, and for this food was given me—much food, fine food, beautiful food, food that I have not tasted in sixty years and shall never taste again. I sometimes think the most wonderful achievement of our tremendous civilization was food—its inconceivable abundance, its infinite variety, its marvellous delicacy. O my grandsons, life was life in those days, when we had such wonderful things to eat."

This was beyond the boys, and they let it slip by, words and thoughts, as a mere senile wandering in the narrative.

"Our food-getters were called *freemen*. This was a joke. We of the ruling classes owned all the land, all the machines, everything. These food-getters were our slaves. We took almost all the food they got, and left them a little so that they might eat, and work, and get us more food—"

"I'd have gone into the forest and got food for myself," Hare-Lip announced; "and if any man tried to take it away from me, I'd have killed him."

The old man laughed.

"Did I not tell you that we of the ruling class owned all the land, all the forest, everything? Any food-getter who would not get food for us, him we punished or compelled to, starve to death. And very few did that. They preferred to get food for us, and make clothes for us, and prepare and administer to us a thousand—a mussel-shell, Hoo-Hoo—a thousand satisfactions and delights. And I was Professor Smith in those days— Professor James Howard Smith. And my lecture courses were very popular—that is, very many of the young men and women liked to hear me talk about the books other men had written.

"And I was very happy, and I had beautiful things to eat. And my hands were soft, because I did no work with them, and my body was clean all over and dressed in the softest garments—" He surveyed his mangy goat-skin with disgust. "We did not wear such things in those days. Even the slaves had better garments. And we were most clean. We washed our faces and hands often every day. You boys never wash unless you fall into the water or go in swimming."

"Neither do you, Granser," Hoo-Hoo retorted.

"I know, I know. I am a filthy old man. But times have changed. Nobody washes these days, and there are no conveniences. It is sixty years since I have seen a piece of soap. You do not know what soap is, and I shall not tell you, for I am telling the story of the Scarlet Death. You know what sickness is. We called it a disease. Very many of the diseases came from what we called germs. Remember that word—germs. A germ is a very small thing. It is like a woodtick, such as you find on the dogs in the spring of the year when they run in the forest. Only the germ is very small. It is so small that you cannot see it—"

Hoo-Hoo began to laugh.

"You're a queer un, Granser, talking about things you can't see. If you can't see 'em, how do you know they are? That's what I want to know. How do you know anything you can't see?"

"A good question, a very good question, Hoo-Hoo. But we did see— some of them. We had what we called microscopes and ultramicroscopes, and we put them to our eyes and looked through them, so that we saw things larger than they really were, and many things we could not see without the microscopes at all. Our best ultramicroscopes could make a germ look forty thousand times larger. A mussel-shell is a thousand fingers like Edwin's. Take forty mussel-shells, and by as many times larger was the germ when we looked at it through a microscope. And after that, we had other ways, by using what we called moving pictures, of making the forty-thousand-times germ many, many thousand times larger still. And thus we saw all these things which our eyes of themselves could not see. Take a grain of sand. Break it into ten pieces. Take one piece and break it into ten. Break one of those pieces into ten, and one of those into ten, and one of those into ten, and one of those into ten, and do it all day, and maybe, by sunset, you will have a piece as small as one of the germs."

The boys were openly incredulous. Hare-Lip sniffed and sneered and Hoo-Hoo snickered, until Edwin nudged them to be silent.

"The woodtick sucks the blood of the dog, but the germ, being so very small, goes right into the blood of the body, and there it has many children. In those days there would be as many as a billion—a crab-shell, please—as many as that crab-shell in one man's body. We called germs micro-organisms. When a few million, or a billion, of them were in a man, in all the blood of a man, he was sick. These germs were a disease. There were many different kinds of them—more different kinds than there are grains of sand on this beach. We knew only a few of the kinds. The micro-organic world was an invisible world, a world we could not see, and we knew very little about it. Yet we did know something. There was the *bacillus anthracis;* there was the *micrococcus;* there was the *Bacterium termo,* and the *Bacterium lactis*—that's what turns the goat milk sour even to this day, Hare-Lip; and there were *Schizomycetes* without end. And there were many others. . . ."

Here the old man launched into a disquisition on germs and their natures, using words and phrases of such extraordinary length and meaninglessness, that the boys grinned at one another and looked out over the deserted ocean till they forgot the old man was babbling on.

"But the Scarlet Death, Granser," Edwin at last suggested.

Granser recollected himself, and with a start tore himself away from the rostrum of the lecture-hall, where to another-world audience, he had been expounding the latest theory, sixty years gone, of germs and germ-diseases.

"Yes, yes, Edwin; I had forgotten. Sometimes the memory of the past is very strong upon me, and I forget that I am a dirty old man, clad in goat-skin, wandering with my savage grandsons who are goat-herds in the primeval wilderness. 'The fleeting systems lapse like foam,' and so lapsed our glorious, colossal civilization. I am Granser, a tired old man. I belong to the tribe of Santa Rosans. I married into that tribe. My sons and daughters married into the Chauffeurs, the Sacramentos, and the Palo-Altos. You, Hare-Lip, are of the Chauffeurs. You, Edwin, are of the Sacramentos. And you, Hoo-Hoo, are of the Palo-Altos. Your tribe takes its name from a town that was near the seat of another great institution of learning. It was called Stanford University. Yes, I remember now. It is perfectly clear. I was telling you of the Scarlet Death. Where was I in my story?"

"You was telling about germs, the things you can't see but which make men sick," Edwin prompted.

"Yes, that's where I was. A man did not notice at first when only a few of these germs got into his body. But each germ broke in half and became two germs, and they kept doing this very rapidly so that in a short time there were many millions of them in the body. Then the man was sick. He had a disease, and the disease was named after the kind of a germ that was in him. It might be measles, it might be influenza, it might be yellow·fever; it might be any of thousands and thousands of kinds of diseases.

"Now this is the strange thing about these germs. There were always new ones coming to live in men's bodies. Long and long and long ago, when there were only a few men in the world, there were few diseases. But as men increased and lived closely together in great cities and civilizations, new diseases arose, new kinds of germs entered their bodies. Thus were countless millions and billions of human beings killed. And the more thickly men packed together, the more terrible were the new diseases that came to be. Long before my time, in the middle ages, there was the Black Plague that swept across Europe. It swept across Europe many times. There was tuberculosis, that entered into men wherever they were thickly packed. A hundred years before my time there was the bubonic plague. And in Africa was the sleeping sickness. The bacteriologists fought all these sicknesses and destroyed them, just as you boys fight the wolves away from your goats, or squash the mosquitoes that light on you. The bacteriologists—"

"But Granser, what is a what-you-call-it?" Edwin interrupted.

"You, Edwin, are a goat-herd. Your task is to watch the goats. You know a great deal about goats. A bacteriologist watches germs. That's his task, and he knows a great deal about them. So, as I was saying, the bacteriologists fought with the germs and destroyed them—sometimes. There was leprosy, a horrible disease. A hundred years before I was born, the bacteriologists discovered the germ of leprosy. They knew all about it. They made pictures of it. I have seen those pictures. But they never found a way to kill it. But in 1984, there was the Pantoblast Plague, a disease that broke out in a country called Brazil and that killed millions of people. But the bacteriologists found it out, and found the way to kill it, so that the Pantoblast Plague went no farther. They made what they called a serum, which they put into a man's body and which killed the Pantoblast germs without killing the man. And in 1910, there was Pellagra, and also the hookworm. These were easily killed by the bacteriologists. But in 1947 there arose a new disease that had never been seen before. It got into the bodies of babies of only ten months old or less, and it made them unable to move their hands and feet, or to eat, or anything; and the bacteriologists were eleven years in discovering how to kill that particular germ and save the babies.

"In spite of all these diseases, and of all the new ones that continued to arise, there were more and more men in the world. This was because it was easy to get food. The easier it was to get food, the more men there were; the more men there were, the more thickly were they packed together on the earth; and the more thickly they were packed, the more new kinds of germs became diseases. There were warnings. Soldervetzsky, as early as 1929, told the bacteriologists that they had no guaranty against some new disease, a thousand times more deadly than any they knew, arising and killing by the hundreds of millions and even by the billions. You see, the micro-organic world remained a mystery to the end. They knew there was such a world, and that from time to time armies of new germs emerged from it to kill men. And that was all they knew about it. For all they knew, in that invisible micro-organic world there might be as many different kinds of germs as there are grains of sand on this beach. And also, in that same invisible world it might well be that new kinds of germs came to be. It might be there that life originated—the 'abysmal fecundity,' Soldervetzsky called it, applying the words of other men who had written before him. . . ."

It was at this point that Hare-Lip rose to his feet, an expression of huge contempt on his face.

"Granser," he announced, "you make me sick with your gabble. Why don't you tell about the Red Death? If you ain't going to, say so, an' we'll start back for camp."

The old man looked at him and silently began to cry. The weak tears of age rolled down his cheeks, and all the feebleness of his eighty-seven years showed in his grief-stricken countenance.

"Sit down," Edwin counselled soothingly. "Granser's all right. He's just gettin' to the Scarlet Death, ain't you, Granser? He's just goin' to tell us about it right now. Sit down, Hare-Lip. Go ahead, Granser."

III

The old man wiped the tears away on his grimy knuckles and took up the tale in a tremulous, piping voice that soon strengthened as he got the swing of the narrative.

"It was in the summer of 2013 that the Plague came. I was twenty-seven years old, and well do I remember it. Wireless despatches—"

Hare-Lip spat loudly his disgust, and Granser hastened to make amends.

"We talked through the air in those days, thousands and thousands of miles. And the word came of a strange disease that had broken out in New York. There were seventeen millions of people living then in that noblest city of America. Nobody thought anything about the news. It was only a small thing. There had been only a few deaths. It seemed, though, that they had died very quickly, and that one of the first signs of the disease was the turning red of the face and all the body. Within twenty-four hours came the report of the first case in Chicago. And on the same day, it was made public that London, the greatest city in the world, next to Chicago, had been secretly fighting the plague for two weeks and censoring the news despatches—that is, not permitting the word to go forth to the rest of the world that London had the plague.

"It looked serious, but we in California, like everywhere else, were not alarmed. We were sure that the bacteriologists would find a way to overcome this new germ, just as they had overcome other germs in the past. But the trouble was the astonishing quickness with which this germ destroyed human beings, and the fact that it inevitably killed any human body it entered. No one ever recovered. There was the old Asiatic cholera, when you might eat dinner with a well man in the evening, and the next morning, if you got up early enough, you would see him being hauled by your window in the death-cart. But this new plague was quicker than that—much quicker. From the moment of the first signs of it, a man would be dead in an hour. Some lasted for several hours. Many died within ten or fifteen minutes of the appearance of the first signs.

"The heart began to beat faster and the heat of the body to increase. Then came the scarlet rash, spreading like wildfire over the face and body. Most persons never noticed the increase in heat and heart-beat, and the first they knew was when the scarlet rash came out. Usually, they had convulsions at the time of the appearance of the rash. But these convulsions did not last long and were not very severe. If one lived through them, he became perfectly quiet, and only did he feel a numbness swiftly creeping up his body from the feet. The heels became numb first, then the legs, and hips, and when the numbness reached as high as his heart he died. They did not rave or sleep. Their minds always remained cool and calm up to the moment their heart numbed and stopped. And another strange thing was the rapidity of decomposition.

No sooner was a person dead than the body seemed to fall to pieces, to fly apart, to melt away even as you looked at it. That was one of the reasons the plague spread so rapidly. All the billions of germs in a corpse were so immediately released.

"And it was because of all this that the bacteriologists had so little chance in fighting the germs. They were killed in their laboratories even as they studied the germ of the Scarlet Death. They were heroes. As fast as they perished, others stepped forth and took their places. It was in London that they first isolated it. The news was telegraphed everywhere. Trask was the name of the man who succeeded in this, but within thirty hours he was dead. Then came the struggle in all the laboratories to find something that would kill the plague germs. All drugs failed. You see, the problem was to get a drug, or serum, that would kill the germs in the body and not kill the body. They tried to fight it with other germs, to put into the body of a sick man germs that were the enemies of the plague germs—"

"And you can't see these germ-things, Granser," Hare-Lip objected, "and here you gabble, gabble, gabble about them as if they was anything, when they're nothing at all. Anything you can't see, ain't, that's what. Fighting things that ain't with things that ain't! They must have been all fools in them days. That's why they croaked. I ain't goin' to believe in such rot, I tell you that."

Granser promptly began to weep, while Edwin hotly took up his defence.

"Look here, Hare-Lip, you believe in lots of things you can't see."

Hare-Lip shook his head.

"You believe in dead men walking about. You never seen one dead man walk about."

"I tell you I seen 'em, last winter, when I was wolf-hunting with dad."

"Well, you always spit when you cross running water," Edwin challenged.

"That's to keep off bad luck," was Hare-Lip's defence.

"You believe in bad luck?"

"Sure."

"An' you ain't never seen bad luck," Edwin concluded triumphantly. "You're just as bad as Granser and his germs. You believe in what you don't see. Go on, Granser."

Hare-Lip, crushed by this metaphysical defeat, remained silent, and the old man went on. Ofter and often, though this narrative must not be clogged by the details, was Granser's tale interrupted while the boys squabbled among themselves. Also, among themselves they kept up a constant, low-voiced exchange of explanation and conjecture, as they strove to follow the old man into his unknown and vanished world.

"The Scarlet Death broke out in San Francisco. The first death came on a Monday morning. By Thursday they were dying like flies in Oakland and San Francisco. They died everywhere—in their beds, at their work, walking along the street. It was on Tuesday that I saw my first death—Miss Collbran, one of my students, sitting right there before my eyes, in my lecture-room. I noticed her face while I was talking. It had suddenly turned scarlet. I ceased speaking and could only look at her, for the first fear of the plague was already on all of us and we knew that it had come. The young women screamed and ran out of the room. So did the young men run out, all but two. Miss Collbrans's convulsions were very mild and lasted less than a minute. One of the young men fetched her a glass of water. She drank only a little of it, and cried out:

" 'My feet! All sensation has left them.'

"After a minute she said, 'I have no feet. I am unaware that I have feet. And my knees are cold. I can scarcely feel that I have knees.'

"She lay on the floor, a bundle of notebooks under her head. And we could do nothing. The coldness and the numbness crept up past her hips to her heart, and when it reached her heart she was dead. In fifteen minutes, by the clock—I timed it— she was dead, there, in my own classroom, dead. And she was a very beautiful, strong, healthy young woman. And from the first sign of the plague to her death only fifteen minutes elapsed. That will show you how swift was the Scarlet Death.

"Yet in those few minutes I remained with the dying woman in my classroom, the alarm had spread over the university; and the students, by thousands, all of them, had deserted the lecture-room and laboratories. When I emerged, on my way to make report to the President of the Faculty, I found the university deserted. Across the campus were several stragglers hurrying for their homes. Two of them were running.

President Hoag, I found in his office, all alone, looking very old and very gray, with a multitude of wrinkles in his face that I had never seen before. At sight of me, he pulled himself to his feet and tottered away to the inner office, banging the door after him and locking it. You see, he knew I had been exposed, and he was afraid. He shouted to me through the door to go away. I shall never forget my feelings as I walked down the silent corridors and out across that deserted campus. I was not afraid. I had been exposed, and I looked upon myself as already dead. It was not that, but a feeling of awful depression that impressed me. Everything had stopped. It was like the end of the world to me—my world. I had been born within sight and sound of the university. It had been my predestined career. My father had been a professor there before me, and his father before him. For a century and a half had this university, like a splendid machine, been running steadily on. And now, in an instant, it had stopped. It was like seeing the sacred flame die down on some thrice-sacred alter. I was shocked, unutterably shocked.

"When I arrived home, my housekeeper screamed as I entered, and fled away. And when I rang, I found the housemaid had likewise fled. I investigated. In the kitchen I found the cook on the point of departure. But she screamed, too, and in her haste dropped a suitcase of her personal belongings and ran out of the house and across the grounds, still screaming. I can hear her scream to this day. You see, we did not act in this way when ordinary diseases smote us. We were always calm over such things, and sent for the doctors and nurses who knew just what to do. But this was different. It struck so suddenly, and killed so swiftly, and never missed a stroke. When the scarlet rash appeared on a person's face, that person was marked by death. There was never a known case of a recovery.

"I was alone in my big house. As I have told you often before, in those days we could talk with one another over wires or through the air. The telephone bell rang, and I found my brother talking to me. He told me that he was not coming home for fear of catching the plague from me, and that he had taken our two sisters to stop at Professor Bacon's home. He advised me to remain where I was, and wait to find out whether or not I had caught the plague.

"To all of this I agreed, staying in my house and for the first time in my life attempting to cook. And the plague did not come out on me. By means of the telephone I could talk with whomsoever I pleased and get the news. Also, there were the newspapers, and I ordered all of them to be thrown up to my door so that I could know what was happening with the rest of the world.

"New York City and Chicago were in chaos. And what happened with them was happening in all the large cities. A third of the New York police were dead. Their chief was also dead, likewise the mayor. All law and order had ceased. The bodies were lying in the streets unburied. All railroads and vessels carrying food and such things into the great city had ceased running, and mobs of the hungry poor were pillaging the stores and warehouses. Murder and robbery and drunkenness were everywhere. Already the people had fled from the city by millions—at first the rich, in their private motor-cars and dirigibles, and then the great mass of the population, on foot, carrying the plague with them, themselves starving and pillaging the farmers and all the towns and villages on the way.

"The man who sent this news, the wireless operator, was alone with his instrument on the top of a loft building. The people remaining in the city—he estimated them at several hundred thousand—had gone mad from fear and drink, and on all sides of him great fires were raging. He was a hero, that man who staid by his post—an obscure newspaperman, most likely.

"For twenty-four hours, he said, no transatlantic airships had arrived, and no more messages were coming from England. He did state, though, that a message from Berlin—that's in Germany—announced that Hoffmeyer, a bacteriologist of the Metchnikoff School, had discovered the serum for the plague. That was the last word, to this day, that we of

America ever received from Europe. If Hoffmeyer discovered the serum, it was too late, or otherwise, long ere this, explorers from Europe would have come looking for us. We can only conclude that what happened in America happened in Europe, and that, at the best, some several score may have survived the Scarlet Death on that whole continent.

"For one day longer the despatches continued to come from New York. Then they, too, ceased. The man who had sent them, perched in his lofty building, had either died of the plague or been consumed in the great conflagrations he had described as raging around him. And what had occurred in New York had been duplicated in all the other cities. It was the same in San Francisco, and Oakland, and Berkeley. By Thursday the people were dying so rapidly that their corpses could not be handled, and dead bodies lay everywhere. Thursday night the panic outrush for the country began. Imagine, my grandsons, people, thicker than the salmon-run you have seen on the Sacramento river, pouring out of the cities by millions, madly over the country, in vain attempt to escape the ubiquitous death. You see, they carried the germs with them. Even the airships of the rich, fleeing for mountain and desert fastnesses, carried the germs.

"Hundreds of these airships escaped to Hawaii, and not only did they bring the plague with them, but they found the plague already there before them. This we learned, by the despatches, until all order in San Francisco vanished, and there were no operators left at their posts to receive or send. It was amazing, astounding, this loss of communication with the world. It was exactly as if the world had ceased, been blotted out. For sixty years that world has no longer existed for me. I know there must be such places as New York, Europe, Asia, and Africa; but not one word has been heard of them—not in sixty years. With the coming of the Scarlet Death the world fell apart, absolutely, irretrievably. Ten thousand years of culture and civilization passed in the twinkling of an eye, 'lapsed like foam.'

"I was telling about the airships of the rich. They carried the plague with them and no matter where they fled, they died. I never encountered but one survivor of any of them—Mungerson. He was afterwards a Santa

Rosan, and he married my eldest daughter. He came into the tribe eight years after the plague. He was then nineteen years old, and he was compelled to wait twelve years more before he could marry. You see, there were no unmarried women, and some of the older daughters of the Santa Rosans were already bespoken. So he was forced to wait until my Mary had grown to sixteen years. It was his son, Gimp-Leg, who was killed last year by the mountain lion.

"Mungerson was eleven years old at the time of the plague. His father was one of the Industrial Magnates, a very wealthy, powerful man. It was on his airship, the Condor, that they were fleeing, with all the family, for the wilds of British Columbia, which is far to the north of here. But there was some accident, and they were wrecked near Mount Shasta. You have heard of that mountain. It is far to the north. The plague broke out amongst them, and this boy of eleven was the only survivor. For eight years he was alone, wandering over a deserted land and looking vainly for his own kind. And at last, travelling south, he picked up with us, the Santa Rosans.

"But I am ahead of my story. When the great exodus from the cities around San Francisco Bay began, and while the telephones were still working, I talked with my brother. I told him this flight from the cities was insanity, that there were no symptoms of the plague in me, and that the thing for us to do was to isolate ourselves and our relatives in some safe place. We decided on the Chemistry Building, at the university, and we planned to lay in a supply of provisions, and by force of arms to prevent any other persons from forcing their presence upon us after we had retired to our refuge.

"All this being arranged, my brother begged me to stay in my own house for at least twenty-four hours more, on the chance of the plague developing in me. To this I agreed, and he promised to come for me next day. We talked on over the details of the provisioning and the defending of the Chemistry Building until the telephone died. It died in the midst of our conversation. That evening there were no electric lights, and I was alone in my house in the darkness. No more newspapers were being printed, so I had no knowledge of what was taking place outside. I heard sounds of rioting and of pistol shots, and from my windows I could see the glare of the sky of some conflagration in the direction of Oakland. It was a night of terror. I did not sleep a wink. A man—why and how I do not know—was killed on the sidewalk in front of the house. I heard the rapid reports of an automatic pistol, and a few minutes later the wounded wretch crawled up to my door, moaning and crying out for help. Arming myself with two automatics, I went to him. By the light of a match I ascertained that while he was dying of the bullet wounds, at the same time the plague was on him. I fled indoors, whence I heard him moan and cry out for half an hour longer.

"In the morning, my brother came to me. I had gathered into a handbag what things of value I purposed taking, but when I saw his face I knew that he would never accompany me to the Chemistry Bulding. The plague was on him. He intended shaking my hand, but I went back hurriedly before him.

"Look at yourself in the mirror," I commanded.

"He did so, and at sight of his scarlet face, the color deepening as he looked at it, he sank down nervelessly in a chair.

" 'My God!' he said. 'I've got it. Don't come near me. I am a dead man.'

"Then the convulsions seized him. He was two hours in dying, and he was conscious to the last, complaining about the coldness and loss of sensation in his feet, his calves, his thighs, until at last it was his heart and he was dead.

"That was the way the Scarlet Death slew. I caught up my handbag and fled. The sights in the streets were terrible. One stumbled on bodies everywhere. Some were not yet dead. And even as you looked, you saw men sink down with the death fastened upon them. There were numerous fires burning in Berkeley, while Oakland and San Francisco were apparently swept by vast conflagrations. The smoke of the burning filled the heavens, so that the midday was as a gloomy twilight, and, in the shifts of wind, sometimes the sun shone through dimly, a dull red orb. Truly, my grandsons, it was like the last days of the end of the world.

"There were numerous stalled motor cars, showing that the gasoline and the engine supplies of the garage had given out. I remember one such car. A man and a woman lay back dead in the seats, and on the pavement near it were two more women and a child. Strange and terrible sights there were on every hand. People slipped by silently, furtively, like ghosts—white-faced women carrying infants in their arms; fathers leading children by the hand; singly, and in couples, and in families—all fleeing out of the city of death. Some carried supplies of food, others blankets and valuables, and there were many who carried nothing.

"There was a grocery store—a place where food was sold. The man to whom it belonged—I knew him well—a quiet, sober, but stupid and obstinate fellow, was defending it. The windows and doors had been broken in, but he, inside, hiding behind a counter, was discharging his pistol at a number of men on the sidewalk who were breaking in. In the entrance were several bodies—of men, I decided, whom he had killed earlier in the day. Even as I looked on from a distance, I saw one of the robbers break the windows of the adjoining store, a place where shoes were sold, and deliberately set fire to it. I did not go to the grocery-man's assistance. The time for such acts had already passed. Civilization was crumbling, and it was each for himself.

IV

I went away hastily, down a cross-street, and at the first corner I saw another tragedy. Two men of the working class had caught a man and a woman with two children, and were robbing them. I knew the man by sight, though I had never been introduced to him. He was a poet whose verses I had long admired. Yet I did not go to his help, for at the moment I came upon the scene there was a pistol shot, and I saw him sinking to the ground. The woman screamed, and she was felled with a fist-blow by one of the brutes. I cried out threateningly, whereupon they discharged their pistols at me and I ran away around the corner. Here I was blocked by an advancing conflagration. The buldings on both sides were burning, and the street was filled with smoke and flame. From somewhere in that murk came a woman's voice calling shrilly for help. But I did not go to her. A man's heart turned to iron amid such scenes, and one heard all too many appeals for help.

"Returning to the corner, I found the two robbers were gone. The poet and his wife lay dead on the pavement. It was a shocking sight. The two children had vanished—whither I could not tell. And I knew, now, why it was that the fleeing persons I encountered slipped along so furtively and with such white faces. In the midst of our civilization, down in our slums and labor-ghettos, we had bred a race of barbarians, of savages; and now, in the time of our calamity, they turned upon us like the wild beasts they were and destroyed us. And they destroyed themselves as well. They inflamed themselves with strong drink and committed a thousand atrocities, quarreling and killing one another in the general madness. One group of workingmen I saw, of the better sort, who had banded together, and, with their women and children in their midst, the sick and aged in litters and being carried, and with a number of horses pulling a truck-load of provisions, they were fighting their way out of the city. They made a fine spectacle as they came down the street through the drifting smoke, though they nearly shot me when I first appeared in their path. As they went by, one of their leaders shouted out to me in apologetic explanation. He said they were killing the robbers and looters on sight, and that they had thus banded together as the only means by which to escape the prowlers.

"It was here that I saw for the first time what I was soon to see so often. One of the marching men had suddenly shown the unmistakable mark of the plague. Immediately those about him drew away, and he, without a remonstrance, stepped out of his place to let them pass on. A woman, most probably his wife, attempted to follow him. She was leading a little boy by the hand. But the husband commanded her sternly to go on, while others laid hands on her and restrained her from following him. This I saw, and I saw the man also, with his scarlet blaze of face, step into a doorway on the opposite side of the street. I heard the report of his pistol, and saw him sink lifeless to the ground.

"After being turned aside twice again by advancing fires, I succeeded in getting through to the university. On the edge of the campus I came upon a party of university folk who were going in the direction of the Chemistry Building. They were all family men, and their families were with them, including the nurses and the servants. Professor Badminton greeted me, and I had difficulty in recognizing him. Somewhere he had gone through flames, and his beard was singed off. About his head was a bloody bandage, and his clothes were filthy. He told me he had been cruelly beaten by prowlers, and that his brother had been killed the previous night, in the defence of their dwelling.

"Midway across the campus, he pointed suddenly to Mrs. Swinton's face. The unmistakable scarlet was there. Immediately all the other women set up a screaming and began to run away from her. Her two children were with a nurse, and these also ran with the women. But her husband, Doctor Swinton, remained with her.

" 'Go on, Smith,' he told me. 'Keep an eye on the children. As for me, I shall stay with my wife. I know she is as already dead, but I can't leave her. Afterwards, if I escape, I shall come to the Chemistry Building, and do you watch for me and let me in.'

"I left him bending over his wife and soothing her last moments, while I ran to overtake the party. We were the last to be admitted to the Chemistry Building. After that, with our automatic rifles we maintained our isolation. By our plans, we had arranged for a company of sixty to be in this refuge. Instead, every one of the number originally planned had added relatives and friends and whole families until there were over four hundred souls. But the Chemistry Building was large, and, standing by itself, was in no danger of being burned by the great fires that raged everywhere in the city.

"A large quantity of provisions had been gathered, and a food committee took charge of it, issuing rations daily to the various families and groups that arranged themselves into messes. A number of committees were appointed, and we developed a very efficient organization. I was on the committee of defence, though for the first day no prowlers came near. We could see them in the distance, however, and by the smoke of their fires knew that several camps of them were occupying the far edge of the campus. Drunkenness was rife, and often we heard them singing ribald songs or insanely shouting. While the world crashed to ruin about them and all the air was filled with the smoke of its burning, these low creatures gave rein to their bestiality and fought and drank and died. And after all, what did it matter? Everybody died anyway, the good and the bad, the efficient and the weaklings, those that loved to live and those that scorned to live. They passed. Everything passed.

"When twenty-four hours had gone by and no signs of the plague were apparent, we congratulated ourselves and set about digging a well. You have seen the great iron pipes which in those days carried water to all the city-dwellers. We feared that the fires in the city would burst the pipes and empty the reservoirs. So we tore up the cement floor of the central court of the Chemistry Building and dug a well. There were many young men, undergraduates, with us, and we worked night and day on the well. And our fears were confirmed. Three hours before we reached water, the pipes went dry.

"A second twenty-four hours passed, and still the plague did not appear among us. We thought we were saved. But we did not know what I afterwards decided to be true, namely, that the period of the incubation of the plague germs in a human's body was a matter of a number of days. It slew so swiftly when once it manifested itself, that we were led to believe that the period of incubation was equally swift. So, when two days had left us unscathed, we were elated with the idea that we were free of the contagion.

"But the third day disillusioned us. I can never forget the night preceding it. I had charge of the night guards from eight to twelve, and from the roof of the building I watched the passing of all man's glorious works. So terrible were the local conflagrations that all the sky was lighted up. One could read the finest print in the red glare. All the world seemed wrapped in flames. San Francisco spouted smoke and fire from a score of vast conflagrations that were like so many active volcanoes. Oakland, San Leandro, Haywards—all were burning; and to the northward, clear to Point Richmond, other fires were at work. It was an awe-inspiring spectacle. Civilization, my grandsons, civilization was passing in a sheet of flame and a breath of death. At ten o'clock that night, the great powder magazines at Point Pinole exploded in rapid succession. So terrific were the concussions that the strong building rocked as in an earthquake, while every pane of glass was broken. It was then that I left the roof and went down the long corridors, from room to room, quieting the alarmed women and telling them what had happened.

"An hour later, at a window on the ground floor, I heard pandemonium break out in the camps of the prowlers. There were cries and screams, and shots from many pistols. As we afterward conjectured, this fight had been precipitated by an attempt on the part of those that were well to drive out those that were sick. At any rate, a number of the plague-stricken prowlers escaped across the campus and drifted against our doors. We warned them back, but they cursed us and discharged a fusillade from their pistols. Professor Merryweather, at one of the windows, was instantly killed, the bullet striking him squarely between the eyes. We opened fire in turn, and all the prowlers fled with the exception of three. One was a woman. The plague was on them and they were reckless. Like foul fiends, there in the red glare from the skies, with faces blazing, they continued to curse us and fire at us. One of the men I shot with my own hand. After that the other man and the woman, still cursing us, lay down under our windows, where we were compelled to watch them die of the plague.

"The situation was critical. The explosions of the powder magazines had broken all the windows of the Chemistry Building, so that we were exposed to the germs from the corpses. The sanitary committee was called upon to act, and it responded nobly. Two men were required to go out and remove the corpses, and that meant the probable sacrifice of their own lives, for, having performed the task, they were not to be permitted to re-enter the building. One of the professors, who was a bachelor, and one of the undergraduates volunteered. They bade goodbye to us and went forth. They were heroes. They gave up their lives that four hundred others might live. After they had performed their work, they stood for a moment, at a distance, looking at us wistfully. Then they waved their hands in farewell and went away slowly across the campus toward the burning city.

"And yet it was all useless. The next morning the first one of us was smitten with the plague—a little nurse-girl in the family of Professor Stout. It was no time for weak-kneed, sentimental policies. On the chance that she might be the only one, we thrust her forth from the building and commanded her to be gone. She went away slowly across the campus, wringing her hands and crying pitifully. We felt like brutes, but what were we to do? There were four hundred of us, and individuals had to be sacrificed.

"In one of the laboratories three families had domiciled themselves, and that afternoon we found among them no less than four corpses and seven cases of the plague in all its different stages.

"Then it was that the horror began. Leaving the dead lie, we forced the living ones to segregate themselves in another room. The plague began to break out among the rest of us, and as fast as the symptoms appeared, we sent the stricken ones to these segregated rooms. We compelled them to walk there by themselves, so as to avoid laying hands on them. It was heartrending. But still the plague raged among us, and room after room was filled with the dead and dying. And so we who were yet clean retreated to the next floor and to the next, before this sea of the dead, that, room by room and floor by floor, inundated the building.

"The place became a charnel house, and in the middle of the night the survivors fled forth, taking nothing with them except arms and ammunition and a heavy store of tinned foods. We camped on the opposite side of the campus from the prowlers, and, while some stood guard, others of us volunteered to scout into the city in quest of horses, motor cars, carts, and wagons, or anything that would carry our provisions and enable us to emulate the banded workingmen I had seen fighting their way out to the open country.

"I was one of these scouts; and Doctor Hoyle, remembering that his motor car had been left behind in his home garage, told me to look for it. We scouted in pairs, and Dombey, a young undergraduate, accompanied me. We had to cross half a mile of the residence portion of the city to get to Doctor Hoyle's home. Here the buildings stood apart, in the midst of trees and grassy lawns and here the fires had played freaks, burning whole blocks, skipping blocks and often skipping a single house in a block. And here, too, the prowlers were still at their work. We carried our automatic pistols openly in our hands, and looked desperate enough, forsooth, to keep them from attacking us. But at Doctor Hoyle's house the thing happened. Untouched by fire, even as we came to it the smoke of flames burst forth.

"The miscreant who had set fire to it staggered down the steps and out along the driveway. Sticking out of his coat pockets were bottles of whiskey, and he was very drunk. My first impulse was to shoot him, and I have never ceased regretting that I did not. Staggering and maundering to himself, with bloodshot eyes, and a raw and bleeding slash down one side of his bewhiskered face, he was altogether the most nauseating specimen of degradation and filth I had ever encountered. I did not shoot him, and he leaned against a tree on the lawn to let us go by. It was the most absolute, wanton act. Just as we were opposite him, he suddenly drew a pistol and shot Dombey through the head. The next instant I shot him. But it was too late. Dombey expired without a groan, immediately. I doubt if he even knew what had happened to him.

"Leaving the two corpses, I hurried on past the burning house to the garage, and there found Doctor Hoyle's motor car. The tanks were filled with gasoline, and it was ready for use. And it was in this car that I threaded the streets of the ruined city and came back to the survivors on the campus. The other scouts returned, but none had been so fortunate. Professor Fairmead had found a Shetland pony, but the poor creature, tied in a stable and abandoned for days, was so weak from want of food and water that it could carry no burden at all. Some of the men were for turning it loose, but I insisted that we should lead it along with us, so that, if we got out of food, we would have it to eat.

"There were forty-seven of us when we started, many being women and children. The President of the Faculty, an old man to begin with, and now hopelessly broken by the awful happenings of the past week, rode in the motor car with several young children and the aged mother of Professor Fairmead. Wathope, a young professor of English, who had a grievous bullet-wound in his leg, drove the car. The rest of us walked, Professor Fairmead leading the pony.

"It was what should have been a bright summer day, but the smoke from the burning world filled the sky, through which the sun shone murkily, a dull and lifeless orb, blood-red and ominous. But we had grown accustomed to that blood-red sun. With the smoke it was different. It bit into our nostrils and eyes, and there was not one of us whose eyes were not bloodshot. We directed our course to the southeast through the endless miles of suburban residences, travelling along where the first swells of low hills rose from the flat of the central city. It was by this way, only, that we could expect to gain the country.

"Our progress was painfully slow. The women and children could not walk fast. They did not dream of walking, my grandsons, in the way all people walk to-day. In truth, none of us knew how to walk. It was not until after the plague that I learned really to walk. So it was that the pace of the slowest was the pace of all, for we dared not separate on account of the prowlers. There were not so many now of these human beasts of prey. The plague had already well diminished their numbers, but enough still lived to be a constant menace to us. Many of the beautiful residences were untouched by fire, yet smoking ruins were everywhere. The prowlers, too, seemed to have got over their insensate desire to burn, and it was more rarely that we saw houses freshly on fire.

"Several of us scouted among the private garages in search of motor cars and gasoline. But in this we were unsuccessful. The first great flight from the cities had swept all such utilities away. Calgan, a fine young man, was lost in this work. He was shot by prowlers while crossing a lawn. Yet this was our only casualty, though, once, a drunken brute deliberately opened fire on all of us. Luckily, he fired wildly, and we shot him before he had done any hurt.

"At Fruitvale, still in the heart of the magnificent resident section of the city, the plague again smote us. Professor Fairmead was the victim. Making signs to us that his mother was not to know, he turned aside into the grounds of a beautiful mansion. He sat down forlornly on the steps of the front veranda, and I, having lingered, waved him a last farewell. That night, several miles beyond Fruitvale and still in the city, we made camp. And that night we shifted camp twice to get away from our dead. In the morning there were thirty of us. I shall never forget the President of the Faculty. During the morning's march his wife, who was walking, betrayed the fatal symptoms, and when she drew aside to let us go on, he insisted on leaving the motor car and remaining with her. There was quite a discussion about this, but in the end we gave in. It was just as well, for we knew not which ones of us, if any, might ultimately escape.

"That night, the second of our march, we camped beyond Haywards in the first stretches of country. And in the morning there were eleven of us that lived. Also, during the night, Wathope, the professor with the wounded leg, deserted us in the motor car. He took with him his sister and his mother and most of our tinned provisions. It was that day, in the afternoon, while resting by the wayside, that I saw the last airship I shall ever see. The smoke was much thinner here in the country, and I first sighted the ship drifting and veering helplessly at an elevation of two thousand feet. What had happened I could not conjecture, but even as we looked we saw her bow dip down lower and lower. Then the bulkheads of the various gas-chambers must have burst, for, quite perpendicular, she fell like a plummet to the earth. And from that day to this I have not seen another airship. Often and often, during the next few years, I scanned the sky for them, hoping against hope that somewhere in the world civilization had survived. But it was not to be. What happened with us in California must have happened with everybody everywhere.

"Another day, and at Niles there were three of us. Beyond Niles, in the middle of the highway, we found Wathope. The motor car had broken down, and there, on the rugs which they had spread on the ground, lay the bodies of his sister, his mother, and himself.

"Wearied by the unusual exercise of continual walking, that night I slept heavily. In the morning I was alone in the world. Canfield and Parsons, my last companions, were dead of the plague. Of the four hundred that sought shelter in the Chemistry Building, and of the forty-seven that began the march, I alone remained—I and the Shetland pony. Why this should be so there is no explaining. I did not catch the plague, that is all. I was immune. I was merely the one lucky man in a million—just as every survivor was one in a million, or, rather, in several millions, for the proportion was at least that.

V

For two days I sheltered in a pleasant grove where there had been no deaths. In those two days, while badly depressed and believing that my turn would come at any moment, nevertheless I rested and recuperated. So did the pony. And on the third day, putting what small store of tinned provisions I possessed on the pony's back, I started on across a very lonely land. Not a live man, woman, or child, did I encounter, though the dead were everywhere. Food, however, was abundant. The land then was not as it is now. It was all cleared of trees and brush, and it was cultivated. The food for millions of mouths was growing, ripening, and going to waste. From the fields and orchards I gathered vegetables, fruits, and berries. Around the deserted farmhouses I got eggs and caught chickens. And frequently I found supplies of tinned provisions in the store-rooms.

"A strange thing was what was taking place with all the domestic animals. Everywhere they were going wild and preying on one another. The chickens and ducks were the first to be destroyed, while the pigs were the first to go wild, followed by the cats. Nor were the dogs long in adapting themselves to the changed conditions. There was a veritable plague of dogs. They devoured the corpses, barked and howled during the nights, and in the daytime slunk about in the distance. As the time went by, I noticed a change in their behavior. At first they were apart from one another, very suspicious and very prone to fight. But after a not very long while they began to come together and run in packs. The dog, you see, always was a social animal, and this was true before ever he came to be domesticated by man. In the last days of the world before the plague, there were many many very different kinds of dogs—dogs without hair and dogs with warm fur, dogs so small that they would make scarcely a mouthful for other dogs that were as large as mountain lions. Well, all the small dogs, and the weak types, were killed by their fellows. Also, the very large ones were not adapted for the wild life and bred out. As a result, the many different kinds of dogs disappeared, and there remained, running in packs, the medium-sized wolfish dogs that you know to-day."

"But the cats don't run in packs, Granser," Hoo-Hoo objected.

"The cat was never a social animal. As one writer in the nineteenth century said, the cat walks by himself. He always walked by himself, from before the time he was tamed by man, down through the long ages of domestication, to to-day when once more he is wild.

"The horses also went wild, and all the fine breeds we had degenerated into the small mustang horse you know to-day. The cows likewise went wild, as did the pigeons and the sheep. And that a few of the chickens survived you know yourself. But the wild chicken of to-day is quite a different thing from the chickens we had in those days.

"But I must go on with my story. I travelled through a deserted land. As the time went by I began to yearn more and more for human beings. But I never found one, and I grew lonelier and lonelier. I crossed Livermore Valley and the mountains between it and the great valley of the San Joaquin. You have never seen that valley, but it is very large and it is the home of the wild horse. There are great droves there, thousands and tens of thousands. I revisited it thirty years after, so I know. You think there are lots of wild horses down here in the coast valleys, but they are as nothing compared with those of the San Joaquin. Strange to say, the cows, when they went wild, went back into the lower mountains. Evidently they were better able to protect themselves there.

"In the country districts the ghouls and prowlers had been less in evidence, for I found many villages and towns untouched by fire. But they were filled by the pestilential dead, and I passed by without exploring them. It was near Lathrop that, out of my loneliness, I picked up a pair of collie dogs that were so newly free that they were urgently willing to return to their allegiance to man. These collies accompanied me for many years, and the strains of them are in those very dogs there that you boys have to-day. But in sixty years the collie strain has worked out. These brutes are more like domesticated wolves than anything else."

Hare-Lip rose to his feet, glanced to see that the goats were safe, and looked at the sun's position in the afternoon sky, advertising impatience at the prolixity of the old man's tale. Urged to hurry by Edwin, Granser went on.

"There is little more to tell. With my two dogs and my pony, and riding a horse I had managed to capture, I crossed the San Joaquin and went on to a wonderful valley in the Sierras called Yosemite. In the great hotel there I found a prodigious supply of tinned provisions. The pasture was abundant, as was the game, and the river that ran through the valley was full of trout. I remained there three years in an utter loneliness that none but a man who has once been highly civilized can understand. Then I could stand it no more. I felt that I was going crazy. Like the dog, I was a social animal and I needed my kind. I reasoned that since I had survived the plague, there was a possibility that others had survived. Also, I reasoned that after three years the plague germs must all be gone and the land be clean again.

"With my horse and dogs and pony, I set out. Again I crossed the San Joaquin Valley, the mountains beyond, and came down into Livermore Valley. The change in those three years was amazing. All the land had been splendidly tilled, and now I could scarcely recognize it, such was the sea of rank vegetation that had overrun the agricultural handiwork of man. You see, the wheat, the vegetables, and orchard trees had always been cared for and nursed by man, so that they were soft and tender. The weeds and wild bushes and such things, on the contrary, had always been fought by man, so that they were tough and resistant. As a result, when the hand of man was removed, the wild vegetation smothered and destroyed practically all the domesticated vegetation. The coyotes were greatly increased, and it was at this time that I first encountered wolves, straying in twos and threes and small packs down from the regions where they had always persisted.

"It was at Lake Temescal, not far from the one-time city of Oakland, that I came upon the first live human beings. Oh, my grandsons, how can I describe to you my emotion, when, astride my horse and dropping down the hillside to the lake, I saw the smoke of a campfire rising through the trees. Almost did my heart stop beating. I felt that I was going crazy. Then I heard the cry of a babe—a human babe. And dogs barked, and my dogs answered. I did not know but what I was the one human alive in the whole world. It could not be true that here were others—smoke, and the cry of a babe.

"Emerging on the lake, there, before my eyes, not a hundred yards away, I saw a man, a large man. He was standing on an outjutting rock and fishing. I was overcome. I stopped my horse. I tried to call out but could not. I waved my hand. It seemed to me that the man looked at me, but he did not appear to wave. Then I laid my head on my arms there in the saddle. I was afraid to look again, for I knew it was an hallucination, and I knew that if I looked the man would be gone. And so precious was the hallucination, that I wanted it to persist yet a little while. I knew, too, that as long as I did not look it would persist.

"Thus I remained, until I heard my dogs snarling, and a man's voice. What do you think the voice said? I will tell you. It said: *'Where in hell did you come from?'*

"Those were the words, the exact words. That was what your other grandfather said to me. Hare-Lip, when he greeted me there on the shore of Lake Temescal fifty-seven years ago. And they were the most ineffable words I have ever heard. I opened my eyes, and there he stood before me, a large, dark, hairy man, heavy-jawed, slant-browed, fierce-eyed. How I got off my horse I do not know. But it seemed that the next I knew I was clasping his hand with both of mine and crying. I would have embraced him, but he was ever a narrow-minded, suspicious man, and he drew away from me. Yet did I cling to his hand and cry."

Granser's voice faltered and broke at the recollection, and the weak tears streamed down his cheeks while the boys looked on and giggled.

"Yet did I cry," he continued, "and desire to embrace him, though the Chauffeur was a brute, a perfect brute—the most abhorrent man I have ever known. His name was . . . strange, how I have forgotten his name. Everybody called him Chauffeur—it was the name of his occupation, and it stuck. That is how, to this day, the tribe he founded is called the Chauffeur Tribe.

"He was a violent, unjust man. Why the plague germs spared him I can never understand. It would seem, in spite of our old metaphysical notions about absolute justice, that there is no justice in the universe. Why did he live?—an iniquitous, moral monster, a blot on the face of nature, a cruel, relentless, bestial cheat as well. All he could talk about was motor cars, machinery, gasoline, and garages—and especially, and with huge delight, of his mean pilferings and sordid swindlings of the persons who had employed him in the days before the coming of the plague. And yet he was spared, while hundreds of millions, yea, billions, of better men were destroyed.

"I went on with him to his camp, and there I saw her, Vesta, the one woman. It was glorious and . . . pitiful. There she was, Vesta Van Warden, the young wife of John Van Warden, clad in rags, with marred and scarred and toil-calloused hands, bending over the campfire and doing scullion work—she, Vesta, who had been born to the purple of the greatest baronage of wealth the world has ever known. John Van Warden, her husband, worth one billion, eight hundred millions and President of the Board of Industrial Magnates, had been the ruler of America. Also, sitting on the International Board of Control, he had been one of the seven men who ruled the world. And she herself had come of equally noble stock. Her father, Philip Saxon, had been President of the Board of Industrial Magnates up to the time of his death. This office was in process of becoming hereditary, and had Philip Saxon had a son that son would have succeeded him. But his only child was Vesta, the perfect flower of generations of the highest culture this planet has ever produced. It was not until the engagement between Vesta and Van Warden took place, that Saxon indicated the latter as his successor. It was, I am sure, a political marriage. I have reason to believe that Vesta never really loved her husband in the mad passionate way of which the poets used to sing. It was more like the marriages that obtained among crowned heads in the days before they were displaced by the Magnates.

"And there she was, boiling fish-chowder in a soot-covered pot, her glorious eyes inflamed by the acrid smoke of the open fire. Hers was a sad story. She was the one survivor in a million, as I had been, as the Chauffeur had been. On a crowning eminence of the Alameda Hills, overlooking San Francisco Bay, Van Warden had built a vast summer palace. It was surrounded by a park of a thousand acres. When the plague broke out, Van Warden sent her there. Armed guards patrolled the boundaries of the park, and nothing entered in the way of provisions or even mail matter that was not first fumigated. And yet did the plague enter, killing the guards at their posts, the servants at their tasks, sweeping away the whole army of retainers —or, at least, all of them who did not flee to die elsewhere. So it was that Vesta found herself the sole living person in the palace that had become a charnel house.

"Now the Chauffeur had been one of the servants that ran away. Returning, two months afterward, he discovered Vesta in a little summer pavilion where there had been no deaths and where she had established herself. He was a brute. She was afraid, and she ran away and hid among the trees. That night, on foot, she fled into the mountains—she, whose tender feet and delicate body had never known the bruise of stones nor the scratch of briars. He followed, and that night he caught her. He struck her. Do you understand? He beat her with those terrible fists of his and made her his slave. It was she who had to gather the firewood, build the fires, cook, and do all the degrading camp-labor—she, who had never performed a menial act in her life. These things he compelled her to do, while he, a proper savage, elected to lie around camp and look on. He did nothing, absolutely nothing, except on occasion to hunt meat or catch fish."

"Good for Chauffeur," Hare-Lip commented in an undertone to the other boys. "I remember him before he died. He was a corker. But he did things, and he made things go. You know, Dad married his daughter, an' you ought to see the way he knocked the spots outa Dad. The Chauffeur was a son-of-a-gun. He made us kids stand around. Even when he was croakin', he reached out for me, once, an' laid my head open with that long stick he kept always beside him."

Hare-Lip rubbed his bullet head reminiscently, and the boys returned to the old man, who was maundering ecstatically about Vesta, the squaw of the founder of the Chauffeur Tribe.

"And so I say to you that you cannot understand the awfulness of the situation. The Chauffeur was a servant, understand, a servant. And he cringed, with bowed head, to such as she. She was a lord of life, both by birth and by marriage. The destinies of millions, such as he, she carried in the hollow of her pink-white hand. And, in the days before the plague, the slightest contact with such as he would have been pollution. Oh, I have seen it. Once, I remember, there was Mrs. Goldwin, wife of one of the great magnates. It was on a landing stage, just as she was embarking in her private dirigible, that she dropped her parasol. A servant picked it up and made the mistake of handing it to her—to her, one of the greatest royal ladies of the land! She shrank back, as though he were a leper, and indicated her secretary to receive it. Also, she ordered her secretary to ascertain the creature's name and to see that he was immediately discharged from service. And such a woman was Vesta Van Warden. And her the Chauffeur beat and made his slave.

"—Bill—that was it; Bill, the Chauffeur. That was his name. He was a wretched, primitive man, wholly devoid of the finer instincts and chivalrous promptings of a cultured soul. No, there is no absolute justice, for to him fell that wonder of womanhood, Vesta Van Warden.

The grievousness of this you will never understand, my grandsons; for you are yourselves primitive little savages, unaware of aught else but savagery. Why should Vesta not have been mine? I was a man of culture and refinement, a professor in a great university. Even so, in the time before the plague, such was her exalted position, she would not have deigned to know that I existed. Mark, then, the abysmal degradation to which she fell at the hands of the Chauffeur. Nothing less than the destruction of all mankind had made it possible that I should know her, look in her eyes, converse with her, touch her hand—ay, and love her and know that her feelings toward me were very kindly. I have reason to believe that she, even she, would have loved me, there being no other man in the world except the chauffeur. Why, when it destroyed eight billions of souls, did not the plague destroy just one more man, and that man the Chauffeur?

"Once, when the Chauffeur was away fishing, she begged me to kill him. With tears in her eyes she begged me to kill him. But he was a strong and violent man, and I was afraid. Afterwards, I talked with him. I offered him my horse, my pony, my dogs, all that I possessed, if he would give Vesta to me. And he grinned in my face and shook his head. He was very insulting. He said that in the old days he had been a servant, had been dirt under the feet of men like me and of women like Vesta, and that now he had the greatest lady in the land to be servant to him and cook his food and nurse his brats. 'You had your day before the plague,' he said; 'but this is my day, and a damned good day it is. I wouldn't trade back to the old times for anything.' Such words he spoke, but they are not his words. He was a vulgar, low-minded man, and vile oaths fell continually from his lips.

"Also, he told me that if he caught me making eyes at his woman he'd wring my neck and give her a beating as well. What was I to do? I was afraid. He was a brute. That first night, when I discovered the camp, Vesta and I had great talk about the things of our vanished world. We talked of art, and books, and poetry; and the Chauffeur listened and grinned and sneered. He was bored and angered by our way of speech which he did not comprehend, and finally he spoke up and said: 'And this is Vesta Van Warden, one-time wife of Van Warden the Magnate—a high and stuck-up beauty, who is now my squaw. Eh, Professor Smith, times is changed, times is changed. Here, you, woman, take off my moccasins, and lively about it. I want Professor Smith to see how well I have you trained.'

"I saw her clench her teeth, and the flame of revolt rise in her face. He drew back his gnarled fist to strike, and I was afraid, and sick at heart. I could do nothing to prevail against him. So I got up to go, and not be witness to such indignity. But the Chauffeur laughed and threatened me with a beating if I did not stay and behold. And I sat there, perforce, by the campfire on the shore of Lake Temescal, and saw Vesta, Vesta Van Warden, kneel and remove the moccasins of that grinning, hairy, ape-like human brute.

"—Oh, you do not understand, my grandsons. You have never known anything else, and you do not understand.

"'Halter-broke and bridle-wise,' the Chauffeur gloated, while she performed that dreadful menial task. 'A trifle balky at times, Professor, a trifle balky; but a clout alongside the jaw makes her as meek and gentle as a lamb.'

"And another time he said: 'We've got to start all over and replenish the earth and multiply. You're handicapped, Professor. You ain't got no wife, and we're up against a regular Garden-of-Eden proposition. But I ain't proud. I'll tell you what, Professor.' He pointed at their little infant, barely a year old. 'There's your wife, though you'll have to wait till she grows up. It's rich, ain't it? We're all equals here, and I'm the biggest toad in the splash. But I ain't stuck up—not I. I do you the honor, Professor Smith, the very great honor of betrothing to you my and Vesta Van Warden's daughter. Ain't it cussed bad that Van Warden ain't here to see?'"

VI

"I lived three weeks of infinite torment there in the Chauffeur's camp. And then, one day, tiring of me, or of what to him was my bad effect on Vesta, he told me that the year before, wandering through the Contra Costa Hills to the Straits of Carquinez, across the Straits he had seen a smoke. This meant that there were still other human beings, and that for three weeks he had kept this inestimably precious information from me. I departed at once, with my dogs and horses, and journeyed across the Contra Costa Hills to the Straits. I saw no smoke on the other side, but at Port Costa discovered a small steel barge on which I was able to embark my animals. Old canvas which I found served me for a sail, and a southerly breeze fanned me across the Straits and up to the ruins of Vallejo. Here, on the outskirts of the city, I found evidences of a recently occupied camp. Many clam-shells showed me why these humans had come to the shores of the Bay. This was the Santa Rosa Tribe, and I followed its track along the old railroad right of way across the salt marshes to Sonoma Valley. Here, at the old brickyard at Glen Ellen, I came upon the camp. There were eighteen souls all told. Two were old men, one of whom was Jones, a banker. The other was Harrison, a retired pawnbroker, who had taken for wife the matron of the State Hospital for the Insane at Napa. Of all the persons of the city of Napa, and of all the other towns and villages in that rich and populous valley, she had been the only survivor. Next, there were the three young men—Cardiff and Hale, who had been farmers, and Wainwright, a common day-laborer. All three had found wives. To Hale, a crude, illiterate farmer, had fallen Isadore, the greatest prize, next to Vesta, of the women who came through the plague. She was one of the world's most noted singers, and the plague had caught her at San Francisco. She has talked with me for hours at a time, telling me of her adventures, until, at last, rescued by Hale in the Mendocino Forest Reserve, there had remained nothing for her to do but become his wife. But Hale was a good fellow, in spite of his illiteracy. He had a keen sense of justice and right-dealing, and she was far happier with him than was Vesta with the Chauffeur.

"The wives of Cardiff and Wainwright were ordinary women, accustomed to toil, with strong constitutions—just the type for the wild new life which they were compelled to live. In addition were two adult idiots from the feeble-minded home at Eldredge, and five or six

young children and infants born after the formation of the Santa Rosa
Tribe. Also, there was Bertha. She was a good woman, Hare-Lip, in
spite of the sneers of your father. Her I took for wife. She was the
mother of your father, Edwin, and of yours, Hoo-Hoo. And it was
our daughter, Vera, who married your father, Hare-Lip—your father,
Sandow, who was the oldest son of Vesta Van Warden and the
Chauffeur.

"And so it was that I became the nineteenth member of the Santa
Rosa Tribe. There were only two outsiders added after me. One was
Mungerson, descended from the Magnates, who wandered alone in the
wilds of Northern California for eight years before he came south and
joined us. He it was who waited twelve years more before he married
my daughter, Mary. The other was Johnson, the man who founded
the Utah Tribe. That was where he came from, Utah, a country that
lies very far away from here, across the great deserts, to the east. It
was not until twenty-seven years after the plague that Johnson reached
California. In all that Utah region he reported but three survivors,
himself one, and all men. For many years these three men lived and
hunted together, until, at last, desperate, fearing that with them the
human race would perish utterly from the planet, they headed west-
ward on the possibility of finding women survivors in California.
Johnson alone came through the great desert, where his two companions died. He was forty-six years old when he joined us, and he
married the fourth daughter of Isadore and Hale, and his eldest
son married your aunt, Hare-Lip, who was the third daughter of
Vesta and the Chauffeur. Johnson was a strong man, with a will of his
own. And it was because of this that he seceded from the Santa Rosans
and formed the Utah Tribe at San José. It is a small tribe—there are
only nine in it; but, though he is dead, such was his influence and the
strength of his breed, that it will grow into a strong tribe and play a leading part in·the recivilization of the planet.

"There are only two other tribes that we know of—the Los Angelitos
and the Carmelitos. The latter started from one man and woman. He
was called Lopez, and he was descended from the ancient Mexicans and

was very black. He was a cow-herd in the ranges beyond Carmel, and his wife was a maidservant in the great Del Monte Hotel. It was seven years before we first got in touch with the Los Angelitos. They have a good country down there, but it is too warm. I estimate the present population of the world at between three hundred and fifty and four hundred—provided, of course, that there are no scattered little tribes elsewhere in the world. If there be such, we have not heard from them. Since Johnson crossed the desert from Utah, no word nor sign has come from the East or anywhere else. The great world which I knew in my boyhood and early manhood is gone. It has ceased to be. I am the last man who was alive in the days of the plague and who knows the wonders of that far-off time. We, who mastered the planet—its earth, and sea, and sky—and who were as very gods, now live in primitive savagery along the water courses of this California country.

"But we are increasing rapidly—your sister, Hare-Lip, already has four children. We are increasing rapidly and making ready for a new climb toward civilization. In time, pressure of population will compel us to spread out, and a hundred generations from now we may expect our descendants to start across the Sierras, oozing slowly along, generation by generation, over the great continent to the colonization of the East—a new Aryan drift around the world.

"But it will be slow, very slow; we have so far to climb. We fell so hopelessly far. If only one physicist or one chemist had survived! But it was not to be, and we have forgotten everything. The Chauffeur started working in iron. He made the forge which we use to this day. But he was a lazy man, and when he died he took with him all he knew of metals and machinery. What was I to know of such things? I was a classical scholar, not a chemist. The other men who survived were not educated. Only two things did the Chauffeur accomplish—the brewing of strong drink and the growing of tobacco. It was while he was drunk, once, that he killed Vesta. I firmly believe that he killed Vesta in a fit of drunken cruelty though he always maintained that she fell into the lake and was drowned.

"And, my grandsons, let me warn you against the medicine-men.

They call themselves *doctors,* travestying what was once a noble profession, but in reality they are medicine-men, devil-devil men, and they make for superstition and darkness. They are cheats and liars. But so debased and degraded are we, that we believe their lies. They, too, will increase in numbers as we increase, and they will strive to rule us. Yet are they liars and charlatans. Look at young Cross-eyes, posing as a doctor, selling charms against sickness, giving good hunting, exchanging promises of fair weather for good meat and skins, sending the death-stick, performing a thousand abominations. Yet I say to you, that when he says he can do these things, he lies. I, Professor Smith, Professor James Howard Smith, say that he lies. I have told him so to his teeth. Why has he not sent me the death-stick? Because he knows that with me it is without avail. But you, Hare-Lip, so deeply are you sunk in black superstition that did you awake this night and find the death-stick beside you, you would surely die. And you would die, not because of any virtues in the stick, but because you are a savage with the dark and clouded mind of a savage.

"The doctors must be destroyed, and all that was lost must be discovered over again. Wherefore, earnestly, I repeat unto you certain things which you must remember and tell to your children after you. You must tell them that when water is made hot by fire, there resides in it a wonderful thing called steam, which is stronger than ten thousand men and which can do all man's work for him. There are other very useful things. In the lightning flash resides a similarly strong servant of man, which was of old his slave and which some day will be his slave again.

"Quite a different thing is the alphabet. It is what enables me to know the meaning of fine markings, whereas you boys know only rude picture-writing. In that dry cave on Telegraph Hill, where you see me often go when the tribe is down by the sea, I have stored many books. In them is great wisdom. Also, with them, I have placed a key to the alphabet, so that one who knows picture-writing may also know print. Some day men will read again; and then, if no accident has befallen my cave they will know that Professor James Howard Smith once lived and saved for them the knowledge of the ancients.

"There is another little device that men inevitably will rediscover. It is called gunpowder. It was what enabled us to kill surely and at long distances. Certain things which are found in the ground, when combined in the right proportions, will make his gunpowder. What these things are, I have forgotten, or else I never knew. But I wish I did know. Then would I make powder, and then would I certainly kill Cross-Eyes and rid the land of superstition—"

"After I am man-grown I am going to give Cross-Eyes all the goats, and meat, and skins I can get, so that he'll teach me to be a doctor," Hoo-Hoo asserted. "And when I know, I'll make everybody else sit up and take notice. They'll get down in the dirt to me, you bet."

The old man nodded his head solemnly, and murmured:

"Strange it is to hear the vestiges and remnants of the complicated Aryan speech falling from the lips of a filthy little skin-clad savage. All the world is topsy-turvy. And it has been topsy-turvy ever since the plague."

"You won't make me sit up," Hare-Lip boasted to the would-be medicine-man. "If I paid you for a sending of the death-stick and it didn't work, I'd bust in your head—understand, you Hoo-Hoo, you?"

"I'm going to get Granser to remember this here gunpowder stuff," Edwin said softly, "and then I'll have you all on the run. You, Hare-Lip, will do my fighting for me and get my meat for me, and you, Hoo-Hoo, will send the death-stick for me and make everybody afraid. And if I catch Hare-Lip trying to bust your head, Hoo-Hoo, I'll fix him with that same gunpowder. Granser ain't such a fool as you think, and I'm going to listen to him and some day I'll be boss over the whole bunch of you."

The old man shook his head sadly, and said:

"The gunpowder will come. Nothing can stop it—the same old story over and over. Man will increase, and men will fight. The gunpowder will enable men to kill millions of men, and in this way only, by fire and blood, will a new civilization, in some remote day, be evolved. And of what profit will it be? Just as the old civilization passed, so will the new. It may take fifty thousand years to build, but it will pass. All things pass. Only remain cosmic force and matter, ever in flux, ever acting and reacting and realizing the eternal types—the priest, the soldier, and the king. Out of the mouths of babes comes the wisdom of all the ages. Some will fight, some will rule, some will pray; and all the rest will toil and suffer sore while on their bleeding carcasses is reared again, and yet again, without end, the amazing beauty and surpassing wonder of the civilized state. It were just as well that I destroyed those cave-stored books—whether they remain or perish, all their old truths will be discovered, their old lies lived and handed down. What is the profit—"

Hare-Lip leaped to his feet, giving a quick glance at the pasturing goats and the afternoon sun.

"Gee!" he muttered to Edwin. "The old geezer gets more long-winded every day. Let's pull for camp."

While the other two, aided by the dogs, assembled the goats and started them for the trail through the forest, Edwin stayed by the old man and guided him in the same direction. When they reached the old right of way, Edwin stopped suddenly and looked back. Hare-Lip and Hoo-Hoo and the dogs and the goats passed on. Edwin was looking at a small herd of wild horses which had come down on the hard sand. There were at least twenty of them, young colts and yearlings and mares, led by a beautiful stallion which stood in the foam at the edge of the surf, with arched neck and bright wild eyes, sniffing the salt air from off the sea.

"What is it?" Granser queried.

"Horses," was the answer. "First time I ever seen 'em on the beach. It's the mountain lions getting thicker and thicker and driving 'em down."

The low sun shot red shafts of light, fan-shaped, up from a cloud-tumbled horizon. And close at hand, in the white waste of shore-lashed waters, the sea-lions, bellowing their old primeval chant, hauled up out of the sea on the black rocks and fought and loved.

"Come on, Granser," Edwin prompted.

And old man and boy, skin-clad and barbaric, turned and went along the right of way into the forest in the wake of the goats.

"Speaking of Operations—"

IRVIN S. COBB

Now that the last belated bill for services professionally rendered has been properly paid and properly receipted; now that the memory of the event, like the mark of the stitches, has faded out from a vivid red to a becoming pink shade; now that I pass a display of adhesive tape in a drug-store window without flinching—I sit me down to write a little piece about a certain matter—a small thing, but mine own—to wit, That Operation.

For years I have noticed that persons who underwent pruning or remodeling at the hands of a duly qualified surgeon, and survived, like to talk about it afterward. In the event of their not surviving I have no doubt they still liked to talk about it, but in a different locality. Of all the readily available topics for use, whether among friends or among strangers, an operation seems to be the handiest and most dependable. It beats the Tariff, or Roosevelt or Bryan, or when this war is going to end, if ever, if you are a man talking to other men; and it is more exciting even than the question of how Mrs. Vernon Castle will wear her hair this season, if you are a woman talking to other women.

For mixed companies a whale is one of the best and the easiest things to talk about that I know of. In regard to whales and their peculiarities you can make almost any assertion without fear of successful contradiction. Nobody ever knows any more about them than you do. You are not hampered by facts. If someone mentions the blubber of the whale and you chime in and say it may be noticed for miles on a still day when the large but emotional creature has been moved to tears by some great sorrow coming into its life, everybody is bound to accept the statement.

316

For after all how few among us really know whether a distressed whale sobs aloud or does so under its breath? Who, with any certainty, can tell whether a mother whale hatches her own egg her own self or leaves it on the sheltered bosom of a fjord to be incubated by the gentle warmth of the midnight sun? The possibilities of the proposition for purposes of informal debate, pro and con, are apparent at a glance.

The weather, of course, helps out amazingly when you are meeting people for the first time, because there is nearly always more or less weather going on somewhere and practically everybody has ideas about it. The human breakfast is also a wonderfully good topic to start up during one of those lulls. Try it yourself the next time the conversation seems to drag. Just speak up in an offhand kind of way and say that you never care much about breakfast—a slice of toast and a cup of weak tea start you off properly for doing a hard day's work. You will be surprised to note how things liven up and how eagerly all present join in. The lady on your left feels that you should know she always takes two lumps of sugar and nearly half cream, because she simply cannot abide hot milk, no matter what the doctors say. The gentleman on your right will be moved to confess he likes his eggs boiled for exactly three minutes, no more and no less. Buckwheat cakes and sausage find a champion and oatmeal rarely lacks a warm defender.

But after all, when all is said and done, the king of all topics is operations. Sooner or later, wherever two or more are gathered together it is reasonably certain that somebody will bring up an operation.

Until I passed through the experience of being operated on myself, I never really realized what a precious conversational boon the subject is, and how great a part it plays in our intercourse with our fellow beings on this planet. To the teller it is enormously interesting, for he is not only the hero of the tale but the rest of the cast and the stage setting as well—the whole show, as they say; and if the listener has had a similar experience—and who is there among us in these days that has not taken a nap 'neath the shade of the old ether cone?—it acquires a double value.

"Speaking of operations—" you say, just like that, even though nobody present has spoken of them; and then you are off, with your new acquaintance sitting on the edge of his chair, or hers as the case may be and so frequently is, with hands clutched in polite but painful restraint, gills working up and down with impatience, eyes brightened with desire, tongue hung in the middle, waiting for you to pause to catch your breath, so that he or she may break in with a few personal recollections along the same line. From a mere conversation it resolves itself into a symptom symposium, and a perfectly splendid time is had by all.

If an operation is such a good thing to talk about, why isn't it a good thing to write about, too? That is what I wish to know. Besides, I need the money. Verily, one always needs the money when one has but recently escaped from the ministering clutches of the modern hospital. Therefore I write.

It all dates back to the fair, bright morning when I went to call on a prominent practitioner here in New York, whom I shall denominate as Doctor X. I had a pain. I had had it for days. It was not a dependable, locatable pain, such as a tummyache or a toothache is, which you can put your hand on; but an indefinite, unsettled, undecided kind of pain, which went wandering about from place to place inside of me like a strange ghost lost in Cudjo's Cave. I never knew until then what the personal sensations of a haunted house are. If only the measly thing could have made up its mind to settle down somewhere and start light housekeeping I think I should have been better satisfied. I never had such an uneasy tenant. Alongside of it a woman with the moving fever would be comparatively a fixed and stationary object.

Having always, therefore, enjoyed perfectly riotous and absolutely unbridled health, never feeling weak and distressed unless dinner happened to be ten or fifteen minutes late, I was green regarding physicians and the ways of physicians. But I knew Doctor X slightly, having met him last summer in one of his hours of ease in the grand stand at a ball game, when he was expressing a desire to cut the umpire's throat from ear to ear, free of charge; and I remembered his name, and remembered, too, that he had impressed me at the time as being a person of character and decision and scholarly attainments.

He wore whiskers. Somehow in my mind whiskers are ever associated with medical skill. I presume this is a heritage of my youth, though I believe others labor under the same impression. As I look back it seems to me that in childhood's days all the doctors in our town wore whiskers.

I recall one old doctor down there in Kentucky who was practically lurking in ambush all the time. All he needed was a few decoys out in front of him and a pump gun to be a duck blind. He carried his calomel about with him in a fruit jar and when there was a cutting job he stropped his scalpel on his bootleg.

You see, in those primitive times germs had not been invented yet, and so he did not have to take steps to avoid them. Now we know that loose, luxuriant whiskers are unsanitary, because they make such fine winter quarters for germs; so, though the doctors still wear whiskers, they do not wear them wild and waving. In the profession bosky whiskers are taboo; they must be landscaped. And since it is a recognized fact that germs abhor orderliness and straight lines they now go elsewhere to reside, and the doctor may still retain his traditional aspect and yet be practically germproof. Doctor X was trimmed in accordance with the ethics of the newer school. He had trellis whiskers. So I went to see him at his offices in a fashionable district, on an expensive side street.

Before reaching him I passed through the hands of a maid and a nurse, each of whom spoke to me in a low, sorrowful tone of voice, which seemed to indicate that there was very little hope.

I reached an inner room where Doctor X was. He looked me over, while I described for him as best I could what seemed to be the matter with me, and asked me a number of intimate questions touching on the lives, works, characters and peculiarities of my ancestors; after which he made me stand up in front of him and take my coat off, and he punched me hither and yon with his forefinger. He also knocked repeatedly on my breastbone with his knuckles, and each time, on doing this, would apply his ear to my chest and listen intently for a spell, afterward shaking his head in a disappointed way. Apparently there was nobody at home. For quite a time he kept on knocking, but without getting any response.

He then took my temperature and fifteen dollars, and said it was an interesting case—not unusual exactly, but interesting—and that it called for an operation.

From the way my heart and other organs jumped inside of me at that statement I knew at once that, no matter what he may have thought, the premises were not unoccupied. Naturally I inquired how soon he meant to operate. Personally I trusted there was no hurry about it. I was perfectly willing to wait for several years, if necessary. He smiled at my ignorance.

"I never operate," he said; "operating is entirely out of my line. I am a diagnostician."

He was, too—I give him full credit for that. He was a good, keen, close diagnostician. How did he know I had only fifteen dollars on me? You did not have to tell this man what you had, or how much. He knew without being told.

I asked whether he was acquainted with Doctor Y—Y being a person whom I had met casually at a club to which I belong. Oh, yes, he said, he knew Doctor Y. Y was a clever man, X said—very, very clever; but Y specialized in the eyes, the ears, the nose and the throat. I gathered from what Doctor X said that any time Doctor Y ventured below the thorax he was out of bounds and liable to be penalized; and that if by any chance he strayed down as far as the lungs he would call for help and back out as rapidly as possible.

This was news to me. It would appear that these up-to-date practitioners just go ahead and divide you up and partition you out among themselves without saying anything to you about it. Your torso belongs to one man and your legs are the exclusive property of his brother practitioner down on the next block, and so on. You may belong to as many as half a dozen specialists, most of whom, very possibly, are total strangers to you, and yet never know a thing about it yourself.

It has rather the air of trespass—nay, more than that, it bears some of the aspects of unlawful entry—but I suppose it is legal. Certainly, judging by what I am able to learn, the system is being carried on generally. So it must be ethical.

Anything doctors do in a mass is ethical. Almost anything they do singly and on individual responsibility is unethical. Being ethical among doctors is practically the same thing as being a Democrat in Texas or a Presbyterian in Scotland.

"Y will never do for you," said Doctor X, when I had rallied somewhat from the shock of these disclosures. "I would suggest that you go to Doctor Z, at such-and-such an address. You are exactly in Z's line. I'll let him know that you are coming and when, and I'll send him down my diagnosis."

So that same afternoon, the appointment having been made by telephone, I went, full of quavery emotions, to Doctor Z's place. As soon as I was inside his outer hallway I realized that I was nearing the presence of one highly distinguished in his profession.

A pussy-footed male attendant, in a livery that made him look like a cross between a headwaiter and an undertaker's assistant, escorted me through an anteroom into a reception-room, where a considerable number of well-dressed men and women were sitting about in strained attitudes, pretending to read magazines while they waited their turns, but in reality furtively watching one another.

I sat down in a convenient chair, adhering fast to my hat and my umbrella. They were the only friends I had there and I was determined not to lose them without a struggle. On the wall were many colored charts showing various portions of the human anatomy and what ailed them. Directly in front of me was a very thrilling illustration, evidently copied from an oil painting, of a liver in a bad state of repair. I said to myself that if I had a liver like that one I should keep it hidden from the public eye—I would never permit it to sit for its portrait. Still, there is no accounting for tastes. I know a man who got his spleen back from the doctors and now keeps it in a bottle of alcohol on the what-not in the parlor, as one of his most treasured possessions, and sometimes shows it to visitors. He, however, is of a very saving disposition.

Presently a lady secretary, who sat behind a roll-top desk in a corner of the room, lifted a forefinger and silently beckoned me to her side. I moved over and sat down by her; she took down my name and my age and my weight and my height, and a number of other interesting facts that will come in very handy should anyone ever be moved to write a complete history of my early life. In common with Doctor X she shared one attribute—she manifested a deep curiosity regarding my forefathers—wanted to know all about them. I felt that this was carrying the thing too far. I felt like saying to her:

"Miss or madam, so far as I know there is nothing the matter with my ancestors of the second and third generations back, except that they are dead. I am not here to seek medical assistance for a grandparent who succumbed to disappointment that time when Samuel J. Tilden got counted out, or for a great-grandparent who entered into Eternal Rest very unexpectedly and in a manner entirely uncalled for as a result of being an innocent bystander in one of those feuds that were so popular in my native state immediately following the Mexican War. Leave my ancestors alone. There is no need of your shaking my family tree in the belief that a few overripe patients will fall out. I alone—I, me, myself—am the present candidate!"

However, I refrained from making this protest audibly. I judged she was only going according to the ritual; and as she had a printed card, with blanks in it ready to be filled out with details regarding the remote members of the family connection, I humored her along.

When I could not remember something she wished to know concerning an ancestor I supplied her with thrilling details culled from the field of fancy. When the card was entirely filled up she sent me back to my old place to wait. I waited and waited, breeding fresh ailments all the time. I had started out with one symptom; now if I had one I had a million and a half. I could feel goose flesh sprouting out all over me. If I had been taller I might have had more, but not otherwise. Such is the power of the human imagination when the surroundings are favorable to its development.

Time passed; to me it appeared that nearly all the time there was passed and that we were getting along toward the shank-end of the Christian era mighty fast. I was afraid my turn would come next and afraid it would not. Perhaps you know this sensation. You get it at the dentist's, and when you are on the list of after-dinner speakers at a large banquet, and when you are waiting for the father of the Only Girl in the World to make up his mind whether he is willing to try to endure you as a son-in-law.

Then some more time passed.

One by one my companions, obeying a command, passed out through the door at the back, vanishing out of my life forever. None of them returned. I was vaguely wondering whether Doctor Z buried his dead on the premises or had them removed by a secret passageway in the rear, when a young woman in a nurse's costume tapped me on the shoulder from behind.

I jumped. She hid a compassionate smile with her hand and told me that the doctor would see me now.

As I rose to follow her—still clinging with the drowning man's grip of desperation to my hat and my umbrella—I was astonished to note by a glance at the calendar on the wall that this was still the present date. I thought it would be Thursday of next week at the very least.

Doctor Z also wore whiskers, carefully pointed up by an expert hedge trimmer. He sat at his desk, surrounded by freewill offerings from grateful patients and by glass cases containing other things he had taken away from them when they were not in a condition to object. I had expected, after all the preliminary ceremonies and delays, that we should have a long séance together. Not so; not at all. The modern expert in surgery charges as much for remembering your name between visits as the family doctor used to expect for staying up all night with you, but he does not waste any time when you are in his presence.

I was about to find that out. And a little later on I was to find out a lot of other things; in fact, that whole week was of immense educational value to me.

I presume it was because he stood so high in his profession, and was almost constantly engaged in going into the best society that Doctor Z did not appear to be the least bit excited over my having picked him out to look into me. In the most perfunctory manner he shook the hand that has shaken the hands of Jess Willard, George M. Cohan and Henry

Ford, and bade me be seated in a chair which was drawn up in a strong light, where he might gaze directly at me as we conversed and so get the full values of the composition. But if I was a treat for him to look at he concealed his feelings very effectually.

He certainly had his emotions under splendid control. But then, of course, you must remember that he probably had traveled about extensively and was used to sight-seeing.

From this point on everything passed off in a most businesslike manner. He reached into a filing cabinet and took out an exhibit, which I recognized as the same one his secretary had filled out in the early part of the century. So I was already in the card-index class. Then briefly he looked over the manifest that Doctor X had sent him. It may not have been a manifest—it may have been an invoice or a bill of lading. Anyhow, I was in the assignee's hands. I could only hope it would not eventually become necessary to call in a receiver. Then he spoke:

"Yes, yes-yes," he said; "yes-yes-yes! Operation required. Small matter—hum, hum! Let's see—this is Tuesday? Quite so. Do it Friday! Friday at"—he glanced toward a scribbled pad of engagement dates at his elbow—"Friday at seven A. M. No; make it seven-fifteen. Have important tumor case at seven. St. Germicide's Hospital. You know the place?—up on Umpty-umph Street. Go' day! Miss Whoziz, call next visitor."

And before I realized that practically the whole affair had been settled I was outside the consultation-room in a small private hall, and the secretary was telling me further details would be conveyed to me by mail. I went home in a dazed state. For the first time I was beginning to learn something about an industry in which heretofore I had never been interested. Especially was I struck by the difference now revealed to me in the preliminary stages of the surgeons' business as compared with their fellow experts in the allied cutting trades—tailors, for instance, not to mention barbers. Every barber, you know, used to be a surgeon, only he spelled it chirurgeon. Since then the two professions have drifted far apart. Even a half-witted barber—the kind who always has the first chair as you come into the shop—can easily spend ten minutes of your time thinking of things he thinks you should have and mentioning them to you one by one, whereas any good, live surgeon knows what you have almost instantly.

As for the tailor—consider how wearisome are his methods when you parallel them alongside the tremendous advances in this direction made by the surgeon—how cumbersome and old-fashioned and tedious! Why, an experienced surgeon has you all apart in half the time the tailor takes up in deciding whether the vest shall fasten with five buttons or six. Our own domestic tailors are bad enough in this regard and the Old World tailors are even worse.

I remember a German tailor in Aix-la-Chapelle in the fall of 1914 who undertook to build for me a suit suitable for visiting the battle lines informally. He was the most literary tailor I ever met anywhere. He would drape the material over my person and then take a piece of chalk and write quite a nice long piece on me. Then he would rub it out and write it all over again, but more fully. He kept this up at intervals of every other day until he had writer's cramp. After that he used pins. He would pin the seam together, uttering little soothing, clucking sounds in German whenever a pin went through the goods and into me. The German cluck is not so soothing as the cluck of the English-speaking peoples, I find.

At the end of two long and trying weeks, which wore both of us down noticeably, he had the job done. It was not an unqualified success. He regarded it as a suit of clothes, but I knew better; it was a set of slip covers, and if only I had been a two-seated runabout it would have proved a perfect fit, I am sure; but I am a single-seated design and it did not answer. I wore it to the war because I had nothing else to wear that would stamp me as a regular war correspondent, except, of course, my wrist watch; but I shall not wear it to another war. War is terrible enough already; and, besides, I have parted with it. On my way home through Holland I gave that suit to a couple of poor Belgian refugees, and I presume they are still wearing it.

So far as I have been able to observe, the surgeons and the tailors of these times share but one common instinct: If you go to a new surgeon or to a new tailor he is morally certain, after looking you over, that the last surgeon you had, or the last tailor, did not do your cutting properly. There, however, is where the resemblance ends. The tailor, as I remarked in effect just now, wants an hour at least in which to decide how he may best cover up and disguise the irregularities of the human form; in much less time than that the surgeon has completely altered the form itself.

With the surgeon it is very much as it is with those learned men who write those large, impressive works of reference which should be permanently in every library, and which we are forever buying from an agent because we are so passionately addicted to payments. If the thing he seeks does not appear in the contents proper he knows exactly where to look for it. "See appendix," says the historian to you in a footnote. "See appendix," says the surgeon to himself, the while humming a cheery refrain. And so he does.

Well, I went home. This was Tuesday and the operation was not to be performed until the coming Friday. By Wednesday I had calmed down considerably. By Thursday morning I was practically normal again as regards my nerves. You will understand that I was still in a state of blissful ignorance concerning the actual methods of the surgical profession as exemplified by its leading exponents of today. The knowledge I have touched on in the pages immediately preceding was to come to me later.

Likewise Doctor Z's manner had been deceiving. It could not be that he meant to carve me to any really noticeable extent—his attitude had been entirely too casual. At our house carving is a very serious matter. Any time I take the head of the table and start in to carve it is fitting to remove the women and children to a place of safety, and onlookers should get under the table. When we first began housekeeping and gave our first small dinner-party we had a brace of ducks cooked in honor of the company, and I, as host, undertook to carve them. I never knew until then that a duck was built like a watch—that his works were inclosed in a burglarproof case. Without the use of dynamite the Red Leary-O'Brien gang could not have broken into those ducks. I thought so then and I think so yet. Years have passed since then, but I may state that even now, when there are guests for dinner, we do not have ducks. Unless somebody else is going to carve, we have liver.

I mention this fact in passing because it shows that I had learned to revere carving as one of the higher arts, and one not to be approached except in a spirit of due appreciation of the magnitude of the undertaking, and after proper consideration and thought and reflection, and all that sort of thing.

If this were true as regards a mere duck, why not all the more so as regards the carving of a person of whom I am so very fond as I am of myself? Thus I reasoned. And finally, had not Doctor Z spoken of the coming operation as a small matter? Well then?

Thursday at noon I received from Doctor Z's secretary a note stating that arrangements had been made for my admission into St. Germicide that same evening and that I was to spend the night there. This hardly seemed necessary. Still, the tone of the note appeared to indicate that the hospital authorities particularly wished to have me for an overnight guest; and as I reflected that probably the poor things had few enough bright spots in their busy lives, I decided I would humor them along and gladden the occasion with my presence from dinner-time on.

About eight o'clock I strolled in very jauntily. In my mind I had the whole programme mapped out. I would stay at the hospital for, say, two days following the operation—or, at most, three. Then I must be up and away. I had a good deal of work to do and a number of people to see on important business, and I could not really afford to waste more than a week-end on the staff of St. Germicide's. After Monday they must look to their own devices for social entertainment. That was my idea. Now when I look back on it I laugh, but it is a hollow laugh and there is no real merriment in it.

Indeed, almost from the moment of my entrance little things began to come up that were calculated to have a depressing effect on one's spirits. Downstairs a serious-looking lady met me and entered in a book a number of salient facts regarding my personality which the previous investigators had somehow overlooked. There is a lot of bookkeeping about an operation. This detail attended to, a young man, dressed in white garments and wearing an expression that stamped him as one who had suffered a recent deep bereavement, came and relieved me of my hand bag and escorted me upstairs.

As we passed through the upper corridors I had my first introduction to the hospital smell, which is a smell compounded of iodoform, ether, gruel, and something boiling. All hospitals have it, I understand. In time you get used to it, but you never really care for it.

The young man led me into a small room tastefully decorated with four walls, a floor, a ceiling, a window sill and a window, a door and a doorsill, and a bed and a chair. He told me to go to bed. I did not want to go to bed—it was not my regular bedtime—but he made a point of it, and I judged it was according to regulations; so I undressed and put on my night clothes and crawled in. He left me, taking my other clothes and my shoes with him, but I was not allowed to get lonely.

A little later a ward surgeon appeared, to put a few inquiries of a pointed and personal nature. He particularly desired to know what my trouble was. I explained to him that I couldn't tell him—he would have to see Doctor X or Doctor Z; they probably knew, but were keeping it a secret between themselves.

The answer apparently satisfied him, because immediately after that he made me sign a paper in which I assumed all responsibility for what was to take place the next morning.

This did not seem exactly fair. As I pointed out to him, it was the surgeon's affair, not mine; and if the surgeon made a mistake the joke would be on him and not on me, because in that case I would not be here anyhow. But I signed, as requested, on the dotted line, and he departed.

After that, at intervals, the chief house surgeon dropped in, without knocking, and the head nurse came, and an interne or so, and a ward nurse, and the special nurse who was to have direct charge of me. It dawned on me that I was not having any more privacy in that hospital than a goldfish.

About eleven o'clock an orderly came, and, without consulting my wishes in the matter, he undressed me until I could have passed almost anywhere for September Morn's father, and gave me a clean shave, twice over, on one of my most prominent plane surfaces. I must confess I enjoyed that part of it. So far as I am able to recall, it was the only shave I have ever had where the operator did not spray me with cheap perfumery afterward and then try to sell me a bottle of hair tonic.

Having shaved me, the young man did me up amidships in a neat cloth parcel, took his kit under his arm and went away.

It occurred to me that, considering the trivial nature of the case, a good deal of fuss was being made over me by persons who could have no personal concern in the matter whatsoever. This thought recurred to me frequently as I lay there, all tied in a bundle like a week's washing. I did not feel quite so uppish as I had felt. Why was everybody picking on me?

Anon I slept, but dreamed fitfully. I dreamed that a whole flock of surgeons came to my bedside and charted me out in sections, like one of those diagram pictures you see of a beef in the Handy Compendium of Universal Knowledge, showing the various cuts and the butcher's pet name for each cut. Each man took his favorite joint and carried it away, and when they were all gone I was merely a recent site, full of reverberating echoes and nothing else.

I have had happier dreams in my time; this was not the kind of dream I should have selected had the choice been left to me.

When I woke the young sun was shining in at the window, and an orderly—not the orderly who had shaved me, but another one—was there in my room and my nurse was waiting outside the door. The orderly dressed me in a quaint suit of pyjamas cut on the half shell and buttoning stylishly in the back, *princesse mode*. Then he rolled in a flat litter on wheels and stretched me on it, and covered me up with a white tablecloth, just as though I had been cold Sunday-night supper, and we started for the operating-room at the top of the building; but before we started I lit a large black cigar, as Gen. U. S. Grant used to do when he went into battle. I wished by this to show how indifferent I was. Maybe he fooled somebody, but I do not believe I possess the same powers of simulation that Grant had. He must have been a very remarkable man—Grant must.

The orderly and the nurse trundled me out into the hall and loaded me into an elevator, which was to carry us up to the top of the hospital. Several other nurses were already in the elevator. As we came aboard one of them remarked that it was a fine day. A fine day for what? She did not finish the sentence.

Everybody wore a serious look. Inside of myself I felt pretty serious too—serious enough for ten or twelve. I had meant to fling off several very bright, spontaneous quips on the way to the table. I thought them out in advance, but now, somehow, none of them seemed appropriate. Instinctively, as it were, I felt that humor was out of place here.

I never knew an elevator to progress from the third floor of a building to the ninth with such celerity as this one on which we were traveling progressed. Personally I was in no mood for haste. If there was anyone else in all that great hospital who was in a particular hurry to be operated on I was perfectly willing to wait. But alas, no! The mechanism of the elevator was in perfect order—entirely too perfect. No accident of any character whatsoever befell us en route, no dropping back into the basement with a low, grateful thud; no hitch; no delay of any kind. We were certainly out of luck that trip. The demon of a joyrider who operated the accursed device jerked a lever and up we soared at a distressingly high rate of speed. If I could have had my way about that youth he would have been arrested for speeding.

Now we were there! They rolled me into a large room, all white, with a rounded ceiling like the inside of an egg. Right away I knew what the feelings of a poor, lonely little yolk are when the spoon begins to chip the shell. If I had not been so busy feeling sorry for myself I think I might have developed quite an active sympathy for yolks.

My impression had been that this was to be in the nature of a private affair, without invitations. I was astonished to note that quite a crowd had assembled for the opening exercises. From his attire and general deportment I judged that Doctor Z was going to be the master of the revels, he being attired appropriately in a white domino, with rubber gloves and a fancy cap of crash toweling. There were present, also, my diagnostic friend, Doctor X, likewise in fancy-dress costume, and a surgeon I had never met. From what I could gather he was going over the course behind Doctor Z to replace the divots.

And there was an interne in the background, playing caddy, as it were, and a head nurse, who was going to keep the score, and two other nurses, who were going to help her keep it. I only hoped that they would show no partiality, but be as fair to me as they were to Doctor Z, and that he would go round in par.

So they placed me right where my eyes might rest on a large wall cabinet full of very shiny-looking tools; and they took my cigar away from me and folded my hands on the wide bowknot of my sash. Then they put a cloth dingus over my face and a voice of authority told me to breathe. That advice, however, was superfluous and might just as well have been omitted, for such was my purpose anyhow. Ever since I can recall anything at all, breathing has been a regular habit with me. So I breathed. And, at that, a bottle of highly charged sarsaparilla exploded somewhere in the immediate vicinity and most of its contents went up my nose.

I started to tell them that somebody had been fooling with their ether and adulterating it, and that if they thought they could send me off to sleep with soda pop they were making the mistake of their lives, because it just naturally could not be done; but for some reason or other I decided to put off speaking about the matter for a few minutes. I breathed again—again—agai——

I was going away from there. I was in a large gas balloon, soaring up into the clouds. How pleasant! . . . No, by Jove! I was not in a balloon—I myself was the balloon, which was not quite so pleasant. Besides, Doctor Z was going along as a passenger; and as we traveled up and up he kept jabbing me in the midriff with the ferrule of a large umbrella which he had brought along with him in case of rain. He jabbed me harder and harder. I remonstrated with him. I told him I was a bit tender in that locality and the ferrule of his umbrella was sharp. He would not listen. He kept on jabbing me. . . .

Something broke! We started back down to earth. We fell faster and faster. We fell nine miles, and after that I began to get used to it. Then I saw the earth beneath and it was rising up to meet us.

A town was below—a town that grew larger and larger as we neared it. I could make out the bonded indebtedness, and the Carnegie Library, and the moving-picture palaces, and the new dancing parlor, and other principal points of interest.

At the rate we were falling we were certainly going to make an awful splatter in that town when we hit. I was sorry for the street-cleaning department.

We fell another half mile or so. A spire was sticking up into the sky directly beneath us, like a spear, to impale us. By a supreme effort I twisted out of the way of that spire, only to strike squarely on top of the roof of a greenhouse back of the parsonage, next door. We crashed through it with a perfectly terrific clatter of breaking glass and landed in a bed of white flowers, all soft and downy, like feathers.

And then Doctor Z stood up and combed the débris out of his whiskers and remarked that, taking it by and large, it had been one of the pleasantest little outings he had enjoyed in the entire course of his practice. He said that as a patient I was fair, but as a balloon I was immense. He asked me whether I had seen anything of his umbrella and began looking round for it. I tried to help him look, but I was too tired to exert myself much. I told him I believed I would take a little nap.

I opened a dizzy eye part way. So this was heaven—this white expanse that swung and swam before my languid gaze? No, it could not be— it did not smell like heaven. It smelled like a hospital. It was a hospital. It was my hospital. My nurse was bending over me and I caught a faint whiff of the starch in the front of her crisp blue blouse. She was two-headed for the moment, but that was a mere detail. She settled a pillow under my head and told me to lie quiet.

I meant to lie quiet; I did not have to be told. I wanted to lie quiet and hurt. I was hurty from head to toe and back again, and crosswise and cater-cornered. I hurt diagonally and lengthwise and on the bias.

I had a taste in my mouth like a bird-and-animal store. And empty! It seemed to me those doctors had not left anything inside of me except the acoustics. Well, there was a mite of consolation there. If the over-hauling had been as thorough as I had reason to believe it was from my present sensations, I need never fear catching anything again so long as I lived, except possibly dandruff.

I waved the nurse away. I craved solitude. I desired only to lie there in that bed and hurt—which I did.

I had said beforehand I meant to stay in St. Germicide's for two or three days only. It is when I look back on that resolution I emit the hollow laugh elsewhere referred to. For exactly four weeks I was flat on my back. I know now how excessively wearied a man can get of his own back, how tired of it, how bored with it! And after that another two weeks elapsed before my legs became the same dependable pair of legs I had known in the past.

I did not want to eat at first, and when I did begin to want to they would not let me. If I felt sort of peckish they let me suck a little glass thermometer, but there is not much nourishment really in thermome-ters. And for entertainment, to while the dragging hours away, I could count the cracks in the ceiling and read my temperature chart, which was a good deal like Red Ames' batting average for the past season—ranging from ninety-nine to one hundred and four.

Also, through daily conversations with my nurse and with the sur-geons who dropped in from time to time to have a look at me, I learned, as I lay there, a great deal about the medical profession—that is, a great deal for a layman—and what I learned filled me with an abiding ad-miration for it, both as a science and as a business. This surely is one profession which ever keeps its face to the front. Burying its past mis-takes and forgetting them as speedily as possible, it pushes straight forward into fresh fields and fresh patients, always hopeful of what the future may bring in the way of newly discovered and highly expensive ailments. As we look backward upon the centuries we are astonished by its advancement. I did a good deal of looking backwards upon the centuries during my sojourn at St. Germicide's.

Take the Middle Ages now—the period when a barber and a surgeon were one and the same. If a man made a failure as a barber he turned his talents to surgery. Surgeons in those times were a husky breed. I judge they worked by the day instead of by piecework; anyhow the records show they were very fond of experiments, where somebody else furnished the raw material.

When there came a resounding knock at the tradesman's entrance of the moated grange, the lord of the manor, looking over the portcullis and seeing a lusty wight standing down below, in a leather apron, with his sleeves rolled up and a kit of soldering tools under his arm, didn't know until he made inquiry whether the gentle stranger had come to mend the drain or remove the cook's leg.

A little later along, when gunpowder had come into general use as a humanizing factor of civilization, surgeons treated a gunshot wound by pouring boiling lard into it, which I would say was calculated to take the victim's mind off his wound and give him something else to think about—for the time being, anyhow. I assume the notion of applying a mustard plaster outside one's stomach when one has a pain inside one's stomach is based on the same principle.

However, one doesn't have to go clear back to medieval times to note the radical differences in the plan of treating human ailments. A great many persons who are still living can remember when the doctors were not nearly so numerous as they are now. I, for one, would be the last to reverse the sentence and say that because the doctors were not nearly so numerous then as they are now, those persons are still living so numerously.

In the spring of the year, when the sap flowed and the birds mated, the sturdy farmer felt that he was due to have something the matter with him, too. So he would ride into the county-seat and get an almanac. Doubtless the reader, if country raised, has seen copies of this popular work. On the outside cover, which was dark blue in color, there was a picture of a person whose stomach was sliced four ways, like a twenty-cent pie, and then folded back neatly, thus exposing his entire interior arrangements to the gaze of the casual observer. However, this party, judging by his picture, did not appear to be suffering. He did not even seem to fear that he might catch cold from standing there in his own draught. He was gazing off into space in an absent-minded kind of way, apparently not aware that anything was wrong with him; and on all sides he was surrounded by interesting exhibits, such as a crab, and a scorpion, and a goat, and a chap with a bow and arrow—and one thing and another.

Such was the main design of the cover, while the contents were made up of recognized and standard varieties in the line of jokes and the line of diseases which alternated, with first a favorite joke and then a favorite disease. The author who wrote the descriptions of the diseases was one of the most convincing writers that ever lived anywhere. As a realist he had no superiors among those using our language as a vehicle for the expression of thought. He was a wonder. If a person wasn't particular about what ailed him he could read any page at random and have one specific disease. Or he could read the whole book through and have them all, in their most advanced stages. Then the only thing that could save him was a large dollar bottle.

Again, in attacks of the breakbone ague or malaria it was customary to call in a local practitioner, generally an elderly lady of the neighborhood, who had none of these latter-day prejudices regarding the use of tobacco by the gentler sex. One whom I distantly recall, among childhood's happy memories, carried this liberal-mindedness to a point where she not only dipped snuff and smoked a cob pipe, but sometimes chewed a little natural leaf. This lady, on being called in, would brew up a large caldron of medicinal roots and barks and sprouts and things; and then she would deluge the interior of the sufferer with a large gourdful of this pleasing mixture at regular intervals. It was efficacious, too. The inundated person either got well or else he drowned from the inside. Rocking the patient was almost as dangerous a pastime as rocking the boat. This also helps to explain, I think, why so many of our forebears had floating kidneys. There was nothing else for a kidney to do.

By the time I attained to long trousers, people in our town mainly had outgrown the unlicensed expert and were depending more and more upon the old-fashioned family doctor—the one with the whisker-jungle—who drove about in a gig, accompanied by a haunting aroma of iodoform and carrying his calomel with him in bulk.

He probably owned a secret calomel mine of his own. He must have; otherwise he could never have afforded to be so generous with it. He also had other medicines with him, all of them being selected on the principle that unless a drug tasted like the very dickens it couldn't possibly do you any good. At all hours of the day and night he was to be seen going to and fro, distributing nuggets from his private lode. He went to bed with his trousers and his hat on, I think, and there was a general belief that his old mare slept between the shafts of the gig, with the bridle shoved up on her forehead.

It has been only a few years since the old-time general practitioner was everywhere. Just look round and see now how the system has changed! If your liver begins to misconduct itself the first thought of the modern operator is to cut it out and hide it some place where you can't find it. The old-timer would have bombarded it with a large brunette pill about the size and color of a damson plum. Or he might put you on a diet of molasses seasoned to taste with blue mass and quinine and other attractive condiments. Likewise, in the spring of the year he frequently anointed the young of the species with a mixture of mutton suet and asafetida. This treatment had an effect that was distinctly depressing upon the growing boy. It militated against his popularity. It forced him to seek his pleasures outdoors, and a good distance outdoors at that.

It was very hard for a boy, however naturally attractive he might be, to retain his popularity at the fireside circle when coated with mutton suet and asafetida and then taken into a warm room. He attracted attention which he did not court and which was distasteful to him. Keeping quiet did not seem to help him any. Even if they had been blindfolded others would still have felt his presence. A civet-cat suffers from the same drawbacks in a social way, but the advantage to the civet-cat is that as a general thing it associates only with other civet-cats.

Except in the country the old-time, catch-as-catch-can general practitioner appears to be dying out. In the city one finds him occasionally, playing a limit game in an office on a back street—two dollars to come in, five to call; but the tendency of the day is toward specialists. Hence the expert who treats you for just one particular thing. With a pain in your chest, say, you go to a chest specialist. So long as he can keep the trouble confined to your chest, all well and good. If it slips down or slides up he tries to coax it back to the reservation. If it refuses to do so, he bids it an affectionate adieu, makes a dotted mark on you to show where he left off, collects his bill and regretfully turns you over to a stomach specialist or a throat specialist, depending on the direction in which the trouble was headed when last seen.

Or, perhaps the specialist to whom you take your custom is an advocate of an immediate operation for such cases as yours and all others. I may be unduly sensitive on account of having recently emerged from the surgeon's hands, but it strikes me now that there are an awful lot of doctors who take one brief glance at a person who is complaining, and say to themselves that here is something that ought to be looked into right away—and immediately open a bag and start picking out the proper utensils. You go into a doctor's office and tell him you do not feel the best in the world—and he gives you a look and excuses himself, and steps into the next room and begins greasing a saw.

Mind you, in these casual observations as compiled by me while bedfast and here given utterance, I am not seeking to disparage possibly the noblest of professions. Lately I have owed much to it. I am strictly on the doctor's side. He is with us when we come into the world and with us when we go out of it, oftentimes lending a helping hand on both occasions. Anyway, our sympathies should especially go out to the medical profession at this particular time when the anti-vivisectionists are railing so loudly against the doctors. The anti-vivisection crusade has enlisted widely different classes in the community, including many lovers of our dumb-animal pets—and aren't some of them the dumbest things you ever saw!—especially chow dogs and love birds.

I will admit there is something to be said on both sides of the argument. This dissecting of live subjects may have been carried to extremes on occasions. When I read in the medical journals that the eminent Doctor Somebody succeeded in transferring the interior department of a pelican to a pointer pup, and vice versa, with such success that the pup drowned while diving for minnows, and the pelican went out in the back yard and barked himself to death baying at the moon, I am interested naturally; but, possibly because of my ignorance, I fail to see wherein the treatment of infantile paralysis has been materially advanced. On the other hand, I would rather the kind and gentle Belgian hare should be offered up as a sacrifice upon the operating table and leave behind him a large family of little Belgian heirs and heiresses—dependent upon the charity of a cruel world—than that I should have something painful which can be avoided through making him a martyr. I would rather any white rabbit on earth should have the Asiatic cholera twice than that I should have it just once. These are my sincere convictions, and I will not attempt to disguise them.

Thanks, too, to medical science we know about germs and serums and diets and all that. Our less fortunate ancestors didn't know about them. They were befogged in ignorance. As recently as the generation immediately preceding our people were unacquainted with the simplest rules of hygiene. They didn't care whether the housefly wiped his feet before he came into the house or not. The gentleman with the drooping, cream-separator mustache was at perfect liberty to use the common drinking cup on the railroad train. The appendix lurked in its snug retreat, undisturbed by the prying fingers of curiosity. The fever-bearing skeeter buzzed and flitted, stinging where he pleased. The germ theory was unfathomed. Suitable food for an invalid was anything the invalid could afford to buy. Fresh air, and more especially fresh night air, was regarded as dangerous, and people hermetically sealed themselves in before retiring. Not daily as at present was the world gladdened by the tidings that science had unearthed some new and particularly unpleasant disease. It never occurred to a mother that she should sterilize the slipper before spanking her offspring. Babies were not reared antiseptically, but just so. Nobody was aware of microbes.

In short, our sires and our grandsires abode in the midst of perils. They were surrounded on all sides by things that are immediately fatal to the human system. Not a single one of them had a right to pass his second birthday. In the light of what we know, we realize that by now this world should be but a barren waste, dotted at frequent intervals with large graveyards and populated only by a few dispossessed and hungry bacteria, hanging over the cemetery fence singing: Driven From Home!

In the conditions generally prevalent up to twenty-five years ago, most of us never had any license, really, to be born at all. Yet look how many of us are now here. In this age of research I hesitate to attempt to account for it, except on the entirely unscientific theory that what you don't know doesn't hurt you. Doubtless a physician could give you a better explanation, but his would cost you more than mine has.

But we digress. Let us get back to our main subject, which is myself. I shall never forget my first real meal in that hospital. There was quite a good deal of talk about it beforehand. My nurse kept telling me that on the next day the doctor had promised I might have something to eat. I could hardly wait. I had visions of a tenderloin steak smothered in fried onions, and some French-fried potatoes, and a tall table-limit stack of wheat cakes, and a few other incidental comfits and kickshaws. I could hardly wait for that meal.

The next day came and she brought it to me, and I partook thereof. It was the white of an egg. For dessert I licked a stamp; but this I did clandestinely and by stealth, without saying anything about it to her. I was not supposed to have any sweets.

On the occasion of the next feast the diet was varied. I had a sip of one of those fermented milk products. You probably know the sort of thing I mean. Even before you've swallowed it, it tastes as though it had already disagreed with you. The nurse said this food was predigested but did not tell me by whom. Nor did I ask her. I started to, but thought better of it. Sometimes one is all the happier for not knowing too much.

A little later on, seeing that I had not suffered an attack of indigestion from this debauch, they gave me junket. In the dictionary I have looked up the definitions of junket. I quote:

JUNKET. *v.* I. *t.* To entertain by feasting; regale. II. *i.* To give or take part in an entertainment or excursion; feast in company; picnic; revel.

JUNKET, *n.* A merry feast or excursion; picnic.

When the author of a dictionary tries to be frivolous he only succeeds in making himself appear foolish.

I know not how it may be in the world at large, but in a hospital, junket is a custard that by some subtle process has been denuded of those ingredients which make a custard fascinating and exciting. It tastes as though the eggs, which form its underlying basis, had been laid in a fit of pique by a hen that was severely upset at the time.

Hereafter when the junket is passed round somebody else may have my share. I'll stick to the mince pie *a la mode*.

And the first cigar of my convalescence—ah, that, too, abides as a vivid memory! Dropping in one morning to replace the wrappings Doctor Z said I might smoke in moderation. So the nurse brought me a cigar, and I lit it and took one deep puff; but only one. I laid it aside. I said to the nurse:

"A mistake has been made here. I do not want a cooking cigar, you understand. I desire a cigar for personal use. This one is full of herbs and simples, I think. It suggests a New England boiled dinner, and not a very good New England boiled dinner at that. Let us try again."

She brought another cigar. It was not satisfactory either. Then she showed me the box—an orthodox box containing cigars of a recognized and previously dependable brand. I could only conclude that a root-and-herb doctor had bought an interest in the business and was introducing his own pet notions into the formula.

But came a day—as the fancy writers say when they wish to convey the impression that a day has come, but hate to do it in a commonplace manner—came a day when my cigar tasted as a cigar should taste and food had the proper relish to it; and my appetite came back again and found the old home place not so greatly changed after all.

And then shortly thereafter came another day, when I, all replete with expensive stitches, might drape the customary habiliments of civilization about my attenuated frame and go forth to mingle with my fellow beings. I have been mingling pretty steadily ever since, for now I have something to talk about—a topic good for any company; congenial, an absorbing topic.

I can spot a brother member a block away. I hasten up to him and give him the grand hailing sign of the order. He opens his mouth to speak, but I beat him to it.

"Speaking of operations—" I say. And then I'm off.

Believe me, it's the life!

Birth

A. J. CRONIN

Though it was nearly midnight when Andrew reached Bryngower, he found Joe Morgan waiting on him, walking up and down with short steps between the closed surgery and the entrance to the house. At the sight of him the burly driller's face expressed relief.

"Eh, Doctor, I'm glad to see you. I been back and forward here this last hour. The missus wants ye—before time, too."

Andrew, abruptly recalled from the contemplation of his own affairs, told Morgan to wait. He went into the house for his bag, then together they set out for Number 12 Blaina Terrace. The night air was cool and deep with quiet mystery. Usually so perceptive, Andrew now felt dull and listless. He had no premonition that this night call would prove unusual, still less that it would influence his whole future in Blaenelly.

The two men walked in silence until they reached the door of Number 12, then Joe drew up short.

"I'll not come in," he said, and his voice showed signs of strain. "But, man, I know ye'll do well for us."

Inside, a narrow stair led up to a small bedroom, clean but poorly furnished, and lit only by an oil lamp. Here Mrs. Morgan's mother, a tall grey-haired woman of nearly seventy, and the stout elderly midwife waited beside the patient, watching Andrew's expression as he moved about the room.

"Let me make you a cup of tea, Doctor, *bach*," said the former quickly, after a few moments.

Andrew smiled faintly. He saw that the old woman, wise in experi-

342

ence, realized there must be a period of waiting, that she was afraid he would leave the case, saying he would return later.

"Don't fret, Mother. I'll not run away."

Down in the kitchen he drank the tea which she gave him. Overwrought as he was, he knew he could not snatch even an hour's sleep if he went home. He knew, too, that the case here would demand all his attention. A queer lethargy of spirit came upon him. He decided to remain until everything was over.

An hour later he went upstairs again, noted the progress made, came down once more, sat by the kitchen fire. It was still, except for the rustle of a cinder in the grate and the slow tick-tock of the wall clock. No, there was another sound—the beat of Morgan's footsteps as he paced in the street outside. The old woman opposite him sat in her black dress, quite motionless, her eyes strangely alive and wise, probing, never leaving his face.

His thoughts were heavy, muddled. The episode he had witnessed at Cardiff station still obsessed him morbidly. He thought of Bramwell, foolishly devoted to a woman who deceived him sordidly, of Edward Page, bound to the shrewish Blodwen, of Denny, living unhappily, apart from his wife. His reason told him that all these marriages were dismal failures. It was a conclusion which, in his present state, made him wince. He wished to consider marriage as an idyllic state; yes, he could not otherwise consider it with the image of Christine before him. Her eyes, shining towards him, admitted no other conclusion. It was the conflict between his level, doubting mind and his overflowing heart which left him resentful and confused. He let his chin sink upon his chest, stretched out his legs, stared broodingly into the fire. He remained like this so long, and his thoughts were so filled with Christine, that he started when the old woman opposite suddenly addressed him. Her meditation had pursued a different course.

"Susan said not to give her the chloroform if it would harm the baby. She's awful set upon this child, Doctor, *bach*." Her old eyes warmed at a sudden thought. She added in a low tone: "Ay, we all are, I fancy."

He collected himself with an effort.

"It won't do any harm, the anæsthetic," he said kindly. "They'll be all right."

Here the nurse's voice was heard calling from the top landing. Andrew glanced at the clock, which now showed half-past three. He rose and went up to the bedroom. He perceived that he might now begin his work.

An hour elapsed. It was a long, harsh struggle. Then, as the first streaks of dawn strayed past the broken edges of the blind, the child was born, lifeless.

As he gazed at the still form a shiver of horror passed over Andrew. After all that he had promised! His face, heated with his own exertions, chilled suddenly. He hesitated, torn between his desire to attempt to resuscitate the child, and his obligation towards the mother, who was herself in a desperate state. The dilemma was so urgent he did not solve it consciously. Blindly, instinctively, he gave the child to the nurse and turned his attention to Susan Morgan who now lay collapsed, almost pulseless, and not yet out of the ether, upon her side. His haste was desperate, a frantic race against her ebbing strength. It took him only an instant to smash a glass ampule and inject pituitrin. Then he flung down the hypodermic syringe and worked unsparingly to restore the flaccid woman. After a few minutes of feverish effort, her heart strengthened; he saw that he might safely leave her. He swung round, in his shirt sleeves, his hair sticking to his damp brow.

"Where's the child?"

The midwife made a frightened gesture. She had placed it beneath the bed.

In a flash Andrew knelt down. Fishing amongst the sodden newspapers below the bed, he pulled out the child. A boy, perfectly formed. The limp warm body was white and soft as tallow. The cord, hastily slashed, lay like a broken stem. The skin was of a lovely texture, smooth and tender. The head lolled on the thin neck. The limbs seemed boneless.

Still kneeling, Andrew stared at the child with a haggard frown. The whiteness meant only one thing: asphyxia pallida, and his mind, unnaturally tense, raced back to a case he once had seen in the Samaritan, to the treatment that had been used. Instantly he was on his feet.

"Get me hot water and cold water," he threw out to the nurse. "And basins too. Quick! Quick!"

"But, Doctor—" she faltered, her eyes on the pallid body of the child.

"Quick!" he shouted.

Snatching a blanket he laid the child upon it and began the special method of respiration. The basins arrived, the ewer, the big iron kettle. Frantically he splashed cold water into one basin; into the other he mixed water as hot as his hand could bear. Then, like some crazy juggler, he hurried the child between the two, now plunging it into the icy, now into the steaming bath.

Fifteen minutes passed. Sweat was now running into Andrew's eyes, blinding him. One of his sleeves hung down, dripping. His breath came pantingly. But no breath came from the lax body of the child.

A desperate sense of defeat pressed on him, a raging hopelessness. He felt the midwife watching him in stark consternation, while there, pressed back against the wall where she had all the time remained,—her hand pressed to her throat, uttering no sound, her eyes burning upon him,—was the old woman. He remembered her longing for a grand-child, as great as had been her daughter's longing for this child. All dashed away now; futile, beyond remedy . . .

The floor was now a draggled mess. Stumbling over a sopping towel, Andrew almost dropped the child, which was now wet and slippery in his hands, like a strange white fish.

"For mercy's sake, Doctor," whimpered the midwife. "It's still-born."

Andrew did not heed her. Beaten, despairing, having laboured in vain for half an hour, he still persisted in one last effort, rubbing the child with a rough towel, crushing and releasing the little chest with both his hands, trying to get breath into that limp body.

And then, as by a miracle, the pigmy chest, which his hands enclosed, gave a short convulsive heave. Another . . . And another . . . Andrew turned giddy. The sense of life, springing beneath his fingers after all that unavailing striving, was so exquisite it almost made him faint. He redoubled his efforts feverishly. The child was gasping now, deeper and deeper. A bubble of mucus came from one tiny nostril, a joyful iridescent bubble. The limbs were no longer boneless. The head no longer lay back spinelessly. The blanched skin was slowly turning pink. Then, exquisitely, came the child's cry.

"Dear Father in Heaven," the nurse sobbed hysterically, "it's come— it's come alive."

Andrew handed her the child. He felt weak and dazed. About him the room lay in a shuddering litter: blankets, towels, basins, soiled instruments, the hypodermic syringe impaled by its point in the linoleum, the ewer knocked over, the kettle on its side in a puddle of water. Upon the huddled bed the mother still dreamed her way quietly through the anæsthetic. The old woman still stood against the wall. But her hands were together, her lips moved without sound. She was praying.

Mechanically Andrew wrung out his sleeve, pulled on his jacket.

"I'll fetch my bag later, Nurse."

He went downstairs, through the kitchen into the scullery. His lips were dry. At the scullery he took a long drink of water. He reached for his hat and coat.

Outside he found Joe standing on the pavement with a tense, expectant face.

"All right, Joe," he said thickly. "Both all right."

It was quite light. Nearly five o'clock. A few miners were already in the streets: the first of the night shift moving out. As Andrew walked with them, spent and slow, his footfalls echoing with the others under the morning sky, he kept thinking blindly, oblivious to all other work he had done in Blaenelly: "I've done something; oh, God! I've done something real at last."

The Operation

ROGER MARTIN DU GARD

WHEN the taxi pulled up near the Tuileries in front of the house in the Rue d'Alger where the Chasles lived, Antoine had pieced together, from the concierge's flustered explanations, an outline of the accident. The victim was a little girl who used to meet "M. Jules" each evening on his way back. Had she tried to cross the Rue de Rivoli on this occasion, as M. Jules was late in coming home? A delivery tri-car had knocked her down and passed over her body. A crowd had gathered and a newspaper-vender who was present had recognized the child by her plaited hair, and furnished her address. She had been carried unconscious to the flat.

M. Chasle, crouching in a corner of the taxi, shed no tears, but each new detail drew from him a racking sob, half muffled by the hand he pressed against his mouth.

A crowd still lingered round the doorway. They made way for M. Chasle, who had to be helped up the stairs as far as the top landing by his two companions. A door stood open at the end of a corridor, down which M. Chasle made his way on stumbling feet. The concierge stood back to let Antoine pass, and touched him on the arm.

"My wife, who's got a head on her shoulders, ran off to fetch the young doctor who dines at the restaurant next door. I hope she found him there."

Antoine nodded approval and followed M. Chasle. They crossed a

347

sort of anteroom, redolent of musty cupboards, then two low rooms with tiled floors; the light was dim and the atmosphere stifling despite the open windows giving on a courtyard. In the further room Antoine had to edge round a circular table where a meal for four was laid on a strip of dingy oilcloth. M. Chasle opened a door and, entering a brightly lit room, stumbled forward with a piteous cry:

"Dédette! Dédette!"

"Now, Jules!" a raucous voice protested.

The first thing Antoine noticed was the lamp which a woman in a pink dressing-gown was lifting with both hands; her ruddy hair, her throat and forehead were flooded with the lamplight. Then he observed the bed on which the light fell, and shadowy forms bending above it. Dregs of the sunset, filtering through the window, merged in the halo of the lamp, and the room was bathed in a half-light where all things took the semblance of a dream. Antoine helped M. Chasle to a chair and approached the bed. A young man wearing pince-nez, with his hat still on, was bending forward and slitting up with a pair of scissors the blood-stained garments of the little girl. Her face, ringed with matted hair, lay buried in the bolster. An old woman on her knees was helping the doctor.

"Is she alive?" Antoine asked.

The doctor turned, looked at him, and hesitated; then mopped his forehead.

"Yes." His tone lacked assurance.

"I was with M. Chasle when he was sent for," Antoine explained, "and I've brought my first-aid kit. I'm Dr. Thibault," he added in a whisper, "house-physician at the Children's Hospital."

The young doctor rose and was about to make way for Antoine.

"Carry on! Carry on!" Antoine drew back a step. "Pulse?"

"Almost imperceptible," the doctor replied, intent once more on his task.

Antoine raised his eyes towards the red-haired young woman, saw the anxiety in her face, and made a suggestion.

"Wouldn't it be best to telephone for an ambulance and have your child taken at once to my hospital?"

"No!" an imperious voice answered him.

Then Antoine descried an old woman standing at the head of the bed—was it the child's grandmother?—and scanning him intently with eyes limpid as water, a peasant's eyes. Her pointed nose and resolute features were half submerged in a vast sea of fat that heaved in billowy folds upon her neck.

"I know we look like paupers," she continued in a resigned tone, "but, believe me, even folk like us would rather die at home in our own beds. Dédette shan't go to the hospital."

"But why not, Madame?" Antoine protested.

She straightened up her back, thrust out her chin and sadly but sternly rebuked him.

"We prefer not," was all she said.

Antoine tried to catch the eye of the younger woman, but she was busy brushing off the flies that obstinately settled on her glowing cheeks, and seemed of no opinion. He decided to appeal to M. Chasle. The old fellow had fallen on his knees in front of the chair to which Antoine had led him; his head was buried on his folded arms as though to shut out all sights from his eyes, and, from his ears, all sounds. The old lady, who was keenly watching Antoine's movements, guessed his intention and forestalled him.

"Isn't that so, Jules?"

M. Chasle started.

"Yes, Mother."

She looked at him approvingly and her voice grew mothering.

"Don't stay there, Jules. You'd be much better in your room."

A pallid forehead rose into view, eyes tremulous behind their spectacles; then, without a protest, the poor old fellow stood up and tiptoed from the room.

Antoine bit his lips. Meanwhile, pending an occasion further to insist, he took off his coat and rolled up his sleeves above the elbows. Then he knelt at the bedside. He seldom took thought without at the same time beginning to take action—such was his incapacity for long deliberation on any issue raised, and such his keenness to be up and doing. The avoidance of mistakes counted less with him than bold decision and prompt activity. Thought, as he used it, was merely the lever that set an act in motion—premature though it might be.

Aided by the doctor and the old woman's trembling hands, he had soon stripped off the child's clothing; pale, almost grey, her body lay beneath their eyes in its frail nakedness. The impact of the car must have been very violent, for she was covered with bruises, and a black streak crossed her thigh transversely from hip to knee.

"It's the right leg," Antoine's colleague observed. Her right foot was twisted, bent inwards, and the whole leg was spattered with blood and deformed, shorter than the other one.

"Fracture of the femur?" suggested the doctor.

Antoine did not answer. He was thinking. "That's not all," he said to himself; "the shock is too great for that. But what can it be?" He tapped her knee-cap, then ran his fingers slowly up her thigh; suddenly there spurted through an almost imperceptible lesion on the inner side of the thigh, some inches above the knee, a jet of blood.

"That's it," he said.

"The femoral artery!" the other exclaimed.

Antoine rose quickly to his feet. The need to make, unaided, a decision gave him a new access of energy and, as ever when others were present, his sense of power intensified. A surgeon? he speculated. No, we'd never get her alive to the hospital. Then who? I? Why not? And, anyhow, there's no alternative.

"Will you try a ligature?" asked the doctor, piqued by Antoine's silence.

But Antoine did not heed his question. It must be done, he was thinking, and without a moment's delay; it may be too late already, who knows? He threw a quick glance round him. A ligature. What can be used? Let's see. The red-headed girl hasn't a belt; no loops on the curtains. Something elastic. Ah, I have it! In a twinkling he had thrown off his waistcoat and unfastened his braces. Snapping them with a jerk, he knelt down again, made with them a tourniquet, and clamped it tightly round the child's groin.

"Good! Two minutes' breathing-time," he said as he rose. Sweat was pouring down his cheeks. He knew that every eye was fixed on him. "Only an immediate operation," he said decisively, "can save her life. Let's try!"

The others moved away at once from the bed—even the woman with the lamp, even the young doctor, whose face had paled.

Antoine clenched his teeth, his eyes narrowed and grew hard, he seemed to peer into himself. Must keep calm, he mused. A table? That round table I saw, coming in.

"Bring the lamp!" he cried to the young woman, then turned to the doctor. "You there—come with me!" He strode quickly into the next room. Good, he said to himself; here's our operating-theatre. With a quick gesture he cleared the table, stacked the plates in a pile. "That's for my lamp." Like a general in charge of a campaign, he allotted each thing its place. "Now for our little patient." He went back to the bedroom. The doctor and the young woman hung on his every gesture and followed close behind him. Addressing the doctor, he pointed to the child:

"I'll carry her. She's light as a feather. Hold up her leg, you."

As he slipped his arms under the child's back and carried her to the table, she moaned faintly. He took the lamp from the red-haired woman and, removing the shade, stood it on the pile of plates. As he surveyed the scene, a thought came suddenly and went: "I'm a wonderful fellow!" The lamp gleamed like a brazier, reddening the ambient shadow, where only the young woman's glowing cheeks and the doctor's pince-nez showed up as high-lights; its rays fell harshly on the little body, which twitched spasmodically. The swarming flies seemed worked up to frenzy by the oncoming storm. Heat and anxiety brought beads of sweat to Antoine's brow. Would she live through it? he wondered, but some dark force he did not analyse buoyed up his faith; never had he felt so sure of himself.

He seized his bag and, taking out a bottle of chloroform and some gauze, handed the former to the doctor.

"Open it somewhere. On the sideboard. Take off the sewing-machine. Get everything out."

As he turned, holding the bottle, he noticed two dim figures in the dark doorway, the two old women like statues posted there. One, M. Chasle's mother, had great, staring eyes, an owl's eyes; the other was pressing her breast with her clasped hands.

"Go away!" he commanded. They retreated some steps into the shadows of the bedroom, but he pointed to the other end of the flat. "No. Out of the room. That way." They obeyed, crossed the room, vanished without a word.

"Not you!" he cried angrily to the red-haired woman, who was about to follow them.

She turned on her heel and, for a moment, he took stock of her. She had a handsome, rather fleshy face, touched with a certain dignity, it seemed, by grief; an air of calm maturity that pleased him. Poor woman! he could not help thinking. . . . But I need her!

"You're the child's mother?" he asked.

"No." She shook her head.

"All the better."

As he spoke he had been soaking the gauze and now he swiftly stretched it over the child's nose. "Stand there, and keep this." He handed her the bottle. "When I give the signal, you'll pour some more of it on."

The air grew heavy with the reek of chloroform. The little girl groaned, drew a deep breath or two, grew still.

A last look round. The field was clear; the rest lay with the surgeon's skill. Now that the crucial moment had come, Antoine's anxieties vanished as if by magic. He went to the sideboard where the doctor, holding the bag, was laying on a napkin the last of its contents. "Let's see," he murmured, as though to gain a few seconds' respite. "There's the instrument-box; good. The scalpel, the artery-forceps. A packet of gauze, cotton-wool, that'll do. Alcohol. Caffeine. Tincture of iodine.

And so forth. . . . **All's ready. Let's begin.**" And yet again there came to him that sense of buoyancy, of boundless confidence, of vital energies tautened to breaking-point, and, crowning all, a proud awareness of being lifted high above his workaday self.

Raising his head, he looked his junior for a moment in the eyes. "Have you the nerve?" his eyes seemed to inquire. "It's going to be a tough job. Now for it!"

The young man did not flinch. And now he hung on Antoine's gestures with servile assiduity. Well he knew that in this operation lay their only hope, but never would he have dared to take the risk, alone. With Antoine, however, nothing seemed impossible.

He's not so bad, this young chap, thought Antoine. Lucky for me! Let's see. A basin? No matter—this will do as well. Grasping the bottle of iodine he sluiced his arms up to the elbow with the liquid.

"Your turn!" He passed the bottle to the doctor, who was feverishly polishing the lenses of his pince-nez.

A vivid lightning flash, closely followed by a deafening clap of thunder, lit up the window.

"A bit previous, the applause," Antoine said to himself. "I hadn't even taken up my lancet. The young woman didn't turn a hair. It'll cool things down; good for our nerves. Must be pretty nearly a hundred degrees in this room."

He had laid out a series of compresses round the injured limb, delimiting the operative field. Now he turned towards the young woman.

"A whiff of chloroform. That'll do. Right!"

She obeys orders, he mused, like a soldier under fire. Women! Then, fixing his eyes on the swollen little thigh, he swallowed his saliva and raised the scalpel.

"Here goes!"

With one neat stroke he cut the skin.

"Swab!" he commanded the doctor bending beside him. "What a thin child!" he said to himself. "Well, we'll be there all the sooner. Hallo, there's little Dédette starting snoring! Good! Better be quick about it. Now for the retractors."

"Now, you," he said aloud, and the other let fall the blood-stained swabs of cotton-wool and, grasping the retractors, held the wound open.

Antoine paused a moment. "Good!" he murmured. "My probe? Here it is. In Hunter's canal. The classical ligation; all's well. Zip! Another flash! Must have landed pretty near. On the Louvre. Perhaps on the 'gentlemen at Saint-Roch.' " He felt quite calm—no more anxiety for the child, none for death's imminence—and cheerfully repeated under his breath: "The ligature of the femoral artery in Hunter's canal."

Zip! There goes another! Hardly any rain, either. It's stifling. Artery injured at the site of the fracture; the end of the bone tore it open. Simple as anything. Still she hadn't much blood to spare. He glanced at the little girl's face. Hallo! Better hurry up. Simple as anything—but could be fatal, too. A forceps; right! Another; that will do. Zip! These flashes are getting a bore; cheap effect! I've only plaited silk; must make the best of it. Breaking a tube, he pulled out the skein and made a ligature beside each forceps. Splendid! Almost finished now. The collateral circulation will be quite enough, especially at that age. I'm really wonderful! Can I have missed my vocation? I've all the makings of a surgeon, sure enough; a great surgeon. In the silent interval between two thunder-claps dying into the distance, the sharp metallic click of scissors snipping the loose ends of the silk was audible. Yes; quickness of eye, coolness, energy, dexterity. Suddenly he picked up his ears and his cheeks paled.

"The devil!" he muttered under his breath.

The child had ceased to breathe.

Brushing aside the woman, he tore away the gauze from the unconscious child's face and pressed his ear above her heart. Doctor and young woman waited in suspense, their eyes fixed on Antoine.

"No!" he murmured. "She's breathing still."

He took the child's wrist, but her pulse was so rapid that he did not attempt to count it. "Ouf!" He drew a deep breath, the lines of anxiety deepened on his forehead. The two others felt his gaze pass across their faces, but he did not see them.

He rapped out a brief command.

"You, doctor, remove the forceps, put on a dressing, and then undo the tourniquet. Quickly. You, Madame, get me some note-paper—no, you needn't; I've my note-book." He wiped his hands feverishly with a wad of cotton-wool. "What's the time? Not nine yet. The pharmacist's open. You'll have to hurry."

She stood before him, waiting; her tentative gesture—to wrap the dressing-gown more closely round her body—told him of her reluctance at going thus, half dressed, into the streets, and for the fraction of a second a picture of the opulent form under the garment held his imagination. He scribbled a prescription, signed it. "A two-pint ampoule. As quickly as you can."

"And if—?" she stammered.

"If the pharmacist's shut, ring, and keep on hammering on the door till they open. Be quick!"

She was gone. He followed her with his eyes to make sure she was running, then addressed the doctor.

"We'll try the saline. Not subcutaneously; that's hopeless now. Intravenously. Our last hope." He took two small phials from the sideboard.

"You've removed the tourniquet? Right. Give her an injection of camphor to begin with, then the caffeine—only half of it for her, poor kid! Only, for God's sake, be quick about it!"

He went back to the child and took her thin wrist between his fingers; now he could feel nothing more than a vague, restless fluttering. "It's got past counting," he said to himself. And suddenly a feeling of impotence, of sheer despair, swept over him.

"God damn it!" he broke out. "To think it went off perfectly—and it was all no use!"

The child's face became more livid with every second. She was dying. Antoine observed, beside the parted lips, two slender strands of curling hair, lighter than gossamer, that rose and fell; anyhow, she was breathing still.

He watched the doctor giving the injections. Neat with his fingers, he thought, considering his short sight. But we can't save her. Vexation rather than grief possessed him. He had the callousness common to doctors, for whom the sufferings of others count only as so much new experience, or profit, or professional advantage; men to whose fortunes death and pain are frequent ministers.

But then he thought he heard a banging door and ran towards the sound. It was the young woman coming back with quick, lithe steps, trying to conceal her breathlessness. He snatched the parcel from her hands.

"Bring some hot water." He did not even pause to thank her.

"Boiled?"

"No. To warm the solution. Be quick!"

He had hardly opened the parcel when she returned, bringing a steaming saucepan.

"Good! Excellent!" he murmured, but did not look towards her.

No time to lose. In a few seconds he had nipped off the tips of the ampoule and slipped on the rubber tubing. A Swiss barometer in carved wood hung on the wall. With one hand he unhooked it, while with the other he hung the ampoule on the nail. Then he took the saucepan of hot water, hesitated for the fraction of a second, and looped the rubber tubing round the bottom of it. That'll heat the saline as it flows through, he said to himself. Smart idea, that! He glanced towards the other doctor to see if he had noticed what he had done. At last he came back to the child, lifted her inert arm, and sponged it with iodine. Then, with a stroke of his scalpel, he laid bare the vein, slipped his probe beneath it and inserted the needle.

"It's flowing in all right," he cried. "Take her pulse. I'll stay where I am."

The ten minutes that followed seemed an eternity. No one moved or spoke.

Streaming with sweat, breathing rapidly, with knitted brows, Antoine waited, his gaze riveted on the needle. After a while he glanced up at the ampoule.

"How much gone?"

"Nearly a pint."

"The pulse?"

The doctor silently shook his head.

Five more minutes passed, five minutes more of sickening suspense. Antoine looked up again.

"How much left?"

"Just over half a pint."

"And the pulse?"

The doctor hesitated.

"I'm not sure. I almost think . . . it's beginning to come back a little."

"Can you count it?"

A pause.

"No."

If only the pulse came back! sighed Antoine. He would have given ten years of his own life to restore life to this little corpse. Wonder what age she is. Seven? And, if I save her, she'll fall a victim to consumption within the next ten years, living in this hovel. But shall I save her? It's touch and go; her life hangs on a thread. Still—damn it!—I've done all I could. The saline's flowing well. But it's too late. There's nothing more to be done, nothing else to try. We can only wait. . . . That red-haired girl did her bit. A good-looker. She's not the child's mother; who can she be then? Chasle never breathed a word about all these people. Not his daughter, I imagine. Can't make head or tail of it! And that old woman, putting on airs. . . . Anyhow, they made themselves scarce, good riddance! Curious how one suddenly gets them in hand. They all knew the sort of man they had to deal with. The strong hand of a masterful man. But it was up to me to bring it off. Shall I now? No, she lost too much blood on the way here. No signs of improvement so far, worse luck! Oh, damn it all!

His gaze fell on the child's pale lips and the two strands of golden hair, rising and falling still. The breathing struck him as a little better. Was he mistaken? Half a minute passed. Her chest seemed to flutter with a faint sigh which slowly died into the air, as though a fragment of her life were passing with it. For a moment Antoine stared at her in perplexity. No, she was breathing still. Nothing to be done but to wait, and keep on waiting.

A minute later she sighed again, more plainly now.

"How much left?"

"The ampoule's almost empty."

"And the pulse? Coming back?"

"Yes."

Antoine drew a deep breath.

"Can you count it?"

The doctor took out his watch, settled his pince-nez, and, after a minute's silence, announced:

"A hundred and forty. A hundred and fifty, perhaps."

"Better than nothing!" The exclamation was involuntary, for Antoine was straining every nerve to withstand the flood of huge relief that surged across his mind. Yet it was not imagination; the improvement was not to be gainsaid. Her breathing was steadier. It was all he could do to stay where he was; he had a childish longing to sing or whistle. *Better than nothing tra-la-la*—he tried to fit the words to the tune that had been haunting him all day. *In my heart tra-la-la. In my heart sleeps* . . . Sleeps—sleeps *what?* Got it. *The pale moonlight.*

> In my heart sleeps the pale moonlight
> Of a lovely summer night . . .

The cloud of doubt lifted, gave place to radiant joy.

"The child's saved," he murmured. "She's *got to be* saved!"

> . . . a lovely summer night!

"The ampoule's empty," the doctor announced.

"Capital!"

Just then the child, whom his eyes had never left, gave a slight shudder. Antoine turned almost gaily to the young woman, who,

leaning against the sideboard, had been watching the scene with steady
eyes for the past quarter of an hour.

"Well, Madame!" he cried with affected gruffness. "Gone to sleep
have we? And how about the hot-water bottle?" He almost smiled at
her amazement. "But, my dear lady, nothing could be more obvious.
A bottle, piping hot, to warm her little toes!"

A flash of joy lit up her eyes as she hastened from the room.

Then Antoine, with redoubled care and gentleness, bent down and
drew out the needle, and with the tips of his fingers applied a compress
to the tiny wound. He ran his fingers along the arm from which the
hand still hung limp.

"Another injection of camphor, old man, just to make sure; and
then we'll have played our last card. Shouldn't wonder," he added
under his breath, "if we've pulled it off." Once more that sense of
power that was half joy elated him.

The woman came back carrying a jar in her arms. She hesitated,
then, as he said nothing, came and stood by the child's feet.

"Not like that!" said Antoine, with the same brusque cheerfulness.
"You'll burn her. Give it here. Just imagine my having to show you
how to wrap up a hot-water bottle!"

Smiling now, he snatched up a rolled napkin that caught his eye
and, flinging the ring onto the sideboard, wrapped the jar in it and
pressed it to the child's feet. The red-haired woman watched him,
taken aback by the boyish smile that made his face seem so much
younger.

"Then she's—saved?" she ventured to ask.

He dared not affirm it as yet.

"I'll tell you in an hour's time." His voice was gruff, but she took his
meaning and cast on him a bold, admiring look.

For the third time Antoine asked himself what this handsome girl
could be doing in the Chasle household. Then he pointed to the door.

"What about the others?"

A smile hovered on her lips.

"They're waiting."

"Hearten them up a bit. Tell them to go to bed. You too, Madame, you'd better take some rest."

"Oh, as far as I'm concerned . . ." she murmured, turning to go.

"Let's get the child back to bed," Antoine suggested to his colleague. "The same way as before. Hold up her leg. Take the bolster away; we'd better keep her head down. The next thing is to rig up some sort of a gadget. . . . That napkin, please, and the string from the parcel. Some sort of extension, you see. Slip the string between the rails; handy things these iron bedsteads. Now for a weight. Anything will do. How about this saucepan? No, the flat-iron there will be better. We've all we need here. Yes, hand it over. Tomorrow we'll improve on it. Meanwhile it will do if we stretch the leg a bit, don't you think so?"

The young doctor did not reply. He gazed at Antoine with spellbound awe—the look that Martha may have given the Saviour when Lazarus rose from the tomb. His lips worked and he stammered timidly:

"May I . . . shall I arrange your instruments?" The faltered words breathed such a zeal for service and for devotion that Antoine thrilled with the exultation of an acknowledged chief. They were alone. Antoine went up to the younger man and looked him in the eyes.

"You've been splendid, my dear fellow."

The young man gasped. Antoine, who felt even more embarrassed than his colleague, gave him no time to put in a word.

"Now you'd better be off home; it's late. There's no need for two of us here." He hesitated. "We may take it that she's saved, I think. That's my opinion. However, for safety's sake, I'll stay here for the night, if you'll permit me." The doctor made a vague gesture. "If you permit me, I repeat. For I don't forget that she's your patient. Obviously. I only gave a hand, as there was nothing else for it. That's so, eh? But from tomorrow on I leave her in your hands. They're competent hands and I have no anxiety." As he spoke he led the doctor towards the door. "Will you look in again towards noon? I'll come back when I'm done at the hospital and we will decide on the treatment to follow."

"Sir, it's . . . it's been a privilege for me to . . . to . . ."

Never before had Antoine been "sirred" by a colleague, never before been treated with such deference. It went to his head, like generous wine, and unthinkingly he held out both hands towards the young man. But in the nick of time he regained his self-control.

"You've got a wrong impression," he said in a subdued tone. "I'm only a learner, a novice—like you. Like so many others. Like everyone. Groping our way. We do our best—and that's all there is to it!"

Allergies and the Man-Eating Carp

HOWARD VINCENT O'BRIEN

At this point, I think I should say something about the delicate subject of constipation. Though why it should be called "delicate," I do not know, since it is almost the principal theme of the radio and is frequently discussed in the advertising pages of the newspapers.

As a matter of fact, constipation is a peculiarly American interest, and children are made aware of it at regrettably tender ages.

One of the first questions a doctor asks of a patient concerns the behavior of the latter's bowels. As a nation, we have become so bowel-conscious that the sales campaigns for laxatives are never based on the desirability of using a laxative but on the superiority of one laxative to another. It is presumed that nobody reaches the age of puberty without becoming addicted to laxatives.

It is heresy, therefore, for me to raise a dissenting voice. Through the years, however, I have come to certain conclusions about physiology; and one of them is that constipation is a phenomenon akin to stuttering. It is a form of self-consciousness. It has a certain analogy to that other great American ailment—insomnia.

I suspect that the chief cause of sleeplessness is the *fear* of sleeplessness. I believe that if a person can get himself into a state of not caring whether he sleeps or not, of believing that he is in repose even if his eyes are open and his mind busy, he will forthwith fall asleep. I have an idea that the insomniac is much like the centipede, who got along all right until he began worrying too much about how his legs worked.

I have the same theory regarding constipation; and I was able to demonstrate its soundness by treating a friend who had suffered from constipation all his life and lived on a diet made up almost wholly of pills, agar-agar and mineral oil.

In a magazine, I read of a scientist who had made some realistic experiments on himself. He had managed to go without a bowel movement for two weeks. (Maybe it wasn't quite that long. I have a treacherous memory for statistics.) But it was long enough to prove that "regularity" was essential neither to health nor happiness. Aside from a sense of congestion and a slight headache, the scientist experienced no ill effects from the experiment.

I told my friend about this, but at first he declined to listen. I insisted, however, that he had nothing to lose. Despite all the thought and money he spent on achieving a daily evacuation of his bowels, he was a walking cadaver, depressed and enervated, really better dead than maintaining the poor semblance of life which was his.

He yielded, finally, to my entreaties, and agreed to make a trial of using no laxatives but fruit and figs—if he could, to get the very thought of laxatives out of his mind.

I didn't see him for several weeks. And what a change. In place of the gaunt picture of misery I had known, was a brisk and hearty fellow, slapping his chest with the joy of living. As if he had discovered the idea for himself, he assured me that the movement of the bowels was exactly like the process of breathing. The royal road to vim and vigor was never to think about either of them.

Believe it or not, that is what he said. And if you don't choose to believe he was right, well, there is certainly no law to compel you to.

I don't mean to suggest, of course, that there is no such thing as intestinal disease. Alas, there is. And it isn't always mental, by any means.

Only the other day a medical friend of mine showed me a new and amazing device for intestinal diagnosis. It looks like a tommy gun with a ten-inch barrel. This is rammed as far as it will go into the customer's interior, and then slowly withdrawn. As it travels, it takes colored movies of the flora and fauna encountered along the way.

Pretty soon, we shall have no privacy left at all!

But enough of such digression. Let us return to our memoirs.

It was in about the fourth year of my travail that the subject of allergies first swam into my ken. The medical world had been making some strange discoveries along this line. And when I heard of a man who ceased to have nervous breakdowns when he stopped taking cream in his coffee, I decided to find out what allergies I had, if any.

I visited a young physician who had made rather a specialty of this branch of medicine and was eager to experiment. He made me strip to the waist, and then, with a sharp knife, made an incision in my back. Into this he rubbed some foreign substance, such as extract of lima beans. In all, he made 144 of these slits, with a different substance in each one.

I couldn't see what was going on, but my wife, who watched the proceedings closely, said I had a back like a New Mexican *penitente* during the Easter Week flagellations.

With all the slitting and rubbing-in completed, the doctor sat down to watch what happened. And that was a pretty discouraging business; for practically nothing happened. The only sign of reaction—shown by a slight reddening of the skin—was around the cut filled with carp. Yes, that's no typographical error. I said carp and I mean carp—C-A-R-P. It's a kind of fish. Goldfish are carp, in case you didn't know.

This reaction was instructive but not particularly helpful, since to the best of my knowledge and belief I have never eaten a carp and never expect to. Someday, though, I am going to eat a brace of carp, just to see what happens. Maybe I shall fizz and explode!

The doctor was nonplussed but not defeated. He was willing to concede that the back-slitting had led up a blind alley, but he was reluctant to quit without exploring the possibility of bacterial allergy. He explained that some people are allergic to certain kinds of viruses, even if not to such things as feathers, face powder, or carp. So he went roaming up my nose, getting samples of the subvisible life lurking there. From these he made cultures, later vaccinating me with them.

The only result of this was a moderately sore arm. The specks continued to dance and sparkle in my vitreous, and the dark archipelagoes of my scotomas continued dark.

Once more I was back to the starting point, and beginning to get discouraged.

Here let me digress for a moment on the subject of the doctor and his problems.

I have often thought that the old Spaniard who sought the fountain of eternal youth looked for it in the wrong place. Instead of chasing around the swamps of Florida, fighting off alligators, red-bugs, and real estate salesmen, and getting older every minute, he should have seen his doctor.

If you feel excessively mature and want to be rejuvenated, just ask your physician a few searching questions about what ails you. His manner of replying is guaranteed to take years off your age. You'll suddenly become young again—about five and a half, and not very bright at that. You'll be made to feel like a kindergarten freshman who wants to know how babies come.

The doctor has a reason for treating you like a low-grade moron, and I'd be the last to say that it isn't a good reason. How, asks the doctor, can a patient be trusted with any important information about himself when just having his pulse taken makes his heart race with terror and the mere recording of his blood pressure scares him half to death?

By painful experience, the doctor has learned that the more a patient knows about his ailment and its possible complications, the more reasons he has for anxiety. Doctors are themselves notoriously pessimistic patients, because they know altogether too much for their own comfort.

Furthermore, people differ in their response to truth. Some patients, when told just how ill they are, fold up and quit. The confidence of such people in their own ability to get well has to be strengthened somehow, even by a whitish lie or two. The ways of nature are mysterious and many a sufferer gets well in the face of a dark outlook, simply by having the doctor tell him cheerily every day that he is getting better and better.

There is, of course, another side to the argument, namely, that warning of a disaster may reduce its effects. If it is in the cards that a man's heart is going to stop ticking in the near future, or if it is reasonably certain that he will be permanently crippled, he ought to know the truth sufficiently in advance to make what provision he can for his family.

There is much to be said on both sides of this argument. My own feeling is that a man has inalienable rights to life, liberty and such knowledge as he can buy concerning the activities inside his person. It seems to me that if he asks for straight talk, the onus is on him, and he ought to get it.

The whole thing boils down, I suppose, to the doctor's judgment of the person with whom he is dealing. Some people respond to a placebo, and some to a poke in the slats. And that is why I suspect that no mass-production system of medicine will ever work. For some things, one doctor is as good as another; and for other things, no doctor at all is best. For purposes of diagnosis there will be an increasing variety of ingeniously effective machines. But for the interpretation of this diagnostic material there must always be the fallible human mind. And for that ultimate mysterious harmony of causes that makes sick men well, there must be an intimately personal relationship—a singularly indefinable compound of art, science—*and* affection.

Hippocrates had that idea, but then the microscope got invented; and there has been a tendency to believe that doctoring is just a matter of drugs and instruments. I do not share this belief. I think the good doctor is more than a mechanic. I think there is a touch of the priest in him.

And with this irrelevant bit of philosophizing, I return to my narrative.

The failure to find me allergic to anything but carp left me a little disheartened. Happily, however, I didn't have an opportunity to brood. The Front Office packed me off to Mexico, and for a couple of months I had other things than my eyes to think about.

In Mexico I had another demonstration of the fact that things are not always what they seem. I made the acquaintance of an aristocratic lady to whom I took an instant dislike. Quite literally, she looked down her nose at me. It seemed to me that her hauteur was almost insulting.

Then, one afternoon, I sat next to her at the bullfight, and I observed that she looked down her nose even at the bulls. This astonished me so much that I made inquiries and found that the reason she looked the way she did was that she couldn't look any other way. Her vision was obscured by scotomas—not unlike mine but in the center of the field.

It was in Mexico, too, that I encountered a fine example of the layman's naive faith in wonder-workers. I had been telling some friends of my trouble, and one of them excitedly gave me the name of an ophthalmologist who had originated in the southwest but was now practicing in New York. This man, I was assured, could cure anything. So I wrote his name and address in my notebook, and when I got home, hastened to ask my doctor if he had ever heard of the miracle man. "Oh, yes," he replied. "He was one of my students. Quite a bright lad, too."

Looking back on that winter, the only new development in my status as a cryptogenic was the appearance of flashes in the eyes, accompanied by gobbets of incandescent blue light, floating lazily across the field of vision and disappearing into the mystery from which they sprang.

It was—and is—difficult to describe these symptoms. The flashing, or scintillance, has a resemblance to what you see in a broken neon sign. The flashes have a definite rhythm, somewhat slower, as near as I can measure them, than that of alternating electric current—about one hundred cycles, I should say, that is, fifty flickers a minute.

My doctor could shed no light on these things. All he could say was that similar phenomena had been observed. He had no idea either as to its cause or cure. He murmured something about "electrical phenomena," and let the subject drop.

So I dropped it, too.

Once established, the flashing never ceased, either by daylight or in the dark, with eyes open or eyes closed. And these pyrotechnical displays have been my inseparable companions ever since, slowly growing in intensity and magnitude.

To get a rough idea of how life looks to a person with these "scintillating scotomas," just imagine some sort of wire arrangement fixed on your forehead, so that bits of glass, blue, white, and black, dangle constantly in front of your eyes. On these bits of glass is fixed a bright light, so that they keep up a never ending sparkle. To complete the scene, you have an assistant stand to one side, shooting Roman candles across your field of view—bright blue balls, mostly, but now and then a "tracer" of fiery yellow. The sparkler show never stops, but the Roman candles are fired only when you least expect them. This adds a needed touch of variety to life with a "scintillating scotoma." Without this it might be monotonous.

I am not going to deny that these "electrical phenomena" have been a great nuisance. At times they have made me extremely jumpy. In weaker moments, I have called them "intolerable." But that is a word altogether too loosely used. Anything can be tolerated. It is really amazing how much we can tolerate when we have to. It is amazing, too, how much of a margin we have been given in our senses. Providence has been especially generous in its allotment of vision. We can get along with much less than the normal equipment. Perfect sight is a pleasant thing to have, but it is by no means essential. When some is lost, it is possible to do quite well with what is left.

Nature seems also to have provided us with a surplus of nervous resistance. Those "scintillating scotomas"—as they are called by people who have heard about them but never experienced them—are another proof. This incessant display of fireworks between you and the visible world is certainly vexing. It "drives you crazy." But you find that you can forget it. You can forget it when you are busy with something that interests you, or when you are occupied with something that has to be done.

I wonder why the human race has always been so obsessed with the idea of *leisure*. Man has always cherished the singularly perverse ideal of a workless world. He has managed to delude himself into thinking that work is a curse, when, obviously, it is the exact opposite of that.

It is considered a pious platitude to say that work is a blessing; but in my opinion it is a platitude which cannot be repeated too often. I know that my worst moments are when I have nothing to do, and can devote my full attention to worry. And I wish to state, from long experience, that nobody puts in such long hours of concentrated effort as an accomplished worrier. A good worrier thinks nothing of worrying for sixteen hours at a stretch, and, with practice, one can even worry in one's sleep.

The Country Doctor

IVAN BEEDE

Wʜɪʟᴇ Dr. Moon waited for a telephone call from the Masheks' it began to snow. A shadow fell across the book he was reading and slowly, slowly, the pale winter light thickened into obscurity. He raised his head to look out the window, then with an effort swung it around and glanced about the room. Although the electric switch was only a few feet away he felt too hopeless to move. Instead he let his head fall to one side in a gesture of fatigue, and closed his eyes.

All this Sunday afternoon, alone in the house, he had been expecting the Mashek call. Sooner or later it would come, and he would have to look at Lily Mashek's deluded smile again. There was nothing more he could do for her, she was beyond aid, but just the same he would go. He felt obliged to go, because last night he had acted like a fool, on her account.

With his head fallen limply, his body slumped in the chair, he waited helplessly for the call to come. He could think of nothing else. The case depressed him, with a depression which he could not shake off, which had been increasing for days.

It was not Lily Mashek so much as the moment she had chosen to die. She had forced herself on his attention just after the long siege of influenza, which had left him physically exhausted, discouraged, and worried by new, strange doubts.

During the epidemic he had been the only available doctor, the others being absent in the Army, and as usual he had taken his work too seriously. He had seemed an almost omnipresent figure in his big fur

369

coat and hunter's cap, his mild face masklike with fatigue. There was no distance he would not drive, no extra effort he would not make, but too many of his patients died. They died by the dozens, throughout the fall and these early months of winter.

The growing toll of deaths threw him into a fit of black discouragement. He was certain that almost any other doctor would have been more useful. But what hurt him most, when he suffered from his own shortcomings so keenly, was to lose patients (and he lost many) who had no right to die. It was dreadful to see them give up without a struggle, killed by fear of the unknown, by lack of faith in themselves, by mental panic arising from the war. Some of them were men whom for years he had respected. He watched them go with tears of anger in his eyes. They were cowards, they did not deserve to live, yet he blamed himself because they died.

When it was all over he was left in a state of mental depression induced by fatigue. He had not only temporarily lost confidence in himself, he was harassed by secret doubts, doubts which he thought too terrible to divulge, about the humanity he had always been so proud to serve. He knew what was wrong. He needed time to forget, to renew his hold on life, but at this moment Lily Mashek fell mortally ill.

He had been her doctor for years, and the spectacle of her life had always annoyed him, but now it took on an exaggerated significance in his mind. She symbolized all the weakness, the fatuity, the shame, of the world he had just discovered. To go every day to that dismal house, to look at her silly smile, grew more and more unbearable, and several days before it seemed he had reached the limit of his patience.

And then last night the nurse had called him up. Her name was Mrs. Thorpe, and she had come from Omaha to help with the influenza cases. He disliked her brisk, efficient ways and the professional manner of her speech. "I think she's going, Moon. Will you come right over?"

He was in bed, with the extension phone pulled to his side. The dry, sharp voice seemed slightly less metallic than the vibration of the receiver. "No, I will not come over," he answered at once, with irrational rage. "I'm in bed. Do you think I'm going to get up and dress just to go over there? There's nothing more I can do."

Mrs. Thorpe's voice buzzed on. It was the reproving voice of humanity. He listened a second to the rasping in his ear, and then without a word slammed the receiver. He did not intend to get out of bed.

But he did get up. He was lying with his hands over his stomach when his wife came in from her room. "What is it, Doctor? Is anything the matter?" "No," he said, sick with discouragement, "nothing's the matter." He climbed out of bed, put on his clothes over his nightshirt, and concealing this makeshift under his coat of fur, went down to the speak-easy. After filling himself full of port he was able to come home and sleep.

But this morning he felt conscience-stricken and made a call at the Masheks'. He found the nurse coldly superior, and Lily not dead after all. There was really nothing to do, there had been nothing last night, but he told Mrs. Thorpe to keep in touch with him through the day. And now when the telephone rang he would go over there again, to no purpose.

He stirred helplessly, and suddenly the book slid from his lap to the floor, pulling his hand with it. He sat there for a moment as he was, with one arm hanging loose, his mind like his body seeming scattered and formless.

With an effort he pulled himself together, picked the book up from the floor, and walked to the window. His head whirled with vertigo, his ears rang, stars streaked across his eyelids. The dizziness passed, and then he looked through the snow at the lonely street lined with square wooden houses. The snow was dropping monotonously, straight from the sky, melting as fast as it fell. While he watched the flakes thickened, the gray deepened, and fringes of white formed on the bare spots of the lawn.

The telephone rang. It was as he expected. Lily was worse again.

He donned his overcoat and cap, discovered that he was still wearing slippers, changed to his shoes, and closed the door of the house.

The snow fell on him in a steady, unending rhythm, on his cap, his shoulders, his nose. He could only see two hundred feet ahead, there were no lights in the houses, the town seemed deserted, tenantless. He walked along a lane of bare trees, through the snow, toward the twilight, alone. He had never felt so alone, and because of his depression his thoughts took on the complexion of the day. He saw the whole world living in these frail, sad houses, in the midst of desolation; victims of the weather, of vague fears, and senseless delusions. It weighed heavily on his spirit. If mankind did not have dignity, how could he hold up his own head? Besides, the humanity to which he ministered with his beautiful hands, had to have dignity.

And Lily Mashek! It was as if she had been unconscious all her life, and she really had that air about her. She was always running from one delusion to another, never touching reality. When Joe took to drink and began to beat her, she turned prohibitionist and tried to save his soul. All these years she had borne up with him, while her expression grew more angelic. And the reason was not because she loved Joe, but because people praised her fortitude, and called her a saint.

And now . . . now she was dying with a happy smile on her face because Joe had promised never to drink again. Joe reform! In a month he would be drunk, in six months he would be beating up some other woman. It was maddening.

The Mashek house was on the east edge of town, near the ice pond. Years ago it had been painted pink but now it loomed through the snow a kind of livid gray, sitting abjectly on a little rise of ground, a tall narrow house on a high foundation, looking both obscene and startled in the abandoned yard. He went up the path—there was no walk—and stamped the wet snow from his shoes on the porch.

A strange young man answered the door. There was no lamp inside, and he could not make out who it was. Then he recognized the Mashek boy, who must have arrived since the morning. While the son was pumping his hand, Dr. Moon remembered him unpleasantly. As a boy he had fought with Joe on the streets, and later had run away.

Going to the stairs he discovered Joe sitting by the table, with his head in his arms. The old man straightened up as he passed.

"It's no good, Doc. She's going to die."

"We'll see, Joe."

"Come on, Joe," he heard the son say from the dimness, "don't bother Doc. You know what's going to happen as well as he does."

Dr. Moon went up the stairs to the sickroom. As soon as he opened the door Mrs. Thorpe hurried on tiptoe toward him. She lifted the sick chart from the bedstand and handed it to him.

She jarred on his nerves.

"Give her some air," he said. "You don't want to choke her, do you?"

He put down the chart without looking at it and approached the iron bedstead. On the stand alongside was a coal oil lamp with a bright pink shade, some ancient peace offering of Joe's. The patient lay beyond the circle of light, in the blue shadows.

She was very thin and wasted, but her eyes were abnormally bright, and there was a strange feverish precocity about the upturned nose and a misplaced look of eagerness on her face. Although she lay weak and still, she seemed in perpetual movement, and at sight of him her lips opened in an ecstatic smile. All he could see was that smile, which maddened and saddened him, and made him want to hurt her even now. Yet when he spoke his voice was very gentle.

"How are you, Lily?"

He felt her pulse, placed his cool palm a moment on her forehead, then arranged her arms more comfortably, and turning to the nurse, signed with his hands that there was nothing more he could do. . . . He walked to the window and raised the sash, which she had lifted a little way, as high as it would go. A draught of damp air came in and brought to his ears the cottony sound of falling snow. The ice pond was all but invisible, limited at one end by the crazy-scattered limbs of scrubwillows, rising like giant witches' brooms, and at the other by the shadowy outlines of the ice house.

A thought was struggling in his mind, but he could not hold it. He could feel it, however, in successive waves, a tremendous affront to him, to everybody who held life in esteem.

The sound of guns brought him back to himself, and then he heard the quick, scared call of ducks. Some one was hunting, he wondered who. It was almost completely dark; they would never find the birds, even if they got them. It worried him. And then he wished he were out there too, in warm high boots, lying in the snow behind a blind of cornstalks, the firm feel of a gun in his hands.

He pulled the window half-way down and started to leave. Mrs. Thorpe cut across to meet him, always on tiptoe, always with her swinging gait. There was something hard and metallic about her, with her bronze hair and sharp features and starched uniform. She awaited him with her hand on the door.

"How long will it be, Moon?"

"Moon, Moon," he thought. What a brittle cat she was.

"How do I know?" he demanded. And then, curtly, "A couple of hours, maybe four."

Mrs. Thorpe nodded, looked speculatively down at the floor, and made a little clucking sound.

He stared at her, then brushed his arm vaguely across his face. She looked so pleased. She was like impersonal nature, which seems to enjoy the manifestation of its phenomena. The expression on her face was just the same as that which he felt in the sun, the trees, the skyline, whenever he left a bed of death.

At the foot of the stairs he saw the son turn from the window, saw him because of the faint blue light which appeared as he moved away. At the same time he felt across the room the full impress of his cheerful bulk on the air.

"Pardon me, Doc, I want to ask you something. Will it be all right to take Joe out for a walk? Just for a little while. He hasn't budged since I come. He's in an awful state."

The son seemed determined to make the best of things. His manner and his personality irritated Dr. Moon. Besides, he could hear behind him Joe milling in a chair, and his stomach was revolted by the cold, stale smell of the house: a sickening egg-shell odour. He longed to get out, but forced himself to be courteous. He went to great lengths.

"It will be all right," he said, "if you don't stay too long, and keep in touch with the house. Nothing will happen right away. It never does." He straightened, and put an arm in his overcoat. "You see, these shocks never come close together, even at the last. A crisis arrives because the heart can't pump blood through the arteries. The condition is accompanied by spasms of pain—your mother has been suffering the past week. We do what we can to ease her with narcotics . . . morphine. Then the condition clears . . . the heart triumphs, so to speak . . . and things go along for a while. Always for a while. . . ."

"I see," the son said. "I see."

Dr. Moon turned toward the table, touching his hat to the obscurity. "Good-bye, Joe."

"Good-bye, Doc. Oh, Doc! Good-bye!"

He closed the door. A slight draught blew curling flakes about his trouser legs, his feet sounded hollow on the porch. He slushed through the snow, already melting on the sidewalk, clinging to his steps, making his feet seem heavy. The smell of the house, the sound of the son's voice, the picture of his patient in that upstairs room, were still with him: he could not shake them off. Lily was going to die, she was going to die as she had lived, deluded. And the snow was falling endlessly, foreshortening the darkness, covering the earth and the houses, imprisoning him with his thoughts.

At the corner of the square he hesitated, standing with his hands in his pockets, his shoulders hunched under the smothering shower. It was completely night, a blackness thickened with gray. The other side of the feebly lighted square looked like the edge of civilization. Beyond, it seemed there could be nothing human, only a limitless waste of falling snow.

Such a wave of hopelessness came over him that he could not think of going home, and he turned toward the speak-easy. He wanted to get drunk, drunker than he had ever been in his life, drunker than he had ever dreamed of being, so drunk that he could fall into a thoughtless sleep.

He walked along the square, which was almost entirely deserted, and into a side street. The speak-easy, a former grocery store in which a full bar equipment had been installed, was packed with men. He edged up to a vacant place half-way down the long rail and ordered a rye, tossing it off at a swallow. Then he ordered another one.

He faced the entrance, lifting his glass, and as he did so the door opened and old Joe appeared, pushed in by his son.

The glass was at his lips; he drank the whisky and turned to the bar again, watching the approach of father and son in the mirror. They were quite close before they saw him. The son greeted him heartily and passed on, but Joe started, then sank his head more deeply into his shoulders.

"You here too, Doc?" he asked huskily.

Dr. Moon did not speak, he only nodded, and faced the mirror again, fingering his glass. He watched in amazement while Joe sat down at a table and the son brought sandwiches, bologna and beer. He felt bewildered, a little hurt, as if they had done him some wrong, and then suddenly, in keeping with his state of mind, with the gloomy weather, with everything that had gone before, an intuition came to him. He was positive the son knew nothing of Joe's promise to reform, because Joe lacked the strength to tell him. Now that they were here it was easy to see what would happen. They would both get drunk and go stumbling home, where Lily was dying in the belief that Joe would never drink again.

It all came to him in a flash, and he was sure, absolutely sure, that he had guessed the truth. It was just such a thing as would happen to the Masheks, as would happen to him, on such a night, feeling as he did.

His conscience bothered him, urging him to interfere, but he pushed it down violently. It was none of his affair.

He waited for developments with flushed cheeks and pounding heart. Everything occurred as he had foreseen: it was like the working out of a play whose action he had guessed. Soon after they had finished eating the son came to the bar for two whiskies. A little later he returned for two more.

Dr. Moon gripped the rail tightly and ordered another one himself.

There was no question now that he was right, that he had been right all along in his shame of humanity. Humanity! The blood rushed to his brain and he saw a whole world of foolish Lilies and weak Joes and well-meaning sons, a world which filled him with disgust.

He wanted to laugh, he wanted to do more than laugh. And then he had an amusing idea, the idea of joining them, to see what would happen.

Taking his glass in his hand, he walked as steadily as he could down the center of the room and stood at their side.

Old Joe started to get up deferentially, but Dr. Moon waved him back to his seat.

"I thought I'd come," he said, with a self-conscious bow, "and join the performance. Since we're all here together."

"Good for you, Doc," the son said. "Sit down and have a drink and listen to what I been saying to Joe. I know you'll agree with me absolutely. We're both in the same boat, I told him. I know it hits him hardest, you can't deny that, but there's only one thing to do. No matter who we are we got to take these things as they come. Ain't I right, Doc?"

Dr. Moon nodded his head gravely. "I'm coming to believe so," he said. "I do agree with you, absolutely. It's a mistake to take things too hard."

Joe looked at him, unimpressed. Slowly he shook his head. "I been a bad man, Doc. I been a drunken, good-for-nothing son of a bitch. But I'm gone to reform. Doc don't believe me, he knows something, Doc does. But I'm gone to, wait and see. You think so, Doc? Listen, Doc. There's things I got to do. I got to have a mass said, and a monument. . . ."

"You can't do that," the son interrupted. "I wish you'd explain to him, Doc. Ma's a Baptist. You can't have no mass said for a Baptist."

"Although I'm not a Catholic," said Dr. Moon, "I'll tell you this: the Catholic church is a great church." He put out his hands, explanatory. "Catholic—universal. Universal—Catholic. . . . I'm not familiar with the laws of the church, but I'm sure that it's possible. You go ahead,

Joe, and do what you want." He turned to the son. "Joe will do what he wants."

"He sure will," the son said, "and I'll help him. Don't you ever doubt that. You ask him what the first thing I said to him was. 'I was a mean kid,' I said, 'and I want to make up for it now. Anything in the world I can do let me know, and,' I said, 'take it from me I didn't come broke.' Don't you worry about the monument, Joe."

"As for the stone . . ." began Dr. Moon and paused. "I wonder . . . I'd like . . ." He hesitated again, while Joe looked at him with a wavering glance. "Lily. All these years. You know what I'm trying to say . . . I never sent you a bill in my life, Joe. If you'd let me help a little now . . ."

Joe began suddenly to weep. His little red watery eyes looked like broken blisters. "You too, Doc," he said. "You like Lily. She's so good, and me . . . Do you know what I am, Doc? I'm . . ."

Dr. Moon put his hand on Joe's shoulder, which collapsed under his touch. "Yes, I know, Joe, but don't worry now. It doesn't matter. Nothing matters. We're no good. Nobody's any good. Hell. Look, Joe—" he brought his hand back and put it to his side, as if expecting to find something wrong. "Some day, Joe, you and I . . ."

"Sure, we all got it coming to us," the son said. "Let's have another drink." He got up and went to the bar.

Dr. Moon watched his retreating back, and then said confidentially: "These young fellows, Joe. They don't understand, as we do. Every time the sun sets it's one less for us, and we wonder why it should be that way when we know what's at the end; nothing. I beg your pardon, Joe. I know you don't believe that, but . . . nothing."

He waited for the son to return, and went on: "You're right, we all have it coming to us. That's just the point I want to make. We've got to remember that every day. Here we are, you and Joe and I. We've got to live. We can't die without living. We've got to be conscious, be human, live strenuously, live beautifully. Live. We've got to mean something. There is a saying" (he waited to fix their attention): "Be noble, and

the nobleness of other men . . . sleeping but not dead . . . will rise in
majesty, to meet thine own."

" 'Will rise in majesty, to meet thine own,' " the son repeated. "That's
beautiful, Doc. That's swell."

"Lily," Joe called. "She's like what you say, ain't she, Doc?"

Dr. Moon suddenly came to himself, and did not say any more. He
remembered his idea and became very reserved, nodding his head and
drinking in silence while both Joe and the son talked at once.

The talking stopped, and all three grew aware that the bartender was
standing before them.

"Somebody telephoned from your house," he said to Joe. "They want
you to come home."

They looked with scared glances at Dr. Moon and then at one another.

"Come," the doctor said. "We'd better hurry."

He pulled Joe up from the chair and the son helped with the overcoat.
They left by the rear door, which opened on an alley, and followed it
to the street. They walked one on each side of Joe, pulling him along,
holding him up when he wanted to drop to his knees and pray. The
weather had grown colder, ice had formed under the deepening layer
of snow. It was difficult going. A wind blew small, hard flakes across
their faces.

Dr. Moon felt intensely curious, but calm. Several times his conscience intruded, but he ignored it. He was only a spectator. He was
going to find out the end of the play.

The son leaned over Joe's back and whispered: "Do you think we'll
be too late, Doc?"

"No, I don't think so," Dr. Moon answered. "Not if we hurry."

He was the first to enter the house. A lamp had been placed below
by the light of which he saw the nurse looking down from the top of
the stairs. He took off his wraps and mounted, followed by Joe and the
son. His step was steady; he felt perfectly sober. He walked across the
sickroom to the little corner washstand and scrubbed his hands and

dried them skillfully on a towel. It was all mechanical, almost unconscious. Then he turned to his patient.

Her eyes stared at the ceiling, her lips moved, her hands crawled back and forth over the covers.

"What is it, Lily?" he asked, and motioned to the nurse to find out what she was saying.

"She wants you to come close," Mrs. Thorpe told Joe and the son.

They leaned awkwardly over the bed and she stared at them, and then smiled in exaltation. Dr. Moon watched the smile, and the troubled but unbroken rhythm of her lips as she prayed. Then he turned away. He had known at once that she could not see them, that she could only realise their presence. She was dying deluded after all.

He walked to the window, watching the white flakes whirl in from the blackness and click against the pane. Behind him he heard Lily's dry, persistent whispering, and an occasional moan from Joe.

So now he knew for sure there was no sense in anything.

He turned around. "I'm going, Joe. I'm going. Good-bye."

He walked quickly from the room, signalling for the nurse to follow him, closing the door behind them. For a second he stared at her, then brushed his hand across his face. Already he felt tired again.

"Do you want to do something for me? Two things. Go downstairs and cook them something hot, some coffee. And the second thing: stay out of there."

She stood still, making no answer, watching him in amazement. At the top of the stairs he turned and looked over his shoulder. "Whatever you do," he added, "don't you touch her."

He descended with eyes looking straight ahead, put on his coat, his cap, his gloves, marched out of the house, across the yard, down the street, through the snow. It was getting bitter; he turned up the collar of his coat and sunk his hands deep in the pockets. He tried not to think: above everything else, he tried not to think of what he had done.

To-morrow, he told himself, would be another day. He would be all right to-morrow.

Morton

LOUISE FIELD COOPER

Early one Saturday morning a while back I went into the hospital and had a baby named Peter. This was no surprise to anyone, and shortly afterward I lapsed into a complacent doze. When I woke, hours later, there was a man in the room. He was a stranger, a thin-faced man in white, pushing a long red handle that had a wide black brush shaped like Groucho Marx's mustache on the end of it. He was watching me as he maneuvered slowly around the foot of the bed toward the waste-basket.

"Good morning," I said, feeling superbly cozy and affable.

"It *is* a good morning," he agreed. "Too good to have to stay in here."

"I can't complain," I said in a brave-little-woman voice.

"I meant me," he said.

His name was Morton and I got to know him well. Certainly I saw a lot more of him than of any other man. Peter made only occasional, very brief visits to my room, and my husband and the doctor were in and ᴄᵘt, but in an irresponsible sort of way, so Morton was about all I could depend on for really steady masculine companionship. The second day, he came in during my breakfast. "Read the paper today?" was his greeting, accompanied by a mournful bending of the head and a sigh.

"No, tell me," I urged politely.

"Well"—he made a few perfunctory swipes with his brush, and then came to rest leaning on the handle—"There's a little item I noticed says a lady away out in Idaho is slowly, slowly dyin' of an unknown disease. Baffles science, the paper says. Terrible, ain't it?"

381

My appetite for coffee and toast and marmalade faded. "What's the matter with her?" I asked.

"Seems she's shrinkin'. Nobody knows why. This Spring she was as all right as you or me. Come July, she begun to shrink." We pondered this interesting case for several silent minutes. Then he fell to work. "Ah, well," he said.

After this little chat he did a brisk, thorough job of sweeping out my room and departed rather happy.

Being so much with Morton colored my point of view. He came in first every day during breakfast, and often he dropped in around noon-time to see if the wastebasket needed emptying and how I was doing, and he always did another bit of tidying early in the evening. It was in the evening that he wielded his greatest power over me.

"Any visitors today?" he would ask, gazing downward, sweeping slowly.

"Oh, it's too soon for me to have visitors," I would say. "I'm not sup-posed to have any until the baby's a week old." But as Peter rapidly approached his second Saturday on earth, I began to feel neglected. The evening of the day Peter was eight days old, Morton neatly corralled the dust into a circle and leaned on his brush. "Any visitors *today?*" he murmured.

"Well, no. Not any today. The doctor came, and my husband, of course, but no visitors. Maybe tomorrow."

Next day I put on my best nightgown and enamelled my fingernails. The flowers around the room were very fresh and fragrant; beyond the hospital windows a warm rain sped to the pavement. I waited for visi-tors for a while, and then I read magazines, turning the pages fre-quently, one eye on the door. No one came to see me; steps passed and passed to other rooms, but only the nurse ever turned in at my door.

At suppertime Morton was at my side, looking at me.

"It rained terribly hard all afternoon," I said quickly. "Nobody would want to go outdoors to visit at a hospital a day like today."

Morton shook his head and said nothing.

The next afternoon I never took my eyes off the door. No one came to visit me, and by night I had worked up a degree and a half of temperature. "Keep her quiet all tomorrow," the doctor said. "And *no visitors.*" Next day was heavenly. I hummed to myself all day, carefree as a flower. Any number of my friends came to the door and were turned away. I told Morton about it at suppertime.

"Of course, I'm frightfully disappointed not to have seen them," I said, gaily tossing a butterball into my baked potato. Morton said, "Ah, well."

It wasn't until I had been about a week at the hospital that I had any clue to the reason for Morton's rather special point of view on life. He brought in the Sunday paper.

"How are you today?" I asked.

"Pretty fair for a Tuesday."

"Tuesday? Today's Sunday."

"It's Tuesday for me. Friday's my day off, so I call it my Sunday, see? That makes Saturday my Monday. Today's Tuesday. That's the way I live—twisted, you might say. I was going to take a little motor trip *my* Sunday, but it rained all day."

"You're fond of driving?"

"Been driving ever since before they made you get a license. Those days, all you had to do was go before the police chief and he give you a piece paper said on it 'This man is illegible to drive a non-horse-drawn vehicle.' "

"That must have made you very proud."

"Naturally it did." He swept beneath the bed. "I like cars. One of the few things I *do* like, you might say. Bought me a motorcycle once, but the first time I was on it I hit a stone in the middle of the road and when I come to I was up in the crotch of a tree, danglin' like. I've drove a car ever since. Four wheels is none too many."

No one who hasn't had a baby on the third floor of the Private Pavilion can ever know how subtle and how penetrating Morton's influence was. Some of my customary lightheartedness, I think, has seeped permanently away. The morning before I went home, I looked up from excavating a boiled egg to find him standing at the foot of the bed.

"Seen the papers?"

"Yes!" I cried. I thought I'd beat him to it for once. "I *loved* the triple slaying in Mississippi."

But he shook his head. "Not that." He moved a little nearer. "I mean the woman in Topeka who's had just one twin."

"What?"

"Yeh." He turned his enormous black eyes from my face and stared out the window. "Just the one. That was last week sometime. The other one, she's still waiting for it. Horrible, wouldn't you say?"

"But why don't the doctors help her have the other?"

Morton drifted to the door, his eyes resting ever so lightly on my helpless, extended form. "Doctors?" he said. "Well . . ." He tipped his head sideways with what might be some fearful secret knowledge and followed his long-handled brush into the hall. I lay clamped in a cold apprehension. What if little Peter, asleep in the hospital nursery, was only half of what Nature had contrived for me. Perhaps *my* doctor . . . I rang and rang and rang for the nurse, and it was an eternity before I heard her firm footsteps coming along the hall and the soothing rustle of her starched white skirt as she turned in at my door.

The Medicine Man

ERSKINE CALDWELL

THERE was nobody in Rawley who believed that Effie Henderson would ever find a man to marry her, and Effie herself had just about given up hope. But that was before the traveling herb doctor came to town.

Professor Eaton was a tall gaunt-looking man with permanent, sewn-in creases in his trousers and a high celluloid collar around his neck. He may have been ten years older than Effie, or he may have been ten years younger; it was no more easy to judge his age than it was to determine from what section of the country he had originally come.

He drove into Rawley one hot dusty morning in mid-August, selling Indian Root Tonic. Indian Root Tonic was a beady, licorice-tasting cure-all in a fancy green-blown bottle. The bottle was wrapped in a black and white label, on which the most prominent feature was the photographic reproduction of a beefy man exhibiting his expanded chest and muscles and his postage-stamp wrestler's trunks. Professor Eaton declared, and challenged any man alive to deny his statement, that his Indian Root Tonic would cure any ailment known to man, and quite a few known only to women.

Effie Henderson was the first person in town to give him a dollar for a bottle, and the first to come back for the second one.

The stand that Professor Eaton had opened up was the back seat of his mud-spattered touring car. He had paid the mayor ten ragged one-dollar bills for a permit to do business in Rawley, and he had parked his automobile in the middle of the weed-grown vacant lot behind the depot. He sold his medicine over the back seat of his car, lifting the

385

green-blown botties from a box at his feet as fast as the customers came up and laid down their dollars.

There had been a big crowd standing around in the weed-grown lot the evening before, but there were only a few people standing around him listening to his talk when Effie came back in the morning for her second bottle. Most of the persons there then were Negroes who did not have a dollar between them, but who had been attracted to the lot by the alcoholic fumes around the mud-caked automobile and who were willing to be convinced of Indian Root Tonic's marvelous curative powers. When Effie came up, the Negroes stepped aside, and stood in a horseshoe at a distance watching Professor Eaton get ready to make another sale.

Effie walked up to the folded-down top in front of Professor Eaton and laid down a dollar bill that was as limp as a piece of wet cheesecloth.

"I just had to come back this morning for another bottle," Effie said, smiling up at Professor Eaton. "The one I took last night made me feel better than I have ever felt before in all my life. There's not another medicine in the whole country like it, and I've tried them all, I reckon."

"Pardon me, madam," Professor Eaton said. "There are hundreds of preparations on the market today, but there is only one Indian Root Tonic. You will be doing me a great favor if you will hereafter refer to my aid-to-human-life by its true and trade-marked name. Indian Root Tonic is the name of the one and only cure for ailments of any nature. It is particularly good for the mature woman, madam."

"You shouldn't call me 'madam,' Professor Eaton," Effie said, lowering her head. "I'm just a young and foolish girl, and I'm not married yet, either."

Professor Eaton wiped the perspiration from his upper lip and looked down at Effie.

"How utterly stupid of me, my dear young lady," he said. "Anyone can see by looking at your fresh young face that you are a mere girl. Indian Root Tonic is particularly good for the young maiden."

Effie turned around to see if any of the Negroes were close enough to hear what Professor Eaton had said. She hoped that some of the women who lived on her street would walk past the corner in time to hear Professor Eaton talk like that about her.

"I never like to talk about myself, but don't you think I am too young yet to get married, Professor Eaton?"

"My dear young lady," he continued after having paused long enough to relight his cigar, "Indian Root Tonic is particularly good for the unmarried girl. It is the greatest discovery known to medical science since the beginning of mankind. I personally secured the formula for this marvelous medicine from an old Indian chief out in our great West, and I was compelled to promise him on my bended knee that I would devote the remainder of my life to traveling over the country offering Indian Root Tonic to men and women like you who would be helpless invalids without it."

He had to pause for a moment's breath. It was then that he looked down over the folded top and for the first time looked at Effie face to face. The evening before in the glare of the gasoline torch, when the lot was crowded with people pushing and shoving to get to the medicine stand before the special introductory offer was withdrawn, he had not had time to look at everyone who came up to hand him a dollar for a bottle. But now when he looked down and saw Effie, he leaned forward to stare at her.

"Oh, Professor Eaton," Effie said, "you are such a wonderful man! Just to think that you are doing such a great work in the world!"

Professor Eaton continued to stare at Effie. She was as good-looking as the next girl in town, not over thirty, and when she fixed herself up, as she had done for nearly two hours that morning before leaving home, she usually had all the drummers in town for the day staring at her and asking the storekeeper who she was.

After a while Professor Eaton climbed out of the back seat of his car and came around to the rear where she was. He relit his cigar, and inspected Effie more closely.

"You know, Professor Eaton, you shouldn't talk like that to me," she said, evading his eyes. "You really don't know me well enough yet to call me 'dear girl.' This is the first time we have been alone together, and—"

"Why! I didn't think that a beautiful young girl like you would seriously object to my honorable admiration," he said, looking her up and down and screwing up his mouth when she plucked at her blouse. "It's so seldom that I have the opportunity of seeing such a charming girl that I must have lost momentarily all sense of discretion. But, now that we are fully acquainted with each other, I'm sure you won't object to my devoted admiration. Will you?"

"Oh, Professor Eaton," Effie said excitedly, "do you really and truly think I am beautiful? So many men have told me that before, I'm accustomed to hearing it frequently, but you are the first man to say it so thrillingly!"

She tried to step backward, but she was already standing against the rear of the car. Professor Eaton moved another step closer, and there was no way for her to turn. She would not have minded that if she had not been so anxious to have a moment to look down at her blouse. She knew there must be something wrong, surely something had slipped under the waist, because Professor Eaton had not raised his eyes from her bosom since he got out of the car and came down beside her. She wondered then if she should not have confined herself when she dressed that morning, putting on all the undergarments she wore to church on Sunday morning.

"My dear girl, there is not the slightest doubt in my mind concerning your beauty. In fact, I think you are the most charming young girl it has been my good fortune to encounter during my many travels over this great country of ours—from coast to coast, from the Lakes to the Gulf."

"You make me feel so young and foolish, Professor Eaton!" Effie said, smoothing her shirtwaist over her bosom. "You make me feel like——"

Professor Eaton turned abruptly and reached into the back seat for a bottle of Indian Root Tonic. He closed his teeth over the cork stopper and popped it out, and, with no further loss of time, handed it to Effie.

"Have this one on me, my dear girl," he said. "Just drink it down, and then see if it doesn't make you feel even better still."

Effie took the green-blown bottle, looking at the picture of the strong young man in wrestler's trunks.

"I drank the whole bottle I bought last night," she said. "I drank it just before going to bed, and it made me feel so good I just couldn't lie still. I had to get up and sit on the back porch and sing a while."

"There was never a more beneficial——"

"What particular ailment is the medicine good for, Professor Eaton?"

"Indian Root Tonic is good for whatever ails you. In fact, merely as a general conditioner it is supreme in its field. And then on the other hand, there is no complaint known to medical science that it has yet failed to allevi—to help."

Effie turned up the bottle and drank down the beady, licorice-tasting fluid, all eight ounces of it. The Negroes standing in a horseshoe around the car looked on wistfully while the fumes from the opened bottle drifted over the lot. Effie handed the empty bottle to Professor Eaton, after taking one last look at the picture on the label.

"Oh, Professor Eaton," she said, coming closer, "it makes me feel better already. I feel just like I was going to rise off the ground and fly away somewhere."

"Perhaps you would allow me——"

"To do what, Professor Eaton? What?"

"Perhaps you would allow me to escort you to your home," he said. "Now, it's almost dinner-time, and I was just getting ready to close up my stand until the afternoon, so if you will permit me, I'll be very glad to drive you home in my automobile. Just tell me how to get there, and we'll start right away."

"You talk so romantic, Professor Eaton," Effie said, touching his arm with her hand. "You make me feel just like a foolish young girl around you."

"Then you will permit me to see you home?"

"Of course, I will."

"Step this way please," he said, holding open the door and taking her arm firmly in his grasp.

After they had settled themselves in the front seat, Effie turned around and looked at Professor Eaton.

"I'll bet you have had just lots and lots of love affairs with young girls like me all over the country."

"On the contrary," he said, starting the motor, "this is the first time I have ever given my serious consideration to one of your sex. You see, I apply myself faithfully to the promotion, distribution, and sale of Indian Root Tonic. But this occasion, of course, draws me willingly from the cares of business. In fact, I consider your presence in my car a great honor. I have often wished that I might——"

"And am I the first young girl—the first woman you ever courted?"

"Absolutely," he said. "Absolutely."

Professor Eaton drove out of the vacant weed-grown lot and turned the car up the street toward Effie's house. She lived only two blocks away, and during the time it took them to drive that distance neither of them spoke. Effie was busy looking out to see if people were watching her ride with Professor Eaton in his automobile, and he was busily engaged in steering through the deep white sand in the street. When they got there, Effie told him to park the machine in front of the gate where they could step out and walk directly into the house.

They got out and Effie led the way through the front door and into the parlor. She raised one of the shades a few inches and dusted off the sofa.

Professor Eaton stood near the middle of the room, looking uneasily through the small opening under the shade, and listening intently for sounds elsewhere in the house.

"Just sit down here on the sofa beside me," Effie said. "I know I am perfectly safe alone with you, Professor Eaton."

Effie closed her eyes and allowed herself the pleasure of feeling scared to death of Professor Eaton. It was an even nicer feeling than the one she had had the night before when she drank the first bottle of Indian Root Tonic and got into bed.

"And this is the ancestral home?" he asked.

"Don't let's talk about anything but you—and me," Effie said. "Wouldn't you just like to talk about us?"

Professor Eaton began to feel more at ease, now that it was evident that they were alone in the house.

"Perhaps," Professor Eaton said, sitting closer to Effie and looking down once more at her blouse, "perhaps you will permit me to diagnose your complaint. You see, I am well versed in the medical science, and I can tell you how many bottles of Indian Root Tonic you should use in your particular case. Naturally, some people require a greater number of bottles than others do."

Effie glanced out the window for a second, and then she turned to Professor Eaton.

"I won't have to——"

"Oh, no," he said, "that won't be at all necessary, though you may do as you like about it. I can just——"

"Are you sure it's perfectly all right, Professor Eaton?"

"Absolutely," he said. "Absolutely."

Effie smoothed her shirtwaist with her hands and pushed her shoulders forward. Professor Eaton bent towards her, reaching for her hand.

He held her hand for a few seconds, feeling her pulse, and then dropped it to press his ear against her bosom to listen to her heartbeat. While he listened, Effie tucked up a few loose strands of hair that had fallen over her temples.

"Perhaps," he said, raising his head momentarily, "perhaps if you will merely——"

"Of course, Professor Eaton," Effie said excitedly.

He bent closer after she had fumbled nervously with the blouse and pressed his head against her breasts. Her heartbeat jarred his eardrum.

After a while Professor Eaton sat up and loosened the knot in his necktie and wiped the perspiration from his upper lip with the back of his hand. It was warm in the room, and there was no ventilation with the door closed.

"Perhaps I have already told you——"

"Oh no! You haven't told me!" she said eagerly, holding her hands tightly clasped and looking down at herself with bated breath. "Please go ahead and tell me, Professor Eaton!"

"Perhaps," he said, fingering the open needlework in her blouse, "perhaps you would like to know that Indian Root Tonic is the only complete aid for general health on the market today. And in addition to its general curative properties, Indian Root Tonic possesses the virtues most women find themselves in need of during the middle and later stages of life. In other words, it imparts a vital force to the glands that are in most need of new vitality. I am sure that once you discover for yourself the marvelous power of rejuvenation that Indian Root Tonic possesses, you will never again be alone in the house without it. In fact, I can say without fear of successful contradiction that——"

Effie laid her blouse aside.

"Do you want me to take——"

"Oh, yes; by all means," he replied hastily. "Now, as I was saying——"

"And this, too, Professor Eaton? This, too?"

Professor Eaton reached over and pinched her lightly. Effie giggled and passed his hands over her bosom as though she were smoothing her shirtwaist.

"I don't suppose you happen to have another bottle of that tonic in your pocket, do you, Professor Eaton?"

"I'm afraid I haven't," he said, "but just outside in my car there are several cases full. If you'll let me, I'll step out and——"

"Oh, no!" Effie cried, clutching at his arms and pulling him back beside her. "Oh, Professor Eaton, don't leave me now!"

"Very well," he said, sitting down beside her once more. "And now as I was saying, Indian Root Tonic's supernatural powers of re——"

"Professor Eaton, do you want me to take off all of this—like this?"

"Absolutely," he said. "And Indian Root Tonic has never been known to fail, whereas in so many——"

"You don't want me to leave anything——"

"Of course not. Being a doctor of the medical science, in addition to my many other activities, I need absolute freedom. Now, if you feel that you cannot place yourself entirely in my hands, perhaps it would be better if I——"

"Oh, please don't go!" Effie cried, pulling him back to the sofa beside her. "You know I have complete confidence in your abilities, Professor Eaton. I know you wouldn't——"

"Wouldn't do what?" he asked, looking down at her again.

"Oh, Professor Eaton! I'm just a young girl!"

"Well," he said, "if you are ready to place yourself entirely in my hands, I can proceed with my diagnosis. Otherwise——"

"I was only teasing you, Professor Eaton!" Effie said, squeezing his hand. "Of course, I trust you. You are such a strong man, and I know you wouldn't take advantage of a weak young girl like me. If you didn't take care of me, I'd more than likely run away with myself."

"Absolutely," he said. "Now, if you will continue removing the——"

"There is only this left, Professor Eaton," Effie said. "Are you sure it will be all right?"

"Absolutely."

"But I feel so—so bare, Professor Eaton."

"'Tis only natural to feel like that," he said, comforting her. "A young girl who has never before experienced the——"

"Experienced the what?"

"Well—as I was saying——"

"You make me feel so funny, Professor Eaton. And are you sure——"

"Absolutely," he said. "Absolutely."

"I've never felt like this before. It feels like——"

"Just place yourself completely in my hands, my dear young girl, and I promise nothing will——"

Without warning the parlor door was thrown open and Effie's brother, Burke, came in. Burke was the town marshal.

"Is dinner ready, Effie?" Burke asked, standing in the doorway and trying to accustom his eyes to the near-darkness of the parlor. "It's a quarter after twelve and——"

Burke stopped in the midst of what he was saying and stared at Effie and Professor Eaton. Effie screamed and pushed Professor Eaton away

from her. He got up and stood beside Effie and the sofa, looking first at
Burke and then at Effie. He did not know what to do. Effie reached for
the things she had thrown aside. Professor Eaton bent down and picked
up something and threw it at her.

The room suddenly appeared to Professor Eaton to be as bright as
day.

"Well, I'll be damned!" Burke said, coming slowly across the floor.
His holster hung from his right hip, and it swung heavily as he swayed
from step to step. "I'll be damned!"

Professor Eaton stood first on one foot and then on the other. He was
between Effie and her brother, and he knew of no way by which he could
change his position in the room. He wished to get as far away from
Effie as he possibly could. Until she had dressed herself, he hoped he
would not be forced to look at her.

Burke stepped forward and pushed Professor Eaton aside. He looked
at Effie and at the herb doctor, but he gave no indication of what he
intended doing.

Professor Eaton shifted the weight of his body to his other foot, and
Burke's hand dropped to the top of the holster, his fingers feeling for
the pearl handle that protruded from it.

Effie snapped a safety-pin and ran between Burke and Professor Eaton.
She was still not completely dressed, but she was fully covered.

"What are you going to do, Burke?" she cried.

"That all depends on what the professor is going to do," Burke said,
still fingering the pearl handle on the pistol. "What is the professor going
to do?"

"Why, Professor Eaton and I are going to be married, Burke," she
said. "Aren't we, Professor Eaton?"

"I had not intended making known the announcement of our engagement and forthcoming marriage at this time," he said, "but since
we are to be married very shortly, Effie's brother should by all means
be the first to know of our intentions."

"Thanks for telling me, professor," Burke said. "It had better by a
damn sight be forthcoming."

Effie ran to Professor Eaton and locked her arms around his neck.

"Oh, do you really mean it, Professor Eaton? I'm so happy I don't know what to do! But why didn't you tell me sooner that you really wanted to marry me? Do you really and truly mean it, Professor Eaton?"

"Sure," Burke said; "he means it."

"I'm the happiest girl in the whole town of Rawley," Effie cried, pressing her face against Professor Eaton's celluloid collar. "It was all so unexpected! I had never dreamed of it happening to me so soon!"

Burke backed across the room, one hand still around the pearl handle that protruded from the cow-hide holster. He backed across the room and reached for the telephone receiver on the wall. He rang the central office and took the receiver from the hook.

"Hello, Janie," he said into the mouthpiece. "Ring up Reverend Edwards for me, will you, right away."

Burke leaned against the wall, looking at Effie and Professor Eaton while Janie at the central office was ringing the Reverend Edwards' number.

"Just to think that I'm going to marry a traveling herb doctor!" Effie said. "Why! all the girls in town will be so envious of me they won't speak for a month!"

"Absolutely," Professor Eaton said, pulling tight the loosened knot in his tie and adjusting it in the opening of his celluloid collar. "Absolutely. Indian Root Tonic has unlimited powers. It is undoubtedly the medical and scientific marvel of the age. Indian Root Tonic has been known to produce the most astounding results in the annals of medical history."

Effie pinned up a strand of hair that had fallen over her forehead and looked proudly upon Professor Eaton.

The Other Room

DON MARQUIS

Dr. Harvey Herbert was not only an M.D. but a Ph.D. His familiars referred to him as a "psychological shark"; but the world in general did not permit itself such slangy informality. What the world saw was a man who had attained an unusual position at thirty-eight years of age, who was acknowledged to be solid as well as brilliant, and who was spoken of with enthusiasm by his professional and academic brethren.

Doctor Herbert specialized as a neurologist, but his private practice was not large, and it was not easy to get him to take a case unless it had some extraordinary feature which piqued his interest. He lectured on psychology in one of the universities and he had written extensively on his subject. He was, among other things, a recognized authority upon criminology. He had devoted a great deal of time to the study of hallucinations.

Some strange cases came to the attention of Dr. Harvey Herbert, cases involving very fine ethical points, at times; cases in which a matter of conscience often lay concealed under the surface of some mental trouble, just as a bit of broken needle may work itself through the flesh of the body for years causing physical disturbances difficult to diagnose because its presence is unknown. Doctor Herbert was a rather acutely conscientious person himself.

But with all his exploration of the shadowy caverns of the subconscious mind, no case ever came to the attention of Dr. Harvey Herbert that was stranger than the case of . . . Dr. Harvey Herbert.

It was one day last spring that Doctor Herbert called at the office of his friend Dr. Howard Vokes, after telephoning to make sure that Doctor Vokes had time for a lengthy consultation, and dropped into the big chair in front of Vokes' desk, a picture of weariness.

Vokes, a general practitioner and a lifelong comrade, looked at Herbert with keen eyes, noted his fag, and offered him a drink. Doctor Herbert nodded his acceptance.

"Which one of my patients has been sneaking off to you, Harvey?" said Doctor Vokes. "I don't think I've sent any one lately."

"None of them," said Doctor Herbert. "I'm here to consult with you about—about myself."

"Quit drinking," said Vokes, with a smile, pouring a liberal allowance of whiskey into a glass for the famous psychologist. "Give up smoking," he went on, pushing his cigarette case towards his friend; "and have your teeth, tonsils, and appendix taken out at once; take a trip to Bermuda, play golf more, raise violets, eat pineapples, and come back in three days and tell me how you feel."

But this facetiousness elicited only the feeblest of smiles from his famous friend; Doctor Herbert was twisting his pointed brown beard with his slender fingers, his face and worried eyes averted. Doctor Vokes went on, seriously:

"Stomach, Harvey? Liver? Kidneys? Something in my line?"

"I wish it were," said Herbert, with a sigh. "But I'm afraid it's—nerves."

"Consult the eminent neurologist, Dr. Harvey Herbert," said Vokes. His remark was really a question as to why the specialist had come to a general practitioner to confer upon a case involving his own specialty; and Doctor Herbert understood it so. He shrugged his shoulders and said in a tired voice:

"I've been to Dr. Harvey Herbert. The man doesn't do me any good." And then, after a brief pause, "Howard, you're the oldest friend I have." He paused again, and resumed, with a smile which made his face very attractive in spite of the ravages of his worry, "And, with the exception of my wife, about the best one, Howard."

The two men exchanged that glance of perfect understanding which is so much more eloquent than words. Presently Vokes suggested, "I suppose you've been down in the sub-cellar of the human mind again, hunting your ghosts—and one of them has turned on you this time."

"Something like that," admitted Doctor Herbert.

"You prowl into some queer, dank places," said Doctor Vokes. "They almost frighten me."

"This time," said Doctor Herbert, "I was frightened. I still am. I saw . . ."

His voice trailed off into a brooding silence.

"What did you see?" insisted Dr. Vokes.

"Myself," said Dr. Harvey Herbert. He shuddered, took another drink, and presently began.

I'm hoping that when I'm finished (said Doctor Herbert) you and I may be able to get together and diagnose my case as something physical— but if we can't, at least I will have told everything to a friend. As a psychologist, I can assure you that there is sometimes great value in a sympathetic father confessor. And now that I've said that word, I recognize that I am really coming to you for the assurance of absolution— an assurance that I've not been able to give to myself.

It was about three weeks ago that I got the jolt I'm still staggering from. You remember Aunt Emma Hastings, who lived with us for so many years? Well, it was three weeks ago that Aunt Emma died.

She was distantly related to both my wife and myself, although Margaret and I are not related to each other. Although we both called her Aunt, she was really a second or third cousin of Margaret's grandmother; she was connected, even more remotely, with my mother's father. We were the only people left in the world who could by any stretch of the imagination be called kinsfolk. So we gave her a home, took care of her.

I don't mean that we took care of her financially. She was a great deal better off than I am. I've grubbed for knowledge, rather than money, as you know; always giving more time to research than to my practice.

We took care of Aunt Emma Hastings physically; and not even our best friends have known what a strain it has been or how Aunt Emma tyrannized over us Entrenched in invalidism, age, sentimentality, the habit of years, she was the very pattern of a petty domestic tyrant. Her death should really be a release and a relief to me; but, for reasons which you will gather, it is anything but that.

The night she died Margaret and I had planned to go to the theater. We had dined early, and at a couple of minutes after eight o'clock I was waiting in the living room for Margaret, who was putting the finishing touches to her dressing. Getting out to the theater was more of a treat to Margaret and me than you might suspect, for Aunt Emma had grown increasingly querulous if one or the other, or both of us, were not with her. In fact, for some time had we foregone almost all social diversions.

Margaret came in from her room, her face shining with pleasant anticipation, and I picked up my top-coat and hat. "Ready at last!" she said, gaily.

But just then Miss Murdock entered. Miss Murdock was Aunt Emma's own attendant—nurse, companion, and maid all at once. There had been a long succession of these companions. Aunt Emma seldom kept one more than six or eight months, and she had had an astonishing variety. But they were all alike in one thing—they seemed to enjoy the tyranny which Aunt Emma exercised over Margaret and myself and to relish the opportunity to participate in it in a minor way. Miss Murdock said, with a prim exterior, but with a certain latent gusto:

"Mrs. Herbert, Miss Hastings sent me to inquire whether you and Doctor Herbert were going out to-night."

"Why, yes," said Margaret; "we're just starting. Does Miss Hastings want anything? I'll go to her if she wishes to speak with me."

Miss Murdock became a composite picture of the petty malice of all her predecessors as she announced:

"Miss Hastings said, in case I found you were going out, that I was to tell you not to do so."

"Not to do so!" I exclaimed. I felt a flush of anger, a sudden red rush of it all over me. If my face looked like Margaret's, I showed what I felt. This was a little too much!

"That's what she said," returned Miss Murdock; and I saw the tip of her tongue run along her lips as if she tasted a creamy satisfaction. "She said, in case you were going out, you must give up your plans and stay at home."

With a triumphant glance, Miss Murdock started for the door. But she paused to give us her final thrust. "Since you will be here with Miss Hastings," she said, "I think I'll go out myself." She left.

Margaret and I sat in silent humiliation for a moment. The anger that had gone all over me seemed to culminate in something that writhed in my head—fluttered and writhed as if a grub were turning to a butterfly all in one instant somewhere among the convolutions of my brain. I rose, with the words forming themselves upon my lips, "Come on, Margaret, let's get out of here at once—she's gone too damned far this time!"

But I did not utter those words. I saw something, suddenly, that made me pause.

I saw another room, with Margaret and myself sitting in it. Listen carefully, Howard; for just here is the beginning of the train of events that has brought me to you.

I say I saw another room. I should have said I saw the room that we were in, or part of it. Our own living room, and she and I sitting in it, dressed to go out for the evening, just exactly as we were.

I saw it as if I were looking into a mirror, only it was dimmer than that, as if a fine gauze were in front of the mirror. No, not so much a gauze as a light mist, a faint fog. A somewhat denser mist, a heavier fog, made a framework around the finer mist—a framework irregularly oval in shape. And through the medium of the fine mist I looked into a room which was the exact replica of the room in which Margaret and I actually were. I looked into it and saw ourselves there.

Our apartment, as you know, is high up in one of the new buildings on the upper East Side. The east windows of our living room look out over the East River. The apartment, which is large, is one of the corner ones. The north windows of the living room overlook Fifty-seventh Street.

My first flickering notion, of course, was that I was seeing the actual reflection of our living room in the east windows, as in a mirror. But that comforting thought lasted only the merest fraction of a second.

For I, Dr. Harvey Herbert, was standing up—and the man who looked just like me in the other room beyond the mist was still sitting down!

I sat down myself and covered my eyes with my hands. I have been, as you know, a student of the various phenomena loosely listed as hallucinations. I have had a certain amount of success in my attempts to analyze the mental states back of these phenomena. But I had had no previous experience of a personal nature. And I realized, in the moment that I sat there with my hands over my eyes, that it is one thing to attempt to diagnose the condition of a patient, and another thing to give an answer to one's own problem during the time when it is actively presenting itself. That wriggling grub, about to become a butterfly, was still stirring in my head, trying to flutter his new, feeble wings; and I thought when he went away, as he should in a moment, that would be the end of my aberration.

Margaret spoke and there was a struggle for kindliness in her voice—a struggle to regain the attitude of forbearance, love and pity, which was usual to her in her relations with Aunt Emma. I knew from her voice that she was not sharing my hallucination with regard to that other room.

"Aunt Emma isn't so well to-night, Harvey," said Margaret, "or I'm sure she would have put her request in some other way."

"Yes," I replied, trying to imitate Margaret's spirit, trying to conquer the anger that possessed me—and that, no doubt, had brought on my queer vision—"yes, she's getting pretty old, and we must remember that she's very fond of us. We'll have to bear with her."

I had hardly finished speaking when I heard another voice—and it was Margaret's voice, but yet it did not have in it the Margaret I knew. It said:

"She gets more spiteful every day! She knows her power; and the more childish she becomes the more malevolent delight she takes in playing tyrant!"

And then a voice answered—a voice that was my voice and yet not the voice of any Harvey Herbert I had ever visualized in the full light of consciousness:

"Cheer up, Margaret! It can't last forever; and if the old hell-cat doesn't change her will before she dies it means fifteen thousand dollars a year for us. That's worth a little trouble, isn't it?"

"A little trouble!" said the voice of the Margaret whom I did not know, with a passionate vibration which I had never heard in the voice of the Margaret I knew. "You're away, at your office or your lectures, most of the time, but I'm here at home with her day and night. A little trouble! It's killing me!"

I took down my hands and opened my eyes. The other room was still there. The Harvey Herbert in it, and the Margaret in it, were on their feet now and were facing each other with a bitterness of face and tone that, surely, my wife and I had never permitted ourselves in any of our rare outbursts of irritation.

The room was still there, but it was not where I had first seen it. I had looked towards the east wall of our real room, where the windows were that overlooked the East River. Now I was looking towards the north wall, where the windows were that overlooked Fifty-seventh Street. I turned and looked towards the west wall which had neither door nor window in it. The other room was there, too. I stepped to the middle of the real room and looked at the south wall, which had two doors in it and no window. The other room was there. I looked above me, and I looked up into it. I looked at the floor, and I stood upon the verge of it, opening below me. And the two figures were in it, the figures of Margaret and of me, walking and talking independently of us.

Let me tell you just what it looked like again, Howard, so that you can realize something of the effect I got, no matter how I turned my head. A thin, fine mist, and around it, framing it, a denser, heavier mist. Beyond the thin, fine mist, the other room. The opening in the thin, fine mist, framed by the denser, heavier fog, an oval in shape. I walked towards the oval entrance, towards the other room. It receded before me. It kept about ten feet ahead of me. When I turned it was still the same distance ahead of me. I went to one of the windows in the east wall and looked out. The other room was out there in the night, overhanging the water front!

I came back and sat down by Margaret. She was brooding.

"Did you see anything peculiar?" I asked her. She moved her head with a brief negative gesture, without looking at me.

"Or hear anything?" I asked.

"Why, no," she said. I was sure she had neither seen nor heard. But she looked at me with a glance that was strained and puzzled, as if she had *almost* heard and seen something, if you follow me.

The two people in the other room looked out at Margaret and me with a faint satirical smile upon their faces. I tried to ignore them, thinking maybe they would go away if I could get my mind off of them. No matter how much this interested me as a student, at the same time it was distinctly uncomfortable. I said to Margaret:

"What are you thinking of?"

"I was thinking, what a poor lonely old soul Aunt Emma is, Harvey."

And as if in answer to this, the man in the other room turned to the woman in there and spoke:

"Damn her! She'll live to be a hundred and ten!"

I made a gesture of repudiation—this creature, this vision, this person, whoever or whatever he was—did not speak for me, although he had somehow seized upon my appearance and my voice. I told myself passionately that I had never thought of Aunt Emma like that! And the man peered out at me with an immense, disconcerting knowingness.

I knew that Aunt Emma had come into the room before I saw her. I knew it by the actions of the people in the other room. They leaned forward eagerly, and there was a tense, rapid interchange of low voices:

"You see," said the man, "she stumbles!"

"She totters," said the woman; "she's getting weaker!"

Aunt Emma had, indeed, stumbled on the edge of a rug just within the door. Margaret and I ran to her and supported her to a chair and settled her in it. And as we did so, those other voices kept on:

"She's not really much weaker. She'll live forever!"

"Perhaps—the mean kind always do!"

Margaret, leaning over Aunt Emma in her big chair, said solicitously: "Shan't I get you a wrap, Aunt Emma?"

Aunt Emma lifted her petulant and sneering face and broke out in her high-pitched, feeble voice:

"You're mighty anxious about a wrap, Margaret! But you were thinking of going out and leaving me practically alone—with nobody but Miss Murdock!"

"But, Aunt Emma," I began, reasonably, "Miss Murdock is employed to—"

"Don't excuse yourself, Harvey!" she interrupted. "Can't I see you were going out? Can't I see your evening clothes?"

I could tell by the look Margaret gave me that she was schooling herself to gentleness—as she always did. I tried to imitate her.

Margaret said, "Aunt Emma, we're going to stay with you the rest of the evening—aren't we, Harvey? We'll go change to something else."

"No!" cried Aunt Emma. "Don't take off your evening clothes. I don't want you to! What do you want to take them off for? Are they too good for me to see? Ain't I as good as any one you'd see if you went out? Eh?"

"But, Aunt Emma, I meant—"

"I know what you meant! You meant to slip out and leave me alone, both of you! It's lucky I caught you in time! It's lucky I have money of my own. I'd be left alone, to starve, if I were poor! I'd die of hunger and neglect!"

Margaret and I looked at each other helplessly. Aunt Emma put her hands in front of her face and began to whimper. Margaret tried to soothe her, to take down her hands and pet her, but Aunt Emma resisted like a spoiled and spiteful child.

In the other room the man murmured:

"This is to be one of Aunt Emma's truly pleasant evenings!"

The woman over there retorted with vehemence, "This sort of thing happens a dozen times a day!"

I looked over Aunt Emma's shoulder at them. They were regarding Aunt Emma with a frowning intentness.

"She's not really crying," said the man.

"Pretense!" said the woman. "She works it up at will."

"The old hell-cat!"

Aunt Emma lifted her head with a startled look, almost as if she had seen and heard; and a puzzled expression, confused and puzzled, flitted across Margaret's countenance. But neither of them had quite got it; it was for me alone that the full perception of this phenomenon was reserved.

"Aunt Emma," said Margaret, soothingly; "you know Harvey and I try to be good to you, don't you?"

"You try to be good to my money!" said Aunt Emma. "But I may fool you! I may fool you yet! It's not too late to change my will! It's not too late yet to leave it all to charity!"

She spoke with a cunning leer. The man in the other room nudged the woman beside him and said, "The old cat's capable of doing just that, too, Margaret!"

Aunt Emma lifted to me a disturbed and pitiable face. She took one of my hands, she took one of Margaret's; she took them in both of hers, and she clung to us. For that moment, everything dropped from her except the expression of her dire need—her need to be loved. Her gestures, her manner, were infinitely pathetic. They were a plea for genuine affection. It was as if she had said that she was an isolated human spirit on the brink of the unknown, and that she dreaded the next step which she must take; dreaded it, and must have our understanding, our kindliness, to go along with her. What she really said was:

"Margaret . . . Harvey . . . you really do care for me, don't you? It isn't all on account of my money, is it?"

I was profoundly touched. All religion, all life, all art, all expression come down to this: to the effort of the human soul to break through its barrier of loneliness of intolerable loneliness, and make some contact with another seeking soul, or with what all souls seek, which is (by any name) God. She pleaded and she clung. She said:

"If you knew I hadn't a cent, you'd still be good to me, wouldn't you?"

"Yes," I said eagerly. And, "Yes!" said Margaret. Eagerly and sincerely. And in that instant I know that both of us were grateful for the patience we had shown to the old woman through the years; grateful that we had been able to rise above our frequent exasperation, to trample it down, and act and speak from worthier impulses.

"If I lost it all . . . if I told you that I'd lost it all," said Aunt Emma, "you'd both still be just the same, wouldn't you?"

"Yes," I said unhesitatingly, still shaken with the vibrations of my own emotion and thankful that I was conscious of nothing in me that did not move spontaneously with my answer. "Yes," I said.

But the man in the other room said to the woman there:

"My God, you don't suppose she's really lost her money, do you?"

"No!" answered the woman. "This is just one of her cunning spells. She can be as crafty as a witch!"

This, while they looked out of their room at the old woman in her agony! I faced them sternly; I was minded to denounce them, these figures, whatever they were, that had stolen the outer aspects of me and of my wife and spoke from sentiments we had never acknowledged or acted upon! I was about to cry out to them that they did not represent us, that they were not we. But I did not cry out. Again they turned upon me that faintly satirical smile, those faces informed with an irony drawn from—from what? From some ulterior deep springs of knowledge? I became confused, and did not speak to them.

"I'm hard on you at times," said Aunt Emma. I have never found it very easy to face expressed sentiment, and now the old woman broke down into a mood that embarrassed me. "I'm unjust," she said, and there was no doubt of the genuineness of her contrition. "I don't mean to be spiteful, but I know I am spiteful. When you get old, you get suspicious of people." I tried to avert my mind from her self-accusations; it is neither pleasant nor inspiring to witness any sort of dissolution, and she was dissolving into a self-pity that I found it harder and harder to face. "Suspicion makes us spiteful and unjust—and I'm suspicious of everybody," she went on. "Oh, I know I'm not easy to live with, Margaret!"

There wasn't anything to say to that—God knows she wasn't easy to live with! The man and woman in the other room grinned at me with a touch of frank malice. My pity for her, momentarily clouded by my embarrassment at her own self-pity, returned. Presently Margaret said:

"Don't you think you'd better go to bed now, Aunt Emma?"

At that she jerked herself up in the big chair she was sitting in, immediately all suspicion and meanness and snarling petulance again, and spluttered at Margaret:

"To bed? Why to bed? Why do you want to pack me off to bed? Oh, I know!" Her pinched countenance was a mask of cunning malignance as she went on: "I know why—so you can talk about me, talk me over! So you can speculate on how long I will live! I know you! I know what you talk about when I'm not around. I know what you've been waiting and hoping for the last ten years!"

She began to cry again. She stretched out her arms towards us. Once more there was that terrible appeal in her manner, terrible to witness, terrible to have directed towards one.

"Well, you won't have long to wait now," she whimpered. "The time's almost come." The tears ran down her cheeks in silence for a moment—those daunting, weak tears of the aged who accuse us and the gods because death cannot be delayed so very much longer—and then she said, "You'll get the money soon enough."

Distressed, Margaret said, "There, there, Aunt Emma; you mustn't go on like this."

"You'll live ten years yet," I added. It is one of the things one says.

"If I thought she'd live ten years—" began the man who was peering out from the other room.

"Well?" cut in the woman beside him."If you thought she would—what?"

"My God—ten more years like the last ten!" he said.

The woman who looked like Margaret turned upon him fiercely and shot at him a tirade that mounted from step to step of bitterness:

"You see it mornings and evenings; but I have it all day long—and every day! I've had it for ten years. I go nowhere. I see no one. I have no pleasures. I have no friends. I'm losing my youth. I'm losing my looks. Harvey, I'm losing my very soul! I shed my life's blood drop by drop to keep that querulous fool, that dying viper, alive—just merely alive! I'm tired of it—I'm sick of it—I'm weary, wearied, wearied to the soul! I'm dying from her, I tell you, dying from her!"

She sank to a chair, shaken and pallid; and there came a silent moment. But something—a note that had been struck—the impulsion of occult wings . . . something . . . vibrated in the silence at that moment.

I say a moment. But what are moments? What is time? Some theologians, some men of science, say there is no such think as time; that we live, always, in eternitl. A moment is long, or it is short, because of the stuff that is packed into it. Can we, somewhere in illimitable space, somewhere in the valleys of infinity, catch up with old moments and live them newly again? Well, I do not think we can ever again take out of a moment what we have put into it, even though we should catch up with it again. Am I speaking foolishly, Howard? I want to cling to the moment before . . . before it had occurred . . . before what happened. did happen. I want to . . .

Listen: for all the events of that night I can advance as good a theory as most psychologists. There are rational explanations for the phenomena I witnessed, and was a part of. I know them very well. The man in the other room—I can write you a thesis on who and what he was, and why I saw him and Margaret did not; I can discourse to you, as cleverly as any one, on every angle of this case.

But it isn't the mechanism of this thing that concerns me now. I am concerned with the things that lie behind the mechanism.

I want to cling to the moment before . . . before it had happened: what did happen. To the moment before what we call the conscience had become involved.

Margaret said, "Come, come, Aunt Emma, you really should go to bed."

"I won't go to bed," she said, with the pettishness of a small child. "I won't go to bed until I've had my medicine. I want my sleeping tablets now."

"Where are they?" asked Margaret.

"In my bathroom," said Aunt Emma. And Margaret went out of the room for them.

"See here," I said to Aunt Emma, "didn't Miss Murdock give you one of those tablets right after dinner?"

"No," she said. And then, "I don't remember. I want one anyhow! My nerves are on the jump. You've got my nerves to jumping! I'll take one and nap here in the chair."

The man in the other room said in a low, speculative tone:

"I suppose if one ever gave her the wrong medicine by mistake it would be called by some ugly name."

The woman answered him:

"People like her never get the wrong medicine given to them by mistake, and never take it by mistake themselves. They live forever."

I turned and spoke to them, "There is a volition in your words," I said sternly, "that is not my volition nor my wife's volition."

"What did you say?" asked Aunt Emma, looking about in bewilderment.

"Nothing," I answered. The two figures in the other room did not reply to me. They looked at me steadily, levelly.

Margaret returned with a small phial. I took it from her and examined it.

"I'm afraid she had one an hour ago," I said. "I don't think it is quite right to let her have another one so soon. They are what Dr. McIntosh prescribed, and they have a powerful, depressing effect on the heart if taken in excess."

As you know, Howard, I did not treat Aunt Emma medically myself —you once had her case until you gave it up—and she has gone from doctor to doctor, always intimating to me that she had little faith in me. That was one of her ways of annoying Margaret and me; but it was no real annoyance, as she did not come within the limits of my specialty.

"You did have one right after dinner, didn't you, Aunt Emma?" said Margaret.

"No! No!" said Aunt Emma. With a sudden monkeylike agility, for which I was not prepared, she reached and snatched the phial from me. She clutched it to her breast, in a childish triumph.

"I didn't have one," she said. "I will take one. You don't want me to get to sleep! You don't want me to get any rest! You want me to die!"

Her hands trembled as she hugged the bottle to her; her jaw chattered, and her lips shook; her victory in getting the bottle had made her all one tremor.

I took hold of her hands, and tried to take the phial away from her gently. She grasped it with her crooked claws until white spots showed on the knuckles, and rocked herself back and forth. Her fingers were interlaced about it.

"See here, Aunt Emma," I said; "you mustn't be stubborn about this. I think you did have a tablet right after dinner, and another one now might be dangerous."

I used a certain amount of force, and she whimpered and actually gnashed her teeth at me. Margaret interposed:

"Don't struggle with her, Harvey. Doctor McIntosh says the least strain is likely to prove fatal."

I knew that was true and released her hands. She had had a dilated heart some years previously, from which she had never really recovered. Emotional strain as well as physical strain was dangerous.

"You want me to die so you can get my money," she said, leering up at me from under her thin white eyebrows.

Tentatively, I reached my hand towards her again. She suddenly grasped it and sank her teeth into it. And then she pulled the cork from the phial.

I was in a quandary as to the right thing to do. If I struggled with her, I should almost certainly kill her. On the other hand, I was not absolutely certain whether she had taken one of the tablets previously or not. She had said she hadn't. I had heard Miss Murdock speak of giving her one; but I hadn't actually seen her take it. I wasn't sure.

I didn't know then what I should have done. And I did the wrong thing—I did nothing. It is easy enough now, Howard, to see that it was the wrong thing. It is easy enough now to say that I should have risked the struggle, risked killing her by the struggle. But I put it to you, man to man, how was I to know then that it was the wrong thing?

She shook two tablets from the bottle and put both of them into her mouth.

"Not two, Aunt Emma!" I cried. I actually tried to take them from her mouth, and I got myself bitten again.

The situation was now changed, in a way that no one could have foreseen.

Two tablets within the hour might not kill her; but three almost certainly would.

"Aunt Emma," I said, "you didn't have one before, did you?"

She had closed her eyes and sunk back into the chair, after swallowing the two tablets, as if thoroughly exhausted by such struggle as there had been. Now she opened them again, and looked up at me with a look indescribably impish—impish and foolish, and puerilely triumphant. She rocked herself from side to side, and she said:

"Yes!" And then, "I've had three, now, and I'm going to sleep—you hate me—you both hate me—but you can't keep me from going to sleep."

And she leaned back in the chair again.

"I don't believe she did have three of them," said Margaret. "She's only saying that now to worry us."

"She says she did," I returned; "but she doesn't know. I think you're right—she's probably only saying it to irritate us. I know she didn't."

She opened her eyes a little, opened and closed them, with a blink of cunning.

"You know I did!" she murmured.

"I hadn't known it—hadn't been sure of it—but evidently the man and woman in the other room had been sure of it.

"She did have one before," said he.

"Yes," said the woman; "I know she did."

Margaret and I stood and looked down on the old woman, whose shaking agitation was now leaving her, who had now begun to breathe quite quietly, in a condition that was strangely helpless; in a sort of suspension of the will-power. I can think now of several things that I should have done. But I give you my word, I could think of nothing then; the only thing that filled my consciousness then was the desperate, working hope that she would not die. And while I looked down on Aunt Emma's silent and shrunken figure I heard the man and woman in the other room speaking. Their voices were cool and quiet; they came to me clearly enough, but they seemed to come from a distance, too.

"Will she die?" said the man. "Shall I see her die?"

"I should hate to look on while she died," said the woman. "But she will die; she is dying and I am looking on."

"She was very old."

"She was very old. She will be better dead."

"She has not died yet."

"She is breathing very quietly. Old people breathe very quietly."

"Old people die very quietly."

"And she is dying."

I heard this monstrous litany, and every fiber in my being was in revolt against it. But, for a time, it seemed impossible for me to speak or to move. I tried to combat, in my own mind, what they were saying in the other room.

Aunt Emma stirred, feebly. Her eyes said that she wanted to say something. Margaret and I bent over her, and she whispered faintly:

"Margaret . . . Harvey . . . you . . . you really love me . . . don't you? You really . . . really . . ."

She relapsed, relaxed. Her head was slightly on one side. She did not speak or move again.

Margaret said, with a note of alarm, "Harvey, she's scarcely breathing! She does not seem to be breathing at all!"

"If I had struggled with her," I said, "it would have killed her."

The man in the other room spoke, "And now she's dead because there was no struggle!"

Margaret cried out, "Phone for Doctor McIntosh! I'm alarmed!"

"Too late for any doctor," said the man in the other room; and the woman there echoed, "Too late!"

Margaret said to me, "Harvey, I'm afraid . . . I'm afraid that Aunt Emma has left us!"

"Thank heaven," I answered, "that we've always tried to be good to her. You've been like an angel to her, Margaret, and I've tried to do my best. Poor Aunt Emma!" For the pathos of her last words clutched at my heart. "Poor Aunt Emma!" I said. Somehow I could not stop saying it for a moment; I chattered it over and over again, "Poor Aunt Emma! Poor Aunt Emma! Poor Aunt Emma!"

"Fifteen thousand a year! Fifteen thousand a year! Fifteen thousand a year!" chattered the man in the other room.

I turned angrily and faced him. I wanted to have it out with him. For he was not I! Oh, I know what had happened—any man in my profession knows what had happened! In that other room I was seeing my other self. The part we all hide and deny, the ungenerous part, the selfish part, the hideous part if you will, had come up out of the caves of the underworld, out of the realm of the unexpressed, out of the repressed subconsciousness, and met me face to face. I need not dwell, in talking with you, on the mechanism of it—as I have said, the mechanism interested me far less than the things behind the mechanism. The man in the other room was compounded of all the unuttered things in my nature which I consciously disavowed, which I fought down, which I never permitted to get into the field of fact and deed. We have all fought them down or there would be no such thing as civilization to-day, not even the imperfect semblance of it which exists.

But I cried out within myself, and I cry out to you now, Howard, that the man in the other room was not and is not the real I! But he was saying that he was! He was claiming to be! It was his will that had triumphed here, for he had willed the old woman's death; while I, the conscious I, had fought against it.

I cried out and I still cry out against the monstrous injustice that he should be able to make the conscious I feel guilty because of a thing that was his doing! Are all the years when I was consciously kind, in spite of my exasperation, to count for nothing—all the years in which I fought down my irritation, all the years in which Margaret had acted, as I told her, like an angel? We had had our ungenerous thoughts, our angers, our selfish impulses; but we had trampled them under our feet, and was that fight, that struggle, that victory, to be as if it had never been? Was not the better part of us, whose deeds were gentle and considerate, to be accepted as the real individual, the real ego? Were these cold and selfish usurpers to be able to pretend that they were we? Able to make us feel that, guiltily? Is the fight towards decency, after it has been won, after its victory has been sealed and signalized by deed and fact, to be lost again merely because of the sneering assertion of these creatures who come bursting up out of the unplumbed depths of life? Are the whispers and nods and looks of those cave men to impose on us and make us think that we are cave men again? I protested, and I protest, that this cannot be! It is not merely my own case that I have brought you, Howard; it is the case of all men, of all humanity.

I turned angrily towards the man in the other room with this protest rising to my lips. But again I was stopped from speaking. He was gazing down on the big chair in his room. Aunt Emma was in it—over there in the other room, beyond the mist. Her eyes were open, and she was looking out at me. On her face was the same faintly satirical smile as on the faces of the other two people in that room.

Margaret was bending over the big chair in our room, weeping. Aunt Emma, from the other room, gazed on Margaret's attitude with something like ironic amusement.

Doctor Vokes was silent for several minutes after Dr. Harvey Herbert paused in his narrative. Then he said, "No, the case is scarcely in my line."

"Nor in mine," said Doctor Herbert. "When I have considered everything that comes within the province of the psychologist, the essence of it all escapes me—the thing behind the thing."

"Why should a sense of guilt cling to you?" said Doctor Vokes. "That sense should belong to the man in the other room. Can't you make him take it and keep it, and dive down with it into whatever strange and shadowy hell he came up out of?"

"He won't stay down there," said Doctor Herbert simply, and with a despairing gesture. "He keeps coming up again, asserting himself."

There was another silence; presently Doctor Vokes said, "And his assertion—" He hesitated; then murmured, "I suppose it turns upon the fact that, after all, he spoke and acted with a direct and vigorous candor."

Dr. Harvey Herbert repeated his gesture.

"I have thought several times I was rid of him," he said; "but he keeps coming back. To-day I knew certainly that I was not rid of him. I discovered it when I found myself arranging with my lawyer to turn over Aunt Emma's fifteen thousand a year to a charity, a home for old ladies."

"You did that?"

"Yes. For a few moments after the transfer was completed I felt a relief. And then there floated in front of me the face of the man who had been in the other room, with a quizzically sarcastic grin upon his lips. The expression said he knew just why I could never touch any of Aunt Emma's money—he knew, that grin said."

The Last Equation

ROGER BURLINGAME

Now that he was sick there was no more responsibility. His job was only to lie there and they would take care of him impersonally, except Megs. The office, Spelman, the men standing at the tables in the drafting room, Miss Kraus, they would all have to get along without him; they were independent of him; now they must call up the hospital until a voice divorced from flesh and warmth answered, "Mr. Drake is resting quietly." So, he was a negative unit in his own scheme: they were glad, in a way, for this interval in which he remained minus. Except Megs.

Stephen closed his eyes and hoped that Megs would not come for a while.

But God, these nurses! How can a human being face another human being so mechanistically? I am a man, they are women, isn't it so? Or is it not so? Can they take that off with their street clothes? No, for Miss Thwing, sitting impassive over there by the window with only half of her showing in the light . . . Miss Thwing must once, twice, sometimes in this silence, reach out to that world beyond the hook she has hung herself on, to someone who does not call her Miss Thwing—a beat must then be skipped by the heart below her starched armor. Yes, occasionally Miss Thwing reaches out.

Miss Thwing has a face, neck, shoulders, hands, feet, and probably lungs, heart, stomach, etc., inside. She must want, once in a while to stretch, belch or scratch herself in the middle of her back but she will not do these things lest I become aware that she is a poor weak human creature. I might even believe that she is a woman. The ultimate breakdown would come if she, in turn, knew then, that I was a man instead of a machine out of order. Still, she must know, secretly, from the frequent evidence I have given her.

Thank God the pain was better.

Stephen sighed and Miss Thwing got up.

"Easier?" she said.

"Yes, easier."

On the whole, it was good, this hanging yourself on a hook. Stephen hoped suddenly that he would never, never, see Miss Thwing with herself on. It would torture him to have her care whether he was worse or better and now he thought uncomfortably about Megs.

"Better, Stephen? A little better, dear?"

Her thin face would draw together and be thinner when she said that. Why was her face so thin, so damn thin! A thousand times she must have said that: "Better Stephen?" the last three days with her familiar thin face close to him. Why did she love him so? She was so sweet, so good, so worried, so utterly unselfish, yet when he looked at her his nerves were acutely conscious of a tooth sticking out further than the other, that her ears lay back too close to her head, that she squinted when she pronounced certain words, that there was one square fleck and one triangular fleck in her right eye.

"I love you, Megs."

But, of course, he must love her; he loved something deep in her beneath these things. Beneath her "Really, Stephen?" when he had made a tremendous joke, beneath her lifting his highball glass from the polished table and wiping it off, beneath the slow, methodical way she picked his clothes off the floor and hung them. Beneath these things, there was something he loved. What?

Well, he was married to Megs. Marriage was an event, 'way back now in the past—a youth when events were important in themselves—events for events' sake. Little china Megs, pale, golden, bric-a-brac Megs, too exquisite to believe and she loved him. Dainty, dainty Megs. A woman? He had quivered with surprise at someone using that word about Megs.

She loved him so much that she submitted that porcelain body to the robustness of marriage. Stephen would never forget how she lay, waiting, that first time, as she might lie, waiting for an operation, heroic, smiling: Yes, kill me, it is for a cause, I love you enough for that. But, child, this is life, not death, love is not negation!

And, always after, too, it was like that—the body ready for the sacrifice. Never, never: Stephen, I am tired tonight; never: Let's sleep Stephen, I love you just the same. No tears.

So a month after the event, Stephen knew it had been a capture. In the first year he learned that the porcelain shepherdess was reinforced by a thin, inflexible steel rod.

Along came the children, dutifully. In her womb, by will, she made them after her pattern, diverted them from him. She made their pale hair, their flecked eyes, their transparent skins, their delicate indestructible hands. Not a toe or a knuckle of Steve's and Margaret's was his. But why?

"Miss Thwing, I'd like some orange juice."

"We cannot start intestinal activity, Mr. Drake, before—"

"Nonsense, Miss Thwing!"

"I'm sorry, Mr. Drake. Your intestines must be empty."

Yet it had seemed inevitable, ordered, chemical, this capture. Certainly Megs had no affinity for his body, but for his essence, perhaps. Well, then, why did his essence not respond? If you put sodium and hydrochloric acid together there is immediate reaction, the sodium is as eager as the acid to form the salt. The atoms fly together to form the new molecules (or did when he went to school) and they fly with equal avidity whether they are sodium or chlorine. The hydrogen gets left out, three is a crowd, poor hydrogen, but it will find its oxygen soon and come down in sweet, warm rain.

A magnet, however, does not move; the iron filings fly to it because it is larger and stronger than they. Some scientists say the magnet does move; they had to work hard to get that . . . Everything moves in an arc. . . .

I love you, Megs.

Well, the habit of marriage is strong. I have never, never been unfaithful to you—hardly, even, in thought. I have looked at other women passing by, been stirred by the sweet curves of their legs, enjoyed occasional, very occasional movies and burlesque shows. But I have not dwelt upon these things.

"Miss Thwing."

"Yes."

Under the starch, Miss Thwing, you have a remarkable body. It is warm and satisfying.

"Miss Thwing, please get me a newspaper."

"You're not supposed to read, Mr. Drake."

"Why?"

"Because you're not supposed to get excited."

"I can read the paper without getting excited. I'll get more excited if I don't."

"No, no, Mr. Drake you must relax."

Relax! Does she know what thinking is? Trying to work it out? The more my body relaxes, the more my mind works. Hunger, tiredness from pain, make it run faster. I must think. No more about Megs except where Megs is chemistry. Perhaps I will die on the operating table: I must think first, think clean and sharp like a knife.

"Miss Thwing."

"Yes."

"Miss Thwing, will you please go away?"

Miss Thwing came to the side of the bed and stood looking down at Stephen.

"No, I'm not feverish, Miss Thwing. Here, feel my forehead. You have fine hands. Now here it is, I can relax if I am quite alone. I believe I can sleep. Do you mind? Usually I like to have you there, I like you very much, Miss Thwing, but now . . ."

She moved the pillows a little, then glided away. Stephen thought she moved purposefully not as if she were going away but as if she were going *somewhere*. God help me if she brings a doctor to see if I am delirious. The door closed slowly against its pneumatic stop.

Now.

The world is full of men and women like me and Megs. It is also full of birds, wolves, woodchucks, trees and grass. One scheme moves chemically, biologically according to a pattern: the other is disordered. Mind has come in there. Now God, we'll say, orders the first scheme: the second he cannot cope with. So mind must be anti-God. That makes two conflicting forces, God and anti-God and the universe is a battle.

Stephen slipped through the circumference of a sphere and now he was in larger, fresher space. It was like slipping through the film of a soap bubble without breaking it.

Now he remembered sharply the drafting room at the office. All day the men stood at their boards in brilliant light making lines which would become houses that would stand up and bear weight on their floors, keep out wet and cold. All day, these men allied their minds with the natural laws: gravity, stress and strain, the mechanical principle of the lever. But at night when they left the drafting room, now close and smelling of their effort, they went home and bucked the natural laws all night. They went home to tight cliff dwellings, fought with their wives, begot undesired and undesirable children or thought miserably or drank.

Joe Beers was a boy and had no wife but he had girls, a string of girls, who fatigued him. Soon there would be nothing left for Joe. Ham Willink found the pressure of his mind intolerable and got drunk to quiet or divert it. Carstairs made futuristic drawings which triumphantly denied his work of the day.

Yet the work these men did kept a part of humanity going.

Now God was the architect for the animals but man fought Him and considered His plans inadequate, uncomfortable and, probably, in bad taste. But all the same, man could not build except by God's laws if, indeed, they were His. The scientists, to be sure, were constantly finding them wrong.

Who is God? Why did he equip man with a vermiform appendix? To try and thwart His enemy, Mind? But Mind had licked the vermiform appendix—that is if you could say you beat a thing by removing it.

Stephen passed into another sphere and observed the stars. Colossal but inanimate. Or, at least, unconscious. Yet here he was in a realm of great activity. The order and business of the animals was nothing to this high-powered organization. Light and energy in the ether, movement and relation motivated and held in check by suns, particles flying off without reducing the bulk of the matter, chemical combination on a large, electric, scale.

Was this superior to mind? No, because mind was conscious of it and it was not conscious of mind. I—or rather Mr. Jeans, say—observe these things, reflect upon them, find their causes. You can weigh a star, Mr. Jeans, weighing so many million times as much as the earth as easily as you can weigh your baby—easier: the star does not squirm or *rebel against being weighed.*

Could Mind destroy the stars? Will it survive them?

Mind, yes; it created them. Not human mind but Mind. Ah, now we are getting somewhere! But what is human mind—a reflection? A particle that is shot off? There, now, I've got it . . . Ah!

The door moved open, men with white coats and the head nurse came in.

"Well, Mr. Drake!"

It was so good just to lie and think.

"Have I got to go now?"

"It's nothing, Mr. Drake. It's very, very easy."

"It seems hard."

"We do twenty a day, Mr. Drake."

"Oh that . . ."

He must be like a feather, they lifted him so easily. Queer to be rolling along feet first. Rubber tires. Balloon . . .

"Ha!" Stephen laughed suddenly.

"All right, Mr. Drake?"

Megs hadn't come! She'd missed it.

When the cone was over his head he breathed deep as they told him; his ears hummed. One, two, three; one *and* two *and* three *and;* one, seven, eleven: symbolic—but always starting with One.

Now he was off through the spheres, not slowly, with labor as before but easily and fast. He recognized them as he went: it was like going in a car over a road you had walked as a child. But he went beyond now, beyond the limits.

So, stop, he was in a room. Men talked and laughed about a long table, moving about, sitting down, getting up, joking in unintelligible language.

"Alpha?"

"To the W minus one."

"Why?"

"Because of epsilon."

"That's diminished by regression."

Stephen sat at an end of the table. Beyond the other end and the men, stretched an unlimited blackboard. Now someone put his hand on Stephen's shoulder and leaned over him. He saw a genial face, dark, smoothshaven, but with eyes almost luminous.

"Now," said this person, "what's the trouble?"

"You *know,* don't you?"

"I can explain it to you, I'm sure. It's absurdly simple."

"You're God, aren't you?"

"No indeed. I'm one of the teachers."

"You're not Christ, that I'm sure."

"No, Stephen, Christ would not help you now. You're not quite up to that. Your thought is very elementary. Christ helps the more advanced pupils like . . . well like your Grandfather Barnes."

"Grandpa could only just read and write."

The person turned away, put his hands in his trousers pockets and faced the blackboard. Now Stephen could see the whole of him: he was short and stocky—his hair was thick and in great disorder.

"Can't we have a higher vibration?" he said.

The light in the room changed from yellow to blue to violet.

"Now look," said Stephen's teacher. "Follow me carefully and don't interrupt. Don't ask me where I get my premises. It will all be clear to you when I'm through. Now: $x + y = 0$. Let me write it down."

He went to the blackboard. The men drew aside, the table seemed to disappear.

"Let's go on from there."

Stephen did not recognize the forms of the equations but he grasped their solutions. The teacher covered the whole blackboard with his symbols. Stephen's excitement rose as he watched: he had never felt such excitement. He could hardly wait for the teacher to write for his eagerness to see these equations resolve. Now they were melting into each other, he could guess the solution before it was written.

The spheres were all there: Megs, the animals, the architects, the stars.

Now Stephen heard the men at the other end whispering and laugh- See this?"

He pounded with his chalk on the board, the dust of the chalk was luminous.

"Now take the kappa root of this."

Stephen cried out.

"There is no kappa root! There's no such thing!"

"Oh, isn't there?" shouted the teacher. "How about this?"

"Don't!" cried Stephen. "Don't, I can't bear it! I see, I see, but stop there for God's sake!"

"Go talk to him, one of you," said the teacher.

A gentle, bearded man came over to Stephen's left side.

"Don't be afraid," he said. "You have every right to know. They've been talking nonsense to you where you live. This is so simple. Now look . . ."

Now Stephen heard the men at the other end whispering and laugh- ing together as pleasantly as if they had just got up from a good stag dinner. So he took his hands away from his eyes and looked back at the blackboard.

"There," said the teacher. "There's the kappa root. Now divide it by the differential . . ."

"The differential of beta!" said Stephen and his voice echoed over the skies where the ceiling of the room had been, but then he put his face in his hands and sobbed a long time because the joy overwhelmed him.

"Now," said the bearded man beside him. "It will be good for you to face it."

So Stephen looked up and saw the final equation glowing in a new color across the sky where the blackboard had been and he understood quietly.

"So X equals . . ." he said.

"Yes," said the teacher. "So it was silly for you to think I was God."

And there it was, still, gigantic, written in light, the last equation. The men all gathered behind Stephen to look at it; the talk and the laughter drew down, the silence was infinite.

When he had fallen back through the spheres and stopped in dark confinement, Stephen could still see the letters: then they moved, turned upside down and faded. He opened his eyes.

"It's gone," he said.

A laugh rang out.

"Yup, gone forever!"

Then a thin familiar voice.

"Oh, doctor, he's coming out."

Stephen closed his eyes trying, trying to go back. It was no good. He could feel the thin face over him, bending close.

"Better, Stephen? Oh, say it's better."

"Yes," said Stephen. "I love you, Megs."

The Surgeon and the Nun

PAUL HORGAN

Here you are. I haven't thought of this for thirty years. I don't know what called it to mind. I'll tell you anyway.

When I was a young doctor just out of interneship I left Chicago to come West, oh, for several reasons. I'd worked hard and they were afraid my lungs might be a little weakened, and then besides, I've always been independent, and wanted to get out on my own, and I'd seen enough of the society doctors back there. Anyway, I came on, and heard of a new section of country in New Mexico, opening up, down toward Texas, and thinks I, I'll just go and see about it. The hottest day I ever spent, yes, and the next night, and the next day, too, as you'll see.

The railroad spur had been pushing down South through the Pecos Valley, a few miles a week, and it was in July that I got on the train and bought a ticket for Eddy, the town I was thinking about trying.

The track was completed all the way, by then, but they had a lot of repairing to do all the time, and no train schedule was maintained, because we'd move, and crawl, and then stop; baking; with nothing but dust to breathe, white dust like filtered sunlight; outside the car window was naked land—with freckles, I remember thinking: spotty bushes and gravel. Above, a blue sky like hot metal. The heat swam on the ground.

You couldn't sleep or read or think.

There was nobody to talk to in the car.

Two seats across the aisle from me was a Sister of Mercy, sitting there in her black robes, skirts and sleeves, and heavy starch, and I wondered at the time, How on earth can she stand it? The car was an oven. She sat there looking out the window, calm and strengthened by her philosophy. It seemed to me she had expressive hands; I recalled the sisters in the hospital in Chicago, and how they had learned to say so much and do so much with their skilled hands. When my traveling nun picked up a newspaper and fanned herself slowly, it was more as if she did it in grace than to get cool.

She was in her early thirties, I thought, plump, placid and full of a wise delicacy and yes, independence, with something of the unearthly knowingness in her steady gaze that I used to see in the Art Institute—those portraits of ladies of the fifteenth century, who look at you sideways, with their eyebrows up.

She wore glasses, very bright, with gold bars to them.

Well, the train stopped again.

I thought I couldn't stand it. When we moved, there was at least a stir of air, hot and dusty, but at that, we felt as if we were getting some place, even though slowly. We stopped, and the cars creaked in the heat, and I felt thick in the head. I put my face out the window and saw that we had been delayed by a work gang up ahead. They were Mexican laborers. Aside from them, and their brown crawlings up and down the little road-bed embankment, there was nothing, no movement, no life, no comfort, for miles. A few railroad sheds painted dusty red stood by the trackside.

I sat for ten minutes; nothing happened. I couldn't even hear the sounds of work, ringing pickaxes or whatnot; I felt indignant. This was no way to maintain a public conveyance!

It was around one o'clock in the afternoon.

Mind you, this was 1905, it isn't a wilderness any more out here. Oh, it was then. Every time I looked out at the white horizon my heart sank, I can tell you. Why had I ever left Chicago?

Then I wondered where the Sister was traveling to.

It was strange how comforting she was, all of a sudden. I had a flicker of literary amusement out of the Chaucerian flavor of her presence—a nun, traveling, alone, bringing her world with her no matter where she might be, or in what circumstance; sober, secure, indifferent to anything but the green branches of her soul; benign about the blistering heat and the maddening delay; and withal, an object of some archaic beauty, in her medieval habit, her sidelong eyes, her plump and frondy little hands. I almost spoke to her several times, in that long wait of the train; but she was so classic in her repose that I finally decided not to. I got up instead and went down to the platform of the car, which was floury with dust all over its iron door and coupling chains, and jumped down to the ground.

How immense the sky was, and the sandy plains that shuddered with the heat for miles and miles! And how small and oddly desirable the train looked!

It was all silent until I began to hear the noises that framed that midsummer midday silence . . . bugs droning, the engine breathing up ahead, a whining hum in the telegraph wires strung along by the track, and then from the laborers a kind of subdued chorus.

I went to see what they were all huddled about each other for.

There wasn't a tree for fifty miles in any direction.

In the heat-reflecting shade of one of the grape red sheds the men were standing around and looking at one of their number who was lying on the ground with his back up on the lowest boards.

The men were mostly little, brown as horses, sweating and smelling like leather, and in charge of them was a big American I saw squatting down by the recumbent Mexican.

"Come on, come on," he was saying, when I came up.

"What's the matter?" I asked.

The foreman looked up at me. He had his straw hat off, and his forehead and brows were shad-belly white where the sunburn hadn't reached. The rest of his face was apple colored, and shiny. He had little eyes, squinted, and the skin around them was white, too. His lips were chapped and burnt powdery white.

"Says he's sick."

The Mexicans nodded and murmured.

"Well, I'm a doctor, maybe I can tell."

The foreman snorted.

"They all do it. Nothin' matter with him. He's just play-actin'. Come on, Pancho, you get, by God, t'hell up, now!"

He shoved his huge dusty shoe against the little Mexican's side. The Mexican drooled a weak cry. The other laborers made operatic noises in chorus. They were clearly afraid of the foreman.

"Now hold on," I said to him. "Let me look him over, anyway."

I got down on the prickly ground.

It took a minute or less to find out. The little cramped up Mexican had an acute attack of appendicitis, and he was hot and sick and when I touched his side, he wept like a dog and clattered on his tongue without words.

"This man is just about ready to pop off," I told the foreman. "He's got acute appendicitis. He'll die unless he can be operated on."

The heat; the shimmering land; something to do; all changed me into feeling cool and serious, quite suddenly.

"I can perform an emergency operation, somehow, though it may be too late. Anyway, it can't do more'n kill him, and he'll die if I don't operate, that's sure!"

"Oh, no. *Oh*-ho, no, you don't," said the foreman, standing up and drawling. He was obviously a hind, full of some secret foremanship, some plainsman's charm against the evil eye, or whatever he regarded civilization as. "I ain't got no authority for anythin' like that on my section gang! And ennyhow, they all take on like that when they're tarred of workin'!"

Oh, it was the same old thing.

All my life I've got my back up over something no more my business than the man in the moon, but seems to me when it's a matter of right and wrong, or good and bad, or the like, thinks I, there's no choice but to go to work and fight.

That blasted foreman infuriated me. And I can swear when I have to. Well, I set to and gave him such a dressing down as you never heard.

I called him everything I ever heard and then I made up some more pretty ones for good measure.

I told him I'd have him up before the nearest district territorial judge for criminal negligence. I told him I was a personal friend of John J. Summerdown, the president of the new railroad, and I'd, by God, have his job so fast he wouldn't know what hit him. I told him that anybody'd stand by and let a man die instead of taking every chance there was to save him, I said was lower'n—Anyway, you can't go through medical school without picking up a few fancy words.

He cocked his elbows and fists at me a couple of times. But when I'm right, I know I'm right, and that's all you need to handle a peasant like that.

He got scared, and we both wiped the sweat off our brows at the same minute, the same gesture, and glared at each other, and I wondered if I looked as hot and messy and ignorant as he did, and I laughed.

The Mexicans were curious and asking questions and clawing at him. I turned around, like a nervous old maid, or a scared child, to see if the train was still there.

It had become a symbol of safety to me, the only way out of that yellow, yellow plain streaming with sunlight. Yes, it was still there, dusty black, and dusty white where the light rested.

The foreman talked to the men . . . there must have been about three dozen of them.

He may have been a fool but he was a crafty one.

He was talking in Mexican and telling them what I wanted to do to Pancho, their brother and friend. He pantomimed surgery—knife in fist and slash and finger-scissors and then grab at belly, and then tongue out, and eyes rolled out of sight, and slump, and dead man: all this very intently, like a child doing a child's powerful ritual of play.

"Oh, yo, yo, yo," went all the Mexicans, and shook their fists at me, and showed their white teeth in rage. No sir, there'd be no cutting on Pancho!

"You see?" said the foreman, "I told 'em what I had to do, and they won't have it."

I am no actor, and certainly no orator, but I turned to those poor peons and tried to show them as best I could how the only way to save Pancho, lying there like a baked peanut, was to operate right now.

The foreman kept up a musical kind of antiphony to my arguments.

You know? It was something like the old lyric struggle between good and evil—enlightenment and superstition.

There we were, miles from everything, on that plain where the heat went up from the fried ground in sheets; nothing but a rickety line of tracks to keep us in the world, so to speak; and a struggle going on over the theory of life or death, as exemplified in the person of a perfectly anonymous wretch who'd eaten too many beans once too often!

I'd be damned if I'd quit.

I went back to the train and had more on my mind now than chivalry and Chaucer and Clouet.

She was still sitting there in her heavy starch and her yards and yards of black serge.

Her face was pink with the heat and her glasses a little moist. But she was like a calm and shady lake in that blistering wilderness, and her hands rested like ferns on the itchy plush of the seat which gave off a miniature dust storm of stifling scent whenever anything moved on it.

I could hear the argument and mutual reinforcement in cries and threats going on and gathering force out there in the little mob. It was like the manifest sound of some part of the day, the heat, the desert life, which being disturbed now filled the quavering air with protest.

When I stopped in the aisle beside her, she looked up sideways. Of course, she didn't mean it to, but it looked sly and humorous, and her glasses flashed.

"Excuse me, Sister," I said. "Have you ever had any hospital experience?"

"Is some one ill?"

Her voice was oddly doleful, but not because she was; no, it had the faintest trace of a German tone, and her words an echo of German accent, that soft, trolling, ach-Gott-in-Himmel charm that used to be the language of the old Germany, a comfortable sweetness that is gone now.

"There's a Mexican laborer out there who's doubled up with appendicitis. I am a surgeon, by the way."

"Yes, for a long time I was dietitian at Mount Mercy Hospital, that's in Clefeland?"

"Well, you see what I think I ought to do."

"So, you should operate?"

"It's the only thing'd save him, and maybe that'll be too late."

"Should we take him in the train and take care of him so? And operate when we reach town?"

Yes, you must see how placid she was, how instantly dedicated to the needs of the present, at the same time. She at once talked of what "we" had to do. She owned responsibility for everything that came into her life. I was young then, and I'm an old man now, but I still get the same kind of pride in doctors and those in holy orders when they're faced with something that has to be done for somebody else. The human value, mind you.

"I don't think they'll let us touch him. They're all Mexicans, and scared to death of surgery. You should've heard them out there a minute ago."

"Yess, I hear them now."

"What I think we'd better do is get to work right here. The poor wretch wouldn't last the ride to Eddy, God knows how long the train'd take."

"But *where,* doctor!"

"Well, maybe one of those sheds."

"So, and the train would wait?"

"Oh! I don't know. I can find out."

I went and asked the conductor up in the next car. He said no, the train wouldn't wait, provided they ever got a chance to go.

"We'd have to take a chance on the train," I told Sister. "Also, those men out there are not very nice about it. Maybe if you came out?"

At that she did hesitate a little; just a moment; probably the fraction it takes a celibate lady to adjust her apprehensions over the things she has heard about men, all of them, the very authors of sin, ancestors of misery, and custodians of the forbidden fruit.

"It would have been more convenient," I said, "if I'd never got off the train. That groaning little animal would die, and when the train went, we'd be on it; but we cannot play innocent now. The Mexican means nothing to me. Life is not that personal to a doctor. But if there's a chance to save it, you have to do it, I suppose."

Her response to this was splendid. She flushed and gave me a terrific look, full of rebuke and annoyance at my flippancy. She gathered her great serge folds up in handfuls and went down the car walking angrily. I followed her and together we went over to the shed. The sunlight made her weep a little and blink.

The men were by now sweating with righteous fury. Their fascinating language clattered and threatened. Pancho was an unpleasant sight, sick and uncontrolled. The heat was unnerving. They saw me first and made a chorus. Then they saw Sister and shut up in awe, and pulled their greasy hats off.

She knelt down by Pancho and examined him superficially and the flow of her figure, the fine robes kneeling in the dust full of ants, was like some vision to the Mexicans, in all the familiar terms of their Church. To me, it gave one of my infrequent glimpses into the nature of religious feeling.

She got up.

She turned to the foreman, and crossed her palms together. She was majestic and ageless, like any true authority.

"Doctor sayss there must be an operation on this man. He is very sick. I am ready to help."

"W', lady," said the foreman, "you just *try* an' cut on that Messican and see what happens!"

He ducked his head toward the laborers to explain this.

She turned to the men. Calmly, she fumbled for her long rosary at her discipline and held up the large crucifix that hung at its end. The men murmured and crossed themselves.

"Tell them what you have to do," she said to me coldly. She was still angry at the way I'd spoken in the train.

"All right, foreman, translate for me. Sister is going to assist me at an appendectomy. We'll move the man into the larger shed over there. I'd be afraid to take him to town, there isn't time. No: listen, this is better. What I *will* do: we could move him into the train, and operate while the train was standing still, and then let the train go ahead after the operation is over. That way, we'd get him to town for proper care!"

The foreman translated and pantomimed.

A threatening cry went up.

"They say you can't take Pancho off and cut on 'im on the train. They want him here."

Everybody looked at Pancho. He was like a little monkey with eyes screwed shut and leaking tears.

The little corpus of man never loses its mystery, even to a doctor, I suppose. What it is, we are; what we are, must serve it; in anyone. My professor of surgery used to say, "Hold back your pity till after the operation. You'll work better, and then the patient will be flattered to have it, and it might show up in the bill."

"Very well, we'll operate here. Sister, are you willing to help me? It'll mean staying here till tomorrow's train."

"*Ja,* doctor, of course."

I turned to the foreman.

"Tell them."

He shrugged and began to address them again.

They answered him, and he slapped his knee and h'yucked a kind of hound dog laugh in his throat and said to us,

"W', if you go ahaid, these Messicans here say *they'll sure 'nough kill you if you kill Pancho!*"

Yes, it was worse than I could have expected.

This was like being turned loose among savages.

You might have thought the searing heat of that light steel sky had got everybody into fanciful ways.

"Why, that's ridiculous!" I said to him. "He's nearly dead now! Osler himself might not save him! Nobody can ever guarantee an operation, but I can certainly guarantee that that man will die unless I take this one chance!"

"W', I dunno. See? That's what they *said* . . ."

He waved at the Mexicans.

They were tough and growling.

Sister was waiting. Her face was still as wax.

"Can't you *explain*," I said.

"Man, you never can 'splain *nothin'* to this crew! You better take the church lady there, and just get back on that train, that's what you better do!"

Well, there it was.

"You go to hell!" I said.

I looked at Sister. She nodded indignantly at me, and then smiled, sideways, that same sly look between her cheek and her lens, which she never meant that way; but from years of convent discretion she had come to perceive things obliquely and tell of them in whispers with many sibilants.

"Come on, we'll move him. Get some help there."

The Mexicans wouldn't budge. They stood in the way.

"Give me your pistol!"

The foreman handed it over. We soon got Pancho moved.

Sister helped me to carry him.

She was strong. I think she must have been a farm girl from one of the German communities of the Middle West somewhere. She knew how to work, the way to lift, where her hands would do the most good. Her heavy thick robes dragged in the dust. We went into the tool shed and it was like strolling into a furnace.

I hurried back to the train and got my bags and then went back again for hers. I never figured out how she could travel with so little and be so clean and comfortable. She had a box of food. It was conventional, in its odors, bananas, waxed paper, oranges, something spicy. Aside from that she had a little canvas bag with web straps binding it. I wondered what, with so little allowed her, she had chosen out of all the desirable objects of the world to have with her and to own.

My instrument case had everything we needed, even to two bottles of chloroform.

I got back into the dusty red shed by flashing the foreman's pistol at the mob. Inside I gave it back to him through the window with orders to keep control over the peasants.

What they promised to do to me if Pancho died began to mean something, when I saw those faces, like clever dogs, like smooth-skinned apes, like long-whiskered mice. I thought of having the engineer telegraph to some town and get help, soldiers, or something; but that was nervously romantic.

It was dark in the shed, for there was only one window. The heat was almost smoky here, it was so dim. There was a dirt floor. We turned down two big tool cases on their sides and laid them together. They were not quite waist high. It was our operating table.

When we actually got started, then I saw how foolish it was to try it, without any hospital facilities. But I remembered again that it was this chance or death for the little Mexican. Beyond that, it was something of an ethical challenge. Yes, we went ahead.

I remember details, but now so long after, maybe not in the right order.

I remember a particular odor, an oily smell of greasy sand, very powerful in the shed; the heat made the very dirt floor sweat these odors up, and they made me ill at ease in the stomach.

It was early afternoon. The sky was so still and changeless that it seemed to suspend life in a bowl of heat. The tin roof of the shed lowered a very garment of heat over us.

Faces clouded up at the window, to see: to threaten: to enjoy. We shook them away with the pistol. The foreman was standing in the doorway. Beyond him we had glimpses of the slow dancing silvery heat on the scratchy earth, and the diamond melt of light along the rails of the track.

The camp cook boiled a kettle of water.

Sister turned her back and produced some white rags from her petticoats.

She turned her heavy sleeves back and pinned her veils aside.

The invalid now decided to notice what was going on and he tried to sit up and began to scream.

Sister flicked me a glance and at once began to govern him with the touch of her hands, and a flow of comforting melody in *Deutsch* noises. I got a syringe ready with morphine. And the mob appeared at the door, yelling and kicking up the stifling dust which drifted in and tasted bitter in the nose.

I shot the morphine and turned around.

I began to swear.

That's all I recall; not *what* I said. But I said plenty. Pancho yelled back at his friends who would rescue him. It was like a cat concert for a minute or so.

Then the morphine heavied the little man down again, and he fell silent.

Then I shut up, and got busy with the chloroform. Sister said she could handle that. It was suddenly very quiet.

My instruments were ready and we had his filthy rags off Pancho. Sister had an instinctive adroitness, though she had never had surgical experience. Yet her hospital service had given her a long awareness of the sometimes trying terms of healing. In fascinated silence we did what had to be done before the operation actually started.

There was a locust, or a cicada, some singing bug outside somewhere, just to make the day sound hotter.

The silence cracked.

"He is dead!" they cried outside.

A face looked in at the window.

Now the threats began again.

I said to the foreman,

"Damn you, get hold of that crowd and make them shut up! You tell them he isn't dead! You tell them—"

I began to talk his language again, very fancy and fast. It worked on him. I never cussed so hard in my life.

Then I turned back and I took up my knife.

There's a lot of dramatic nonsense in real life; for example: my hand was trembling like a wet dog, with that knife; and I came down near the incisionary area, and just before I made the first cut, steady? that hand got as steady as a stone!

I looked at Sister in that slice of a second, and she was biting her lips and staring hard at the knife. The sweat stood on her face and her face was bright red. Her light eyebrows were puckered. But she was ready.

In another second things were going fast.

I once told this story to someone, and later heard it repeated to someone else. I hardly recognized the events as my friend described them, because he made it all sound so dramatic and somehow like a scene in the opera, grand and full of high notes. No, it seems to me that the facts are more wonderful than all the things time and play-going can do to a person's imagination. The whole situation couldn't have been meaner; more dangerous from forces like dirt and stupidity, instead of forces like fate or fascinating Mexican bandits. There was the hazard, too, of my own youth, my inexperience as a surgeon. There was my responsibility for Sister, in case any trouble might start. There was the heat and a patient with temperature and no way to cool off boiled water in a hurry, and the dust rising through the cracks of the door and window and walls of the shed, as the outraged men kicked and shuffled outside. We could see the sheets of dusty light standing in the room's dusk, sliced from the gloom by a crack of that sunlight and its abstract splendor.

Oh, my surgery professor and my colleagues would've been shocked to see some of the things I did, and didn't do, that day!

I tried to hum a little tune instead of talk.

But now and then the noise outside would get worse.

Or the foreman would creak the door open and stick his varlet face in to peer.

Or the patient would almost swallow his tongue making a noise like a hot sleeping baby.

So I'd swear.

Sister said nothing all the time.

She obeyed my instructions. Her face was pale, from so many things that she wasn't used to—the odors, the wound, manipulation of life with such means as knives and skill, the strain of seeing Pancho weaken gradually; she was glassy with perspiration. Her starched linen was melted. There was some intuitive machinery working between us. Aside from having to point occasionally at what I needed, things she didn't know the name of, I've never had a more able assistant at an operation in all my long life of practice.

I think it was because both she and I, in our professions, somehow belonged to a system of life which knew men and women at their most vulnerable, at times when they came face to face with the mysteries of the body and the soul, and could look no further, and needed help then.

Anyway, she showed no surprise. She showed none even at my skill, and I will admit that I looked at her now and then to see what she thought of my performance. For if I do say it myself, it was good.

She looked up only once, with a curious expression, and I thought it was like that of one of the early saints, in the paintings, her eyes filmed with some light of awareness and yet readiness, the hour before martyrdom; and this was when we heard the train start to go.

She looked rueful and forlorn, yet firm.

The engine let go with steam and then hooted with the exhaust, and the wheels ground along the hot tracks.

If I had a moment of despair, it was then; the same wavy feeling I'd had when the train had stopped here a couple of hours before.

The train receded in sound.

It died away in the plainy distance.

Shortly after there was a rush of voices and cries and steps toward the shack.

It was the laborers again, many of whom had been put back to work on the track ahead of the engine, in order to let the train proceed. Now they were done. Now they were crazy with menace.

It was about four o'clock, I suppose.

Fortunately, I was just finishing up. The door screeched on its shaken hinges and latch. I heard the foreman shouting at the men.

Then there was a shot.

"Most sacred Heart!" said Sister, on her breath, softly. It was a prayer, of course.

Then the door opened, and the foreman came in and closed it and leaned back on it.

He said they sent him in to see if Pancho were still living. I told him he was. He said he had to see. I said he was a blankety-blank meddling too, must have looked like a challenge, an alien force, to him. done, and if he had to smell around he could come.

I showed him the pulse in the little old Mexican's neck, beating fast, and made him listen to the running rapid breath, like a dog's.

Then he looked around.

He was sickened, first, I suppose; then he got mad. The place *was* dreadful. There were unpleasant evidences of surgery around, and the and low-down blank to come bothering me now; but that I was just heat was absolutely weakening, and the air was stifling with a clash of odors. Sister had gone to sit on a box in the corner, watching. She,

He grew infuriated again at the mysterious evidences of civilization.

He began to wave his gun and shout that next time, by God, he'd fire on us, and not on them Messicans out yander. He declared that he, too, was agin cuttin' on anybody. He was bewildered and sick to his stomach and suffering most of all from a fool's bafflement.

He bent down and tried to grab back the meager sheeting and the dressing on Pancho's abdomen. He was filthy beyond words. I butted him with my shoulder (to keep my hands away and reasonably clean) and he backed up and stood glaring and his mouth, which was heavy and thick, sagged and contracted in turn, like loose rubber.

Sister came forward and without comment, knelt down by the wretched operating table which might yet be, for all I knew, a bier, and began to pray, in a rich whisper, full of hisses and soft impacts of r's upon her palate, and this act of hers brought some extraordinary power into the room; it was her own faith, of course; her own dedication to a simple alignment of life along two channels, one leading to good, the other to evil.

I was beginning to feel very tired.

I had the weakness after strain and the almost querulous relief at triumph over hazard.

I'd been thinking of her all along as a woman, in spite of her ascetic garb, for that was natural to me then. Now for the first time, listening to her pray, I was much touched, and saw that she was like a doctor who thinks enough of his own medicine to take some when he needs a lift.

The foreman felt it all too, and what it did to him was to make him shamble sullenly out of the shed to join the enemy.

We watched all night.

It got hardly any cooler.

Late at night Sister opened her lunch box with little delicate movements and intentions of sociability, and we made a little meal.

I felt intimate with her.

I had a sense of what, together, we had accomplished, and over and over I tried to feel her response to this. But none came. We talked rather freely of what we still had to do, and whether we thought the Mexicans *meant* it, and whether the train crew knew what was going on, and if they'd report it when they reached Eddy.

We had an oil lamp that the foreman gave us.

When I'd get drowsy, my lids would drop and it seemed to me that the flame of the wick was going swiftly down and out; then I'd jerk awake and the flame would be going on steadily, adding yet another rich and melancholy odor to our little surgery.

I made Sister go to sleep, on her corner box, sitting with her back against the wall.

She slept in state, her hands folded, her body inarticulated under the volume of her robes, which in the dim lamplight looked like wonderful masses carved from some dark German wood by trolls of the Bavarian forests . . . so fancifully ran my mind through that vigil.

I saw morning come, like a cobweb, on the little window; then steal the whole sky that I could see; and then just as a flavor of cool sweetness had begun to lift into the air off the plains, the sun appeared (rapidly, I thought, but then it was I, not the sun, whose fever hurried life along that day).

Early that day Pancho became conscious.

We talked to him and he answered.

He was enclosed in the mystery of pain and the relief of weakness.

When he identified Sister by her habit, he tried to cross himself, and she smiled and crowed at him and made the sign of the cross over him herself.

I examined him carefully, and he was all right. He had stood the shock amazingly well. It was too early for infection to show to any degree, but I began to have a certain optimism, a settling of the heart. It had come off. I began to think the day was cooler. You know: the sweetness over everything that seems to follow a feeling of honest satisfaction.

Then the crowd got busy again.

They saw Pancho through the window, his eyes open, his lips moving, smiling faintly, and staring at Sister with a child's wonder toward some manifest loveliness, hitherto known only in dream and legend.

In a second they were around at the door, and pushing in, babbling like children, crying his name aloud, and eager to get at him and kiss him and gabble and marvel and felicitate.

They were filthy and enthusiastic, flowing like life itself toward that which feeds it. They were, then, infection personified.

I shouted at them and made them stay back. I let them see Pancho, but from a distance of three feet.

He spoke to them, thinly, and they cried "Aiee!" with astonishment, and nodded their heads as if sagely, and blinked their eyes at me, ducking their little bodies in homage. They couldn't have been more friendly now. They went yes-yes, and my-my, and how wonderful to have such a man! and he is my friend, and so forth.

But their very presence was dangerous, for they kicked up the dirt floor, and they hawked and spat on their words, and I finally put them out.

The foreman's mood was opposite to theirs.

He was now surly and disgruntled that we had pulled it off successfully.

He knew, as I had known, that the Mexicans really would kill if Pancho died.

We had the unpleasant impression that he felt cheated of a diverting spectacle.

We watched Pancho carefully all morning; he grew uncomfortable as the heat arose. But then, so did we. It rose and rose, and the bugs sang, and the tin roof seemed to hum too, but that must have been dramatic imagination. I had all our plans made. When the noon train came along, we would flag it, and carefully move Pancho on board, and take him down the valley to Eddy, where he could spend two weeks in the company hospital.

Mid-morning, I stepped outside and called the men together and the foreman, and made them a speech. Now they had their hats off, listening to me. Their little eyes couldn't have looked more kindly and earnest. *Sure,* I could take Pancho off on the train. *Sure,* they wanted him to get well. *By all means* the senior medico must do what he thought best. So with a great show of love for them, I shook hands with myself at the little mob, feeling like a gifted politician.

The train finally arrived, and as it first showed, standing down the tracks in the wavering heat, it looked like a machine of rescue.

There was only one more thing there.

When we went to take Pancho on the train, the foreman refused to help.

"I won't he'p you," he declared. "I ain't got no authority t'move none of my men, and I won't he'p you."

I picked out two of the less earthy natives and they helped me to bring the patient on board the train. We carried him on a camp cot. It belonged to the foreman. When he saw that, he got so mad he threw down his hat and jumped on it. The dust flew. His fish-white brow broke into sweat. Then he came running to stop us. We barely got Pancho on the train in time, and the door closed and latched. It was a state of siege until the train went again. It must have been ten minutes. Fortunately I'd brought my bags on board the first thing, and Sister's.

We finally pulled out.

We looked out the rear window, and saw our desert hospital recede into the slow pulsing glassy air.

We could see the little figures, most of them waving.

Just at the last, one of them held forth his arm, and we saw a puff of smoke, and heard an explosion in our imaginations, and then heard the actual ring and sing-off of a bullet as it struck the rear of the car.

It was the foreman's farewell, the last, and futile, opinion of the ignorant.

The afternoon passed slowly in the train.

The heat and the dust were hard on everyone, and especially Pancho. I kept wetting down the cracks of the windows, and the doors, to keep the dust out if I could.

But soon the water was gone, and we had to sit there and hope.

We reached Eddy in the evening, and it was like a garden, after the endless plains and their sear life. We found green trees and artesian wells and fields of alfalfa.

There is little more to tell, and what there is, is not about Pancho, except that he made a recovery in the proper time.

It is about my saying good-by to Sister.

It seemed to me we had been through a good deal together.

Now we were going to separate, for she was taking a stage-coach from

Eddy on down into Texas somewhere, and I was going to stay a few days and see my patient out of the woods.

So we said good-by in the lobby of the wooden hotel there, where she was going to spend the night.

Nobody knew what a good job I had done except Sister, and after we shook hands, and I thanked her for her wonderful help, I waited a moment.

She knew I was nervous and tired, and it was vanity of course, but I needed the little lift she could give me.

But she didn't say anything, while I waited, and then as I started to turn off and go, she did speak.

"I will pray for you, doctor."

"What?"

"That you may overcome your habit of profanity."

She bowed and smiled in genuine kindliness, and made her way to the stairs and disappeared.

Duty is an ideal and it has several interpretations, and these are likely to be closely involved with the character that makes them.

You might say that Sister and I represented life eternal and life temporal.

I never saw her again, of course, but if she's still alive, I have no doubt that she's one of the happiest people in the world.

The Three Veterans

LEANE ZUGSMITH

As far back as the memory of Miss Riordan, which was three months, for she had been the attending nurse in the clinic for that long, the three old women regularly appeared twice a week. Only when they managed to sit together on the bench, with their old, high-veined legs stiff ahead of them, was she able to distinguish one from the other. Otherwise, Mrs. Farrell could be mistaken for Mrs. Gaffney, or either of the two for Mrs. Betz. Each showed gaps in her front teeth when she broke into her cackle; each had yellow-gray hair wisping from beneath a moldy hat; each wore stained, shapeless outer garments; and each had the same kind of bad leg.

Outside the dispensary, the three old women did not lay eyes on one another from one clinic day to the next, but inside they formed a sisterhood. Together, they would question newcomers and advise them on their ills, but once The Doctor was in the room, they would remain respectfully silent unless he made one of his lame jokes or scolded them. Promptly then, they would cackle. Anything The Doctor said was a signal for their ingratiating brays of laughter.

The first three to enter Room 4 this morning, they sat together on the long bench, eyes alert on the door as Miss Riordan called to the patients outside, "Number 6 and 7 for Room 4."

When the pale young woman with the fretful infant came in, relinquishing her numbered green ticket for Room 4, and sat opposite them, Mrs. Betz crooked her soiled finger. "Gutsie-goo," she said to the baby. Then she addressed the mother. "Something wrong with it?" Mrs. Far-

445

rell and Mrs. Gaffney turned professional eyes on the child.

"She had an infected arm, and now she don't eat." The young woman jogged the whimpering infant with her knee.

"Only your first?" asked Mrs. Farrell, who had borne nine.

"Yes," said the young mother.

The three old women smiled knowingly at one another. Mrs. Gaffney flapped her hand down from the wrist. "Sure, you're always worrying your poor head off about the first. Isn't it the truth?" Mrs. Farrell and Mrs. Betz vigorously nodded their heads, and their moldy hats gave off a little puff of dust.

"When it don't eat, you want to pull out ten hairs from the right side of your head and braid them and twist them around its little toe," said Mrs. Betz.

"Give it honey and tea," said Mrs. Gaffney.

"It's always that way with the first of them," said Mrs. Farrell. "You'll be wanting to—"

"Who's in attendance around here? You or me?" It was The Doctor, his voice harsh, his face red.

Mrs. Gaffney and Mrs. Betz nudged Mrs. Farrell, who left her mouth open to giggle quickly with them.

"Just let me know when you want to take my job," he said, and stalked to the end of the room to visit the patients behind the screens.

The old women held their forefingers against their simpering lips. Now they would not even look at the ailing baby.

"Anyone else for Room 4?" called Miss Riordan, out in the corridor.

The eyes of the three old women frogged at the sight of the beautiful peroxide-blonde lady in a beautiful imitation-fur jacket. Everything about her seemed sweet and ripe as she handed over her green ticket and sat on the bench beside them. The three old women watched her pull down her silk stocking; she had only a little two-inch scratch on her fine, shapely leg and her skin was whiter than milk.

But Mrs. Gaffney could no longer stare at her, for now The Doctor was pressing his finger into her highest vein and she must keep her eyes submissive on his face. He whispered to the nurse and then, without looking into Mrs. Gaffney's submissive eyes, said, "You better quit staying out dancing all night, or that'll never get right."

The three old women cackled with delight. Mrs. Betz kept a meek smile on her face as The Doctor examined her leg. When he came to Mrs. Farrell, he wrinkled up his nose. "Suppose you wash your leg off yourself," he said. "Give the poor nurse a break. Just rub it up and down with *soap* and *water*. Ever heard of it?"

This time the brays of laughter from the three old women were wilder than ever. Seeing him turn to the baby, all three of the old women tried to retard Miss Riordan's manipulations of their leg wrappings so that they could remain to watch The Doctor and the beautiful peroxide-blonde lady in the beautiful imitation-fur jacket. Mrs. Gaffney elbowed Mrs. Betz as The Doctor stood before the lady.

"What's wrong with you?" he said.

She smiled invitingly up at him. "I tripped on the stairs—my landlord doesn't know enough to have safe stairs in his house—and it's been bothering me." She pointed a tapering white finger at the abrasion.

He looked at it carefully before whispering his orders to Miss Riordan. Mrs. Gaffney started to edge out of her seat, disappointed, when the beautiful lady said, "Is it serious, Doctor?"

"It hurt you, didn't it?" he said, sarcastically.

At the familiar tone, Mrs. Gaffney, Mrs. Farrell, and Mrs. Betz chuckled, but softly for fear of being sent away, now that their legs were wrapped.

"Yes," said the beautiful lady, "but I want to know what to tell my lawyer, in case—"

"Oh, your lawyer?" said The Doctor, witheringly. "I see. You want to bring suit. Well, Madam, you can tell your lawyer that anyone who's so careless as to trip on the stairs deserves more than the little scratch you have there."

The three old women lowered their heads, their soiled fingers at their mouths to curb their explosions of laughter. The beautiful lady's eyes flashed. "I don't see why you have to use that tone of voice!" she exclaimed with resentment. "Just because it's free is no reason why we can't be treated like human beings!"

The three old women waited breathlessly, their lips ready to stretch at his sally. Their waiting ears were met by silence. Their rheumy eyes saw The Doctor turn his back and regard the table of ointments and bandages. As he stood there, whistling softly, the three old women found themselves staring at one another, and not one was smiling. With gray tired faces, they rose together. At the door, their way was blocked by the man in white whom they called The Specialist Doctor.

"Just the old friends I may want!" he cried in his ringing tones. He turned to The Doctor. "Are they varicose?"

"All three, Chief," said The Doctor.

"Are they interesting? Good enough for my Friday-night lecture?"

"I'll show you their charts," said The Doctor.

The Specialist Doctor rubbed his hands. "How would you girls like to dance in my chorus Friday night?" he boomed cheerfully.

The three old women looked at one another. The beautiful peroxide-blonde lady clack-clacked her high heels across the floor.

"No," said Mrs. Betz, heavily.

"No," said Mrs. Farrell, without looking up.

"No," said Mrs. Gaffney, plucking at the edge of her stained wrap "Just because it's free don't mean we aren't human beings."

Then, with lowered heads and sombre faces, the three old women trudged out.

The Testimony of Dr. Farnsworth

FRANCIS LEO GOLDEN

THE ambulance from Mercy Hospital glided into the tunneled passage-way and drew up with pin-point brakeage at the door of the Emergency Room.

An orderly came out to help the chauffeur. The man was lifted from the stretcher on to the table. "Easy boys," cautioned the interne, "be careful of his left side."

Ordinarily, Dr. Larry Wayne would not have been within two wards of Emergency. But the evening had horrible portents for him and he could not explain his inward jumpiness. It was peculiar the way that Delaine had brushed him off when he suggested the movies. Had she not consecrated Thursday nights to the attachment that had sprung up between them?

The nurse looked up at his approach. The interne barely nodded. "What have you got, Ben?"

"Tough, Dr. Wayne. Entire left side of the head bashed in."

Larry scrubbed up. "Hemorrhage?"

The interne was cryptic. "Profuse. Zygomatic process may be exposed."

Dr. Wayne peered into the lesion. "H'm, not so good. The tempero-mandibular joint is completely crushed. Whoever slugged him wasn't fooling. Better get the Chief down here. We're in sacred territory—territory that's his special province."

That was why the telephone was so insistent. The quiet of the red-brick and green stuccoed home atop Madison Avenue fought the challenge until, wearily, Dr. Mark A. Farnsworth lifted the receiver.

449

"Larry thinks I should come down, eh? Very well, I shan't be long."

Just as wearily he replaced the phone on its outswinging bracket. The house was cold. Through the casement windows he could see below —to the Hudson where the twinkling lights of the ferry-boats were furrowing a path toward New York.

His finger touched the buzzer. Mrs. Grady bustled in. "If you're going into the movies, Midge, leave word with Robert I'll be at the Hospital."

"Shouldn't have to be a-gettin' up of a night like this." She sniffed the air. "Yer work too hard as it is."

"My dear Midge," he said roguishly, "you have served me well and faithfully these past thirty-odd years. And during that time you have, by your patient effort and deep devotion to duty, exemplified my constant preachment: that there is in every living creature an obscure but powerful impulse to active functioning. Life demands to be lived. Inac tion is foreign to the healthy organism. Only the dead can be really idle."

She looked up at his venerable figure. The long, blue jowls always so smoothly shaven; the closely-cropped, gray mustache that shet off ad- smoothly shaven; the closely-cropped, gray mustache that set off ad- No wonder the Judge always says yer right. He can't understand yer!"

Dr. Wayne was handling the transfusion when the Chief reached Emergency. "Call out the trauma, Larry, while I'm scrubbing." Dr. Farnsworth cocked his ear toward the table.

"I've ridden the old wagon for years," said Larry, "and I've seen many a chap conked on the cocoanut, but this is a honey. The blow covers the parietal and temporal region."

"Extradural hemorrhage?"

"Right, Chief. The middle meningeal artery."

"Pulse?"

"Not so hot."

"Respiration?"

"Slowing up."

The Chief accepted the towel from the student nurse. He beamed fatherly on the young man in white who in the seriousness of the case had forgotten his uneasiness of the early evening. Dr. Farnsworth knew the fibre of Wayne. He had carefully checked the progress of Larry since that day at Mrs. Gaudeau's bedside when Wayne had insisted on a diagnosis of diabetes because of the presence of acetone on the breath. The Chief had been guiding him these past three years as his logical successor in the field of forensic medicine. Running to Court several times a week was tiring on legs that were fast losing their elasticity. Dr. Farnsworth enjoyed his days as the Expert Witness, but now the vascular demands on his system were imperative. He had to slow his pace. That was where Larry Wayne was so helpful.

Wayne stepped aside. Dr. Farnsworth surveyed the field of injury. "I think transfusion has only been a reprieve, Larry. He has been dealt a savage blow. The fracture is compound." His sensitive fingers located the depression of the fragments. "Extends to the base of the skull," he said.

Dr. Farnsworth spoke on. "He must have lain a while after the blow. Police case, I suppose?"

Larry looked at the interne. "What's the story, Ben?" The interne looked away. The nurse spoke through her gauze mask. "Ben doesn't want to tell you, Dr. Wayne."

"What do you mean?"

"Apartment on Commonwealth Avenue. This patient here is the party of the first part. There were two weeping dames in the room. Bending over this fellow when the police arrived was the lady pharmacist of our Hospital, Miss Delaine Kennedy, your dimpled, little red-head."

Larry looked at her querulously. "You don't mean—"

"Ask the Homicide Squad. They're out in the reception room waiting to ask you a few questions."

"It just couldn't be," whispered Larry.

Dr. Farnsworth glared at the nurse. "We usually save personalities until disposition has been made of the patient. Next time, Miss Howard, a little restraint, please!"

"I'm sorry, Dr. Farnsworth."

Larry gazed at the man on the table. "I don't know who he is. But Delaine is not the type who—" He could not finish the sentence.

Dr. Farnsworth snapped him out of the mood. "If our Hospital pharmacist means that much to you, Larry, we'll go radical. There are some cerebral concussions that might respond to venesection. You young fellows know little about it. But we can't debate here. This man is going out—and going fast. And, evidently, Larry, two lives are at stake. This chap's and our Miss Kennedy's."

It was well after midnight before Dr. Farnsworth threw his gown and gloves into the hamper. Larry was disconsolate.

"We've done all we could, boy. It was just hopeless. He must have been nailed by an exceptionally heavy instrument. What did the police say?"

Larry looked up dejectedly. "A hammer. The fellow is a section foreman on the railroad. It was his own hammer. He was the boy-friend of Miss Kennedy's sister. They have Delaine at Headquarters. I'm going down there now."

Dr. Farnsworth called out from the shower-room. "Better call Pawlston, Larry. He's a good lawyer. You'll probably need some bail, too. Get in touch with Townsend. He'll rout the Fidelity man out of bed."

Robert was sitting up for Dr. Farnsworth when he reached his citadel atop Madison Avenue. The brass kettle over the fireplace was whistling a happy tune. "I'll have your tea in a moment, sir." Robert wheeled the table over to the easy chair.

"You didn't have to wait up, Robert."

"Lor' bless you, sir, if I didn't, Mrs. Gray would pay me off in the mornin'. A spot of brandy in it, sir?"

Dr. Farnsworth nodded. "And have you any cheese and crackers, Robert?"

The man looked nervously to the door. "I'm under special orders, sir. She says cheese don't agree with you and you're not to have it."

"Nonsense, Robert. That old termagant is in a constant conspiracy to rob me of all my gustatory pleasures. Ah, well. I daresay she's right. Never mind, Robert. I'll just sip away."

"That will be all, sir?"

"Yes, Robert. You may put out the lights, too. I have some meditation before I turn in." The man's steps went softly across the rug as he doused the lamps.

"Robert?"

"Yes, sir."

"What happens when you love two young people who love each other?"

"Don't know as I understand, sir." The man paused at the door.

"You've heard of Damon and Pythias, Robert? And Jonathan and David? Friendship, to endure, must be tested in the fires of suffering."

"Dare say you're right, sir."

"I've got to think out a great problem, Robert. It involves that great crucible of physiology—the human mind. Friendship survives, Robert, only if we have faith."

"Good-night, sir. If you need more logs, you'll find them in the box."

Robert closed the door. Dr. Farnsworth reached into the drawer for his queer-bowled pipe. He recalled the first day he met Miss Kennedy. He was passing the pharmacy in the basement of Mercy when he heard a contralto-ish voice call after him. There was vibrancy in the tones. Binet could have written a new chapter on its sonorescence. It was Wordsworthian "beauty born of murmuring sound."

"Dr. Farnsworth, please?"

He turned his head toward the doorway. She was slightly below average height, but you failed to see that in the cherry-tinted hair that was drawn back from the forehead in a series of terraces. There were dimples, too, that caught the shadows of her smile.

"Yes."

"I'm worried about this prescription for Mrs. Grayson."

"Prescription?" He smiled disarmingly. H'm, she had cerulean eyes. "Prescription? My, my, yes. You're the new pharmacist, aren't you?

Little lady, I'll let you in on a great State secret." He had pretended to look up and down the corridor for eavesdroppers. "When we had the vacancy as pharmacist, the Board was reluctant to engage a girl. But I rose to the defense of Female Rights. I said to them, rather sternly, 'What are we going to do when our boys leave for the front? We've got to realize woman's importance in every field of endeavor heretofore reserved exclusively for men.' Did you ever hear me make a speech, Miss—Miss?"

"Kennedy. Delaine Kennedy."

"I'm a rough, growling, old bear, Miss Kennedy." His smile had softened the fierceness of the grimace. They both laughed, but she had carried the melody. That had reminded him of something else. Her application stated that she had four years at the Conservatory of Music; then there was that hiatus of several years before she enrolled at the College of Pharmacy. He'd ask sometime about this.

"Now, about that prescription?"

'It calls for a grain of morphine," she had answered. "Surely, there must be some mistake." He looked the paper over carefully. "H'm, Mrs. Grayson, eh? Make it one-quarter grain."

"Thank you, Dr. Farnsworth. I just had to make sure."

She was a sweet portrait framed there in the doorway. He could understand why Larry Wayne, so wholesome himself, loved this girl. "In making sure, Miss Kennedy, you've saved a patient's life."

He had periodically studied her work in the pharmacy. She was vigilant, trustworthy, and always cheerful. She had further endeared herself to him the night when little Gloria cried for her mother. That was a nasty case. He had been in the Staff Room reading a paper on the Pituitary Hormones when they brought in Mrs. Allerton on the stretcher. He had been called to Emergency. There was no hope for the mother, but the child had come through the accident with merely a few scratches and a twisted ligament.

The youngster cried pitifully. Each sob was punctuated by the yearning call: "I wan' my mamma." Miss Kennedy, off duty, had been passing by. She quieted the child without apparent effort.

"There, there, Gloria. Your mama isn't far away." She led the child, with the assistance of Dr. Farnsworth, into the Play Room. "Your mama can't be far away because mamas never are. Look around the room, darling. Aren't the wall paintings lovely? See the Three Bears? Someone has taken their breakfast. And what have we here? A piano. A teeny-weeny piano. Let me play for you, Gloria."

A very light sob had escaped the child. "I like to hear moosic."

He had listened, too. It was a miniature piano. The sounds were quite metallic, but, yet, soothing to the child. Miss Kennedy's left hand caressed the key-board; her right arm was around the child's waist.

The chords were familiar and yet he could not recall the name of the piece in the greater contemplation of Miss Kennedy's gift of lulling a motherless child to sleep. Not until he had reached the cloistered comfort of Mrs. Gray's tea-before-the-fireplace did the melody bestir him. He had to make several pilgrimages to the piano and copious references to his music library before his curiosity was appeased. Miss Kennedy had been dashing off excerpts of Richard Strauss's symphonic study, *Panathenaenzug.* . . .

And now, Miss Kennedy was in great trouble. The tabloids would be screaming their innuendos; Larry would be in a daze; Pawlston would be adopting new thespian attitudes in wooing the jury. The courtroom would be crowded; the Judge would feel important. Yes, all that was familiar ground to Dr. Mark Farnsworth, sitting here in a darkened room and watching the River through the casement windows. He would appear at the trial as a witness. But this time he would be more than The Expert giving telescopic testimony. He was in "at the kill." His eyes had penetrated the traumatic depths of the man's skull. His words, reluctantly drawn from his lips by an ambitious District Attorney, would send Miss Kennedy to the "chair."

The reverie was disturbed by Mrs. Grady. "Angels and saints, would you look at him now! Sitting in a cold room and him thinkin' he's as young and healthy as a squirrel. Off to bed wi' yer and none of yer big talk."

"You wouldn't be harsh to me, Midge, you old meanie, if you knew that I just received consolation from one of your favorites."

"Meanin' what?" She had turned up the lamp to find him chilblainish. Her shawl went over his shoulders.

"I was thinking of St. Paul. A great man, Midge. He once said that no obedience to moral rules can take the place of Love. Where Love is genuine, it will, if combined with intelligence, suffice to generate whatever moral rules are necessary."

"St. Paul said that? Sure them is lovely words comin' from him."

"Lovely, Midge, and quite sustaining."

The Principal Keeper greeted Dr. Farnsworth warmly. "We don't get to see much of you, Doctor."

"It isn't lack of good fellowship, Tom. These walls could never be inviting. How is she?"

"Miss Kennedy? No rest at all. Paced the floor all night. That young doctor of yours is on his way over. He couldn't get a Judge to consider bail. It's a murder charge, you know."

"I never thought about that, Tom. Or maybe it's because I have some doubts that she is a ..." He could not say the word.

The P.K. interrupted: "The police don't have any doubts. She screamed to them that she was guilty and would they please let her kid sister alone."

The buzzer sounded. Through the intercommunicating phone boomed the voice of a guard. "P.K.? Dr. Wayne in the outer reception room."

The P.K. answered with a switch of the key. "Send him in."

Dr. Farnsworth could see that Larry, too, had had a restless night. His eyes were glassy and red. His collar was smudged and his overcoat was draped over his shoulders carelessly.

"You'll have to talk to her, Chief. I just can't."

"What about the sister?"

Larry drew his palms across his unshaven cheeks in a gesture that spelled despair. "From what I can piece together, the guy has been treating the sister shamefully. No—they weren't married. He's a dipso.

And when he goes on a binge, it's a beaut. Del insists she walked in while he was belaboring the kid. That's what she told the cops."

"She clipped him, eh?" Dr. Farnsworth patted Larry affectionately. "Wait for me. I'll go see her now."

Miss Kennedy looked up at his approach. When the door rolled back, she threw herself into his arms. "Oh, Dr. Farnsworth," she sobbed.

"It's all right, little lady, let it all out." The story came in tearful staccato.

"I love her so much, Dr. Farnsworth. I know you can understand that. And when he started to hit her . . ." She was biting her lips and struggling for control. "I couldn't stand it, I just couldn't stand it!"

He quieted her with all the blandishments he possessed. Her head drooped on his chest, and unconsciously, he found himself stroking her hair. "You'll be calm, won't you? Larry and I have retained a good lawyer. And we'll have to testify."

She looked at him. "I'm sorry you were dragged into this sordid mess. And Larry. What must he think of me?"

"Think of you? Why, that juvenile baboon loves you—and you know I'm so jealous of him that—that I must love you, too."

He arose to go. She clung to him for a moment. "My sister. She's been pushed around so much. Would you see that . . ."

He nodded his head affirmatively. "She's been held as a material witness. But I'm sure we can send her down South for a little rest until the trial begins."

She brushed back the tears. "I feel stronger already," she said. And looking at her he could see that inner strength.

The trial opened in the glare of the headlines that Dr. Farnsworth predicted. Additional space had to be arranged for the newspapermen and photographers. The syndicates were represented by gushing Love-lorn advisers and visiting sociologists. The columnists were there in force, seeking tomorrow's paragraphs. Only the stern attitude   Judge Haynes's gavel prevented the atmosphere from becoming hippo-dromish.

Pawlston, in his defense of Miss Kennedy, summoned all his adroit mannerisms to the scene.

He confused the coroner and the police repeatedly. The theme was reiterative. "But you did not see either of these girls actually strike the fatal blow? How do you know that some person or persons unknown, but bearing a grudge against the deceased, might not have struck him? Do you realize that Miss Kennedy weighs only one hundred and twenty-four pounds? Do you realize that her sister weighs a mere one hundred and eighteen pounds? Could either one have wielded a hammer weighing *forty-one* pounds?"

At the counsel table, Miss Kennedy fought to control the storm rising within her. She pleaded with Dr. Wayne. "Stop him, Larry. He's violating our agreement."

"Agreement?"

"Pawlston is casting doubt on my confession. I killed Mulgrew. They can't—they dare not pin it on Carol. Tell him to stop, Larry."

He patted her hand. "Hush, darling. We're here to help you."

"I don't want that kind of help!"

Judge Haynes glared at her. "The defendant will restrain her conduct," he warned.

The District Attorney was enjoying the performance. Here was a defendant so cooperative that all he had to do was place her on the stand and she assumed the entire guilt. The D.A. knew all the artifices in this arena, too. When to feint, when to lead, when to dodge. He was lenient with Carol; he was unctuous with Miss Kennedy.

The confession, as given to Lieutenant Decker, was admitted in evidence over the objections of Pawlston. The hammer became Exhibit S-2, over the further objections of Pawlston.

The testimony of the interne and that of Dr. Wayne followed. Their presence on the stand was brief. "What was the condition of Paul Mulgrew on the night he was brought into Mercy Hospital? What was the clinical picture? What was the hour he expired?"

"Dr. Farnsworth," the bailiff called out with the pride he felt in the Doctor's friendship. Bulbs flashed from the corners of the room.

Larry studied the face of Dr. Farnsworth. There was nobility of character and intellect in the way his preceptor placed his hand on the Bible and swore "to tell the whole truth and nothing but the truth."

Last night in Dr. Farnsworth's library this scene had been rehearsed.

"You see, Larry, one's presence on the witness stand is as sacred an endowment as a call to Holy Orders. The oath that you take is a direct communication to the All-Highest."

Larry knew the inward fires that must now be burning in Dr. Farnsworth's mind. They had recruited eight nurses from the Hospital, all of whom weighed the same as Miss Kennedy. And all of them had, with some effort and using both hands, lifted a forty-one pound bar and crashed it against the face of a skeleton.

It would be driving a stake in his heart when the D.A. would pin him down to the direct question. Dr. Farnsworth's expert, as well as eyewitness opinion, would influence any jury. Miss Kennedy's fate was sealed.

The voice of the D.A. boomed across the courtroom. "Dr. Farnsworth, I understand that you are a regularly licensed physician and surgeon of this state; that you hold a degree of Doctor of Medicine from Johns Hopkins University; that you are also a graduate of the University of Heidelberg, and have done post-graduate work at the University of Vienna; that you have specialized in neurology and traumatic surgery; that you are a consultant in neurology in the State Hospital; senior visiting surgeon at the local hospital; clinical professor at the Graduate School of Medicine, and attending neurologist at the Mercy Hospital?"

Dr. Farnsworth's hands were clasped during the recital of this introduction. He nodded at its conclusion. "And may I add, with pardonable modesty, that I am also a Fellow of the American College of Surgeons, and a member of the American Neurological Association?"

Pawlston had been on his feet during this ritual. "If Your Honor pleases, I do not think any of us could question either Dr. Farnsworth's eminent qualifications or his established sense of probity."

Dr. Farnsworth's eyes strayed toward the defense table. Miss Kennedy had a protective arm linked within her sister's.

The D. A. was now on the firing line. "I'm not going to bore the Court, nor you, Dr. Farnsworth, with repetitious medical history of one Paul Mulgrew, now deceased. Your associate, Dr. Wayne, and the attending interne have described the traumatic picture."

Dr. Farnsworth leaned forward. The Court Stenographer's pen dangled loosely in his hand.

"Doctor," continued the D.A., "you performed an emergency operation on the deceased? What was the cause of death?"

"Multiple blows in the tempero-occipital-parietal area of the skull. As Dr. Wayne testified, we usually find that at the point of impact fractures by irradiation—in other words, continued fractures—result." He looked toward the jury as though he had drawn up a chair in their living rooms for a fireside chat. "The fractures begin on the convexity of the skull and follow the shortest route from that point to the base of the skull. We call it Aran's Law."

"Thank you, Doctor. Now will you be specific in the injuries that resulted in Paul Mulgrew's death?"

"The fracture passed from a line between the parietal-temporal region toward the occipital, taking in the middle fossa of the skull between the wings of the sphenoid and the petrous portion of the temporal bone. There was extradural hemorrhage from the middle meningeal artery, as Dr. Wayne explained on the chart."

The D.A. edged in closer. Any minute now, a greater blow would fall. Dr. Farnsworth wet his lips nervously and for the first time since he began his medico-legal career he was uneasy. "Dr. Farnsworth, the deceased was a railroad section foreman. A hammer, weighing forty-one pounds, was found at his body. Could his death, could the injuries which you have just described, have been caused by such an instrument?"

The answer was slow and painful. "I . . . would . . . say . . . yes."

"Dr. Farnsworth," continued the D.A., "you have heard the defense Opening? Opposing counsel has inferred that the defendant, despite her confession to the police, Exhibit H-3, was physically unable to wield a hammer, Exhibit S-2, weighing forty-one pounds. Could the defendant, weighing one hundred and twenty-four pounds strike the deceased with this hammer, inducing injuries that resulted in death?"

A thousand imps were pounding in Dr. Farnsworth's ear. This is IT. But Pawlston was on his feet. "I object, Your Honor! It's irrelevent and immaterial what the Doctor *thinks*. The District Attorney knows he can only get this into the record by asking the witness a hypothetical question."

The D.A. smiled. "I withdraw the question, Your Honor, and I shall abide by my learned friend's suggestion. Now, Dr. Farnsworth, assuming that the deceased, on the fourth day of December, was struck in the parietal and temporal region, sustaining a compound fracture as described, and assuming that the defendant weighs one hundred and twenty-four pounds, as has been testified, and that a hammer weighing forty-one pounds, admitted in evidence as Exhibit S-2, is assumed to be the weapon of death, would it be possible for the defendant to have wielded the hammer, Exhibit S-2, in such a way as to produce the injuries to the head that you described?"

The blood was coursing madly through his temples. Now his tongue was dry. He had to gulp before he could frame his answer. His fingers clutched at the chair for support. "No. I do not believe that the defendant was physically able to lift such a hammer."

There, the lie was out. And all the St. Pauls could not rebut what St. Augustine wrote to Consentius, could they? He who says some lies are just might also say that some sins are just, and therefore, some things are just which are unjust: what can be more absurd?

Zeus gives no aid to liars, so Homer said. Congreve had his measure, too: Thou liar of the first magnitude.

Dr. Farnsworth looked down from the witness chair toward the girl. Her handkerchief, now in threads, lay on the counsel table. There were two extra big tears ski-ing down her cheeks. "Gratitude's liquid," he mumbled to himself. But he would need more than tears to purge himself.

The D.A. was undaunted. He strode challengingly toward the box.

"Isn't it possible, Dr. Farnsworth, that the close association of your assistant, Dr. Wayne, with the defendant may have obscured your judgment?"

The Judge frowned on the District Attorney. "Is it possible, sir, you are impugning your own witness?"

The D.A. bristled up. "If it pleases the Court, this testimony comes as a complete surprise to me."

Pawlston rose to object. Dr. Farnsworth motioned him to silence. "The District Attorney is sugar-coating his inference. If Your Honor permits, I would call Mr. Shakespeare as a witness. 'For my part, if a lie may do thee grace, I'll gild it with the happiest terms I have.'"

The Judge quelled the ripple of laughter with a light tap of the gavel. "The answer will be stricken from the record. Henry IV has no legal entity in this Court."

Dr. Farnsworth smiled at the jurist. But perhaps the jury had not yet been convinced. To tell a lie is bad enough; not to have it believed is worse. "Too regrettable, Your Honor. For I might also have added to the District Attorney, and quoting the same Bard, 'If I tell thee a lie, spit in my face; call me horse.'"

The jury joined in the laughter that swept the courtroom. Dr. Farnsworth sighed with relief. Miss Kennedy no longer was in danger.

He was in a half-doze when Midge ushered in Larry and the girl. Dr. Farnsworth sat up hurriedly. His hands extended toward Miss Kennedy. She sank her head in his lap while a gripping hysteria brought alternate tears and laughter. Larry shook her roughly. "Come, Del, snap out of it. You promised no scenes."

Delaine kissed the wrinkled hands fervently. "I shall never forget your kindness."

"Your testimony stopped them cold, Chief," said Larry admiringly. "The D.A. didn't know whether he was coming or going."

"I feel that way myself, Larry." He motioned to Midge. "Some tea, please, and I'm sure they'll like your cookies, Midge." He sat up in his chair and pointed to the writing table. "I've just one more letter to dash off, Larry. Suppose you tell me what happened after I left the court-room."

Dr. Wayne began the recital with gestures. First he was the D.A. Then he was Pawlston. Midge spread the tea things just where the jury box should have been. They all chuckled.

Larry reached into the tray for a cup and passed it to Dr. Farnsworth. Below him on the table were the letters. "Haven't you paid your dues, Chief?"

"A different picture, Larry. I'm resigning from the State and County Medical Societies."

Larry stared at the letters. "And the A.M.A.? Why Chief, you can't—"

"I'm unworthy, Larry. I feel soiled. I can't help it if that's my sense of ethics."

"But this is your life, Chief! The courtroom is your other surgery. You can't fold up like that. Forget what I said about your testimony today, Chief. It was Pawlston who convinced the jury that Delaine's confession was obtained by duress."

Dr. Farnsworth smiled wanly. He pointed to the pit of his stomach. "The seat of our emotions, Larry, is here in the viscera. And that's where I feel low. If Justice has been led away, I have no basin as Pilate had. But enough of that. Let's not be dispirited. No pall of gloom for this happy occasion. Midge, have Robert open a bottle of Pinet Noir. We must have a toast to these young people." He looked over his read-ing glasses toward Miss Kennedy. "And before we become exuberant, young lady, let's remember that you haven't a job any more."

Larry held up the girl's chin and planted a kiss on her lips. "She won't need one, Chief. As soon as we bundle sister Carol off to New York, Delaine and I are going to rhumba down the aisle."

Midge sniffed. "You don't dance in church, you heathen." She gathered up the tea dishes. Dr. Farnsworth was in a thoughtful mood. "I had some plans for her, Larry."

"Plans?" Delaine was curious. Dr. Farnsworth smiled her way. "Your application at the Hospital mentioned several years at the Conservatory of Music. I thought, perhaps, you might care to . . . return to the piano.

The concert stage? Larry and I could underwrite the program."

Delaine fought the tears that seemed to come so easily now. "Oh, you're so generous, Dr. Farnsworth."

"Not at all, my dear. Purely selfish of me. I love the piano. It's an old Italian proverb that he who plays the piano keeps sane. That's my piano over there in the corner. Won't you play for us now?"

Larry added his coaxing. "Yes, Del, please do."

"If you wish." She stepped to the far end of the room and adjusted the bench. "I may be somewhat rusty. You'll be indulgent, I hope."

Dr. Farnsworth settled himself back in the easy chair. The river was quiet down there tonight. The sea-gulls were circling the harbor for their twilight whirl before nesting for the night. It had been a hectic day and now this repose was delightfully welcome. The music was flooding the room.

Ravel, eh? A real craftsman and not a sentimentalist as Dr. Farnsworth was. He recalled a visit he had made to Montfort l'Amaury, outside of Paris, while on a tour through Europe. He had found Ravel polite but inwardly cold.

Dr. Farnsworth's reverie continued. This girl's technique was flawless. H'm. The *Concerto For One Hand*. Difficult and intricate fingering even for two hands. And that night when Miss Kennedy soothed the child in the Hospital . . . h'm, wasn't all this odd? He lifted his creaking limbs from the chair and quietly approached Miss Kennedy. Larry's eyes followed him.

Dr. Farnsworth stood over the piano. He watched her left hand weaving up and down, from treble to bass and from bass to treble. Her right hand rested motionless on the keyboard. Could it be that . . . ? He reached over and fastened both hands on her right shoulder. The music ended in her scream. "Stop, Dr. Farnsworth! You're hurting my arm."

Larry sprang forward. "What is it, Chief? You're trembling."

"I should have known, Larry! What a dullard I am." Miss Kennedy was sobbing softly. "Do you remember, Larry," Dr. Farnsworth continued, "that night when she quieted the little girl? I've told you about it so often. Not until I returned home did I learn what she had been playing on that tiny hospital piano. It was Richard Strauss's symphonic study, *Panathenaenzug.*"

"I still don't know what you're driving at, Chief."

"Strauss composed it for Paul Witgenstein, the Viennese pianist *who lost an arm in the War.* And just now, while we listened, she was playing Ravel's *concerto for one hand.* Here, Larry, feel her deltoideus. The muscle is partially paralyzed. Look at the clavicle—how awkwardly it is set."

Larry's fingers ran up and down the girl's arm. "The deltoid and the triceps are certainly weak. What is it, Delaine? What have you been hiding from us?" Her sobbing continued.

Dr. Farnsworth raised her to her feet. "Lift your right arm, Miss Kennedy. Up—up—this high."

"I can't, Dr. Farnsworth, I can't."

Tenderly his arm went about her waist and he led her to the divan. "Now, let's have the story, my dear."

Midge handed her a table napkin and she dried her eyes. "I had to forego the concert stage," she spoke haltingly, "when I was thrown from my horse. That's the story. Simple, isn't it? I had to find some income. And . . . well, I had always loved chemistry."

"You loved Carol, too." A radiance had come over Dr. Farnsworth. "You loved her so much you were willing to die for her." He hugged her warmly. "My dear, you have no idea how happy this moment is. And say, Midge, where's Robert with that wine? I must drink to St. Augustine. I thought he had let me down. But now it's all so clear." He tapped the little black book on the table. "*Quid est enim fides, nisi credere quod non vides.*"

"There he goes again," said Midge, "with more of thim fancy words."

"Meaning what, Chief?"

"The Homilies on Saint John. Augustine asks what is faith save to believe what you do not see."

The Bedchamber Mystery

C. S. FORESTER

Now THAT a hundred years have passed one of the scandals in my family can be told. It is very doubtful if in 1843 Miss Forester (she was Eulalie, but being the eldest daughter unmarried, she of course was Miss Forester) and Miss Emily Forester and Miss Eunice Forester ever foresaw the world of 1943 to which their story would be told; in fact it is inconceivable that they could have believed that there ever would be a world in which their story could be told blatantly in public print. At that time it was the sort of thing that could only be hinted at in whispers during confidential moments in feminine drawing rooms; but it wa. whispered about enough to reach in the end the ears of my grandfather, who was their nephew, and my grandfather told it to me.

In 1843 Miss Forester and Miss Emily and Miss Eunice Forester were already maiden ladies of a certain age. The old-fashioned Georgian house in which they lived kept itself modestly retired, just like its inhabitants, from what there was of bustle and excitement in the High Street of the market town. The ladies indeed led a retired life; they went to church a little, they visited those of the sick whom it was decent and proper for maiden ladies to visit, they read the more colorless of the novels in the circulating library, and sometimes they entertained other ladies at tea.

And once a week they entertained a man. It might almost be said that they went from week to week looking forward to those evenings. Dr. Acheson was (not one of the old ladies would have been heartless enough to say "fortunately," but each of them felt it) a widower, and several years older even than my great-great-aunt Eulalie. Moreover, he was a keen whist player and a brilliant one, but in no way keener or more brilliant than were Eulalie, Emily, and Eunice. For years now the three nice old ladies had looked forward to their weekly evening of whist—all the ritual of setting out the green table, the two hours of silent cut-and-thrust play, and the final twenty minutes of conversation with Dr. Acheson as he drank a glass of old Madeira before bidding them good night.

The late Mrs. Acheson had passed to her Maker somewhere about 1830, so that it was for thirteen years they had played their weekly game of whist before the terrible thing happened. To this day we do not know whether it happened to Eulalie or Emily or Eunice, but it happened to one of them. The three of them had retired for the night, each to her separate room, and had progressed far toward the final stage of getting into bed. They were not dried-up old spinsters; on the contrary, they were women of weight and substance, with the buxom contours even married women might have been proud of. It was her weight which was the undoing of one of them, Eulalie, Emily or Eunice.

Through the quiet house that bedtime there sounded the crash of china and a cry of pain, and two of the sisters—which two we do not know—hurried in their dressing gowns to the bedroom of the third— her identity is uncertain—to find her bleeding profusely from severe cuts in the lower part of the back. The jagged china fragments had inflicted severe wounds, and, most unfortunately, just in those parts where the injured sister could not attend to them herself. Under the urgings of the other two she fought down her modesty sufficiently to let them attempt to deal with them, but the bleeding was profuse, and the blood of the Foresters streamed from the prone figure face downward on the bed in terrifying quantity.

"We shall have to send for the doctor," said one of the ministering sisters; it was a shocking thing to contemplate.

"Oh, but we cannot!" said the other ministering sister.

"We must," said the first.

"How terrible!" said the second.

And with that the injured sister twisted her neck and joined in the conversation. "I will not have the doctor," she said. "I would die of shame."

"Think of the disgrace of it!" said the second sister. "We might even have to explain to him how it happened!"

"But she's bleeding to death," protested the first sister.

"I'd rather die!" said the injured one, and then, as a fresh appalling thought struck her, she twisted her neck even further. "I could never face him again. And what would happen to our whist?"

That was an aspect of the case which until then had occurred to neither of the other sisters, and it was enough to make them blench. But they were of stern stuff. Just as we do not know which was the injured one, we do not know which one thought of a way out of the difficulty, and we shall never know. We know that it was Miss Eulalie, as befitted her rank as eldest sister, who called to Deborah, the maid, to go and fetch Dr. Acheson at once, but that does not mean to say that it was not Miss Eulalie who was the injured sister—injured or not, Miss Eulalie was quite capable of calling to Deborah and telling her what to do.

As she was bid, Deborah went and fetched Dr. Acheson and conducted him to Miss Eunice's bedroom, but of course the fact that it was Miss Eunice's bedroom is really no indication that it was Miss Eunice who was in there. Dr. Acheson had no means of knowing; all he saw was a recumbent form covered by a sheet. In the center of the sheet a round hole a foot in diameter had been cut, and through the hole the seat of the injury was visible.

Dr. Acheson needed no explanations. He took his needles and his thread from his little black bag and he set to work and sewed up the worst of the cuts and attended to the minor ones. Finally he straightened up and eased his aching back.

"I shall have to take those stitches out," he explained to the still and silent figure which had borne the stitching stoically without a murmur. "I shall come next Wednesday and do that."

Until next Wednesday the three Misses Forester kept to their rooms. Not one of them was seen in the streets of the market town, and when on Wednesday Dr. Acheson knocked at the door Deborah conducted him once more to Miss Eunice's bedroom. There was the recumbent form, and there was the sheet with the hole in it. Dr. Acheson took out the stitches.

"It has healed very nicely," said Dr. Acheson. "I don't think any further attention from me will be necessary."

The figure under the sheet said nothing, nor did Dr. Acheson expect it. He gave some concluding advice and went his way. He was glad later to receive a note penned in Miss Forester's Italian hand:

DEAR DR. ACHESON,

We will all be delighted if you will come to whist this week as usual.

When Dr. Acheson arrived he found that the "as usual" applied only to his coming, for there was a slight but subtle change in the furnishings of the drawing room. The stiff, high-backed chairs on which the three Misses Forester sat bore, each of them, a thick and comfortable cushion upon the seat. There was no knowing which of the sisters needed it.

A Day's Wait

ERNEST HEMINGWAY

He came into the room to shut the windows while we were still in bed and I saw he looked ill. He was shivering, his face was white, and he walked slowly as though it ached to move.

"What's the matter, Schatz?"

"I've got a headache."

"You better go back to bed."

"No. I'm all right."

"You go to bed. I'll see you when I'm dressed."

But when I came downstairs he was dressed, sitting by the fire, looking a very sick and miserable boy of nine years. When I put my hand on his forehead I knew he had a fever.

"You go up to bed," I said, "you're sick."

"I'm all right," he said.

When the doctor came he took the boy's temperature.

"What is it?" I asked him.

"One hundred and two."

Downstairs, the doctor left three different medicines in different colored capsules with instructions for giving them. One was to bring down the fever, another a purgative, the third to overcome an acid condition. The germs of influenza can only exist in an acid condition, he explained. He seemed to know all about influenza and said there was nothing to worry about if the fever did not go above one hundred and four degrees. This was a light epidemic of flu and there was no danger if you avoided pneumonia.

Back in the room I wrote the boy's temperature down and made a note of the time to give the various capsules.

"Do you want me to read to you?"

"All right. If you want to," said the boy. His face was very white and there were dark areas under his eyes. He lay still in the bed and seemed very detached from what was going on.

I read aloud from Howard Pyle's *Book of Pirates;* but I could see he was not following what I was reading.

"How do you feel, Schatz?" I asked him.

"Just the same, so far," he said.

I sat at the foot of the bed and read to myself while I waited for it to be time to give another capsule. It would have been natural for him to go to sleep, but when I looked up he was looking at the foot of the bed, looking very strangely.

"Why don't you try to go to sleep? I'll wake you up for the medicine."

"I'd rather stay awake."

After a while he said to me, "You don't have to stay in here with me, Papa, if it bothers you."

"It doesn't bother me."

"No, I mean you don't have to stay if it's going to bother you."

I thought perhaps he was a little lightheaded and after giving him the prescribed capsules at eleven o'clock I went out for a while.

It was a bright, cold day, the ground covered with a sleet that had frozen so that it seemed as if all the bare trees, the bushes, the cut brush and all the grass and the bare ground had been varnished with ice. I took the young Irish setter for a little walk up the road and along a frozen creek, but it was difficult to stand or walk on the glassy surface and the red dog slipped and slithered and I fell twice, hard, once dropping my gun and having it slide away over the ice.

We flushed a covey of quail under a high clay bank with overhanging brush and I killed two as they went out of sight over the top of the bank. Some of the covey lit in trees, but most of them scattered into brush piles and it was necessary to jump on the ice-coated mounds of brush several times before they would flush. Coming out while you were poised unsteadily on the icy, springy brush they made difficult shooting and I killed two, missed five, and started back pleased to have found a covey close to the house and happy there were so many left to find on another day.

At the house they said the boy had refused to let any one come into the room.

"You can't come in," he said. "You mustn't get what I have."

I went up to him and found him in exactly the position I had left him, white-faced, but with the tops of his cheeks flushed by the fever, staring still, as he had stared, at the foot of the bed.

I took his temperature.

"What is it?"

"Something like a hundred," I said. It was one hundred and two and four tenths.

"It was a hundred and two," he said.

"Who said so?"

"The doctor."

"Your temperature is all right," I said. "It's nothing to worry about."

"I don't worry," he said, "but I can't keep from thinking."

"Don't think," I said. "Just take it easy."

"I'm taking it easy," he said and looked straight ahead. He was evidently holding tight onto himself about something.

"Take this with water."

"Do you think it will do any good?"

"Of course it will."

I sat down and opened the *Pirate* book and commenced to read, but I could see he was not following, so I stopped.

"About what time do you think I'm going to die?" he asked.

"What?"

"About how long will it be before I die?"

"You aren't going to die. What's the matter with you?"

"Oh, yes, I am. I heard him say a hundred and two."

"People don't die with a fever of one hundred and two. That's a silly way to talk."

"I know they do. At school in France the boys told me you can't live with forty-four degrees. I've got a hundred and two."

He had been waiting to die all day, ever since nine o'clock in the morning.

"You poor Schatz," I said. "Poor old Schatz. It's like miles and kilometers. You aren't going to die. That's a different thermometer. On that thermometer thirty-seven is normal. On this kind it's ninety-eight."

"Are you sure?"

"Absolutely," I said. "It's like miles and kilometers. You know, like how many kilometers we make when we do seventy miles in the car?"

"Oh," he said.

But his gaze at the foot of the bed relaxed slowly. The hold over himself relaxed too, finally, and the next day it was very slack and he cried very easily at little things that were of no importance

Family in the Wind

F. SCOTT FITZGERALD

The two men drove up the hill toward the blood-red sun. The cotton fields bordering the road were thin and withered, and no breeze stirred in the pines.

"When I am totally sober," the doctor was saying—"I mean when I am totally sober—I don't see the same world that you do. I'm like a friend of mine who had one good eye and got glasses made to correct his bad eye; the result was that he kept seeing elliptical suns and falling off tilted curbs until he had to throw the glasses away. Granted that I am thoroughly anæsthetized the greater part of the day—well, I only undertake work that I know I can do when I am in that condition."

"Yeah," agreed his brother Gene uncomfortably. The doctor was a little tight at the moment and Gene could find no opening for what he had to say. Like so many Southerners of the humbler classes, he had a deep-seated courtesy, characteristic of all violent and passionate lands—he could not change the subject until there was a moment's silence, and Forrest would not shut up.

"I'm very happy," he continued, "or very miserable. I chuckle or I weep alcoholically and, as I continue to slow up, life accommodatingly goes faster, so that the less there is of myself inside, the more diverting becomes the moving picture without. I have cut myself off from the respect of my fellow man, but I am aware of a compensatory cirrhosis of the emotions. And because my sensitivity, my pity, no longer has direction, but fixes itself on whatever is at hand, I have become an exceptionally good fellow—much more so than when I was a good doctor."

As the road straightened after the next bend and Gene saw his house in the distance, he remembered his wife's face as she had made him promise, and he could wait no longer: "Forrest, I got a thing——"

The doctor brought his car to a sudden stop in front of a small house just beyond a grove of pines. On the front steps a girl of eight was playing with a gray cat.

"This is the sweetest little kid I ever saw," the doctor said to Gene, and then to the child, in a grave voice: "Helen, do you need any pills for kitty?"

The little girl laughed.

"Well, I don't know," she said doubtfully. She was playing another game with the cat now and this came as rather an interruption.

"Because kitty telephoned me this morning," the doctor continued, "and said her mother was neglecting her and couldn't I get her a trained nurse from Montgomery."

"She did not." The little girl grabbed the cat close indignantly; the doctor took a nickel from his pocket and tossed it to the steps.

"I recommend a good dose of milk," he said as he put the car into gear. "Good-night, Helen."

"Good-night, doctor."

As they drove off, Gene tried again: "Listen; stop," he said. "Stop here a little way down. . . . Here."

The doctor stopped the car and the brothers faced each other. They were alike as to robustness of figure and a certain asceticism of feature and they were both in their middle forties; they were unlike in that the doctor's glasses failed to conceal the veined, weeping eyes of a soak, and that he wore corrugated city wrinkles; Gene's wrinkles bounded fields, followed the lines of rooftrees, of poles propping up sheds. His eyes were a fine, furry blue. But the sharpest contrast lay in the fact that Gene Janney was a country man while Dr. Forrest Janney was obviously a man of education.

"Well?" the doctor asked.

"You know Pinky's at home," Gene said, looking down the road.

"So I hear," the doctor answered noncommittally.

"He got in a row in Birmingham and somebody shot him in the head." Gene hesitated. "We got Doc Behrer because we thought maybe you wouldn't—may you wouldn't——"

"I wouldn't," agreed Doctor Janney blandly.

"But look, Forrest; here's the thing," Gene insisted. "You know how it is—you often say Doc Behrer doesn't know nothing. Shucks, I never thought he was much either. He says the bullet's pressing on the—pressing on the brain, and he can't take it out without causin' a hemmering, and he says he doesn't know whether we could get him to Birmingham or Montgomery, or not, he's so low. Doc wasn't no help. What we want——"

"No," said his brother, shaking his head. "No."

"I just want you to look at him and tell us what to do," Gene begged. "He's unconscious, Forrest. He wouldn't know you; you'd hardly know him. Thing is his mother's about crazy."

"She's in the grip of a purely animal instinct." The doctor took from his hip a flask containing half water and half Alabama corn, and drank. "You and I know that boy ought to been drowned the day he was born."

Gene flinched. "He's bad," he admitted, "but I don't know——You see him lying there——"

As the liquor spread over the doctor's insides he felt an instinct to do something, not to violate his prejudices but simply to make some gesture, to assert his own moribund but still struggling will to power.

"All right, I'll see him," he said. "I'll do nothing myself to help him, because he ought to be dead. And even his death wouldn't make up for what he did to Mary Decker."

Gene Janney pursed his lips. "Forrest, you sure about that?"

"Sure about it!" exclaimed the doctor. "Of course I'm sure. She died of starvation; she hadn't had more than a couple cups of coffee in a week. And if you looked at her shoes, you could see she'd walked for miles."

"Doc Behrer says——"

"What does he know? I performed the autopsy the day they found her on the Birmingham Highway. There was nothing the matter with her but starvation. That—that"—his voice shook with feeling—"that Pinky got tired of her and turned her out, and she was trying to get home. It suits me fine that he was invalided home himself a couple of weeks later."

As he talked, the doctor had plunged the car savagely into gear and let the clutch out with a jump; in a moment they drew up before Gene Janney's home.

It was a square frame house with a brick foundation and a well-kept lawn blocked off from the farm, a house rather superior to the buildings that composed the town of Bending and the surrounding agricultural area, yet not essentially different in type or in its interior economy. The last of the plantation houses in this section of Alabama had long disappeared, the proud pillars yielding to poverty, rot, and rain.

Gene's wife, Rose, got up from her rocking-chair on the porch.

"Hello, doc." She greeted him a little nervously and without meeting his eyes. "You been a stranger here lately."

The doctor met her eyes for several seconds. "How do you do, Rose," he said. "Hi, Edith. . . . Hi, Eugene"—this to the little boy and girl who stood beside their mother; and then: "Hi, Butch!" to the stocky youth of nineteen who came around the corner of the house hugging a round stone.

"Goin' to have a sort of low wall along the front here—kind of neater," Gene explained.

All of them had a lingering respect for the doctor. They felt reproachful toward him because they could no longer refer to him as their celebrated relative—"one of the best surgeons up in Montgomery, yes, suh"—but there were his learning and the position he had once occupied in the larger world, before he had committed professional suicide by taking to cynicism and drink. He had come home to Bending and bought a half interest in the local drug store two years ago, keeping up his license, but practicing only when sorely needed.

"Rose," said Gene, "doc says he'll take a look at Pinky."

Pinky Janney, his lips curved mean and white under a new beard, lay in bed in a darkened room. When the doctor removed the bandage from his head, his breath blew into a low groan, but his paunchy body did not move. After a few minutes, the doctor replaced the bandage and, with Gene and Rose, returned to the porch.

"Behrer wouldn't operate?" he asked.

"No."

"Why didn't they operate in Birmingham?"

"I don't know."

"H'm." The doctor put on his hat. "That bullet ought tc come out, and soon. It's pressing against the carotid sheath. That's the—anyhow, you can't get him to Montgomery with that pulse."

"What shall we do?" Gene's question carried a little tail of silence as he sucked his breath back.

"Get Behrer to think it over. Or else get somebody in Montgomery. There's about a 25 per cent chance that the operation would save him; without the operation he hasn't any chance at all."

"Who'll we get in Montgomery?" asked Gene.

"Any good surgeon would do it. Even Behrer could do it if he had any nerve."

Suddenly Rose Janney came close to him, her eyes straining and burning with an animal maternalism. She seized his coat where it hung open.

"Doc, you do it! You can do it. You know you were as good a surgeon as any of 'em once. Please, doc, you go on and do it."

He stepped back a little so that her hands fell from his coat, and held out his own hands in front of him.

"See how they tremble?" he said with elaborate irony. "Look close and you'll see. I wouldn't dare operate."

"You could do it all right," said Gene hastily, "with a drink to stiffen you up."

The doctor shook his head and said, looking at Rose: "No. You see, my decisions are not reliable, and if anything went wrong, it would seem to be my fault." He was acting a little now—he chose his words carefully. "I hear that when I found that Mary Decker died of starvation, my opinion was questioned on the grounds that I was a drunkard."

"I didn't say that," lied Rose breathlessly.

"Certainly not. I just mention it to show how careful I've got to be." He moved down the steps. "Well, my advice is to see Behrer again, or, failing that, get somebody from the city. Good-night."

But before he had reached the gate, Rose came tearing after him, her eyes white with fury.

"I did say you were a drunkard!" she cried. "When you said Mary Decker died of starvation, you made it out as if it was Pinky's fault— you, swilling yourself full of corn all day! How can anybody tell whether you know what you're doing or not? Why did you think so much about Mary Decker, anyhow—a girl half your age? Everybody saw how she used to come in your drug store and talk to you——"

Gene, who had followed, seized her arms. "Shut up now, Rose. . . . Drive along, Forrest."

Forrest drove along, stopping at the next bend to drink from his flask. Across the fallow cotton fields he could see the house where Mary Decker had lived, and had it been six months before, he might have detoured to ask her why she hadn't come into the store that day for her free soda, or to delight her with a sample cosmetic left by a salesman that morning. He had not told Mary Decker how he felt about her; never intended to—she was seventeen, he was forty-five, and he no longer dealt in futures—but only after she ran away to Birmingham with his vicious nephew, Pinky Janney, did he realize how much his love for her had counted in his lonely life.

His thoughts went back to his brother's house.

"Now, if I were a gentleman," he thought, "I wouldn't have done like that. And another person might have been sacrificed to that dirty dog, because if he died afterwards Rose would say I killed him."

Yet he felt pretty bad as he put his car away; not that he could have acted differently, but just that it was all so ugly.

He had been home scarcely ten minutes when a car creaked to rest outside and Butch Janney came in. His mouth was set tight and his eyes were narrowed as though to permit of no escape to the temper that possessed him until it should be unleashed upon its proper objective.

"Hi, Butch."

"I want to talk to you, Uncle Forrest. I want to tell you you can't talk to my mother thataway. I'll kill you, you talk to my mother like that!"

"Now shut up, Butch, and sit down," said the doctor sharply.

"She's already 'bout sick on account of Pinky, and you come over and talk to her like that."

"Your mother did all the insulting that was done, Butch. I just took it."

"She doesn't know what she's saying and you ought to understand that."

The doctor thought a minute. "Butch, what do you think of Pinky?"

Butch hesitated uncomfortably. "Well, I can't say I ever thought so much of him"—his tone changed defiantly—"but after all, he's my own brother——"

"Wait a minute, Butch. What do you think of the way he treated Mary Decker?"

But Butch had shaken himself free, and now he let go the artillery of his rage:

"That ain't the point; the point is anybody that doesn't do right to my mother has me to answer to. It's only fair when you got all the education——"

"I got my education myself, Butch."

"I don't care. We're going to try again to get Doc Behrer to operate or get us some fellow from the city. But if we can't, I'm coming and get you, and you're going to take that bullet out if I have to hold a gun to you while you do it." He nodded, panting a little; then he turned and went out and drove away.

"Something tells me," said the doctor to himself, "that there's no more peace for me in Chilton County." He called to his colored boy to put supper on the table. Then he rolled himself a cigarette and went out on the back stoop.

The weather had changed. The sky was now overcast and the grass stirred restlessly and there was a sudden flurry of drops without a sequel.

minute ago it had been warm, but now the moisture on his forehead was suddenly cool, and he wiped it away with his handkerchief. There was a buzzing in his ears and he swallowed and shook his head. For a moment he thought he must be sick; then suddenly the buzzing detached itself from him, grew into a swelling sound, louder and ever nearer, that might have been the roar of an approaching train.

II

Butch Janney was halfway home when he saw it—a huge, black, approaching cloud whose lower edge bumped the ground. Even as he stared at it vaguely, it seemed to spread until it included the whole southern sky, and he saw pale electric fire in it and heard an increasing roar. He was in a strong wind now; blown débris, bits of broken branches, splinters, large objects unidentifiable in the growing darkness, flew by him. Instinctively he got out of his car and, by now hardly able to stand against the wind, ran for a bank, or rather found himself thrown and pinned against a bank. Then for a minute, two minutes, he was in the black center of pandemonium.

First there was the sound, and he was part of the sound, so engulfed in it and possessed by it that he had no existence apart from it. It was not a collection of sounds, it was just Sound itself; a great screeching bow drawn across the chords of the universe. The sound and force were inseparable. The sound as well as the force held him to what he felt was the bank like a man crucified. Somewhere in this first moment his face, pinned sideways, saw his automobile make a little jump, spin halfway around and then go bobbing off over a field in a series of great helpless leaps. Then began the bombardment, the sound dividing its sustained cannon note into the cracks of a gigantic machine gun. He was only half conscious as he felt himself become part of one of those cracks, felt himself lifted away from the bank to tear through space, through a blinding, lacerating mass of twigs and branches, and then, for an incalculable time, he knew nothing at all.

His body hurt him. He was lying between two branches in the top of a tree; the air was full of dust and rain, and he could hear nothing;

it was a long time before he realized that the tree he was in had been blown down and that his involuntary perch among the pine needles was only five feet from the ground.

"Say, man!" he cried aloud, outraged. "Say, man! Say, what a wind! Say, man!"

Made acute by pain and fear, he guessed that he had been standing on the tree's root and had been catapulted by the terrific wrench as the big pine was torn from the earth. Feeling over himself, he found that his left ear was caked full of dirt, as if someone had wanted to take an impression of the inside. His clothes were in rags, his coat had torn on the back seam, and he could feel where, as some stray gust tried to undress him, it had cut into him under the arms.

Reaching the ground, he set off in the direction of his father's house, but it was a new and unfamiliar landscape he traversed. The Thing—he did not know it was a tornado—had cut a path a quarter of a mile wide, and he was confused, as the dust slowly settled, by vistas he had never seen before. It was unreal that Bending church tower should be visible from here; there had been groves of trees between.

But where was here? For he should be close to the Baldwin house; only as he tripped, in the gathering night, over great piles of boards, like a carelessly kept lumberyard, did Butch realize that there was no more Baldwin house, and then, looking around wildly, that there was no Necrawney house on the hill, no Peltzer house below it. There was not a light, not a sound, save the rain falling on the fallen trees.

He broke into a run. When he saw the bulk of his father's house in the distance, he gave a "Hey!" of relief, but coming closer, he realized that something was missing. There were no out-houses and the built-on wing that held Pinky's room had been sheared completely away.

"Mother!" he called. "Dad!" There was no answer; a dog bounded out of the yard and licked his hand. . . .

. . . It was full dark twenty minutes later when Doc Janney stopped his car in front of his own drug store in Bending. The electric lights had gone out, but there were men with lanterns in the street, and in a minute a small crowd had collected around him. He unlocked the door hurriedly.

"Somebody break open the old Wiggins Hospital." He pointed across the street. "I've got six badly injured in my car. I want some fellows to carry 'em in. Is Doc Behrer here?"

"Here he is," offered eager voices out of the darkness as the doctor, case in hand, came through the crowd. The two men stood face to face by lantern light, forgetting that they disliked each other.

"God knows how many more there's going to be," said Doc Janney. "I'm getting dressing and disinfectant. There'll be a lot of fractures——" He raised his voice, "Somebody bring me a barrel!"

"I'll get started over there," said Behrer. "There's about half a dozen more crawled into town."

"What's been done?" demanded Doc Janney of the men who followed him into the drug store. "Have they called Birmingham and Montgomery?"

"Telephone wires are down, but the telegraph got through."

"Well, somebody get Doctor Cohen from Wettala, and tell any people who have automobiles to go up the Willard Pike and cut across toward Corsica and all through those roads there. There's not a house left at the crossroads by the nigger store. I passed a lot of folks walking in, all of them hurt, but I didn't have room for anybody else." As he talked he was throwing bandages, disinfectant, and drugs into a blanket. "I thought I had a lot more stuff than this in stock! And wait!" he called. "Somebody drive out and look down in that hollow where the Wooleys live. Drive right across the fields—the road's blocked. . . . Now, you with the cap——Ed Jenks, ain't it?"

"Yes, doc?"

"You see what I got here? You collect everything in the store that looks like this and bring it across the way, understand?"

"Yes, doc."

As the doctor went out into the street, the victims were streaming into town—a woman on foot with a badly injured child, a buckboard full of groaning Negroes, frantic men gasping terrible stories. Everywhere confusion and hysteria mounted in the dimly illumined darkness. A mud-covered reporter from Birmingham drove up in a side car, the wheels crossing the fallen wires and brushwood that clogged the street, and there was the siren of a police car from Cooper, thirty miles away.

Already a crowd pressed around the doors of the hospital, closed these three months for lack of patients. The doctor squeezed past the melée of white faces and established himself in the nearest ward, grateful for the waiting row of old iron beds. Doctor Behrer was already at work across the hall.

"Get me half a dozen lanterns," he ordered.

"Doctor Behrer wants iodine and adhesive."

"All right, there it is. . . . Here, you, Shinkey, stand by the door and keep everybody out except cases that can't walk. Somebody run over and see if there ain't some candles in the grocery store."

The street ouside was full of sound now—the cries of women, the contrary directions of volunteer gangs trying to clear the highway, the tense staccato of people rising to an emergency. A little before midnight arrived the first unit of the Red Cross. But the three doctors, presently joined by two others from near-by villages, had lost track of time long before that. The dead began to be brought in by ten o'clock; there were twenty, twenty-five, thirty, forty—the list grew. Having no more needs, these waited, as became simple husbandmen, in a garage behind, while the stream of injured—hundreds of them—flowed through the old hospital built to house only a score. The storm had dealt out fractures of the leg, collar bone, ribs, and hip, lacerations of the back, elbows, ears, eyelids, nose; there were wounds from flying planks, and odd splinters in odd places, and a scalped man, who would recover to grow a new head of hair. Living or dead, Doc Janney knew every face, almost every name.

"Don't you fret now. Billy's all right. Hold still and let me tie this. People are drifting in every minute, but it's so consarned dark they can't find 'em——All right, Mrs. Oakey. That's nothing. Ev here'll touch it with iodine. . . . Now let's see this man."

Two o'clock. The old doctor from Wettala gave out, but now there were fresh men from Montgomery to take his place. Upon the air of the room, heavy with disinfectant, floated the ceaseless babble of human speech reaching the doctor dimly through layer after layer of increasing fatigue.

". . . Over and over—just rolled me over and over. Got hold of a bush and the bush came along too."

"*Jeff! Where's Jeff?*"

". . . I bet that pig sailed a hundred yards——"

"—just stopped the train in time. All the passengers got out and helped pull the poles——"

"*Oh, Jeff! Where's Jeff?*"

"He says, 'Let's get down cellar,' and I says, 'We ain't got no cellar'——"

". . . If there's no more stretchers, find some light doors."

". . . Five seconds? Say, it was more like five minutes!"

At some time he heard that Gene and Rose had been seen with their two youngest children. He had passed their house on the way in and, seeing it standing, hurried on. The Janney family had been lucky; the doctor's own house was outside the sweep of the storm.

Only as he saw the electric lights go on suddenly in the streets and glimpsed the crowd waiting for hot coffee in front of the Red Cross did the doctor realize how tired he was.

"You better go rest," a young man was saying. "I'll take this side of the room. I've got two nurses with me."

"All right—all right. I'll finish this row."

The injured were being evacuated to the cities by train as fast as their wounds were dressed, and their places taken by others. He had only two beds to go—in the first one he found Pinky Janney.

He put his stethoscope to the heart. It was beating feebly. That he, so weak, so nearly gone, had survived this storm at all was remarkable. How he had got there, who had found him and carried him, was a mystery in itself. The doctor went over the body; there were small contusions and lacerations, two broken fingers, the dirt-filled ears that marked every case—nothing else. For a moment the doctor hesitated, but even when he closed his eyes, the image of Mary Decker seemed to have receded, eluding him. Something purely professional that had nothing to do with human sensibilities had been set in motion inside him, and he was powerless to head it off. He held out his hands before him; they were trembling slightly.

"Hell's bells!" he muttered.

He went out of the room and around the corner of the hall, where he drew from his pocket the flask containing the last of the corn and water he had had in the afternoon. He emptied it. Returning to the ward, he disinfected two instruments and applied a local anæsthetic to a square section at the base of Pinky's skull where the wound had healed over the bullet. He called a nurse to his side and then, scalpel in hand, knelt on one knee beside his nephew's bed.

III

Two days later the doctor drove slowly around the mournful countryside. He had withdrawn from the emergency work after the first desperate night, feeling that his status as a pharmacist might embarrass his collaborators. But there was much to be done in bringing the damage to outlying sections under the ægis of the Red Cross, and he devoted himself to that.

The path of the demon was easy to follow. It had pursued an irregular course on its seven-league boots, cutting across country, through woods, or even urbanely keeping to roads until they curved, when it went off on its own again.Sometimes the trail could be traced by cotton fields, apparently in full bloom, but this cotton came from the insides of hundreds of quilts and mattresses redistributed in the fields by the storm.

At a lumber pile that had lately been a Negro cabin, he stopped a moment to listen to a dialogue between two reporters and two shy pickaninnies. The old grandmother, her head bandaged, sat among the ruins, gnawing some vague meat and moving her rocker ceaselessly.

"But where is the river you were blown across?" one of the reporters demanded.

"There."

"Where?"

The pickaninnies looked to their grandmother for aid.

"Right there behind you-all," spoke up the old woman.

The newspapermen looked disgustedly at a muddy stream four yards wide.

"That's no river."

"That's a Menada River, we always calls it ever since I was a gull. Yes, suh, that's a Menada River. An' them two boys was blowed right across it an' set down on the othah side just as pretty, 'thout any hurt at all. Chimney fell on me," she concluded, feeling her head.

"Do you mean to say that's all it was?" demanded the younger reporter indignantly. "That's the river they were blown across! And one hundred and twenty million people have been led to believe——"

"That's all right, boys," interrupted Doc Janney. "That's a right good river for these parts. And it'll get bigger as those little fellahs get older."

He tossed a quarter to the old woman and drove on.

Passing a country church, he stopped and counted the new brown mounds that marred the graveyard. He was nearing the center of the holocaust now. There was the Howden house where three had been killed; there remained a gaunt chimney, a rubbish heap and a scarecrow surviving ironically in the kitchen garden. In the ruins of the house across the way a rooster strutted on top of a piano, reigning vociferously over an estate of trunks, boots, cans, books, calendars, rugs, chairs and window frames, a twisted radio and a legless sewing machine. Everything there was bedding—blankets, mattresses, bent springs, shredded padding—he had not realized how much of people's lives were spent in bed. Here and there, cows and horses, often stained with disinfectant, were cropping again in the fields. At intervals there were Red Cross tents, and sitting by one of these, with the gray cat in her arms, the doctor came upon little Helen Kilrain. The usual lumber pile, like a child's building game knocked down in a fit of temper, told the story.

"Hello, dear," he greeted her, his heart sinking. "How did kitty like the tornado?"

"She didn't."

"What did she do?"

"She meowed."

"Oh."

"She wanted to get away, but I hanged on to her and she scratched me—see?"

He glanced at the Red Cross tent.

"Who's taking care of you?"

"The lady from the Red Cross and Mrs. Wells," she answered. "My father got hurt. He stood over me so it wouldn't fall on me, and I stood over kitty. He's in the hospital in Birmingham. When he comes back, I guess he'll build our house again."

The doctor winced. He knew that her father would build no more houses; he had died that morning. She was alone, and she did not know she was alone. Around her stretched the dark universe, impersonal, inconscient. Her lovely little face looked up at him confidently as he asked: "You got any kin anywhere, Helen?"

"I don't know."

"You've got kitty, anyhow, haven't you?"

"It's just a cat," she admitted calmly, but anguished by her own betrayal of her love, she hugged it closer.

"Taking care of a cat must be pretty hard."

"Oh, no," she said hurriedly. "It isn't any trouble at all. It doesn't eat hardly anything."

He put his hand in his pocket, and then changed his mind suddenly.

"Dear, I'm coming back and see you later—later today. You take good care of kitty now, won't you?"

"Oh, yes," she answered lightly.

The doctor drove on. He stopped next at a house that had escaped damage. Walt Cupps, the owner, was cleaning a shotgun on his front porch.

"What's that, Walt? Going to shoot up the next tornado?"

"Ain't going to be a next tornado."

"You can't tell. Just take a look at that sky now. It's getting mighty dark."

Walt laughed and slapped his gun. "Not for a hundred years, anyhow. This here is for looters. There's a lot of 'em around, and not all black either. Wish when you go to town that you'd tell 'em to scatter some militia out here."

"I'll tell 'em now. You come out all right?"

"I did, thank God. With six of us in the house. It took off one hen, and probably it's still carrying it around somewhere."

The doctor drove on toward town, overcome by a feeling of uneasiness he could not define.

"It's the weather," he thought. "It's the same kind of feel in the air there was last Saturday."

For a month the doctor had felt an urge to go away permanently. Once this countryside had seemed to promise peace. When the impetus that had lifted him temporarily out of tired old stock was exhausted, he had come back here to rest, to watch the earth put forth, and live on simple, pleasant terms with his neighbors. Peace! He knew that the present family quarrel would never heal, nothing would ever be the same; it would all be bitter forever. And he had seen the placid countryside turned into a land of mourning. There was no peace here. Move on.

On the road he overtook Butch Janney walking to town.

"I was coming to see you," said Butch, frowning. "You operated on Pinky after all, didn't you?"

"Jump in. . . . Yes, I did. How did you know?"

"Doc Behrer told us." He shot a quick look at the doctor, who did not miss the quality of suspicion in it. "They don't think he'll last out the day."

"I'm sorry for your mother."

Butch laughed unpleasantly. "Yes, you are."

"I said I'm sorry for your mother," said the doctor sharply.

"I heard you."

They drove for a moment in silence.

"Did you find your automobile?"

"Did I?" Butch laughed ruefully. "I found something—I don't know whether you'd call it a car any more. And, you know, I could of had tornado insurance for twenty-five cents." His voice trembled indignantly: "Twenty-five cents—but who would ever of thought of getting tornado insurance?"

It was growing darker; there was a thin crackle of thunder far to the southward.

"Well, all I hope," said Butch with narrowed glance, "is that you hadn't been drinking anything when you operated on Pinky."

"You know, Butch," the doctor said slowly, "that was a pretty dirty trick of mine to bring that tornado here."

He had not expected the sarcasm to hit home, but he expected a retort—when suddenly he caught sight of Butch's face. It was fish-white, the mouth wide open, the eyes fixed and staring, and from the throat came a mewling sound. Limply he raised one hand before him, and then the doctor saw.

Less than a mile away, an enormous, top-shaped black cloud filled the sky and bore toward them, dipping and swirling, and in front of it sailed already a heavy, singing wind.

"It's come back!" the doctor yelled.

Fifty yards ahead of them was the old iron bridge spanning Bilby Creek. He stepped hard on the accelerator and drove for it. The fields were full of running figures headed in the same direction. Reaching the bridge, he jumped out and yanked Butch's arm.

"Get out, you fool! Get out!"

A nerveless mass stumbled from the car; in a moment they were in a group of half a dozen, huddled in the triangular space that the bridge made with the shore.

"Is it coming here?"

"No, it's turning!"

"We had to leave grampa!"

"Oh, save me, save me! Help me! Help me!"

"Save my soul!"

There was a quick rush of wind outside, sending little tentacles under the bridge with a curious tension in them that made the doctor's skin crawl. Then immediately there was a vacuum, with no more wind, but a sudden thresh of rain. The doctor crawled to the edge of the bridge and put his head up cautiously.

"It's passed," he said. "We only felt the edge; the center went way to the right of us."

He could see it plainly; for a second he could even distinguish objects in it—shrubbery and small trees, planks and loose earth. Crawling farther out, he took out his watch and tried to time it, but the thick curtain of rain blotted it from sight.

Soaked to the skin, he crawled back underneath. Butch lay shivering in the farthest corner, and the doctor shook him.

"It went in the direction of your house!" the doctor cried. "Pull yourself together! Who's there?"

"No one," Butch groaned. "They're all down with Pinky."

The rain had changed to hail now; first small pellets, then larger ones, and larger, until the sound of their fall upon the iron bridge was an ear-splitting tattoo.

The spared wretches under the bridge were slowly recovering, and in the relief there were titters of hysterical laughter. After a certain point of strain, the nervous system makes its transitions without dignity or reason. Even the doctor felt the contagion.

"This is worse than a calamity," he said dryly. "It's getting to be a nuisance."

IV

There were to be no more tornadoes in Alabama that spring. The second one—it was popularly thought to be the first one come back; for to the people of Chilton County it had become a personified force, definite as a pagan god—took a dozen houses, Gene Janney's among them, and injured about thirty people. But this time—perhaps because everyone had developed some scheme of self-protection—there were no fatalities. It made its last dramatic bow by sailing down the main street of Bending, prostrating the telephone poles and crushing in the fronts of three shops, including Doc Janney's drug store.

At the end of a week, houses were going up again, made of the old boards; and before the end of the long, lush Alabama summer the grass will be green again on all the graves. But it will be years before the people of the county cease to reckon events as happening "before the tornado" or "after the tornado," and for many families things will never be the same.

Doctor Janney decided that this was as good a time to leave as any. He sold the remains of his drug store, gutted alike by charity and catastrophe, and turned over his house to his brother until Gene could rebuild his own. He was going up to the city by train, for his car had been rammed against a tree and couldn't be counted on for much more than a trip to the station.

Several times on the way in he stopped by the roadside to say good-by—once it was to Walter Cupps.

"So it hit you, after all," he said, looking at the melancholy back house which alone marked the site.

"It's pretty bad," Walt answered. "But just think; they was six of us in or about the house and not one was injured. I'm content to give thanks to God for that."

"You were lucky there, Walt," the doctor agreed. "Do you happen to have heard whether the Red Cross took little Helen Gilrain to Montgomery or to Birmingham?"

"To Montgomery. Say, I was there when she came into town with that cat, tryin' to get somebody to bandage up its paw. She must of walked miles through that rain and hail, but all that mattered to her was her kitty. Bad as I felt, I couldn't help laughin' at how spunky she was."

The doctor was silent for a moment. "Do you happen to recollect if she has any people left?"

"I don't, suh," Walt replied, "but I think as not."

At his brother's place, the doctor made his last stop. They were all there, even the youngest, working among the ruins; already Butch had a shed erected to house the salvage of their goods. Save for this the most orderly thing surviving was the pattern of round white stone which was to have inclosed the garden.

The doctor took a hundred dollars in bills from his pocket and handed it to Gene.

"You can pay it back sometime, but don't strain yourself," he said. "It's money I got from the store." He cut off Gene's thanks: "Pack up my books carefully when I send for 'em."

"You reckon to practice medicine up there, Forrest?"

"I'll maybe try it."

The brothers held on to each other's hands for a moment; the two youngest children came up to say good-by. Rose stood in the background in an old blue dress—she had no money to wear black for her eldest son.

"Good-by, Rose," said the doctor.

"Good-by," she responded, and then added in a dead voice, "Good luck to you, Forrest."

For a moment he was tempted to say something conciliatory, but he saw that it was no use. He was up against the maternal instinct, the same force that had sent little Helen through the storm with her injured cat.

At the station he bought a one-way ticket to Montgomery. The village was drab under the sky of a retarded spring, and as the train pulled out, it was odd to think that six months ago it had seemed to him as good a place as any other.

He was alone in the white section of the day coach; presently he felt for a bottle on his hip and drew it forth. "After all, a man of forty-five is entitled to a little artificial courage when he starts over again." His mind jumped to something else: "She hasn't got any kin, because if she had they'd have sent word after the first storm."

He patted the bottle, then looked down at it as if in surprise.

"Well, we'll have to put you aside for a while, old friend," he said aloud, for he often talked to himself. "You're expensive in more ways than one, and any cat that's worth all that trouble and loving care is going to need a lot of grade-A quality milk."